D0387242

Odd & True

AMULET BOOKS
NEW YORK

Odd & True

CAT WINTERS

PUBLISHER'S NOTE: This is a work of fiction. Names, characters, places, and incidents are either the product of the author's imagination or used fictitiously, and any resemblance to actual persons, living or dead, business establishments, events, or locales is entirely coincidental.

Cataloging-in-Publication Data has been applied for and may be obtained from the Library of Congress.
ISBN 978-1-4197-2310-0

Text copyright © 2017 Catherine Karp
Jacket illustrations copyright © 2017 Nathália Suellen
Book design by Alyssa Nassner

Published in 2017 by Amulet Books, an imprint of ABRAMS. All rights reserved. No portion of this book may be reproduced, stored in a retrieval system, or transmitted in any form or by any means, mechanical, electronic, photocopying, recording, or otherwise, without written permission from the publisher.

Amulet Books and Amulet Paperbacks are registered trademarks of Harry N. Abrams, Inc.

Printed and bound in USA
10 9 8 7 6 5 4 3 2 1

Amulet Books are available at special discounts when purchased in quantity for premiums and promotions as well as fundraising or educational use. Special editions can also be created to specification. For details, contact specialsales@abramsbooks.com or the address below.

ABRAMS The Art of Books
115 West 18th Street, New York, NY 10011
abramsbooks.com

FOR MY SISTER

We are the music-makers,
And we are the dreamers of dreams,
Wandering by lone sea-breakers,
And sitting by desolate streams;
World-losers and world-forsakers,
On whom the pale moon gleams:
Yet we are the movers and shakers
Of the world for ever, it seems.

—ARTHUR O'SHAUGHNESSY, "ODE"

ONCE UPON A TIME . . .

T ell me the story again," I urged my sister in the night-time blackness of our attic bedroom.

Odette rolled toward me on her side of the bed. The straw mattress crunched and shifted beneath her weight, and her brown eyes shone in the trace of moonlight straining through the shadows.

"Please," I said with a hopeful squeak in my voice, which made me sound such a baby compared to her, an eight-year-old girl, almost nine.

"Oh, Tru." My sister burrowed her right cheek against her pillow. "You know the story so well."

"Tell me again. My leg hurts, and I really, really want to hear it."

She sighed with a force that rustled the curls peeking out from beneath my nightcap.

"Please, Od," I begged. "Tell me about the day I was born . . . and Papa's horse . . . and the tower."

Downstairs, our uncle William readjusted his chair and coughed on the pipe smoke that clogged up his throat every evening. I stiffened, fearful that Od would tell me to be quiet and go to sleep. Outside, the wind howled across the roof with a mournful wail that shook the rafters and turned my insides tingly and cold. Mama's hand mirror lay propped on the windowsill, the glass turned toward the trees behind the house to capture anything diabolical that might creep toward us while we slept. Sometimes I wondered if the mirror was enough . . .

"All right." Od sighed again. "Since it is your birthday, I suppose I could tell you the story . . ."

"Thank you, thank you, thank you!" I smiled and wriggled my shoulders beneath the wool blankets.

"Are you ready?"

"Yes."

"Here it goes, then." My sister leaned close to my left ear and whispered, "Once upon a time, on a cold January morning, five years ago today, a girl named Trudchen Maria Grey was born in a castle built to resemble a stone Scottish fortress called Dunnottar . . ."

I swallowed, while rain pelted the thin glass of our windowpane. The wind—that fierce and tempestuous witch borne from high on the snowcapped peaks of the Cascade Range—blew through the cracks in the walls and turned our sheets to ice.

Odette snuggled close enough that the warmth of her body and her long cotton nightgown burned away the chill. Our elbows touched. I closed my eyes, and the splattering of the rain turned into the galloping of hooves tearing across a golden canyon.

"Tell me more," I whispered, even though I knew what was coming next.

"Papa hurried home from selling one of his grandest paintings to a rich ranchero who lived in an old adobe by the Pacific Ocean. He loosened the reins and urged his handsome black stallion forward, and he smiled when he spied the first stone tower of the palace he'd built high on the side of a California hill. I'm sure you don't even remember that tower."

"But I do." I nodded and saw in my mind's eye a rounded tower made of gray blocks of stone, topped by a brilliant scarlet flag that rippled in a breeze. "I think I do remember it."

"We moved away from there when you were just two, Tru. You couldn't possibly—"

"I remember!"

"Well . . . then you must remember how magnificent it was. The castle was filled with furniture made of velvet, rugs from the Far East, and other spellbinding treasures from across the world. And it was, oh, so colorful . . . greens and reds and gold and bright royal blue. Performers arrived the night after you were born. Persian dancers, an Arabian flutist, a lady opera singer in a horned Viking hat . . . They celebrated. Everyone was always celebrating inside our castle, and the place smelled of roasted turkey and gingerbread cakes and . . . and . . . and little chocolate pastries sprinkled with powdered sugar that looked just like fresh, sweet snow."

"Didn't the noise of the party wake me up, if I was a sleeping little baby?"

"Not at all, silly." Od pulled on one of my blond curls and let it spring back against my cheek. "Mama kept you wrapped in a heavy cloth to muffle the noise."

"Mmm," I said in a dreamy murmur, and I saw it all: our beautiful, brown-haired mother holding a swaddled, infant version of me close to her chest while music, dancing, and feasting surrounded us. I saw vast stone walls that stretched three stories high; windows carved into the stone in the shape of thimbles; women with hair the color of ravens, swiveling their hips, hypnotizing the room with the movements of their arms, which jangled with gleaming bracelets.

In the real version of life, I smelled Uncle William's pipe smoke from downstairs and heard the clicking of Aunt Viktoria's knitting needles, but I told myself they were the scents of the roasting turkey on the crackling fire, the *tap-tap-tap*s of ladies' heels gliding across a marble floor.

"Wasn't there an elephant?" I asked.

"Oh, yes, of course," said Od. "Papa knew all sorts of people—artists, poets, actors, explorers, a magician, fortune-tellers, circus folk. He invited P. T. Barnum, who happened to be in California that very night. In the front garden, I rode Barnum's famous elephant, Jumbo, while Papa painted a portrait of me doing so. The magician even managed to levitate the beast off the ground."

"But the magician was bad, wasn't he?" I tugged the quilt over my right shoulder. "He once took you away and made Mama cry. And he hurt Papa."

Od drew her bottom lip inside her mouth and hesitated, the way she always stopped and left me waiting—gaping, holding my breath—before speaking about the magician.

"He wasn't entirely bad," she said. "He practiced his most wondrous spells on us. You probably don't remember, but he used to raise us into the air without any strings attached to us, like he did with the elephant. Long before that awful old polio attacked you, you were flying up to the tallest tapestries inside our castle walls, as free as a sparrow."

"I flew?" I asked, my eyes widening, for I had never heard this part of the tale.

"Yes. The magician wore a cape lined in red silk, and he'd lift his arms—"

I heard the flap of a long black cape and saw the sheen of the crimson lining.

"—and he'd utter a magical phrase: '*Lifto magicus Escondido.*'" Od raised her head off the pillow and propped herself up on an elbow. "We rose off the ground, floated into the air like two Russian ballerinas, and ran our fingertips through the top tassels of tapestries with pictures of golden-haired ladies on swings. Mama even gave me a feather duster so I could swipe away all the cobwebs up there."

I laughed and covered my mouth.

Another chair scraped across the floor beneath us.

"Are you two girls still awake up there?" called Aunt Viktoria in her rumbling thunderclap of a voice from the bottom of the ladder that led to our attic—a ladder I could not climb because my right leg didn't work like a proper leg. A rope, a pulley, and a wooden chair hoisted me off the ground and into our bedroom every night.

"Tru wanted a bedtime story," said Od to our aunt.

"It's nine thirty, for goodness' sake. Go to sleep."

My stomach tightened. *Nine thirty!* So close to ten o'clock, when Wee Willie Winkie knocked at children's windows and cried at the lock to ensure we all lay asleep in our beds.

I turned to check the window for signs of Willie's face, when something rapped on the glass and clanked Mama's mirror against the sill. I jumped and screamed and thought I saw the flash of yellow eyes peering in from the dark.

"What's wrong?" asked Od.

"Odette!" called our aunt, her voice as sharp as the blade of her carving knife. "Are you scaring your sister half to death with your stories again?"

"It's Wee Willie Winkie"—I buried my face in my pillow—"at the window. I hear him! I hear him!"

"It's hail, Tru," said our aunt. "Go to sleep, the both of you, before you turn into terrible cowards with wild, unharnessed imaginations."

"What's wrong with that?" whispered Od to me with a snicker.

I snorted through my tears and hiccups, even though I did not know why she would want to be a coward in a harness. I cast another glance over my left shoulder and saw nothing but storm clouds writhing beyond the glass.

Aunt Viktoria's knitting needles went back to work with little *click, click, click, click, click*s. The storm—or Wee Willie Winkie—continued hurling hailstones at our window, and the witchy wind whistled through the cracks in the walls and chilled my skin with gooseflesh.

"Tell me about Papa disappearing," I whispered.

Od flopped her head back down against the pillow. "That is not a story for a birthday."

"I want to hear it, though." I nudged her arm, just above her wrist. "Please . . . tell me again why we don't have a mama and papa."

"Well . . ." Od swallowed. "As you know, it had something to do with the magician."

"Why did they let him into our house if he was so bad?"

"I just said, he wasn't entirely bad. Weren't you listening?"

"Yes."

My sister fidgeted on the mattress and could not seem to bend her long, storklike legs into just the right position. "There's something I haven't yet told you about the magician, Tru."

"What?"

She sniffed. "He was Mama's younger brother. Our other uncle. Aunt Vik's younger brother, too."

"He was?"

"Yes, I never told you because I didn't want to upset you, but now that you are five, you ought to know that's why Aunt Viktoria is always a little . . . well . . . *grumpy*. Long ago, she shared Mama's monster-hunting skills and a touch of our uncle's magic, but now that they're both gone, she's stopped believing in the marvelous. Her life lacks enchantment."

I wrinkled my forehead, not quite understanding the last part of that sentence. Od was always using grown-up phrases she found in the books she borrowed from a neighbor who received novels in the mail from relatives in the east. She would conjure up long and complicated words that perplexed even Aunt Viktoria.

"What does that mean?" I asked. "'Lacksen' . . . 'Lacksen-chant' . . . ?"

"I said, she lacks enchantment. She ignores her magical powers to give herself an excuse to be boring."

"Go back to the magician and Papa's part of the story."

"All right, all right." Od uncoiled one of my locks of hair again, this time with less of a spring. "The magician did not like that Papa kept Mama trapped inside our castle walls like Rapunzel. Papa was always leaving us to sell his paintings and to write poetry by the ocean. We would stay behind, all alone in that California canyon, with Mama forced to protect us from all sorts of terrible creatures—werewolves and bogeymen and *La Llorona,* the Weeping Woman. *La Llorona* was particularly horrible, Tru. I saw her one frightful night after you were born. She banged on my window and threatened to snatch you away while she shrieked and wept in the moonlight, wailing for her own children that she'd drowned."

I sucked air through my teeth and dared another peek at our present-day window in Oregon.

"So, one night," continued Od, "when he was visiting us, the magician put on his cape and raised his hands over the chair where Papa dozed . . ." Od raised both of her hands in the air in the dark, and the shadowy shapes of her fingers lengthened into claws that made my neck shrink down into my shoulders. "And Papa vanished." She dropped her hands to the bed. "Forever."

I threw the quilt over the top of my head and drew my good knee to my chest. "Where did he go, Od? Where is he?"

"He's just . . . gone. Never to be seen again." She tugged the blanket off my shoulder and pulled on my right earlobe. "Come now, Tru. You were the one who asked for the story."

My right leg throbbed from the attic's frigidness. I whimpered and grabbed my calf while my eyes watered.

"What's wrong?" asked my sister.

"Where's our mama?" I asked through gritted teeth.

The shine of my sister's eyes disappeared, and the room slipped deep into a darkness that reminded me of the sludge that oozed from the bottoms of molasses jars. "I don't want to talk about Mama and Papa anymore tonight," she said.

I grumbled and rubbed at my leg. One week earlier, our physician, Dr. Dunn, had declared that we might need to remove the leg, because it didn't do anything but dangle and ache, and it looked like a withered old tree branch. He did not say *how* he would get rid of it, so I imagined him snipping it off with a pair of giant pruning shears, which petrified me, of course. I had lived with that leg's strangeness ever since a bout of fevers overtook me and paralyzed me two years earlier. I would miss it, despite its uselessness.

Outside, the hail changed back into a steady rain.

I snuggled closer to my sister. "I'm scared Dr. Dunn is going to take away my leg."

"No, don't worry about that." Od stroked my head with a touch that relaxed my shoulders. "I won't let him. You're going to get better. One day soon, Mama will return and find a way to help you."

"Is she truly a monster-hunter?"

"Yes."

"In Oregon?"

"No, all over the United States, for the land is filled with wild and mystical beasts that terrify even the bravest huntsmen. If she lived in Oregon, we'd see her all the time, silly. Aunt Vik certainly wouldn't keep her from coming here and hugging her babies."

"And you're certain she'll make my leg better?"

Od nodded hard enough to cause the muslin fabric of her pillowcase to crinkle. "Yes."

"When?"

"After she's earned enough money for her bravery. People pay her in gold for her heroism, and one day we'll join her on her expeditions."

"We will?"

"Yes. It's our destiny to embark upon a daring quest to save the world. I've viewed the future in a mystical set of cards called the tarot, and I swear to you, Tru, we'll be heroes, just like Mama."

The pain shrank down to a mere twitch beneath my knee, as if Od had uttered one of the magician's spells to tame my discomfort.

With my eyes still shut, I imagined our mother dressed like the huntsman who rescued Little Red Riding Hood and her grandmother by chopping open the wolf's belly with an ax. She wore a long forest-green coat, a scarlet vest, black boots that stretched up to her knees, and a hat shaped like an upside-down flower pot. She carried a rifle nearly as long as she stood tall, and she smiled with the softness and adoration of a true mother, despite her bloody brutality with beasts.

I reached out and took hold of my sister's hand. "I liked the story. Thank you."

"You're welcome."

"Good night."

"Good night, Tru. Happy birthday."

My sister kissed my cheek, and I fell asleep amid dreams of castles and magicians and a mother who slayed the bogeyman.

Throughout the years, we would repeat that very same scene, over and over and over again, with Od and me tucked together in the bone-chilling attic until I grew too heavy for Uncle William to lift with the pulley. Eventually, he built an extra bedroom for us at the back of the house, but no matter where we slept or how big I got, my leg would ache, rain would drum against the glass, and my sister would spin her tales.

"Once upon a time . . ." she would always say in the beginning, "on a cold January morning in the year 1894, a girl named Trudchen Maria Grey came into the world in a castle built to resemble a stone Scottish fortress called Dunnottar . . ."

Up until the day Aunt Viktoria sent Od away when she was just seventeen, my sister spoon-fed me fairy tales to anesthetize my heart from the pain of truth, just as mothers slipped tonics laced with morphine into the mouths of teething babes. Instead of teaching me who we were and why we'd been banished to a small wooden house in the middle of an Oregon filbert farm, Od had stuffed my brain full of legends, tall tales, fables, ghost stories, myths, magic, monsters, and promises of an epic adventure.

In other words, *lies*.

HOW TO READ TEA LEAVES

As written in a letter from Odette Grey to Trudchen Grey, detailing Odette's months performing in a circus, dated August 4, 1907.

1. First and foremost, ensure that Aunt Vik has left the room and will not be observing this delicate process.

2. Sneak a spoonful of leaves into your cup and then pour the tea as usual.

3. Sip the tea with your eyes closed, elbows tucked against your ribs. Direct your mind toward the future. Silently ask the leaves to show what lies ahead. Drink the entire cup.

4. Rotate the teacup three times in the saucer.

5. Gently tilt the cup so that the excess liquid may drip into a napkin on the saucer. With utmost care, flip the cup upside down. Do be careful of this part, Tru. Try not to let too many leaves slide.

6. Turn the teacup upright.

7. Peer down at the shapes of the leaves stuck against the sides of the china.

8. Those lovely shapes are little windows into the moments yet to come, my dear Tru. If I can convince the girl who taught me these secrets to pen a guide illustrating what each shape means, I will send it straightaway. For now, use your best judgment and interpret the shapes yourself. I have a feeling you will see that greatness awaits.

CHAPTER ONE

Trudchen
January 14, 1909—Oregon

The creature, yet again, clung to the wall of my teacup.

Unlike my older sister, I held no interest in pursuing "real-life monsters," for I no longer believed in such poppycock. I read tea leaves for the mere fun of it, to see how many coincidences emerged whenever I compared the patterns of the leaves—essentially soggy clumps of dirt by that particular stage in the tea-drinking process—to the ordinary occurrences of my life. Sometimes I would see a flower in my cup and then spy a new bloom in the front garden. Before Christmas, the shape of a jacket manifested, and Aunt Viktoria surprised me with a new coat made of wool the bright purple of spring irises to replace the ill-fitting jacket I'd owned since I was twelve. Nothing of consequence ever resulted from my attempts at divining the future, nor did I expect it to.

And yet there he sat, my fourth sighting of the curious little figure in a week. An odd greeting to find on the morning of one's fifteenth birthday.

Beyond the wooden partition that separated the kitchen from our house's main room, Aunt Viktoria scrubbed the breakfast dishes clean and sneezed from another one of her colds. I had used her brief absence from the table as an opportunity to prepare the leaves for the reading, and now I willed her to remain in the kitchen for at least another five minutes.

Careful not to block the candlelight that twitched across the tabletop, I bent my face over the rim of the bone-colored teacup and contemplated the creature-shaped cluster within. He stood in profile on the rightmost side of the cup, and he was a spindly fellow with the wings of a bat and a head like a loaf of bread. Remnants of tea trickled down to the cup's bottom from his twiggy little legs, which ended in hooves. He inhabited the right side, which I always interpreted to mean "the east" whenever I pointed the handle toward me, "the south," and he lingered one inch below the rim, which I took as a sign that he represented an event that would occur in one to two weeks. The shape of a bell hung to his left. Crisscrossing lines—train tracks, perhaps—occupied the space to the left of the bell.

A twinge of dread pinched at my stomach. Every time I viewed the wee devil in a reading, he edged farther and farther up the side of the teacup, as though he prowled closer and closer on his tea-colored hooves to the point in time when our paths would cross. If he thought I would climb aboard a train and lug myself across the world to find him . . .

"Oh, don't be ridiculous," I scolded myself in a whisper, for I knew I was fretting over mere smudges in a cup.

"Are you finished yet, Trudchen?" asked Aunt Viktoria in her no-nonsense accent—part German (meaning that every phrase she uttered sounded blunt), part Oregon pioneer (meaning her voice offered no comfort for any hardship that did not involve transcontinental migration. Please note, however, that Aunt Viktoria had traveled to Oregon via train, not covered wagon).

I wiped away the leaves with my napkin. "Yes, Auntie."

Auntie clomped around the corner in her thick house shoes while drying her hands on a milk-stained apron. Her pinned-up hair, her cotton dress, her shoes—even the fine little hairs that sprouted across her upper lip—were all the same watery brown as the tea stains crumpled inside my napkin.

She reached for my plate, but I grabbed all the items that involved the reading.

"I'll get my cup and napkin, thank you," I said.

"I don't want you dropping the china. Does your hip still hurt?"

I averted my eyes from hers, never liking to discuss any new discomforts.

"Trudchen?" she asked, her head cocked. "Are you well enough to help with chores today?"

"I'm fine," I said. "You need my help."

I wrapped my left fingers around the curved handle of the hickory cane Uncle William had carved for me not long before he died, two years earlier. The ball of my thumb brushed the cold metal of the letter *T*, for *Trudchen*, set into the wood below the handle. Using my free hand, I crammed the soiled napkin into my cup. I then rose to my feet, accompanied by the usual *clink* of my leg brace as it locked into place at my knee.

Ever since small quivers of muscle movement had returned to my right leg when I was ten years old, I had worn a heavy iron brace that buckled around my knee and upper thigh with leather straps. The brace kept the limb as stiff as a wooden peg beneath my petticoats and skirts, but it allowed me to walk short distances. The bones of that leg hadn't grown quite right, so it was two and a half inches shorter than my left leg. To compensate, I wore a special black shoe with an oversize heel that was as ugly as sin but quite useful. For longer travels, Auntie pushed me around in a wicker wheelchair.

As always, I tromped to the kitchen with that special shoe thumping against the floorboards, then dragging across the wood like the whooshing of sandpaper. The leg brace creaked; the tip of my cane rapped against the wood. No matter how hard I tried, I could never creep about the house in secret, as Od often had as a child.

Aunt Viktoria followed with my plate and the teapot. She sighed, and I sighed, and the house itself seemed to wilt along with us. The floorboards sagged beneath our feet, and the curtains filled with a weak breath of air from a draft before promptly deflating.

Ever since she'd thrown Od out, ever since I'd left school to help with the farm full-time, Auntie and I had exchanged few words. We whiled away the hours by tending to the orchards and hunching over housework, cooking, scrubbing, chopping, scouring, mending, gutting, stirring, darning, *dying* . . .

The postmarks on my sister's correspondence from the past nineteen months ranged from Missouri to various cities throughout California. Elaborate tales of circuses, fortune-tellers, and wealthy supporters of her "supernatural studies" littered her letters, but I did not actually know what she was doing, how she managed to feed herself, or why our aunt had forced her to leave in the first place. Auntie sent her away shortly after Od started working for a lawyer's family in the town of Hillsboro, about seven miles away, and I always feared that Od had stolen something from the family to help pay for my care. I prodded Aunt Viktoria for this information dozens of times, but no one ever told me—delicate, fragile Trudchen—*anything*.

"Do you know what I wish I could do for my birthday?" I asked Auntie when we buttoned up our long woolen coats to embark upon the chores outdoors. I would undertake the more sedentary tasks—feeding the chickens, milking the cows—while Auntie pruned the winter-bare filbert trees.

"What do you wish?" she asked with a sniff, her nose already red from the chill emanating from beyond the door.

I drew a deep breath and tightened my grip on my cane. "I wish I could visit my sister. I'm certain she could cure my melancholy."

"You're not meant to go gallivanting about, Trudchen." Auntie swung open the door. "And there's no need for melancholy. You have a good life. Believe me, things could be far worse." She marched out to the toolshed beyond the chicken coop.

I limped after her, my right leg stiffer than ever. I had to thrust the leg forward with a great deal of force in order to make it move, which aggravated the joints in my right hip. "I would like to see my sister," I called after my aunt. "I miss her and worry about her all the time."

Auntie continued on to the little gray shed without another word. I stopped and watched her go, hope fluttering away, as it was apt to do on those freezing January mornings, without even the chatter of birdsong in the air to ease the loneliness and silence. A breeze filled my nose with the scents of chimney smoke, of last night's rain, along with whiffs of sweetness from the Pacific Coast Condensed Milk Company's big white condensary that sat beside the railroad tracks in nearby Carnation, Oregon.

The tracks that led out of town . . .

After supper that evening, Aunt Viktoria presented me with a gift wrapped in burlap: a hat she'd knitted with yarn the same shade of purple as my coat.

"Thank you," I said.

"Happy birthday, Trudchen."

That was that. We never exchanged any hugs or kisses. Aunt Viktoria did not seem to think them necessary, or else she had frightened Od and me so terribly as children, we never dared to get close to her for any semblances of affection.

Auntie cleared the dishes with a cough that turned into sneezes, and once again, I took advantage of her absence by finishing my tea to embark upon another attempt at divination. I rotated the cup three times and inhaled the fragrance of the leaves deeply into my nostrils.

Show me the future, I willed to the china, holding the cup upside down, my eyes closed, my posture erect, palms pressed against the warm, circular base. *If divination is real, please, I implore you, reveal what is to come.*

I opened my eyes, flipped the cup upright, and leaned over the china without breathing.

The creature was back.

Oh, he did not simply reappear in a nonchalant way. He had grown taller. He'd swelled to twice his previous thickness. He'd darkened. Moreover, he now hovered a mere half inch beneath the rim of the cup, once again in the region I believed to represent the east, and beside him hung that bell again, as well as the crisscrossing tracks and, now, four letters.

PHIL

Phil, as in . . . Philip?

How peculiar! I thought. *The creature now has a name. A regular, human name.*

Or . . . perhaps, I then surmised, *the figure represents a man and not a beast at all.*

Phil.

And a bell.

A bell with a little line weaving through it.

A bell with, perhaps, a crack.

The Liberty Bell, maybe.

Phil.

Philadelphia?

"Whatever is the matter with your teacup, Tru?" asked Auntie, catching me in the act of frowning down at the leaves.

I jerked my chin upward. "Nothing. It's just in need of some washing."

Once again, I crammed my napkin down inside the cup to hide my little game.

And again, I scolded myself for getting spooked and swayed by petty clusters of leaves.

✭

At nine o'clock, I retired to my bedroom, more fatigued than usual. My right hip burned as though on fire, and both legs lagged, even my left one. Everything popped and cracked and clicked when I walked.

After changing into my nightgown and unfastening the leather straps from my right leg, I used my hands to hoist the limb out of the iron brace, dropped it onto the mattress, and scooted backward on my bed until my spine met the wall. My long white nightgown hid the leg's scrawniness, the shortness, the ghostly paleness, but I didn't care all that much how it looked when I was alone. What I fretted about was the way my leg stopped me from seeing any true future for myself. Auntie had hinted more than once it would be rather difficult, if not impossible, for me to find a husband. I wasn't sure I believed her, for boys at school had always been kind to me, and just the year before I'd received a sweet valentine from a fellow named Peter, but that's what she said all the same. I could sew and embroider but had no means of traveling to work, even if I could take time off from helping Auntie with the farm.

Fine examples of my embroidery, in fact, surrounded my head at that very moment. Hummingbirds, blue jays, robins, sparrows, nuthatches, eagles, and cranes—all stitched with bright threads on square-shaped cloths. I couldn't afford to frame them, so I pinned the swatches to the bare boards of my walls with great care. No signs of my sister remained in the small quarters, however, aside from Mama's gold and copper hand mirror, propped on the windowsill, the reflective glass still pointed at the world beyond. On the back of the mirror was etched a circle divided into four parts by an intricately knotted rope. A "protective symbol," according to my sister.

Sometimes, when we'd slept side by side as children, Od would nudge me in the ribs and whisper, "Did you see that, Tru?"

"What?" I'd ask with a lift of my head.

"The mirror just flashed again—like a burst of lightning. That's what it always looks like when I catch it working."

I never personally saw the mirror casting even the smallest wink of light. I never witnessed any of it—the castle, the tarot cards, a mysterious old case of monster-hunting tools Od claimed our mother once owned. On my eleventh birthday, I experienced a vivid dream about a woman screaming outside our front door, and Od explained afterward it had been the ghost called *La Llorona*, a tragic, vengeful spirit who shared the same first name as our mother: Maria. Od had feared *La Llorona* ever since our early-childhood years in California.

But, as I said, it was only a dream. Everything about my life with Od had dripped with fantasy, reveries, whimsy, and bunkum.

My head ached. Tired of all those superstitions—tired of paying heed to legends and divination simply because they made me feel close to my sister—I lifted my leg back into the brace, fastened the straps, and grabbed my cane and that silly hand mirror. I then walked across the room to my pine wardrobe and buried the mirror deep beneath my summer dresses.

✹

In the middle of the night, something rapped against my window.

Mama's mirror remained tucked away in the wardrobe. For the first time in my fifteen years of life, I'd slept without that tarnished old piece of glass pointing toward the orchard, and now SOMETHING WAS RAPPING AGAINST MY WINDOW!

With my teeth clenched, I forced my eyes to my right with an agonizing strain of ocular muscles. I peered through the darkness at the drawn curtains that hung no more than two feet from my bed. The rapping, initially a tap, soon loudened to a full-fledged knock that vibrated across my skull and the walls of my bedroom.

BANG! BANG! BANG! BANG!

Chills coated my arms and my neck, and my hands and feet went numb. *Why, oh, why didn't you just leave that mirror in the window?* I asked myself. *Why on earth did you believe that being torn to shreds by a half-dog, half-human monstrosity —or whatever horrific wretch is pounding on the glass out there . . . oh, God, listen to it pound! Why did you think a painful death involving sharp teeth and ripped flesh would be better than boredom? Why didn't you listen to your sister? She's been warning you about this very moment ever since you could first understand words! It's going to hurt so terribly to die this way!*

"Tru?" I heard someone ask—a muffled sound.

My eyes stretched wider.

"Tru?" called the voice again, and my mind scrambled to interpret what it had heard, to decipher the voice—a female voice a tad higher than Aunt Viktoria's.

"Are you in there?" she asked again.

I gasped and sat upright.

"Tru? Are you there?"

I sprang off the side of the bed, but my right leg, unsupported by the brace, gave way, which led to my falling and crashing onto my left knee in the dark. Ignoring the pain and the bruising, I scrambled up to a kneeling position and lifted the bottom of my curtain, discovering *my sister's* face glowing in the light of a lantern, directly outside my window. She wore a black hat with little red roses, and the curls that snuck out from beneath the brim looked a tad darker than when she was younger; her face seemed a mite fuller and older. Without a doubt, though, it was my Odette, peering at me with warm brown eyes.

I pressed my right hand against the glass. "Od?"

She pushed a glove-covered palm against mine. "Please, open up."

I raised the sash as far as I could from my kneeling position, my hands slipping, shaking, unable to function quite right.

"What in heaven's name are you doing here?" I asked.

She lifted the window the rest of the way open and spread the curtains apart. "Is Aunt Vik asleep?"

"Yes."

"May I come in?"

"Why didn't you knock on the front door?"

"I don't want her to know I'm here just yet." She hoisted a tan bag—an iron-bottom Gladstone, the type that folded into two compartments—through the open window and plopped it down with a thud on the floor below the sill. She turned away for a moment, then somehow climbed into the room with a mahogany-colored case gripped in her right hand and the lantern dangling from the crook of her left fingers. She wore a plum-colored coat with a high collar and flared cuffs that reminded me of Aunt Viktoria's old dresses from the 1880s. She smelled of ashes and dust. I almost believed she'd just appeared outside my window in a puff of smoke.

I remained on the floor, my mouth agape.

Od shut the window and the curtains and plunked herself down in front of me, the lantern and luggage parked by her sides. "My heavens." She grabbed hold of my shoulders. "Look how much you've grown, Tru. Just look at you! Happy birthday."

"You . . . y-y-you came," I said, and the room spun and tilted, the air too thin to breathe. All I could think of was the vision of an Odette-style monster in my teacup, and the railroad tracks, and how this all must be a dream.

Od pulled me to her and squeezed her arms around me, her clasp real and solid and not like a hallucination at all. The felt of her hat brushed my left cheek; her warmth washed through me and stopped the room from tilting. We cried quiet tears against each other, careful not to wake Aunt Viktoria, who snored on the other side of the wall. In an instant, that embrace transported us back into our former selves, tucked together in our attic bed with nothing between us—not time, nor heartbreak, nor secrets.

"Why did you finally come back?" I asked in a whisper.

"I wanted to surprise you for your birthday."

"Where have you been?"

"Didn't you receive my letters?"

I sniffed. "Where have you *really* been?"

She lifted her head away from mine. "I've also returned because of matters most urgent."

"What matters?"

"Tell me honestly, and this is vital, Tru"—her grip on my arms strengthened—"has anything troubled you now that you've just turned fifteen? Has anything peculiar occurred?"

My thoughts turned again to the beast with bat wings in my teacup. A shiver trembled through me, but I clamped my lips shut and refrained from discussing anything supernatural with my sister.

"Tru?"

"No." I wiped my eyes. "The only thing that's troubled me is boredom and tiredness. And not being able to see you, of course. I've missed you terribly. It's hurt so much."

"I know," she said, her voice a mere whisper. She held my hands, and her eyes glistened in the lamplight. "Aunt Vik will have a conniption when she sees me here, but there's something I absolutely must tell you."

"What?"

She swallowed. "I know I've buried you in all sorts of wild tales throughout the years, but there's truth to the stories about our mother, Tru. You must believe me—she was special. She wasn't an ordinary mother, and I've learned she didn't leave Oregon just to save our uncle Magnus from dying of asthma, as Aunt Vik's claimed all these years."

The excitement in Od's voice warned she was about to dump another one of her "wild tales" into my lap. A sharp stab of disappointment punctured my elation.

"What did . . ." I cleared my throat and squirmed. "What did you learn?"

Od leaned closer. "As I've already told you hundreds of times before, it runs in our family, this ability to protect others. Before she came to America, our mother's mother was a fierce Protector of villages in the Black Forest of Germany, and Mama inherited that talent from her. But the gifted people in our bloodline don't just hunt down dark creatures." Od's gloved fingers grew warmer against my hands. "They attract them. The creatures come to them."

My shoulders sank. "Od, please. I don't want any tales of monsters right now . . ."

"Listen to me." She cast a quick glance toward the bedroom door. "It started sometime when Mother was fifteen, after her parents both died. Aunt Vik, Uncle Magnus, and Mama lived on their parents' farm in the hills west of Portland, and *things*—terrifying things beyond normal animal and human categorization—fought to get into the house late at night, despite all the charms and bells they hung from the eaves, just like the amulets hanging outside your very own window. They were forced to kill the creatures or to send them away through special mirrors." Od turned toward the window and lifted the bottom edge of the curtain. "Oh, Lord!" She whipped her head my way and glowered. "Where's the hand mirror I left with you?"

"Od, please, stop—"

"Where is it? Why isn't it protecting you anymore?"

"I've hidden it."

She jumped to her feet. "Where?"

"It doesn't matter."

"Yes, it does." She dragged me up to a standing position. "Fetch it, please! Hurry! This isn't a joke, Tru."

"I can't hurry anywhere."

"You must. You're fifteen now. The same thing that happened to our mother could happen to you."

"Od, stop!" I yanked my arms out of her grip, but without my brace to support me, I fell backward to the floor and landed on my rump with a jolt of my neck.

"Tru! Are you all right?" Od reached down to help me, but I shoved her hand away.

"I'm not hurrying anywhere," I said, "and I'm certainly not going to chase after any monsters, real or otherwise. If you think my leg miraculously healed while you were gone, then you're even more childish than you sound."

Od froze at those words, her arm still outstretched, her eyes round with shock.

I lowered my face and heard how callous I had sounded—even though it was true: her refusal to face reality seemed worse than ever.

"I'm sorry," I said. "I shouldn't have said that."

Aunt Viktoria's mattress squeaked in the room next door. Od and I whipped our heads in that direction.

A moment later, another snore rumbled from beyond the wall, behind my embroidery collage of birds frozen mid-flight. In unison, my sister and I released held breaths.

Od kneeled in front of me and removed her gloves. "I didn't mean to make you fall. I'm so sorry, Tru. Are you hurt?"

"Just this morning," I said in a whisper, "I told Auntie that more than anything in the world, I wished to be with you."

"You see, then?" She grabbed my hands. "Birthday wishes do come true."

"Ever since you left, I've longed to leave this farm and find you, to live with you, but I've always known I would have to be reasonable about it. I want a real life that would make me happy, not a pretend one."

Od pursed her eyebrows. "This isn't pretend, Tru. I've saved up money. I can buy us train tickets, food, and shelter. I want to take you far away from this place and seek our destiny."

"Where do you expect us to go?"

"Anywhere you wish."

"I would love that—truly I would. But I'm still growing a bit and need to make sure I'm in a leg brace the proper size. I need my wheelchair. I require care and money."

"I'll take care of you."

"It's one thing to dream about seeing the world, but, honestly, Od"—I shook my head—"it wouldn't be practical."

Od withdrew her hands from mine. "We would hire ourselves out as specialists. We'd earn money."

I shrank back. "What type of specialists?"

"Let's get you off this floor"—she wrapped an arm around my back—"and onto the bed."

She helped me up and supported my full weight against her. Without the brace and my raised shoe, I had to hop on my left leg to avoid falling, but she clutched me through every hop.

I sank down on the edge of the bed. Od kept her arms around me until she was certain I was safely situated.

"What did you mean by specialists?" I asked again.

My sister stood upright and wriggled her shoulders out of

the plum-colored coat. Her attention strayed again to the window. "I honestly would feel a hundred times better if I could put that mirror back on the sill. Something rustled through the bushes when I was out there, and it sounded hungry."

"How did you get here?" I asked. "Is someone with you?"

"No, I took the last electric streetcar to Carnation and waited at the Colonial Hotel until nightfall." She draped her coat across the foot of the bed and then fussed with a little pearl that adorned her black hat. "Do you remember that porter at the hotel—the one who grew up believing in a horrifying creature called Rawhead and Bloody Bones?"

"Od, I don't care about creatures right now . . ."

"He still works there. The porter, that is, not the creature. He arranged for me to eat a free supper."

From the depths of the black felt of her chapeau, Od withdrew a hatpin ten inches in length, topped by that innocent little pearl. I shuddered, for it looked as if she were wielding a small sword with a lethally sharp tip. I'd heard a story of a woman who jabbed at a gentleman caller's chest with a hatpin as a joke but punctured his heart by mistake. The man died!

"Do you mean monster-hunters, Od?" I asked, gripping the edge of the mattress. "Is that the type of specialists you're talking about?"

Something fell against the wall outside, and we both gasped and flinched. Od raised the hatpin in her fist like a dagger.

"Just go get the mirror," I said, a quaver in my voice. "It's tucked in the bottom drawer of the wardrobe."

Od tossed the pin onto my bedside table and bolted to the wardrobe. I eyed the window, my heart pounding, but I knew in my gut that the wind, nothing worse, had tipped over a rake or a shovel out there. The bells and charms that hung from our eaves tinkled in a breeze.

Beneath the window sat Od's tan traveling bag and that mahogany-colored case she'd carried inside. On the latter, next to the handle, I spotted a word of some sort, engraved on an oval plate of silver. I bent forward at my waist and read the engraving.

MarViLUs

My lips parted with a sense of wonder.

MarViLUs.

How familiar that strange spelling of the word seemed. I recalled a long-ago moment, bathed in the fuzzy haze of my earliest memories, in which Od had lifted the dust ruffle of a bed the size of a pirate ship and showed me those silver letters on that very same case.

Marvelous, she had said. *It says marvelous.*

"How long has the mirror been missing from the window?" asked Od in a voice that startled me enough to forget about the case. She parted the curtains and arranged the mirror just so. The reflective glass again faced the craggy silhouettes of the filbert trees outside.

"Where have I seen that leather case before?" I asked.

Od peeked at me over her shoulder. "Do you mean Mother's case?"

"Is this *the* case?" I scooted myself sideways on the bed to better see it. "The famous case of tools you always told me about?"

Od lifted the case as though it weighed nothing at all and perched herself beside me on the bed. "It most certainly is."

I smelled the case's antiquity in the dust and the leather and realized what an old relic of the past it seemed. Our entire childhood was rapidly turning into a precious antique.

"Od?" I asked, my heart heavy. "Is our mother . . . is she dead?"

"Thankfully, no."

"Have you seen her?"

"Yes."

I sat up straight. "Where? When?"

"Do you know what this means?" Od ran her right index finger across the silver letters.

"Od, tell me the truth," I said, sliding closer to her on my backside. "Where is she?"

"Look at the letters." She pointed to the first three of the eight characters. "'Mar . . .'" Her finger moved to the next two. "'Vi . . . ,'" she said, and she pronounced the syllable as though she were about to add a *k* at the end. "And Us." Her eyes met mine and urged me to listen—to *truly* listen.

I dropped my gaze to the letters.

"Mar," she said again, enunciating each letter with great care. "Vi. Us."

I gasped, suddenly understanding. "Is it 'Mar' for Maria and 'Vi' for Viktoria? And . . . the 'Us' is for . . ." I squinted at the letters. "Is it for the last two letters of our uncle Magnus's name?"

"Clever girl." Od beamed with pride, the way she had whenever she'd taught me how to complete some complex task, such as buckling shoes or sounding out words in Uncle William's monthly bulletins from the Oregon Agricultural Experiment Station.

"And what is that bizarre, gargantuan *L* doing in the middle of the word?" I jabbed at that awkward-looking letter, which reminded me of a six-foot-tall boy named Ernest Cole, who stood at the center of a photograph taken of all of us schoolchildren years ago.

"It's for their surname, Lowenherz," said Od. "In German, the name means 'lionheart.'"

"I see a lock," I said, picking at the silver metal, "but is there a key?"

"It doesn't require a key."

I spotted a brass key dangling from a gold chain around her neck. "Then what is that key doing there"—I flicked the brass with the back of a finger—"hanging around your neck?"

Od squeezed her left hand around the key, swallowing up the metal in her fist. "It's for a little box that's sitting in my Gladstone bag."

"What's in the box?"

"Heavens!" She rolled her eyes. "You do still bubble over with questions, don't you?"

"What is in the box, Od?"

She took a deep breath. "Just a story I wrote. I'll show you it later. That's not what's important at the moment. Right now I need you to agree to come away with me."

I cast her a sidelong glance. "To hunt down monsters, you mean?"

"They'll be coming for you, and it's far better we find them first instead of the other way around. We must also continue cataloging otherworldly beasts. Do you remember all those stories we collected from neighbors and condensary workers about where they were born and what types of monsters they believed in?"

"Of course I remember."

"Remember their eye-widening tales of flying serpents, owl men, dog men, thunderbirds, water dragons . . . Oh!" She sat up straight and palmed her cheeks. "There was even the Kalapuya legend of a water monster named Amhuluk who enjoyed drowning children five miles away from this very house."

I nodded. Like an expert folklorist, Od had, indeed, catalogued our findings in a black leather journal, grouping the supernatural creatures by regions, defining traits, and their proclivity for eating—or at least *murdering*—wicked children. I, being a budding naturalist, had sat beside her during these interviews and drawn crude sketches of whatever half-human animal or fantastical winged beast our subjects described. Od had taken the book along with her when she left home.

The exhilaration in her eyes now made me fear that she viewed our old catalog not as a lark but as a legitimate guidebook that would tell her where to travel with a rifle, a sword, or whichever lethal weapon she happened to acquire, and she would one day kill a person whom she mistook for a beast—just as Don Quixote attacked windmills he mistook for giants.

If my sister, a girl one month shy of her nineteenth birthday—technically, a woman—still believed in monsters and mystical leather cases, then one of two scenarios was now true.

1. Od and I genuinely hailed from a family with the ability to fight evil.

2. Od's stories were the mutterings of a broken girl who'd lost her lovely mind.

I feared the latter possibility far more than the first.

"Tru." She gripped my right shoulder. "Future generations desperately require our help. They'll need to know how to eradicate these creatures. We've got to head out and actually experience battling the darkness so we can pass on this knowledge and save them."

My throat thickened. For a moment, I couldn't swallow or breathe.

Od took hold of my left hand. "Let me tell you the history of this leather case."

I drew my hand away. "I told you, I don't want any more stories."

"Not a story—a *history*," she said. "You see, whatever the Lowenherzes required to fend off trouble could be found within this receptacle. Uncle Magnus enchanted the case, Aunt Vik created the charms to protect it, and Mama used it to fight off their unsettling attackers. That's how they worked together after their parents died tragically and they lived all alone in their house in the forested hills." Od ran her fingers over the leather with a soft and fluttery sound. "When battling monstrous creatures became too much, too tiring, and Uncle Magnus struggled with asthma and almost died, Mama took him down to San Diego, where the air was better for breathing and fewer demons dwelled. Aunt Vik stayed behind, for she had fallen in love with Uncle William. Plus, she possessed no glamour that beckoned dark creatures to her. That's one of the reasons Mama left us here: we'd be safe from monsters, guarded by Aunt Viktoria's amulets, and far from the person who attracts the darkness . . . until we would grow old enough to attract the darkness ourselves."

"If all of this is true," I said with a tilt of my head, my eyes narrowed, "then why didn't monsters approach you when *you* turned fifteen?"

Od averted her eyes from mine. "Oh, I've battled many a dark demon, Tru."

Again, I couldn't swallow. My throat squeezed shut, my nostrils swelled, and tears blurred my vision.

"You must be awfully tired from your journey," I said, a quaver cutting through my voice. "I'm sure you traveled a great distance . . ."

She frowned. "You don't believe me."

I wiped my eyes. "Please, tell me honestly . . . are you well, Od?"

She wrapped her hands around the sides of the case. "I am now. I will be if you leave this house with me tomorrow morning. We mustn't waste time, Tru . . ."

"Were you lonely when you were gone?"

She mustered a weak smile. "Oh, there were dozens of other troublemakers like me out in the world. We all helped each other get through any homesickness and tears."

"Where were you?"

She shook her head. "I already told you, in my letters."

"Od . . ." I placed my hand in the space between the two of us on my quilted bedspread. "Will you please believe that I'm no longer a child and that I can face reality, no matter how harsh that reality might be?"

She lowered her face and breathed through her nose. Her spine shortened. The brim of her hat sank down her forehead. She no longer seemed the confident girl who'd just launched herself through my window.

"Was I even born in a castle?" I asked.

She smiled a genuine smile then. In the time it took me to blink, however, her lips sank, and she picked at the case's bottom right corner.

"Was I, Od? Did our father come galloping in from the coast and ride up to towers made of stone?"

"What do you think?"

"I think . . ." I cleared my throat. "I think that I was probably born in a regular house or a hospital, and there was nothing magical in the slightest about my entrance into the world."

Od turned her face my way, her left eyebrow cocked. "Ah," she said, "now that's where you're wrong . . ."

CHAPTER TWO

Odette
January 14, 1894—California

O n the morning Trudchen Maria Grey entered the world, the eastern sky blazed with a magnificent orange light that made me believe someone had struck a match to the heavens. I dangled from the branch of an olive tree in front of our California ranch house, the thick bark scratching at my palms, the muscles of my arms straining to keep my hands attached to the crooked bough. The ground below my bare feet brightened to the color of flames, and I gasped in wonder at its grandeur. If I had peeked into one of the little protective mirrors that Mama hung by the windows and doors—her *Hexenspiegels*—I would have seen my face glowing orange, as well, and my eyes reflecting clouds made of streaks of molten lava.

I wasn't quite four years old yet. Mama lay in bed inside our house, her belly swollen, her mood foul. She had vomited all night, and the house reeked of a stench like spoiled milk that no amount of nose-pinching could hide. I had stolen outside as soon as the first rays of light nudged between my curtains.

On the back step, our white cat, Renoir, watched me hanging from the branch. His fur, too, reflected the conflagration of the sunrise, and his icy blue eyes latched upon me without blinking. No one else watched over me, so he seemed to take it upon himself to ensure I didn't fall and crack open my skull. Mama could not budge beneath that belly, and Papa rode about by the sea, selling his paintings to men with a taste for fine art and pockets bulging with money.

So, there I dangled, my muscles quivering, the sky shining in my eyes, Renoir flicking his tail, Mama hidden away inside our eggshell-brown farmhouse that also glowed bright orange . . . when all of a sudden a scream ripped through the silence.

I dropped to the dirt below me. Every hair on my body stood on end, and the echo of the scream pulsated inside my head, right behind my eyeballs. Mama's collection of bells and charms tinkled from the eaves of the front porch.

A second shriek followed. An unholy howl. I thought of the diabolical Weeping Woman my father had warned me about— *La Llorona*—and my feet froze to the earth. My knees smarted from my sudden drop to the ground, and my heart shuddered in my chest. Renoir no longer sat on the back step. He had launched himself into the safety of the olive grove, far from that yowl of horror, and I did not blame him one bit.

I waited in a crouched position on the cold winter soil for what seemed like the rest of my life. The house stood still in front of me, and the bright wildfire sky dimmed to a muted peach, almost white. The only thing that caused me to move from that spot was another hideous cry.

"ODETTE!"

My mother.

I sprang off the ground and shot into the house and up the stairs. I found Mama in her bedroom, bent over her washbasin, panting, sweating, her eyes squeezed shut. The protruding stomach that held my sister drooped below her like the hump of a capital D, and she stood with her legs akimbo. The thin fabric of her nightgown failed to completely conceal her naked hip and backside beneath, which made her seem so exposed and fragile and *alien* to me.

She groaned and clutched the washbasin, her arms and legs shaking.

"Mama?" I asked.

"Go fetch Mrs. Alvarado!" she yelled through a curtain of brown hair slick with sweat. "NOW!"

I retraced my path through the house and bolted out the front door. The soles of my feet slammed across the dry dirt road, and I wished I had taken time to put on a pair of shoes. The skirt of my plaid dress and my long brown hair flapped into the air behind me like the sails of a ship, speeding me forward.

A movement to my right caught my eye. In a flash, the lean body of a coyote dashed through the canyon's scrubby bushes and disappeared beyond the live oaks that populated the pale green hills. The sky to the east now shone in an empty shade of blue, all the fire in the clouds snuffed out. The world looked faded and desolate and unfathomably huge.

Another mile down the road lived Mrs. Alvarado—mother of eight—who would help Mama push her baby into the world. Mrs. Alvarado's husband hailed from a family of rancheros who had owned the land beneath our feet when California belonged to Mexico. Mrs. Alvarado's family once owned a rancho to the west.

Halfway to the Alvarados' house, while imagining Mama fixing me a breakfast of toast and jam, I ran across something in the dirt so sharp, it made the sole of my left foot sing with pain.

"Nooooo!"

I screamed and hopped about on my good leg to slow myself down and then lifted the foot to investigate the gore. A dark red gash stretched across the wrinkly skin of my entire sole. Blood oozed to the surface and dripped to the ground as crimson raindrops.

"Oh, no! Mama!"

I plopped down on the dirt in the middle of the canyon and plunked my forehead against my left knee. Insects hummed near the oak trees that shadowed the road ahead of me, and their high-pitched buzzing made my foot throb all the more. Blood trickled into the cold, hard ground, beneath which rattlesnakes slumbered for the winter. I imagined them awakening, their tongues flicking, rattles shaking, while I sat above them on the road, alone, bleeding, sobbing.

I could cry all I wanted, but Mama wailed through her own throes of agony back at the house while Papa tried his darnedest to keep us warm and fed. Handsome Uncle Magnus, just nineteen years old at the time, slept in a saloon down in San Diego. My mama's mama lay dead in a cemetery in Oregon, gone since 1887. My mama's father rested beside her, also dead. Aunt Viktoria was eating breakfast with her husband on a nut farm more than a thousand miles away.

No one would help me.

So . . . I helped myself.

I closed my eyes and told myself a tale of a girl who saved

the world by running a mile on a foot that leaked a trail of blood behind her. Because of the girl's astounding bravery, her blood seeped through the pebbles and dirt of the bone-hard ground and transformed into a garden of red, red roses that pushed their way out of the rocks and the soil. Blossoms bloomed for the child when she returned home on that same path, and not one single thorn protruded from the stems. She picked every last flower and carried a bouquet to her mother, who held a brand-new baby girl with the fuzzy blond hair of a duckling. Her mother thanked her and promised she would never be alone—never suffer any more pain—ever again.

And they lived happily ever after.

Mrs. Alvarado—a tall, sturdy woman with hair as dark as our canyon nights—tossed me a pair of one of her children's brown boots for the journey back home. She rushed about in a blur of black skirts and billowing white sleeves. She threw on her shoes and a coat, barked orders to the older children, and fetched a basket containing supplies such as cloth and scissors that would somehow be used for the birth. Her oldest daughter, Josefina, wrapped my bleeding foot in a rag and helped me stuff my toes into the left boot. The house smelled of frying eggs and peppers, and my stomach groaned with hunger.

"Are you excited about a baby coming in your house?" asked Josefina, her pretty brown eyes smiling.

I shrugged and wished I could simply stay in her house and eat their scrumptious eggs, which Mrs. Alvarado called *huevos*.

"You are a brave girl, running all this way by yourself," added Josefina.

With my tongue poking out of the right side of my mouth for added strength, I forced the rest of my left foot into the boot. "I saw a coyote," I said through my straining and squeezing, my voice creaking like an old man's.

Josefina grinned. "You did?"

"He wanted to eat me up like Red Riding Hood's wolf, but I kept running and running and running."

"Good girl." She patted my knee. "You are protecting your baby brother or sister already by ignoring trouble and coming straight here for help. Guarding your younger sibling is something you will need to do for the rest of your life."

"*Vámonos,* Odette!" cried her mother, and I jumped out of the chair and followed.

Mrs. Alvarado half walked, half jogged back home with me, her arms pumping, her shoulders and torso swinging from side to side as she huffed and puffed through the oaks and the scrub. The basket dangled off her left arm.

I spotted dots of blood from my foot, left behind like a trail of bread crumbs. I had to hop on my right foot most of the way. Mrs. Alvarado hissed her disapproval whenever I fell down from all the hopping.

We found Mama sitting on her bed, her legs bent and spread wide open, her hands clutching her knees, her knuckles white. She gritted her teeth and bellowed like our neighbor's old dairy cow when it broke its leg in a ditch and had to be shot.

Mrs. Alvarado threw her basket at me and ripped off her coat. "The baby's already crowning."

I caught a glimpse of the view between my mother's legs. Vomit charged up my throat.

Mama tipped her head back and roared with so much ground-shaking force, my father probably heard her all the way out by the ocean and stopped selling his paintings mid-sentence. Uncle Magnus probably awoke with a start and a belch in the saloon. Even Grandma and Grandpa Lowenherz probably heard her in their Oregon graves. I dropped the basket and covered my ears, but Mrs. Alvarado, unfazed by the ruckus, propped her left foot on the bed and yanked my sister out of my mother.

Trudchen Maria Grey sprang into the world as a purple, slimy, blood-covered creature with trembling hands and a face scrunched up with fury. She let out a cry that sounded like the bleating of an angry goat, and she looked as if she wanted to get put straight back into my mother, which I wouldn't have minded one bit. Mama collapsed against the pillows. Mrs. Alvarado chuckled from deep within her chest and said, "You have another feisty little girl, Maria." I puked all over Mrs. Alvarado's daughter's boots.

It was not love at first sight.

Four days after the birth, my uncle Magnus came to visit us. Mama, Tru, and I had been sleeping in the front room, and we missed the telltale clip-clops of the dappled horse, Glancer, that he rented from a livery down in San Diego in order to reach us every couple of months. The front door blew open, and Mama sat up on the sofa, clutching Tru to her chest.

"Louis?" she asked, hope ringing in her voice.

"No, it's me," said my uncle, and he rounded the corner with a yellow-haired rag doll tucked beneath one arm and a crocheted green and blue blanket nestled under the other. His hair—reddish brown like mine and Mama's—looked damp and mussed from the hat he must have left hanging on a hook on the front porch, and his face needed a shave. Prickly-looking whiskers sprouted all over his chin and above his upper lip, even though he couldn't yet grow a mustache even half as thick as Papa's.

"Uncle Magnus!" I cried, and I flew across the room and attached myself to his left leg. The rich scents of his horse and leather saddle flooded my nose.

"Hello, darling." He rubbed his hand through the hair on the top of my head, which hadn't been brushed in four days. The blanket he carried slipped down to my face with the harsh stink of a flowery perfume. "What have we got here?"

I thought he meant the baby sleeping against my mother, but he reached down and pulled a shiny copper penny out from behind my right ear. As always, I slapped my hand against the place from which the coin had materialized, looking for the mysterious slot in my skin that produced money— and sometimes even candy—whenever Uncle Magnus came around. He smiled and rubbed my head again, although his expression soured when his fingers became ensnared in one of my tangles.

"So . . ." He wrestled his hand out of the knot and swaggered over to my mother and sister. "I think introductions are in order."

Mama sighed and pulled back the white blanket shielding my sister's face. "I had another girl. Four days ago. Trudchen. Trudchen Maria."

Uncle Magnus straightened his neck. "You . . . you named her after Mama?"

My mother nodded, and a moment later her bottom lip trembled and she burst into tears. She'd cried at least three times every hour ever since my sister came screeching into the world.

I crept over to my uncle's side and grabbed hold of his warm left hand. He peeked down at me with concern in his eyes and gave my palm a squeeze.

"Well"—he swallowed and cleared his throat—"I've got presents for both children. A new doll for you, Od." He lifted his left elbow, which allowed the doll to fall straight into my arms. "And a blanket for little Tru."

"*Trudchen*," said Mama. "Don't start calling her nicknames, the way you make Odette sound like she's odd. Who made the blanket?"

"A kind lady."

"What type of lady?"

Uncle Magnus loosened his fingers from mine. "One who wanted to make a blanket for my new niece or nephew."

Mama grabbed the blanket and sniffed it. Her hair hung over her face like seaweed—like the ratty locks of a sea witch. Bruise-colored bags bulged beneath her red-rimmed eyes, and the long black nightgown she wore didn't help her frightful appearance. "It smells of cheap perfume, Magnus." She threw the blanket at my uncle's stomach. "Get it out of here."

"I was just trying to be nice." He glanced over his shoulder. "Where's Louis?"

Mama pressed her cheek against Tru's cheek and cried again.

Uncle Magnus stepped forward. "Are you all right, Maria?"

"Go take a bath!" she screamed. "You smell like whores!"

He jumped back, and I clung fast to my doll.

"Go!" She pointed toward the kitchen. "Clean that filthy stink off you, and take Odette with you. I can't stand looking at the two of you anymore, always wanting something from me."

"Come on!" Uncle Magnus steered me away by my shoulders.

"You're always wanting something from me!" cried Mama again, and her words slapped me in the back and pushed me forward.

My uncle led me into a room just off the front door that served as my father's art studio whenever Papa came home to create his work. Paint-spattered tarps blanketed the floor, and an easel bearing a portrait of a redheaded woman with bushy eyebrows stood in one corner, below a crinkled old poster for P. T. Barnum's famous elephant, Jumbo.

Uncle Magnus perched himself on Papa's work stool and hoisted me onto his lap. The stool's legs squeaked against the floor with a hiccup sort of sound, and the wood creaked and sagged beneath our shared weight. I buried my face against my uncle's scratchy coat and tried not to cry like Mama. Tears and snotty sniffles erupted, nonetheless.

My uncle cupped a warm hand around the back of my head. "Has she been like that since the birth?"

I nodded against him.

"And your father hasn't been here?"

I shook my head.

"Has she been feeding you?"

"No."

"She hasn't?"

"I hate Mama right now. And I hate Trudchen. Everything's ruined. I almost got eaten by a coyote."

"When?"

"When I ran to tell Mrs. Alvarado the baby was coming. I saw him running through the bushes. Snakes tried to get me, too."

My uncle nestled his whiskery chin against the top of my head and pulled me close against him. "Your mama would never let anything eat you or steal you away. I don't know if she's ever told you her secret, Od . . ."

I kept my face smashed against his coat, but I lifted my eyes toward his when he didn't say anything more. "What secret?"

"Your mother, just like her mama before her"—he brushed his fingers through my tangled hair—"hunts monsters."

I gasped. *Oh, heavens!* I had always wondered about all those bells and amulets made of various metals that jangled above the doors and windows . . . and Mama's rule that we put our shoes next to our beds with the toes facing the bedroom door every night, her insistence that I wear my special *Hexenspiegel* necklace—a copper flower with a mirror the size of a half-dollar positioned in the center. Any evil entity who saw himself in such a mirror would have his evilness reflected three times back at him.

"Have you ever seen the leather case she keeps hidden under her bed?" asked Uncle Magnus.

My eyes expanded. "No."

"It's a special case from Germany that once belonged to our mother—your grandmother, who, as a young woman, protected her village from *Alps* and werewolves and all sorts of other nefarious beasts."

I wrapped my fingers around the lapel of his coat. "What is an *Alp*?"

"If you don't know what it is, darling"—Uncle Magnus grinned—"then that must mean your mother has kept those nasty nightmares away from you."

Tru wailed again in the other room. My shoulders jerked from the suddenness of her cry.

"Mama can't fight monsters anymore," I said in a whisper. "Tru broke her."

"No, give her time. She's simply exhausted from having the baby. We all need to be nice and quiet and very, very helpful, and she'll be back to protecting you and your sister soon."

I lifted my face and saw the reflection of myself in my uncle's dark irises and pupils. He had deep brown eyes that made women and men alike turn their heads when he walked down streets, or so Mama said. She didn't like to think of him alone in the wild city of San Diego and always spoke of people wanting to devour him. She loved him more than anything. Uncle Magnus always told me that she'd saved his life by moving him to California when he was a sickly boy who couldn't breathe. Now I imagined monsters sitting on his chest when he was little, squashing the air from his lungs while he slept.

"I'm going to marry you when I'm older, Uncle Magnus," I said.

He smiled. "Well, that's very sweet of you, but you can't marry me, Od. I'm your uncle."

"Papa says I can't marry you because you're a jackass."

At that, Uncle Magnus laughed, and his cheeks flushed pink.

I snickered, but I didn't actually understand the reason behind his laughter. Papa was always calling Uncle Magnus a "jackass" and a "ne'er-do-well" whenever he wasn't around. Uncle Magnus played piano and took odd jobs to earn his keep, and when he was eighteen he'd spent a night in jail for wandering around drunk in public. Papa predicted he would soon get something called "the clap," and when I asked what that meant, my father said, "Well, it certainly doesn't mean people will be applauding him."

My uncle reached behind my right ear and pulled out some sort of object that rustled against my hair.

"This is a tarot card, Od." He handed me a card illustrated with the image of a woman in a red robe with her hair wrapped in a white headdress. She sat in a fancy, high-backed chair, and a lion lay at her feet like a regal pet cat.

I pinched the card between my fingers. My breath fluttered against the thick paper, making it tremble.

"How do you play?" I asked.

"It's not a game. The tarot predicts your future." He tapped the back of the card with the ball of his left index finger. "This one is *La Force*, which foretells that you'll become a woman of great strength and courage. You yourself will be able to conquer dangerous creatures. And this"—with a swish of his hand, he pulled another card from the enchanted spot behind my ear—"is the Two of Cups, which may mean you'll fall in love, or it may mean you will find yourself with another type of powerful partnership. You will be at your strongest when you are with someone else. Seek the company of loved ones who can help you."

I took the card and studied the image of two yellow chalices. The cups were not half as exciting as the woman with the pet lion. I peeked back up at my uncle and squeezed my lips together.

"What is it?" He cocked his head. "Do you want another card?"

I nodded. "Show me one that says I'll be a magician like you."

Uncle Magnus grinned with a spark in his eye and withdrew a third card from behind my right ear. He regarded the picture for a few silent moments and then turned the image my way. The card showed a funny fellow in an outfit that looked like pajamas with stripes of red, yellow, and green. He wore a floppy hat with bells on the ends and pointy black shoes, and he covered his eyes with both hands.

I wrinkled my nose, unimpressed. "That doesn't look like a magician."

"It's *Folie*, or the fool, but he is not always as foolish as he seems. He embarks upon grand adventures. He's a dreamer, but he carries the lessons of his journeys around with him."

"Am I going to have grand adventures?"

"Yes." He arched a dark eyebrow. "Numerous adventures. You will be exactly what your mother and I always wanted to be. You will be a hero."

I smiled and again buried my forehead against his chest.

Uncle Magnus bathed and shaved in a copper tub in the middle of our kitchen. I waited outside the entrance of the room on a small stepstool and pored over the beautiful black-and-white illustrations in our copy of *Grimm's Fairy Tales*, the only book we owned aside from a musty old Bible written in German. I wrapped a blanket around my shoulders and huddled under its fuzzy warmth, for I had turned ever so cold since the day my sister was born.

My uncle usually sang for me as he scrubbed, but on this particular day, he kept quiet. I heard the sloshing of his bathwater and the whooshing of the scrub brush as he scoured his back, but no boisterous refrains of "Ta-ra-ra Boom-de-ay" or "The Cat Came Back" echoed through the house. In the other room, Mama nursed Tru, but the endeavor somehow was not going well and involved much huffing and growling on my mother's part.

Tru cried. Again.

Mama cried. Again.

The idea of a special case—one potentially packed full of monster-hunting weapons, a case hiding somewhere *inside our very house*—distracted me from the Grimms' tales of woodsmen and princesses, and it even drew my attention away from all the caterwauling in the parlor. Without a sound, I lowered the book to the floor and tiptoed up the staircase.

At the top of the steps, the plain wooden door to my parents' bedroom rose before me: a gateway to a forbidden fortress. I pushed it open with the tips of my fingers and stole inside the sun-bathed quarters, which now held a wooden cradle and a foul-smelling pail for soiled diapers. In the center of the room stood Mama and Papa's bed, covered in a burgundy bedspread embroidered with swirls of gold that always made me think of curled-up mermaids. I lowered myself to my knees and peeked beneath the dust ruffle.

The bottom edge of a mahogany-brown case made of leather caught my eye. I lifted the ruffle and came face-to-face with the thick handle, a silver lock, and a peculiar word, engraved on a metal plate, positioned next to the lock.

MarViLUs

I could not yet read, but I could sound out four or five letters, thanks to Mama teaching me the alphabet when she read to me each night. I pressed my lips together and produced a deep and quite impressive "*Mmm*" that thrummed inside the middle of my throat. The rest of the word remained a mystery. That tall *L* in the middle made the name resemble no other word I had seen.

I stroked the letters with the tips of my fingers, finding the metal cold, the engraving bumpy. The trunk revealed no secrets to me, but just from touching it, breathing on it, the utter weight of its importance sank deep into my bones.

After Uncle Magnus dressed himself, I trailed him back into Papa's studio, where he combed his hair before swiveling toward me and battling the knots in my own hair. I cried out "Ow!" with each stroke of the comb, but he told me to stay as quiet as a mouse for the sake of my mother and sister. He did not smell of horses any longer. He smelled like my father's shaving soap—a spicy, citrusy scent that made me hungry for fresh fruit. My stomach growled.

"I saw the case," I told him.

"Did you, now?"

I nodded, a movement that made the brushing twice as painful. I clutched my temples and squeezed my eyes shut and yet managed to say, "It had a word on it."

"Ah, yes," said my uncle. "I know that word."

"What does it say?"

"'Marvelous,' although it's spelled a little differently than the regular way."

"Why does it say that?"

"MarViLUs, dear Od, was the name of an old and highly secret club."

"Who was in it?"

Uncle Magnus stopped brushing and answered in a deep voice, "Monster-wranglers. Amulet-makers. Diviners of the future."

My lips parted. "Was Mama a part of it?"

"Yes, and so was I."

I shivered, due to awe of this fantastical secret society but also because of that achy, oozing old foot of mine.

"There's a scratch on my foot that hurts and itches," I said, and I lifted the injured sole and showed Uncle Magnus the angry red stripe running across it.

"Oh, God, Od!" He dropped the comb. "When did that happen?"

"The day Trudchen came, when I ran to Mrs. Alvarado's."

"Four whole days ago?"

I wrinkled my nose at the gash's unfathomable stink. "Something yellow keeps coming out of it. And I'm so, so cold." Again, I shivered, but this time I couldn't stop. My teeth chattered so much, I bit the tip of my tongue and tasted blood.

"Damn!" My uncle raked a hand through his hair. "Damn! Damn! Damn!" He scooped me up and hurried me to the kitchen. "Maria!" he called out to my mother in the front room. "Odette's walking around with an infected foot. Did you know that?"

"Leave me alone!" called Mama, and she sobbed yet again, which, of course, made Tru sob, too. My sister's lungs had grown so fierce in four short days that her cries tore straight through the walls and smacked against my ears.

Uncle Magnus sat me down in a chair in the kitchen, grabbed a bottle of Papa's brandy, and poured some of the contents onto a dishcloth. "This is going to hurt, Od. Close your eyes and think of something happy."

I squeezed my eyes shut and imagined Papa galloping our way on his black stallion, Vulcan, which he'd named after a Roman god.

Uncle Magnus then kneeled down on one knee and set the bottom of my foot on fire.

"Nooooooo!" I hollered, louder than even Tru's wails from the other room. "Damn! Damn! Damn!"

Uncle Magnus's mouth fell open.

The house went silent. Even Tru stopped squalling.

"*What* did Odette just say?" called Mama—now, indeed, sounding like a warrior who could slay a thousand vile beasts.

Uncle Magnus stood to his full height, and his face blanched to the color of his button-down shirt. Footsteps thundered toward us from the front room, and the entire house shook so hard, the copper bathtub rattled against the floor.

Mama stopped in the kitchen doorway and glared at her brother. She cradled Tru in her right arm like a loaf of bread, and the front of her nightgown hung open, exposing a shockingly large right breast.

Uncle Magnus turned his head away, but I gaped at my mother, who just stood there, exposed and horrifying, her hair still witchy and wild, my sister tucked against her side.

"What did you say, Odette?" she asked.

I pinched my lips together and shook my head, refusing to speak. I did not know what that word meant, but I knew it contained power if it had prompted Mama to finally leave the sofa.

"Take her out of this house, Magnus."

"Her foot's badly infected, Maria. She looks malnourished, too."

"Take her out! Take them both out." Mama forced Tru upon my uncle and yanked me by my right arm to the back door. "Get out. All of you!" She shoved me onto the back step, and Renoir scrambled away with a yowl. "You want too much from me. I'm done protecting everyone. Do you hear me? I'm done!" She slammed the door behind us.

With Tru bawling in his arms, Uncle Magnus stumbled off the last step beside me. We both staggered more than walked, he from the shock of his half-naked sister throwing an infant into his arms, me from the foot that burned from the brandy. We collapsed to the ground in the shade of the leathery leaves of one of the nearest olive trees and sat with our legs stretched in front of us. A bitter chill rose from the sparse grass.

My uncle bounced Tru in his arms and tried to shush her, but my sister shook her fists and squealed like a piglet with her eyes shut tightly. She didn't produce any tears when she cried, I noticed, but her face turned a purplish red and reminded me of my own fists when I squeezed them with all my might. I smelled our mother's milk and a dirty diaper, as well as my stinky old foot, and pinched my nose to block the stenches.

Uncle Magnus huffed. "Your father should be here, not me."

"When is he coming home?"

"How am I supposed to know? I'm not his private secretary." He shot me a glare that made my blood run cold. "Don't ever swear again. Do you hear me?"

"You said that word first."

"I know, and that's why I'm in trouble, too." He turned toward the house, still bouncing Tru. "Just look at this place. Look what he's done to your mother. I'm going to kill him one day. I swear to God, I'll kill him."

I dropped my hand to my lap and stared at my uncle with narrowed eyes. He knitted his eyebrows and tightened his jaw, and I believed he might, indeed, kill my father, a man twenty-five years older than he, a man with gray hair and a beard and colorful coats who looked as if he could have stepped out of one of the tarot cards.

Tru cried and shook her arms until she turned as purple as the day she was born. I reached out and maneuvered her out of my uncle's arms.

"Be careful of her, Od."

"Of course I will. She's my sister." I laid the baby in the folds of my skirt and leaned down to kiss her cheek, which felt rubbery and soft and tasted like tears, even though she couldn't make any. "*I'll* take care of you, Tru. There's no need to cry, little one."

She shuddered and drew a deep breath, reining in her need to squeal. To my surprise, her purple face even relaxed into a doughy shade of white, and her little lips soon closed and made a sucking movement. I tickled the dimpled knuckles of her left hand, and she squeezed her fingers around my right index finger and looked me in the eye with her large gray irises.

A hush fell over the canyon. A mockingbird trilled from a branch in the crooked olive tree across from us, and Uncle Magnus sighed and leaned back against the trunk behind him. My foot still screamed in pain, but I couldn't help but smile down at Tru, who peered up at me with fascinated eyes, as though she had just discovered I existed.

"If you stay quiet, I'll tell you a story," I told her. "Do you want to hear a story?"

She wiggled her legs in her blanket and continued to stare at my face with a dazed expression of wonder.

"Once upon a time," I said, and I bent my head close to hers, "on a cold January morning, a girl named Trudchen Maria Grey came into the world in a castle . . ."

Mama slept for hours that day. While she rested and recovered, Uncle Magnus took my sister and me to downtown Fallbrook and stocked up on food with some of the money Papa had left us. That evening, my uncle miraculously figured out how to roast a chicken for supper, even though I'd never seen him cook before.

While he bustled about in the kitchen, trying not to burn the house down, I again swung from the branch of one of the olive trees out front, licking the taste of lemon from the corners of my mouth from a stick of candy Uncle Magnus had bought me at the general store. I scanned the road for signs of dust stirred up by an approaching horse, for I believed Papa would charge home that night to meet his brand-new baby girl. Three crows landed on the road, and they cawed and laughed and pecked at the ground. They felt me foolish for wishing for my father; I heard the skepticism in their cackles and saw the teasing way they cocked their heads at me. My father's adventures mattered to him more than we did. The crows knew it. I knew it. Mama knew it. But only the crows voiced the ridiculousness of my waiting for him.

"Suppertime, Od," called Uncle Magnus from the back door. "Come inside."

I jumped to the ground, and the crows flapped away with one last round of chuckles.

Uncle Magnus gathered us all around the dining room table, which was topped with a platter of carved chicken and bowls of fresh vegetables and fruit. He poured Mama and himself glasses of a white wine that smelled vinegary.

"I'm taking care of a baby, Magnus," said Mama, waving the bottle away. "I shouldn't."

"Oh, come now." He filled her glass a little higher and rested a hand on her left shoulder. "After all you've been through, I should think you deserve at least one glass."

He seated himself in my father's chair, and we dove into the food while Tru slept in a little basket by the fireplace. Uncle Magnus coaxed Mama into chatting, even laughing, about the olden days, when they were little children in Philadelphia, fresh from Germany, as well as their ride across the country on the rails to live on a dairy farm near cousins already established in Oregon. They spoke of the past as if it were a time so far away, it had evolved into a tale they'd merely imagined. Mama insisted Uncle Magnus had made up half of his memories, or at least embellished them, and my favorite part was when he described witnessing magnificent green dragons flying over the prairie during their westward travels on the steaming locomotive.

Sometimes their eyes grew dark and haunted when they mentioned the house where they had lived in the Oregon hills, but they drank more wine, and their moods again lightened.

After Mama fed Tru, my sister fell sound asleep in her cradle. I planned to enjoy some rest without the usual ruckus of Tru crying in my parents' bedroom, but my mother and uncle laughed with such a commotion, I still couldn't manage to sleep. I tiptoed down the staircase with small sighs gasping from the steps below my feet and spied on the two of them through the wooden spindles of the banister. Mama lay against the back cushions of the sofa, positioned on her right side, her left thumb tucked inside my uncle's shirt between two of the buttons, her left leg resting over both his knees. Uncle Magnus reclined on his back, his right arm bent behind his head, his left hand stroking Mama's long brown hair. They snickered and spoke of a girl named Amelia whom Uncle Magnus used to love, long ago. A fire crackled on the hearth and turned both of their faces golden.

Watching them that night, seeing the way they clung to each other, as though they braved unfamiliar waters while rocking about in a lifeboat, I understood that Uncle Magnus was Mama's Tru.

I climbed back up the staircase—the arches of my feet straining to remain silent, my toes stretched out in front of me—and I peeked in on my sister, who slept in the moonlight with her hands folded into tiny fists by her head, as if she imagined holding on to my fingers . . . as if we, too, bobbed about together on choppy seas.

Two nights after Uncle Magnus arrived to take care of Mama, Tru, and me, a pack of coyotes howled in the hills surrounding our house. I clutched my new rag doll to my chest and tasted the yarn of her yellow hair, smelling the perfume Mama hated. At first the howls—so strange, so of another world—resembled the cackling of witches, but soon the sounds merged into one long and keening cry that froze me to my sheets. Those cries no longer belonged to coyotes, I realized, but to a woman, wailing from the depths of her belly, down by the creek that flowed just beyond our olive trees. I turned my head toward the window to ensure that Mama's copper hand mirror stood in place, wedged between the frame and the sill. She'd never told me why she insisted on placing it there, but a twitchy feeling in my gut now made me understand that the mirror belonged to the world of MarViLUs and monsters—just like all the charms and bells tinkling around the house, attached to the eaves with red ribbons and silver strings.

"Please protect Tru and me from *La Llorona*," I called to the mirror in a whisper. "Please, please, *please*, don't let her come any closer."

That past December, when Papa had spent a Christmastime evening with us, painting his pictures, rubbing Mama's swollen belly, he had plopped me down in his lap by the fireplace.

"When I was a lad in England, Odette"—he fluffed his gray beard, as coarse and as thick as sheepskin—"my father told us ghost stories every Christmas Eve. You're almost four years old now." He bounced me on his knee. "Are you brave enough for a story that will make the little hairs on the back of your neck stand on end?"

Mama shook her head from where she lay on the sofa, half in darkness, half in the flickering light of a candle's flame wavering by her side, and she smoothed her hand over the curve of her stomach. "Don't scare the poor girl, Louis."

"Bah. I was younger than she when people filled my head with stories of Spring-heeled Jack and London ghosties." Papa drew me closer against him, radiating a brandy-infused heat. His sky-blue eyes twinkled down at me. "You're a courageous one, aren't you, little monkey?"

"Yes," I said, and I folded my hands in my lap, ignoring the shadows crouching behind the furniture, as well as the breeze ringing the bells outside. "Please, tell me the tale."

"It's a story told to me by a chap I know from Mexico." Papa's voice went as rumbly and rich as the lowest string of the violin he often played for us in the evenings. "He said that if you reside by a river or a creek, just like the little body of water that trickles through this very canyon, and if you wander outside late at night, as every good child knows she ought not to do, you will hear the mournful screams and cries of the terrible *La Llorona*."

My heart beat with a wildness in my chest. "What is *La Llorona*?" I asked.

"She is a woman . . ." Papa wiggled his fingers, and the shadow of his hand seemed poised to grab me from the wall. "A betrayed woman who, as it so happens, was also named Maria, like your own, dear mother. She drowned her children to spite their unfaithful father and in death repents her sins. She roams by the rivers of Mexico, the Southwest, and even California, weeping, wailing, asking, 'Where shall I find my children?'"

I shuddered.

"And," he continued, "if she finds a child walking about on her own in the dark"—he grabbed both of my arms—"she'll snatch her away!"

"Louis!" snapped Mama from the sofa. "That's a horrible story to tell a little girl before bedtime. Stop it, please."

My fingers, I realized, now clung to Papa's vest, wrapped like little claws around the smooth brocade. "Is it true?" I dared a peek at our closed front door. "Is she out there right now, looking for children?"

Papa's pink lips spread into a smile above his beard. "You had better not go outside on your own to find out, little one. Had you?"

That January night when the coyotes howled and Uncle Magnus slept downstairs, while my mother and sister slumbered in the room beside mine, I was so certain I heard her— *La Llorona*—roaming the land beside our creek. Her wails rose and strengthened, building up into an ear-shattering crescendo that shook my windowpane and sent the bells around the house clanging and warning, *She's coming! She's coming! She's coming!*

"Mama!" I called out into the darkness.

The Weeping Woman's cries rushed toward my upstairs window. The hand mirror rattled from her howls, and the curtains billowed with a scream.

"Mama!" I called until my throat blazed with fire.

"Quiet, Odette!" Mama flew into my room with a swish of her nightgown and a flash of a candle's flame. "You'll wake the baby."

"Do you hear her?"

"Who?"

"*La Llorona.*"

Mama wheeled toward my window.

"Do you hear her?" I asked again.

She huffed a sigh. "It's only coyotes."

"No, Papa said—"

"Papa knows nothing of monsters."

"She'll steal Tru away—I know it. She wants a baby, and she's going to take Tru, because she's the best one."

"Go back to sleep." The black sleeves of Mama's gown flapped in my direction, and I pushed the fabric away, for they felt like bird wings rustling against my face. Again, I shrieked.

"What's happening?" asked Uncle Magnus, his brown eyes shining in the light of a kerosene lantern behind Mama.

"Louis told Odette about *La Llorona* last Christmas. She thinks the coyotes are her."

"It's *La Llorona*, Uncle Magnus." I put out my arms to my uncle. "She wants Tru."

"Come now, darling." My uncle rounded my mother and arrived at my side posthaste. "Bring your pillow. You're sleeping downstairs with me so your poor mama can rest."

From around the corner, Tru burst out crying.

"Someone's taking her!" I bolted upright. "Save her, Mama! Why aren't you saving her?"

"She's crying because of *you*." Mama grabbed me by the hand and coaxed me out of bed. "Go downstairs with Magnus. Let your sister sleep so I may sleep. No one has ever been snatched away from this house, and I'm certainly not going to allow that to happen now that there are two of you."

I grabbed my rag doll from the sheets before my mother could herd me out of the room, and I walked between the grown-ups through the near-darkness of the upper landing. The flames of the lamplight bobbed and shivered around me. Shadows stretched and darted across the deep blue wallpaper, and my stomach churned, but, somehow, I managed to follow Uncle Magnus downstairs without tripping and crashing to the bottom. *La Llorona*'s howls retreated into the farthest reaches of the canyon, as though she knew I now possessed Protectors and light.

Upstairs, Mama shut her door and tended to Tru, who soon stopped crying.

Uncle Magnus tossed my pillow next to his on one of the paint-spattered cloths in Papa's studio. He set the lantern beside his beige blankets and slid his legs beneath the covers. I did the same, laying my head against his chest so that the beats of his heart blocked the last of the screams outside. His blood pumped in a steady rhythm against my ear.

"Is Mama's hand mirror one of her monster-hunting tools?" I asked. "Is that why she puts it in my window?"

"Yes," he said, wrapping his left arm around me. "Sometimes, nasty little fiends find their way into our realm, and special mirrors like that one send them straight back to where they belong."

"Why does Mama need a case full of other tools, then?"

"I didn't say it was filled with tools."

"What's in it, then?"

"Something extremely special. She'll always keep you safe, Od. Don't ever doubt her bravery."

I blinked and studied the thin slice of moonlight that shimmered in the darkness where the curtains parted.

"Od," said Uncle Magnus, his voice now sounding heavy, tired, impossibly deep.

"What?" I asked.

"Your father is finally coming to meet your sister tomorrow."

I listened to five more ticks of his heart before asking, "How do you know that?"

He flicked his left wrist and, without even a breath of a sound, another one of his tarot cards manifested in his hand in the dim haze of the lantern. This one showed a man with a pointy brown beard and a large hat. He sat in a gold chair and held a coin as large as his face.

"The King of Pentacles told me so." He tucked the card inside his right sleeve. "I can't be here when your papa arrives."

"Why not?"

"I just can't." Uncle Magnus swallowed. "I can't look at your father ever again. He makes me furious, the way he keeps your mother trapped here like Rapunzel. He always has."

I raised my head off his chest and played with one of the frayed drawstrings hanging from his nightshirt. "Are you going to kill him?"

The corners of his lips twitched into a smile. "Such a dark question for a little girl."

"You said you would, when we sat beneath the tree and Tru was crying."

He swallowed again, and the smile faded. "After he's left the three of you alone again, whenever your mother seems sad and in dire need of help, I want you to close your eyes and wish with all your might for me to come back here." He brushed a lock of hair out of my eyes. "Will you promise me that?"

"That won't work."

"Yes"—he nodded—"it will. You and I are very much alike, Od. We form connections to the people we love—connections stronger than regular bonds."

I frowned and twirled his string between my fingers. "Is that true?"

"I've heard you call to me before. Your soul, Od, pulsates with enchantment. I told you, you're going to grow up to be something rather special."

I lay my cheek back down on his chest, and his heart again boomed against my ear. He cupped a warm hand over my left ear, and all I could hear was the symphony of his internal rhythms. All other sounds slipped away.

"Please don't kill Papa," I said in a whisper.

He removed his hand from my ear and wrapped it around my shoulder. "Please don't grow up and make the same mistakes as your mother."

CHAPTER THREE

Trudchen
January 15, 1909—Oregon

After stealing through my window, Od slept with me in the bed we used to share in our days of schoolbooks and childhood chores, of folktale collecting and sky-high dreams. We now lay on a mattress composed of coiled springs and cushioned coverings instead of one made of cloth and straw and the occasional wriggling mouse, but the bed stretched no wider or longer than before, and we had to sleep with our knees knocking against each other. I drifted off while wondering if the little creature in my teacup had somehow predicted Od's return—if any smidgens of truth percolated in the thick stew of her outlandish stories.

In the morning, I awoke to the warmth of sunlight brightening my face and the sight of my sister and her rumpled brown hair lying next to me. On the back of her neck gleamed the little clasp of the gold chain that held the key to the mystery box she'd spoken of the night before—the box that contained a story of some sort.

How my fingers itched to reach out and unfasten that clasp, to unlock the box.

Od stirred.

I propped myself up on my left elbow and said, "Stay here with us."

She emitted a confused-sounding murmur and peeked over her shoulder at me with eyes barely cracked open. "I beg your pardon?"

"I'm going to talk Aunt Viktoria into letting you stay with us. We need your help here, and I think you need us."

Od sighed in the direction of the ceiling, rustling a lock of her hair that wobbled against her forehead. "I can't stay in this house, Tru. And neither can you." She tossed the blankets off her legs. "Let's get you packed so we can leave."

"Wait! I never said I would go."

"I don't even want to see Aunt Vik while I'm here. We shall sneak out the window." She climbed over my legs and tripped over her own brown shoes, left next to the bed with the toes pointed toward the door to keep away the *Alps* that used to worry her as a child. After regaining her balance, she threw open the doors of the wardrobe.

Behind her, the bedroom door squeaked open, and, lo and behold, there stood our aunt.

Od paled.

Aunt Viktoria stiffened and squeezed her lips together until they lost all shape and color. "What are you doing here, Odette?"

Od withdrew from the wardrobe and hid her hands behind her back, even though she didn't hold anything in them. "Are you still so angry with me after the past two years, Aunt Viktoria," she asked, "that the first words out of your mouth must sound like an accusation?"

Auntie's hand remained clamped around the knob. "You weren't to return."

Od stood up straight. "I'm tired of living without my sister. I'm taking her with me."

"Taking her where?"

"Away. She's languishing here."

Auntie didn't move a muscle. She didn't blink. "There are medical bills to consider, Odette, accommodations for Tru's leg . . ."

"I've put aside money this past year. I want to save her."

"Save her from what?"

"From you." Od lifted her chin. "And other monsters."

Auntie's hand dropped away from the doorknob. "Leave this house."

"Not without Tru."

Auntie pointed out the doorway. "Leave!"

"Don't fight, please," I said, reaching for my leg brace on the floor. "Od arrived at my window last night, desperate to see me, and I want her here, terribly. Please, allow her to stay for breakfast—that's all I ask. Allow me to at least share one meal with my sister. She didn't mean what she just said. Did you, Od?"

My sister and aunt remained locked eye to eye in a wordless battle that raised my pulse.

"Please!" I said again.

Auntie's gaze dropped to Od's pile of belongings, and a flash of recognition—of tenderness—softened her face for the breadth of a second. "Why is your mother's old coat here?"

"You made it for her, years ago, didn't you?" asked Od. "You chose purple because of the color's protective powers, because she was attracting trouble—because she'd turned fifteen."

Auntie swallowed and hardened back into the stoic version of herself. "Your mother drew the attention of unfavorable young men after she turned fifteen years old, if that's what you mean. She still does. I hope you don't think you're taking Trudchen anywhere near her."

Od stepped forward. "I know you weren't always this way, Aunt Viktoria. I know you used to believe in the marvelous and magic. Uncle Magnus told me all about the girl you once were."

"Magnus was always as full of hogwash as you are. Don't believe a word my brother said."

Od glowered at our aunt and readjusted her stance. "Why do you hang amulets around the house, Aunt Vik, if you don't believe anything exists beyond the ordinary? Why are you so damn superstitious?"

"Mind how you speak, Odette!"

"Why do you hang them?"

"Out of habit. Out of tradition. Now please—"

"You even affixed a crucifix to Tru's cane." Od grabbed up my cane from the side of the bed.

"That's a *T*, Od, not a crucifix," I said, and I shifted toward our aunt. "Isn't it?"

Auntie snatched the cane from Od and handed it back to me. "You may stay for breakfast, for Tru's sake. But I'm driving you to the depot afterward and putting you on the afternoon train. You're still obviously nothing but trouble."

Od snorted. "A train to where? Where have you expected me to go all this time?"

"You chose to follow in your mother's footsteps, and you may continue to do so if you please, but don't bring your sister into this. She's a good girl. An honest girl. I intend to keep her that way." Aunt Viktoria turned and slammed the bedroom door shut behind her.

"She's a prisoner is what she is!" Od called after her, and she smacked a fist against the door. "You're keeping her trapped out here, just like our father did to our mother. Danger still sniffs you out, even when you're hiding—even when you don't know it's coming for you."

"Od, please stop quarreling with her," I said. "I'm not sure I have the strength to go anywhere with you, or the courage, for that matter."

My sister slumped against the door. "If you stay here without me, you're going to need to learn how to fight."

"But . . ."

"If she won't allow you to leave, then at least let me teach you how to prepare for what's coming. I'm not taking one step outside of this house until I know you're ready."

What's coming, she had said, a phrase that hardened my stomach into a lump of stone. I eyed the orchard outside the window, and beyond it the woods with its Douglas firs that scraped the bleak winter sky.

I nodded, for agreeing seemed simpler than arguing at the moment. "All right, then. Teach me how to fight."

After enduring the most silent and uncomfortable breakfast in the history of all breakfasts, Od and I buried ourselves in mittens, scarves, hats, and boots for our journey out of doors.

Naturally, Aunt Viktoria knew nothing of the true intention of our excursion. She believed Od was taking me out for a breath of fresh air in my wheelchair.

Auntie called after us from the doorway, "Wear your hat and coat at all times, Tru. It's cold out there. Odette, bring her straight back home in an hour. Not a second later or I'm coming after you!"

Od didn't reply.

The MarViLUs case hid beneath a crocheted blanket that my sister had draped across my lap in the wicker wheelchair, and upon the case wobbled the hand mirror. Od insisted we wear the old, protective *Hexenspiegel* necklaces our mother had looped over our heads when we were little, and at my side in the chair rested my hickory cane, the tip propped against the footrest.

Od pushed the wheelchair over the frozen ground of the path that led through our rows of filberts. The trees reached toward the sky with a tangle of spiraling branches thick with moss and lichen. I rocked about in the chair with the leather case jostling on my legs, while the two pairs of wheels—large ones in back and smaller ones in front—whined from the cold.

We passed the last row of trees in the orchard, and Od suddenly called out, "Onward!"

She picked up her pace and broke into a jog. Now more than ever she seemed a young Don Quixote de La Mancha, guiding her steed, Rocinante, toward windmills she mistook for belligerent giants. That made me, I supposed, her reluctant squire, Sancho Panza.

I tried to remember whether Sancho Panza ever actually

believed in the giants. I feared I myself was straying into my family's realm of quixotic madness for placing stock in the wisdom of teacups.

We neared the forest of evergreens that rose beyond the orchard. Fog drifted over the Coast Range, brewed in the air that blew down from Alaska and across the Pacific Ocean, and the woods appeared darker, more cloistered and ominous than usual. Od and I wore our calf-length coats of purple wool, hers that rich plum color, mine the bright iris, both creations of Aunt Viktoria, or so I had just learned. Below the cane's handle, the silver T—or *crucifix*—caught in one of the loops of yarn in the thumb of my left glove.

Od broke into a full-fledged run, now hurtling me toward the forest, shaking me about in the seat.

"Must you go so fast?" I asked, gripping the armrests.

"Our hour is slipping away." She sprinted as though something chased us. "We mustn't waste a second."

Moments later, firs engulfed us. The chair's wheels wobbled and screeched, and Od panted near my ear from all that running and pushing, and yet no other sounds—no twittering birds, no chattering squirrels—met my ears. The stillness of the gray winter air unsettled me. It hinted that animals knew better than to venture through those woods. My breath chilled into mist before my eyes and blurred my view of the firs ahead.

Od shoved the chair over the roots and stones that riddled the deer trail we followed. "Tru," she said, out of breath, "no matter what Aunt Vik says, come with me this afternoon. You must."

"What do you expect me to do," I asked with a laugh, "spring out of my chair and jump into the train before Aunt Viktoria can tug me back out?"

"Precisely."

I squeezed my hands around the armrests. "I can't spring or jump. You know that."

"Then I'll grab you by the wrists and hoist you into the train. I've worked so hard to return to you." She slowed the chair to a stop in a clearing thick with ferns. "Don't let her trap you here."

I rubbed at my right hip beneath the blanket.

"Did you hear me?" she asked.

"Yes."

"We're meant to be together."

"I'm scared to leave."

She kneeled down in front of me. "There's absolutely no need to be frightened."

"Yes, there is! No matter how brave or confident you try to make me feel, no matter how much money you have at this moment, I know I can't survive out there."

"Yes, you can, Tru."

"I can't, Od. I'm a cripple."

"Don't use that word."

"But it's what I am. I'm deformed."

Od recoiled, and her eyes turned moist and bloodshot. She angled her face away from me, toward the trees to the south, and I heard my words echo across the woods.

"I'm sorry." I gulped down a lump in my throat. "But I'm not like you. I can't simply run off."

She sniffed. I lowered my head. For a solid minute neither of us said a word, and I worried she regretted her return. Down in the footrest of the wheelchair, my left leg felt as though it were lengthening, stretching longer and longer and longer, until the sole of the high-button boot at the end of it crunched against the wicker. The raised black shoe at the end of my short leg, however, disappeared beneath the hem of my skirt, stuck at an angle.

"Maybe you should take me back to the house now," I said.

Od raised her face. "This seems a good spot for your training."

I blinked, not expecting that particular response.

"Here's what you need to do." She slid the crocheted blanket off our cache of supplies that teetered on my lap. "Grip the hand mirror with all your might and close your eyes. I'm going to hide behind one of the trees and then lunge at you when you least expect it. Your job will be to react as swiftly as possible. Raise the mirror the second you detect me and shout at the top of your lungs, 'Be gone!'"

I sat there with my lips sealed shut, unsure whether I should go along with the game.

She stared down at me with pleading brown eyes. I thought again of her long absence, of the years she'd spent shielding me from hardships, bolstering me up, filling me with so much love, I no longer hurt from the loss of the missing members of our family.

I drew a sharp breath. "Must I really shout that?"

"Yes," she said, a smile forming on her lips. "You'll stun your attacker."

I glanced around, worried that a neighbor might catch me waving a hand mirror about and shouting like a ninny.

"And what about the leather case?" I asked with a lift of the handle.

"We'll get to that later. That's mainly with us right now so Aunt Vik won't see I have it." She backed away, toward the towering evergreens behind her. "For now, concentrate on using the mirror."

I nodded, with some reluctance. "All right."

"Close your eyes."

I did as she asked and heard her feet swishing through piles of decomposed leaves, rustling behind the trees—then silence. My arms and neck bristled with gooseflesh. My spine tingled. I shifted about to get more comfortable in my chair, and the wicker crackled like flames.

Od didn't lunge at me straightaway. She left me sitting there in agonizing suspense. I kept my eyes closed, for I felt her watching me. Or . . . at least, something watched me from behind the trees. The weight of a steady gaze pressed upon me, making my chest feel tight.

A twig snapped.

I gasped and raised the mirror, and for a moment, I saw a figure leaping at me from the trees.

"Be gone!" I shouted. "Be gone!"

"Well done!" said Od, and my mind settled enough to transform the ferocious shadow into a girl in a purple overcoat.

"Od!" I sank back in the chair. "You genuinely frightened me."

"Good," she said, kicking aside a pinecone. "You need to learn to react when fear threatens to overtake you. Let's try it again."

"Let's not."

She batted away my sour attitude with a wave of a hand. "Close your eyes."

"Od . . ."

"Close your eyes, Trudchen Maria."

I sighed, lowering my lids during the exhale.

Again I waited, and again she burst forth when I least expected her.

"Be gone!" I cried, the mirror raised like a sword. Od's skirts and coat billowed behind her as she pounced through the branches with the intensity of a fiend blasted out of hell.

We repeated that horrifying exercise at least seven times in a row, and each time she assailed me, she emerged from a different direction, making me flinch in my chair so hard, I would roll a foot backward. My arms ached from swinging the mirror about with my fear-fueled muscles, and my heart pounded as though I were the one dashing about in the trees. I craved an end to the whole rigmarole and realized the best way to bring it about.

"Od," I called out to her when she turned to hide for the ninth time. "I'll trade you a secret for a secret."

She stopped and glanced over her shoulder at me. "*You* have a secret?"

"I do." I leaned my elbows on the leather case in my lap.

She tucked her hands inside her coat pockets and strolled my way with an air of caution. "What type of secret would you be asking for in return?"

"I have a question about our father. A simple question that would require a mere yes or no answer."

She shifted her weight between her legs. "I don't know . . ."

"Mine's an enormous secret."

She stood up taller.

"I believe," I said, "I may be able to foretell the future."

Her hands slipped out of her pockets. Her lips parted, but she couldn't seem to speak.

I gulped. "And now to my question . . ."

"No, no, no—you need to elaborate." She braced her hands against my armrests and leaned down toward me. "*How* do you foretell the future?"

Another gulp. "I've followed your guide to reading tea leaves."

"You have?"

I nodded. "At first I did it for a lark . . . and sometimes small coincidences occurred. A sign in my cup would match an insignificant moment in my life, and I'd smile and then forget all about it. But . . . during this past week . . ." I cleared my throat and fidgeted in the chair.

"Go on," said Od. "Please, what's happened this week?"

"Well . . . things have taken a peculiar turn."

She let go of my chair. "How so?"

"I saw train tracks, which I interpreted to mean a journey of some sort."

"A journey?" Her eyes bulged. "You . . . you mean to say that you predicted my return . . . and our expedition?"

"I know you're counting on me being something extraordinary, but really, I'm just a girl who's placing an awfully high importance on the ability of tea leaves to gum together."

"What else have you seen?"

To that, I looked away and twirled the mirror between my fingers.

"Tru?" She clutched my chair again, rocking me backward. "What else have you viewed in the leaves?"

I spun the mirror all the faster.

"Trudchen?"

"I'm worried if I tell you, it'll only encourage you to keep on with these monster tales."

She drew back. "Did you see something monstrous in the leaves?"

I dropped the mirror against the case. "I'm not entirely sure what it is I'm seeing. It . . . it strikes me as being some sort of demon. It has wings and hoofed feet and a head shaped like a loaf of bread. Its name might be Phil."

Her forehead creased. "*Phil?*"

"Either that or he lives in Philadelphia. A bell persists in appearing with him, too."

"What are you saying?" Od stepped backward two feet. "You've seen this 'Phil the Demon' multiple times?"

I scooted myself up to a more comfortable position in the wheelchair and tried to remember if she had ever mentioned anyone named Philip. Before she was sent away, she once spoke of a boy named Cy, whose name I first thought to have been spelled "Sigh," for that's what she did when she talked about the fellow: sighed with a dreamy, lovesick sound.

"Do you know any Phils?" I asked.

"No, not one. How many times have you seen him?"

I shrugged. "I've lost track. Five times. Maybe six."

"Six?" She grabbed her temples. "Holy smoke, Tru!"

"I might simply be bored. I might be making more out of the smudges than what's actually there."

"Six times!" she said, and she paced the dirt in front of me. "Are you meant to go to Philadelphia, do you think? Our mother's family lived there, before they came to Oregon, after Germany . . ."

"We can't go running across the country because of tea leaves. Do you realize how ridiculous that sounds?"

Od dropped her hands to her sides. "When did you last see the shape of the demon in your cup?"

"Well . . ." I cleared my throat. "Yesterday evening, after supper. Not long before you arrived."

She put her hands on her hips and gaped. "Trudchen! You foretold an encounter with a monster just hours before I arrived and told you my plan?"

"The truth of the matter is, even if I could hunt down monsters, I wouldn't want to. If you ask me, it sounds like a terrible job. And if turning fifteen means I'll lure vicious creatures to me"—I plunked the leather case down on the ground beside me—"then I don't want to be fifteen, either. That sort of 'talent' would be a horrifying inheritance I'd gladly decline. No, thank you."

"I see. Well . . ." She crossed her arms over her chest. "I suppose I could understand why it might sound intimidating."

"Yes, it 'might.'" I rubbed my gloved hands together, for the temperature had dropped in the past few minutes. "And now to my question about our father . . ."

She frowned.

"I want to know," I said before she could object to my asking, "if what you said is true. If our uncle made him . . . *disappear*."

"Yes," said Od without hesitation, still frowning.

"Do you mean"—I leaned forward with a creak of the chair—"'disappear' disappear, or are you saying, in a delicate manner, that our uncle was a murderer?"

She met my eye. "You said you would ask a simple yes or no question."

"Od, please tell me."

She sidled behind my chair and rotated me counterclockwise, back toward the path out of the woods. "We'll need to be discreet"—she pushed me forward—"about the way we pack your belongings. I'll squeeze your clothing inside my bag."

"Was it murder, then?" I craned my neck so I could better see her behind me. "If you don't tell me, I'm going to assume it's murder."

"That's a story for another day. For now, let's discuss the packing."

"I can't go, Od. It's impossible."

"You'll find the strength to leave when we arrive at the station." She pushed onward, guiding me up and over a tree root thicker than me. "We're going on a quest foretold not only by you and your marvelous tea leaves, but also by a tarot card, years ago. We're meant to be together, and I'm not going to let any obstacles block us."

Aunt Viktoria remained steadfast in her insistence that we whisk my sister straight off to the depot to catch the afternoon train to Portland, where Od could either choose to stay in the city and find an honest job or board a train bound for destinations unknown. I sat in my wheelchair by the fire, the case and the hand mirror buried back beneath the blanket in my lap, and I pondered, *What to do? What to do? What to do?*

Od lugged her Gladstone out of my bedroom and shot our aunt a poisonous glare. "You may have been unbothered to part ways with your brother and sister when you were my age, Aunt Viktoria, but I am not so heartless."

"Don't assume the worst of people, Odette." Aunt Viktoria fitted her wool gloves over her freckled hands. "Sending your mother and uncle to California broke my heart, but I agreed to stay behind and sort out matters with our parents' farm, just as your mother agreed to save Magnus. I was left with responsibilities and anguish, but we were forced to do what we could—grow up before we were ready—in order to survive."

"Did anything else at your farm cause our mother and uncle to leave?" I asked, thinking of Od's claim about the "terrifying things beyond normal animal and human categorization" that "fought to get into the house late at night."

Auntie struggled with the left glove, as though she couldn't quite squeeze her longest fingers into their proper compartments. "A brother gasping for air in the middle of the night was reason enough," she said in a voice that quavered. "Why do you ask?"

My face warmed. "Never mind."

Aunt Viktoria lifted an envelope off the table. "I've written a letter vouching for your character, Odette, so that you may find work in a factory. Inside this envelope you'll also find your mother's latest address, should you decide to seek her assistance. She might understand you better than I. That's the best I can offer."

Od gripped her luggage in her right hand. "You could forgive me," she said. "Family should stand by family."

Aunt Viktoria shook her head. "No, Odette. I made my rules quite clear when I first hired you out to work at the Leedses' two years ago. You chose to leave this house for good by breaking those rules. You have nothing and no one but yourself to blame."

Huddled in my chair by the fireplace, I listened to the sternness and guilt-laden bitterness spewing from our aunt's thin lips, and I trembled with rage.

Family should stand by family was all Od had said—a statement with which I agreed wholeheartedly. And yet my aunt had essentially answered, *No, they shouldn't. Family has every right to abandon family, even when a loved one is desperately needed.*

The steam engine bound for Portland arrived all too soon. Auntie could have put Od on one of the electric interurban streetcars that now linked Carnation to Forest Grove to the north, then to Portland to the east, but she distrusted anything that carried the "threat of electrocution." I supposed her decision meant she cared at least a tad about my sister's safety.

Od watched the arrival of the train from beside my wheelchair, her big iron-bottom bag in hand. She pressed her lips together and stood absolutely still while the train's bell clanged and the smokestack billowed. She already looked as if she were alone, even though Auntie and I both flanked her.

Down the platform, I noticed a boy who buried his face deep in a book—a crimson, clothbound beauty with a cover illustrated with a fanged and bat-eared gargoyle. The title looked to have been *Marvelous and Monstrous*, but I wondered if my jangled nerves were blurring reality and causing Od's tales to invade my brain.

"Aboard!" shouted the conductor.

From within the depot behind me, the *TAP-TAP-tap, TAP-TAP-TAP* of arriving telegraphs urged my legs, *RUN-RUN-run, RUN-RUN-RUN*.

Aunt Viktoria cleared her throat. "Well, then . . . I wish you the best of luck, Odette."

Odette gripped my left arm and bent her lips next to my ear. "Are you sure you won't come?"

Other travelers climbed aboard the train. My gaze darted between my sister and the green train car swallowing up the passengers' dark coats and hats.

TAP-TAP, tap-TAP, tap-TAP-tap.

"Let me at least stand up to properly hug you," I said, and I passed her the MarViLUs case and the mirror, which I'd brought along for her to keep.

"What is that case doing here?" asked Aunt Viktoria from the other side of my sister. "Odette, what . . . Have you . . . have you seen your uncle Magnus recently?"

Using my cane for support, I rose out of the wheelchair and

wrapped my free arm around my sister. "I don't know what to do," I whispered in her ear.

"I packed some of your clothing."

Tap-tap-tap-TAP, tap-tap, tap-TAP-tap-tap.

"What about Aunt Viktoria?" I asked. "She needs me."

"We wouldn't have to leave her forever. We could come back and visit. We'll send her money."

"Odette," said Auntie, "I asked, have you seen your uncle?"

Tap-tap-TAP, tap-tap-tap.

"Odette?" Desperation squeaked through Auntie's voice. "Did you hear me? The train is starting to move. Answer me."

Od pulled me close enough for me to feel her heart pounding against my chest. I couldn't let her go. I feared she might die if I didn't watch over her.

"All right," I told her with a nod. "I'll go."

"Hurry over to the train as best as you can. I'll distract Aunt Vik." She collected her luggage and the case and turned toward our aunt. "Thank you for your hospitality, Aunt Viktoria. I appreciate the time you allowed me to spend with my sister this morning. It was awfully kind of you to cook that lovely breakfast, but because you refuse to forgive me my errors, I refuse to say a word about Uncle Magnus, whom I've heard you also rejected from your life when you learned he played piano in brothels down in San Diego."

While Od horrified Auntie with words like *brothel*—a word I didn't quite understand—I lumbered toward the railcar at the briskest pace I could muster. The train lurched forward. Wheels creaked and groaned, and steam gusted from the smokestack with exasperated hisses. The sole of my left shoe smacked against the platform, while my right leg—suddenly nothing but dead weight—dragged behind. I felt as though my cane were an oar I was using to row through a sea of concrete.

"Tru?" called Auntie. "Where on earth are you going?"

I broke into my best semblance of a run, more of a hop—a desperate hop that made my left hip click and pop.

A porter at the top of the steps reached out a gloved hand and asked, "May I help you aboard, miss?"

"Yes, please." I extended my right arm and clasped his fingers.

He yanked me up to the first step with a mighty strength.

"Trudchen Maria!" screamed Auntie. "Do not get on that train!"

The porter's forehead wrinkled in confusion. His grip loosened. Shouts from both my sister and aunt cracked through the air behind me, but I didn't look back—I couldn't; I'd lose my nerve. I staggered up the next step, swaying, fearful of falling backward.

"Keep climbing, Tru!" called Od, now directly behind me. She pushed against my backside and boosted me up to the third step, and before long I was on that train, and down below on the platform, Od was running to keep up, then jumping inside, tearing up the steps behind me with the mirror, the Gladstone bag, the leather case, and the broadest smile I had ever witnessed on a person, her eyes as luminescent as the sun stealing through the clouds behind her. Back on the platform, Aunt Viktoria screamed my name, a hand to her chest, the abandoned wheelchair parked behind her, but the shrill cry of the train's whistle muffled her voice. All I saw out the window was her mouth frozen into the shape of an O.

The train chugged down the tracks, gaining speed, rushing off into worlds unfamiliar and terrifyingly new.

"Let the quest begin," said Od, and she took my hand and steered me to a seat.

CHAPTER FOUR

Odette
June 19, 1896—California

For the first two years of my little sister's life, we followed a particular routine. Every other month, Papa would trot up to the house on his big black stallion and spend a week with us. He painted his pictures, regaled me with stories, played his violin, strolled through the olive groves without wearing any shoes, and kept our mama company. Sometimes he even took us on carriage rides through the oak-covered hills and valleys. My favorite excursion entailed his driving us along a trail below a fairy-tale castle that a man had built high in the hilltops.

"An artist and poet named Mr. Frazee built it," Papa explained, "in honor of the Scottish home of his ancestors, a great feudal castle called Dunnottar."

Dunnottar. One of my new favorite words. Almost as delicious as *marvelous.*

Each alternate month, when Papa specifically *wasn't* visiting, Uncle Magnus would ride up on Glancer and help Mama take care of Tru and me. He would lift both us girls high above his head, one at a time, and run us through the house or among the trees ripening with olives, while we flew above him, our arms outstretched, and I felt just like the hawks and falcons that circled our land.

Whenever Papa and Uncle Magnus weren't around, Mama stayed up late at night, pacing the floorboards. During the days, worry lines wrinkled her forehead, and she started at each jarring creak of the house, even though she claimed, with a tight smile, "It's only the house settling. Nothing to fear, girls."

Throughout the years, the coyotes continued to cackle while we lay in our beds, and the growls and howls of other night-time creatures threatened the sanctuary of our home. Several times I heard the back door swing open and caught sight of Mama disappearing into the darkness behind our house in a long purple coat. Within a mere matter of minutes, the eerie baying and laughter would cease. Mama would then reemerge in the moonlight, her gait slowed, her coat tucked under one arm, as though she'd grown too warm. And without fail, the following morning, she would always be standing in our kitchen, cooking breakfast, claiming to have been inside the house the entire night.

"Don't be foolish, Odette," she'd tell me when I questioned her nighttime wanderings, her back facing me, bacon sizzling on the skillet. "I'm not going to run around out of doors after dark." She would then glance over her shoulder, her eyes as sharp as knives. "And don't you dare think of doing so, either. Do you understand me?"

"Yes, ma'am," I'd say, and I'd back away like a dog with its tail tucked between its legs, both curious and terrified to sneak off into the darkness, to see what she saw.

✖

Everything changed the summer I was six and Tru, two.

Mama changed.

Without warning, she dropped whatever she was carrying and vomited into buckets and wastebins, just like the day Tru had come into the world. She took naps in the middle of the day and told me to wake her up when the clock struck three. She cried over the stews and soups she cooked in the kitchen, and she stopped sneaking out in the night in her deep-purple coat. Strange sounds scraped against the window while Tru slept beside me in our shared bed—even though our room stood on the second floor, too high for a regular animal to reach. In the morning, I'd find nail marks scratched across the glass, and my neck went cold, as though the nails had scraped my own skin.

One night, when something barked and snorted down in our backyard, I clasped Tru to my chest and whispered, "Please come help us, Uncle Magnus. Please, please, please, please, please."

Well, as sure as I'm alive, the following evening, when Tru and I chased each other around beneath the tiny green olives awakening on the branches, Uncle Magnus galloped up on Glancer.

He brought the horse to a stop in front of us and dismounted on the left, his feet landing with a *thump*, a frown darkening his face. He pulled his hat off his sweaty brown hair and asked, "Od, is everything all right?"

I took hold of Tru's hand and said, "Mama's sick."

"Sick? What's wrong with her?"

"She's puking into buckets. All she wants to do is sleep."

Uncle Magnus put his hands on his hips and huffed, "Not again."

"Is she dying?" I asked.

"No, she's not dying." With movements stiff and brusque, he guided his horse toward the hitching post and called over his shoulder, "You two stay outside. I'm going to have a talk with your mother, and I don't want you eavesdropping."

So, of course, after he slammed the front door shut behind him, I snuck over to the side of the house and bent down on hands and knees beneath the kitchen window. Tru kneeled by my side in the exact same position and panted with her tongue hanging out one side of her mouth, her right eye squeezed shut, pretending to be a one-eyed dog named McMurray that nosed around downtown Fallbrook. Her eyes were as clear blue as Papa's, and her little round head was covered in short blond curls as fine and delicate as silken threads.

"This is none of your business, Magnus!" yelled Mama from the kitchen. "Leave me alone."

"You brought us to California to make a better life for the both of us, Maria. What do you think you're doing, having another baby?"

"I came here to give *you* a better life, and you're wasting it in God knows what sorts of hellholes down in San Diego. If anyone should be angry, it's me for giving up everything so you could behave like a fool."

"He's keeping you trapped up here," said Uncle Magnus over the clanking of pots in the sink. "Every time he saddles you with another baby, you get stuck deeper and deeper."

"I don't have any money. I can't go anywhere else."

"Take *his* money!"

"I can't just take it. He's got responsibilities."

"His pockets are brimming with cash. Steal it from him if you have to."

"I can't—"

"Get yourself out of here so you don't have to keep swelling up with his babies and living like a prisoner in the middle of this godforsaken rattlesnake country. This isn't the life you were put on this earth to live. Protect *yourself* for a change."

"I've got two children. What do you expect me to do?"

"It'll be three children soon."

"I'm not going back to Oregon. I've got no place to go but Viktoria's, and she's already made it quite clear what she thinks I've done to the family name."

"I'll take you and the girls elsewhere."

"You've got less money than I do. There's nothing either of us can do, Magnus, so keep your mouth shut about my choices."

"They've been atrocious choices, Maria, which has been highly disappointing, when you started out so smart."

Something heavy then crashed against one of the walls—a pot that had whizzed by Uncle Magnus's head, or so I guessed from the string of curse words that followed. A moment later, the front door flew open, and someone stormed out of the house. I jumped to my feet, grabbed Tru's hand, and ran us into the olive grove. Through a V-shaped crook between a tree trunk and a low branch, I watched Uncle Magnus mount his horse and ride off toward Fallbrook in a cloud of dust. He appeared to just be leaving to simmer down for a spell, not to return to the "hellholes" down in San Diego.

✹

No more than an hour after Uncle Magnus fled his argument with Mama, my father's regal black Vulcan came prancing our way up the dirt road, and atop the horse rode Papa in his red-and-white-striped summer coat. From the house's open windows wafted the scents of freshly baked bread and a potato soup Mama called *Kartoffelsuppe*. After her fight with her brother and all that vomiting, I knew she would crave a peaceful supper.

"Uh-oh," I said to Tru from the shade of the tree where we played on the ground with our rag dolls. "Best not misbehave this evening. There's going to be an awful battle."

"Best not misbehave!" she parroted me in her loud, slurred, two-year-old voice, glowering down at her doll.

Just like Uncle Magnus, Papa rode his horse over to us, a smile brightening his blue eyes. His forehead and cheeks shone with sweat and a fresh sunburn, and his beard carried a dusting of dirt and tiny twigs from the winds, as well as a peppering of dead gnats. He spat something black from his tongue.

"Ah, there's my two little monkeys," he said, and he dismounted Vulcan. "Why the long faces?"

"Best not misbehave!" said Tru again, wagging a finger at Papa, the way Mama did whenever she scolded Renoir for dragging dead mice into the house.

"Uncle Magnus is here," I said before fear kept me from speaking the truth.

Papa ran his tongue along the inside of his cheek and glanced at the house. "Is he in there with your mother?"

"No. He rode into town after they had an awful spat."

Papa patted his horse's gleaming black neck. "And what did the jackass and your mother spat about?"

"Mama's sick."

"How sick?"

"I think she's going to swell up with another baby," I said, borrowing Uncle Magnus's rather frank yet accurate description of what had happened to Mama's body in the months leading up to Tru.

"You two girls stay out here." Papa swung his horse around to the hitching post. "Let your mother and I enjoy a moment of privacy."

After he secured his horse and entered the house with the brim of his hat pressed flat against his chest, Tru and I once again scrambled toward the kitchen window and kneeled beneath the open pane. This time, Mama spoke through tears when she discussed the possibility of another baby, but Papa soothed her in his crisp English accent, promising he would always take care of her, no matter what, forever and ever.

Uncle Magnus did not return for supper. Nightfall shrouded the house in darkness after the clock struck eight, and still he did not return. The rest of us sat in the parlor in candlelight, listening to Papa read "The Robber Bridegroom" from our book of the tales of the Grimms. Tru lounged on Papa's lap with her feet propped on his right arm, and I leaned against his cushiony right side, my face pressed against his striped shirtsleeves, which he'd rolled to the elbows because of the heat. He smelled of smoke and brandy and warmth.

Just as Papa reached the last paragraph, Uncle Magnus threw open the front door, and we collectively started.

"Aha!" My uncle slammed the door shut behind him. "Look who decided to honor us with his presence." His eyes looked strange—dazed and unnatural and wild. His dark hair was tousled, and the longer strands in front dangled over his eyebrows.

"Magnus!" Mama jumped to her feet. "You're drunk!"

"Did you tell him the news?" Uncle Magnus wobbled across the floorboards toward us. "Did you tell him he's got you further pinned to the walls of this house? A chloroformed butterfly in his collection of treasures."

"Go lie down." Mama grabbed her brother by his right arm. "Don't let the children see you like this."

"Odette, take your sister up to bed," said Papa, lowering Tru to the floor. "I need to have a little talk with your uncle."

"You don't get to talk to me like I'm a child, old man," said Uncle Magnus, lunging forward, but Mama held him back before he could reach Papa. "You may be older, but you're nothing like a father to *anyone*—not to these children, not to any other children—"

"I'll stop talking to you like you're a child, Magnus," said Papa, "when you stop acting like a twenty-one-year-old brat who's in love with his sister."

Mama and Uncle Magnus froze at those words, and their faces flushed bright red. An ugly taste coated my tongue. My skin felt too tight, and the air turned stale.

"Odette!" snapped Mama, as though the words I'd just heard were my own fault. "Take Tru upstairs at once. Close the door. Cover your ears."

I took hold of Tru's shoulders and steered her past our uncle, who stepped toward us, but Mama yanked him back so hard, he whimpered.

"Stay down here, Od," he called to me, "so you can learn what your father's hiding from you. You shouldn't grow up thinking he's a saint."

"Go upstairs, Odette," barked Papa. "Don't listen to a word this drunken imbecile says."

My eyes watered from the burn of whiskey and hate in the air.

I held my breath and hurried Tru upstairs to our bedroom, where I ushered her beneath the sheet and blankets. "Cover your ears like Mama said," I told her, and I jumped into the bed with her. We lay side by side with our palms clamped against our ears, while the grown-ups waged their battles below. Objects crashed against walls, voices shuddered through the house, and the little mirror on the windowsill trembled with their rage and their secrets.

I wondered if the mirror would flash with a blinding light and snatch one of them away.

I wondered which of them might have been a monster in our midst.

The morning afterward, silence gripped the house. The heart-stopping stillness reminded me of an October afternoon almost three years earlier when the world had gone so quiet, I expected the earth to shake beneath my feet—which, in fact, it did. An earthquake had rattled the dishes in the cupboard and sent rocks tumbling down the hillside behind our house.

I didn't expect an earthquake to now strike, but an awful coldness crept across my arms, warning that something far worse awaited. I stole out of my bedroom, found Mama and Papa's door closed, and then attempted to tiptoe down the staircase. My feet drew deep croaks from each step, as though pressing against the backs of frogs.

"You don't have to sneak around, Od," said Uncle Magnus from down below.

I stiffened.

"I hear you on the stairs."

I continued down the steps without breathing and spied my uncle sitting in Papa's armchair; he was sipping coffee. His brown hair was now combed in a somewhat tidier fashion than the unkempt mess on his head the night before, and he wore a maroon vest over fresh white shirtsleeves and black trousers. His eyes remained bloodshot and clouded, however. He didn't look quite like himself, and the fact that he reigned over the empty room in my father's chair paralyzed me.

I gripped the handrail, which my chin just barely grazed. "Where's Mama and Papa?"

"Your mama's still in bed," he said, "resting. She's tired this morning."

"Where's Papa?"

His eyelids closed with a languid blink that lasted about a hundred years, but then he opened them again and peered straight at me. "Gone."

I shivered. The earth, indeed, quaked. My throat strained to form sounds. "Wh-wh-where is he?"

"He's not coming back." Another swallow. "Not ever."

My gaze switched to an object sitting next to the chair: Mama's mahogany-brown case from under her bed. *The* case! My hands slipped off the handrail. All I could imagine was Uncle Magnus chasing after Papa among the moonlit shapes of the olive trees and stabbing his heart with a knife from that box of tools reserved for the most fiendish of monsters—not fathers.

I climbed up the staircase backward, my eyes trained on my uncle, and he watched me ascend, never blinking. For the first time in my life, I hated him. I wanted him out of our house. He had transformed into a creature we needed to banish.

I hid in my bedroom with Tru until Mama stirred in her room next door, and even when she fetched my sister and put her on the chamber pot, I remained in bed, the blankets pulled to my chin. Eventually, Mama called me down for breakfast, but not once did I speak to Uncle Magnus at the table. Using my front teeth—now proper grown-up teeth, not puny baby ones—I crunched deeply into my hot buttered toast and refused to look at him seated in Papa's chair at the head of the table, as cocky as a rooster with a puffed-up chest.

"We're moving soon, Odette," said Mama in a voice that sounded flat. She spoke to a scratch that zigzagged across the table in front of her plate of untouched food. "You'll need to pack up your toys and your clothing. We can't take much, but we must leave soon."

"Why?" I asked.

"No, Odette." She shook her head. "No questions today. Do as you're told. We can't stay, and that's simply how it is."

Papa's dead, I thought while watching her pick at her crust, her fingers shaking. *Uncle Magnus killed him and buried him somewhere on our land, and now we're supposed to run away and abandon him before anyone else finds him. He's dead, and nobody cares but me.*

After breakfast, I changed into a brown cotton dress as colorless as moth wings, and I slipped out of doors without a peep. We owned thirty acres of land, including half of the hill behind our house, and it would take a rather long time to dig up every square inch of it. But dig I would.

I fetched a splintery old shovel from the toolshed and dragged its blade across the ground behind me. The soil in the olive groves would be moister, easier for digging, as opposed to the crusty dirt in the open brush.

I stopped below one of the largest trees. With a grunt, I raised the shovel an inch off the ground and thrust the blade into the dirt, making a dent no bigger than one of my footprints. The morning sun baked my bare head; sweat already rolled down my chest. My nostrils dried enough to bleed. Nonetheless, I sliced that blade into the earth and searched for my daddy, certain he lay somewhere down in the dust and the rocks.

The muscles above my wrists hardened into lumps that made my hands tingle. I remembered the fairy tale Papa had read to us the night before, "The Robber Bridegroom." It involved a band of robbers who filled a maiden with wine, removed her clothing, and chopped her up to eat on a table. They salted her first, before eating her. They even cut off her ring finger to steal her gold wedding band. The jackasses.

It did not seem like a story meant for little girls.

Our house no longer seemed like a place meant for little girls.

The hole I dug expanded into the size of an upside-down turtle shell, which I considered quite impressive, worthy of the pain and perspiration of creating it. My rate of digging doubled, and my back muscles strained and quivered.

"What are you doing, Od?" asked a voice behind me.

I spun around and found Uncle Magnus sauntering toward me, his thumbs tucked into the front pockets of his black trousers. His long and lanky shadow spread across my face, chilling my skin, shrinking me downward. A splinter caught in my left thumb.

My uncle peered down at me from high above. "Why are you digging?"

"I . . ." I stepped back. "I'm looking for something."

"What?"

I pressed my lips together.

"Od?"

"It's a secret."

He frowned. "I don't think your mother needs any secrets right now. She's packing up the house and wants you to help."

A streak of courage—of desperation—coursed through me. "I'm looking for Papa."

Uncle Magnus turned his chin an inch to his left and narrowed his eyes. "Why are you looking for him down in the ground?"

I lowered my head. My throat tightened, which made me cough, then cry. All of my bravery seeped away into the dirt.

"Oh . . . no, Od . . ." Uncle Magnus stepped closer. "I said he was gone. I didn't mean he's dead."

"You did something to him—I know it. You made him disappear."

"No, I didn't. He left on his own. He got angry and marched out, saying he wants your mother to pack up and leave for good." He withdrew his thumbs from his pockets. "Od? Did you think I killed him? Is that why you're digging?"

"You've said you wanted to kill him since the day Tru was born, and you were sitting there in his chair with that case of tools."

"Your mother gave me that case because she said she's done with it. She's given up on magic, which breaks my heart. Your father's not what he claims. He's not a poet, or an artist, or a loving family man. He's living down in San Diego, filthy rich from an allowance he receives from his parents back in England."

"No, he's not!" I dropped the shovel and covered my ears. "You killed him. I know you did."

"No, I didn't." Uncle Magnus squatted down and yanked my hands away from my ears. "Stop saying that. You're ripping my heart to pieces, Od. Look at me."

I did as he asked, and the old, familiar compassion shone in my uncle's brown eyes.

"Do you want me to take you to him?" he asked. "Shall I prove to you he's alive?"

The absence of my father gnawed all the harder at my belly. Snot and tears ruined my brown dress.

"Don't cry, darling." Uncle Magnus gave my hands a tender squeeze. "I don't want to hurt you by showing you the truth, but I think you deserve to know why your mother has seemed so sad and trapped all these years. Do you want to see him one last time?"

I managed a nod.

"Your mother won't want me taking you," he said, his voice softening. "You'll need to run upstairs and pack a bag in secret. Can you do that?"

I hiccupped. "Yes."

"She doesn't want you ever seeing him again."

"I want to see him."

"Then pack your bags—quickly." He cast a glance at the house. "It's an all-day journey. We'll leave in fifteen minutes. No dilly-dallying."

Never having traveled any farther than the two-hour carriage ride to the castle in the hills—and being only six years old—I did not know what to pack for a journey. I owned a small quilted satchel for storing scraps of fabric for my sewing lessons with Mama and decided it would do as a traveling bag. I left the hand mirror on the windowsill to guard Tru but crammed my yellow-haired rag doll beneath my balled-up dresses, under-clothes, stockings, and blue sunbonnet. My *Hexenspiegel* would serve as my sole article of protection.

In her bedroom Mama packed up two trunks for whatever horrible, far-off destination she intended for our move. Tru crawled around on Mama and Papa's bed, barking again like poor, one-eyed McMurray. I bolted past them and hustled down the staircase.

Uncle Magnus ducked out of Papa's studio with his saddle-bags. "Hurry, hurry!" He held the front door open for me.

I ran outside to Glancer, hitched to the post.

"Magnus?" called Mama from upstairs. "What are you and Odette doing?"

"We'll be back in a while," he called over his shoulder, sprinting behind me, passing me. "Don't worry."

"What do you mean, you'll be back?" cried Mama from the house.

Before Mama could fly out the door behind us, Uncle Magnus scooped me up and lifted me up to the saddle. He plopped me down so that my legs straddled the dappled horse. "Hang on to your bag for now," he said. "We'll tie it on later."

"Magnus?" Mama swung open the door, her eyes wide, her voice shrill. "Where are you taking her?"

Uncle Magnus tossed his own bags over the horse and unhitched him from the post.

"Magnus?" She lifted the hem of her dress and bolted our way. "What are you doing?"

He climbed up behind me. "Don't worry, Maria."

"Where are you taking her?"

He grabbed up the reins, his arms around me. "To see her father."

"Don't you dare, Magnus!"

"She thought I killed him. She needs to see the truth."

"Don't you dare!"

Uncle Magnus kicked his heels into Glancer's sides and sent the horse galloping away. I gripped the saddle with one hand, clutched my bag with the other, and squinted into the oven-hot wind whipping past my cheeks. Mama ran after us in the wake of our dust, her long hair flying behind her, her face disappearing into a smaller and smaller speck. Even when we rounded a bend in the canyon, I still heard her screaming my uncle's name, as though someone were chopping her to bits, as though she were laid out on a table, a victim of "The Robber Bridegroom" murderers.

CHAPTER FIVE

Trudchen
January 15, 1909—Oregon

W here are you planning to take us?" I asked Od when we collapsed into our seats on the train to Portland. "I'm so terribly proud of you for leaving, Tru. Terribly proud!" Od hooked her right arm through the crook of my left elbow. "I've been dreaming of this very moment for the past two years."

I felt disoriented and dizzy and strangled by the starched white collar of my blouse. I kept envisioning my wheelchair and Aunt Viktoria—my tethers to safety and comfort—both abandoned back at the depot. Oh, and that look of absolute horror on Auntie's face! The velveteen seats and the passengers' hats and coats around me smeared into a blur of greens and browns and grays.

"I still don't—" I broke into a fit of coughing from the stink of a cigar smoked by a man in a cowboy hat two seats in front of us. "I don't entirely understand this plan of yours. Where are we going, precisely?"

"Philadelphia, of course." Od unfastened the glass buttons of her coat. "Never second-guess a premonition, Tru. *Never.*"

My blood drained to my toes at the thought of the two of us

trekking clear across the country because of my teacup game. It was one thing to toy with the idea of a Philadelphia monster when I sat in a chair inside my own home . . .

"I think we ought to go, instead, to our mother," I said.

Od did not respond. She pulled her arms out of the coat's purple sleeves.

"In that note Aunt Viktoria gave you," I continued, "what did she list for Mother's address?"

"I haven't yet opened the envelope." She squished the jacket into the space between her left hip and the armrest. "But I know we shouldn't go to our mother."

"Why not?"

"Because . . ." Od sighed. "She's not proud of her living conditions. I don't want to embarrass her. And I don't want to stop for any visits and chitchat. We mustn't get attached to any one place if we're going to be productive."

She stood up and rummaged around in her canvas bag in the compartment above our seat. The train swung around a bend and tipped her forward at the waist, but she soon dropped back down beside me with an object I hadn't seen since Auntie had tossed her out of the house: the black leather journal from our childhood. *Odd & True Tales* we had called it. Our catalog of strange creatures and monsters we had heard of.

Instead of proceeding with our conversation about our mother, my sister opened the journal to sheets of paper filled with her handwriting from childhood—a fanciful assortment of loops and swirls and curlicues.

"Your illustrations are still tucked inside some of the pages"—she pulled out a folded piece of paper—"still stained with berries from all the pies and tarts the farmers' wives gave us as they told us their stories."

I smelled the faint whiff of blackberries and smiled at the memory of all those baked goods, and of Od's determination to cart me across the farmlands in either our little toy wagon or my wheelchair, just so I could join her on her story-collection travels. She also pushed me in my chair down the dirt roads to reach our schoolhouse, a mile and a half journey each way, through sunshine, rain, and snow.

I unfolded the paper and found a rough sketch I had drawn of Od stabbing a creature that seemed part moose, part human skeleton. My sister was a stick figure with two lines of Xs denoting the braids in her hair. Her round face bared square teeth. She shoved the tip of a sword into the fiend's belly. Little dots of blood squirted from its flesh.

I wrinkled my nose and refolded the page. "I don't remember adding violence to my drawings."

Od took the illustration and tucked it back into the journal. "You can't enter our profession without a little violence, Tru."

"Profession?" I furrowed my brow. "We don't have a profession, Od."

My sister bent her face over a page devoted to water monsters.

"We're simply having a bit of fun," I continued, "searching to see if there's anything to the tea leaves. Isn't that correct?"

Od thumbed through the journal. "If we're to complete *Odd & True Tales*—if we're to instruct future generations how to stay safe—then it's vital we try killing off any evil we encounter. I envision this book as a survival guide that will appear in stores and catalogs across the country."

As my sister spoke, I surveyed the seriousness in her eyes and her knitted eyebrows. She continued to pore over her old notes.

"Od, you don't want to hurt any . . . *people* . . . do you?"

Od flinched and looked up. "What type of question is that?"

"You're talking about killing things." I quickly lowered my voice, for a woman in front of us had just glanced over her shoulder. "I want to make sure you're thinking rationally. How much money do you have for this quest of yours?"

"Quest of *ours*," she corrected me. "Nearly two hundred dollars." She continued to page through the journal with a crisp rustle of the pages. "I'm trying to see if we ever recorded any accounts of creature sightings in Philadelphia."

"Please, let me see our mother's address. I want to know where she is so I don't keep imagining her dead."

"Oh, Tru." Od's voice softened. "She's not dead."

"Prove it to me. Open Aunt Viktoria's envelope. Please."

She rubbed her lips together, and behind her pensive eyes I sensed the whirring of her mind as she calculated the risks and the advantages of abiding my wishes.

A half minute later, she closed the journal, and after a sigh and a sniff, she rose to her feet and fetched the envelope from her bag.

"Here . . ." She handed the envelope to me. "I'll consider adding her location to our expedition, but I strongly believe we should visit Philadelphia before traveling anywhere else. If that message in your teacup—"

"I require more rest than you do," I said. "Walking is tiring, and Philadelphia is practically on the other side of the world."

"I know that, Tru. I'm the one who used to take care of you more than anyone, remember?"

"Of course, but I want to make sure you truly remember."

"Well, I do." She dropped back down into the seat. "You'll receive ample rest."

I ripped open the envelope and pulled out two pieces of paper, the first being Aunt Viktoria's letter, in which she vouched for Od's character with phrases such as "hard worker" and "punctual," without any heart in the praise.

On the second sheet I found an address for our mother.

A Philadelphia address.

I slapped a hand over my mouth.

"What is it?" asked Od.

I couldn't speak. All I could do was sit there, clasping my fingers over my lips, while that cowboy fellow's cigar smoke crept up my nostrils with a sickening sourness that settled in my stomach. Again the train blurred, as did all the numbers and letters on the paper.

"What does it say?" Od took the address from me and must have spotted the name of the city, for her jaw dropped; her face blanched.

"How could I . . . ?" I leaned over her right arm and reread the words, which shook in her hands. Mother's address still said Philadelphia. "I . . . I couldn't have known . . . that creature!

I'm not seeing the future in tea leaves, Od. I can't be. Tell me you wrote down that address yourself as a joke."

"No, I didn't write it." Od swiveled my way, and her brow creased with a glower that made me feel I'd somehow just betrayed her.

"What's wrong?" I asked.

"You didn't make up the story of the Philadelphia monster, did you?"

"Why on earth would I do that?"

"So I would want to go find our mother with you."

"No!" I shook my head. "I wasn't even sure I would climb aboard this train with you."

She shoved the paper back into the envelope. "Our mother is busy, Tru. She doesn't have the means to take care of us. Now that I think of it, Philadelphia *is* awfully far away."

I rubbed the handle of the cane between my fingers and searched for the right words to persuade her.

"What if we're meant to save her?" I asked. "What if this creature I'm seeing is about to attack her? What if that's what the tea leaves meant?"

Od stiffened, and a streak of guilt shot through me for playing upon her fears. The more I thought about our mother, however, the more I believed she would be the one person in the world who could help Od recover from whatever it was that haunted her—from whatever hardships she'd just endured. If Mama couldn't save my sister from these bizarre fantasies, I didn't know who would.

"I swear I've never seen this address," I said. "But I have seen that creature."

"You just said a trip to Philadelphia would be too hard for you."

"That's before I knew our mother was there. I want to meet her, more than anything else in the world. I need her. And I think you need her, too."

Od traced a finger along the envelope's right edge, risking the sting of a wicked paper cut.

"You said to never second-guess a premonition, Od . . ."

"Oh, all right. I'll purchase fare for Philadelphia when we reach Portland." She stood up and stored the envelope back inside the Gladstone above. "We'll check on Mama's safety. We'll search for talk of the supernatural in her neighborhood. But we can't stay for long. I don't want her bringing up my last visit with her."

I blinked.

She did not elaborate.

"How recently did you visit her?" I asked.

"I don't want to talk about it."

"Didn't it go well?"

"Tru, I don't want to talk about." She plopped back down in the seat and returned to reading the journal.

Od and I disembarked the train in Portland at a grand depot—more of a palace—with a terra-cotta roof and a clock tower that loomed almost two hundred feet over the rail yard. I had only dim snippets of memories from living in that city when our mother first moved us to Oregon from San Diego: a shadowy tenement house; neighbors shouting in different languages on the other sides of the walls; a hospital; my mother watching me through a window with crisscrossing lines as I lay in a cold bed, my right leg cramping with muscle spasms that made me holler and cry.

"Let's go check the timetables," said Od.

My sister carried the luggage and could not spare a hand for support, so I grabbed hold of her left elbow with my right hand and clutched my cane with my left.

Not long after we sifted our way through the crowd inside the depot, we turned straight back around and boarded a train bound for Chicago, where we would then need to transfer to a train to Pennsylvania after spending a night in a Chicago railway station—according to the older gentleman behind the ticket counter who showed us complicated timetables. Od depleted most of her savings to pay for our fare, which cost over seventy-five dollars apiece! She agreed, quite kindly, to lend me ten more cents to send a telegram to Aunt Viktoria, to tell her I was safe and on a mission to find our mother in Pennsylvania.

My sister and I sat side by side in a Pullman passenger car that porters would somehow transform into a sleeping compartment while we ate supper in the dining car. Until that fascinating-sounding alteration occurred, we rode down the tracks—hurling eastward, miles away from the city—in springy green seats that faced other passengers. Beneath us, the wheels of the train drummed a beat in a hypnotizing rhythm that made my eyelids sag.

Across from Od lounged a gray-haired woman in an ostrich-feather hat who slept and snored with her mouth tipped open. Every time she exhaled, she cooed like a pigeon, and her pink lips sputtered.

"I wonder if she's witnessed any bogeymen in her life," said Od in a whisper to me. "Perhaps I'll ask when she's awake. Just getting to Chicago to switch trains will take three days, so we'll have time to interview dozens of passengers."

I nodded. Weariness—and wariness—kept me from formulating a response.

Next to the snorer sat a brunette girl of about twelve or so. She had legs so long and grasshopper-like, she didn't quite know how to position herself without her shoes sliding next to mine. She read the same crimson-bound book I had spied at the depot in Carnation: *Marvelous and Monstrous*.

I nudged Od with an elbow. "Do you suppose the author of that *Marvelous* book across the way ever met our mother and her siblings?"

My sister shifted her attention from the window to the book and drew a short breath. "Our family never knew any authors, but what a splendid title." She cupped her hands around her knees and called over to the girl, "Excuse me."

The girl peeked up with the startled look of a person yanked out of an enthralling story.

"What types of monsters are in your book?" asked Od.

The girl grinned. "All sorts."

Od smirked. "What's the worst one in it?"

The girl eyed the sleeping woman, possibly her grandmother. "I don't want to frighten anyone . . ." She bent forward. "But there's this *thing* in there that attacks people while they're sleeping."

"Isn't that always the case?" asked Od. "It's the worst time for a 'thing' to attack."

The girl nodded. "It's currently trying to kill a boy named Augustus. I'll let you know if it succeeds."

"Please do."

The girl tucked her chin against her chest and resumed reading.

Od sat back and ran a knuckle across the window. "I hope we're not missing anything important by passing through so many states without stopping."

I eyed the dark outlines of trees beyond the glass. "We can't collect monster tales in every state, Od."

"I don't want to miss anything," she said again, her voice dreamy, distant. "Or anyone . . ."

I leaned back against the seat and gazed at the golden gargoyle on the cover of *Marvelous and Monstrous* until my vision blurred and my head drooped . . . until all I saw were dozens of gargoyles, bouncing around on the laps of passengers.

In the dining car that evening, Od asked me to read the tea leaves again.

"I don't know if I can do it when someone is watching," I said as the last swallow of a bitter black tea trickled down my throat. "There'd be so much pressure."

"I'll look away." She readjusted herself in the chair so that she faced a family at the table across from us: a mother and father with three little girls in white dresses. The youngest, a baby, gurgled on the mother's lap.

"How old are your sweet children?" asked Od.

The mother sat up straight and answered with a smile.

"Frances is eight, Evelyn, five, and baby Florence here is nine months old."

"Nine months?" asked Od. "It's been so long since my sister was a baby, I'd forgotten how much they can sit up and chatter at that age."

"Oh, yes, Florence has plenty to say."

Od closed her eyes and drew a long breath, and I appreciated the fact that she did not proceed to press the parents about the monster legends of their youth.

I rotated my teacup on the saucer three times, then turned it over with care. After a few light taps to scare away leftover drops, I pressed my palms against the base of the cup and willed myself to see what was to come in our travels. I implored the leaves to show me our mother. And safety.

I flipped the cup upright and peered down into the china, which was beige and marred by hairline cracks that branched down to the bottom. My eyes strained to decipher our future in the jumble of leaves below me. I saw globs and splotches and squiggly brown lines, but no discernible shapes. No hoofed beast with the wings of a bat. No bell. No train tracks. No mother. The teacup merely looked dirty. I rubbed my eyelids and wondered if I might be trying too hard.

"What do you see?" asked Od.

"It's too hard with all these people around. I feel silly."

"Don't. Ignore them. Take a long breath, and—"

Baby Florence released an ear-shattering wail.

Od cringed. "Don't pay attention to that. Push it away. You can do this."

I gazed down again and crossed my eyes to see if that would help. I may have spotted a dog. Or perhaps it was a cat. Or a table . . .

"What is it?" asked Od. "You're frowning. Is it something awful?"

"I might see a dog."

"A hellhound?"

I snorted. "I was going to say a poodle. But, really, Od, I can't do this here. It only seemed to work when Auntie stood around the corner in the kitchen and I sat by myself." I nudged the cup and saucer away. "I'm tired. I'll need to sleep soon, even if there are poodles or hellhounds on this train."

Od wiped a corner of her mouth. "Poodles can be deceptively devilish."

I worried for a moment she was serious, but then I caught her cracking a small grin.

The baby's cries loudened at the next table.

"Very well." Od took one last sip of her own tea. "Let's get out of here."

I unbuckled my leg brace in the confines of our bed in a bottom bunk. Od tried to stay far enough away to allow me room to scoop my leg up and out of the iron frame, but her head bumped the bottom of the bed above, and she banged her elbow on the wood behind her.

"I'm sorry, Od."

"No, don't apologize." Od moved the brace to the foot of the bed, where my cane also lay. "We'll make this work, I promise."

She adjusted the cane so that the tip stopped pushing against the green curtain that concealed us from the aisle. "I was just thinking about our old days of sword fighting, when you'd be armed with your cane or crutch, and you'd knock my broomstick sword out of my hands every single time. Do you remember that?"

I laughed. "Yes, I do. You said my brace was part of my suit of armor."

"You were a knight who was missing your suit except for the right leg, and I was a foe from another kingdom. Aunt Viktoria was the dragon."

"Oh." My stomach sank, and my face sobered. "Poor Aunt Viktoria."

"She'll be just fine. We sent the telegram. There's no need for her to call out the cavalry to rescue you."

We tucked ourselves beneath the blankets, and the other passengers soon settled in the beds around us. I imagined Auntie pacing the floorboards of her bedroom, wringing her hands, muttering insults about my sister.

You chose to follow in your mother's footsteps, she had yelled at Od that morning, *and you may continue to do so if you please, but don't bring your sister into this. She's a good girl. An honest girl. I intend to keep her that way.*

Od kissed the top of my head and said, "Good night, Tru. I love you."

"I love you, too," I said, and my guilt over my aunt dissipated.

The lights dimmed, and I thought again of the possible figure of the dog in my teacup. I snickered.

"What's so funny?" asked Od.

"I was just thinking about our different interpretations of that dog formation in the tea leaves. I thought poodle, but, of course, you naturally thought hellhound."

"Our father told me about monstrous black demon dogs that roamed the English moors," she said through a yawn. "They smelled of burning brimstone and heralded death." She tilted her face away, toward the thick curtain that glowed with a light from the aisle. "What would you do if one were out there right now, Tru?"

"No, I don't want to imagine that." I sighed. "I'm too tired for more of your monster training."

"Our father was a remittance boy."

"A what?"

"The second child of an aristocratic family in England. I extracted that information from Aunt Vik over the years. He wasn't permitted to inherit land like his older brother, but his family gave him an allowance that enabled him to come to America and buy land in California." Od tickled the curtain with her fingers, and the cloth rippled at her touch.

My bleary eyes thought they saw the silhouette of a large and silent creature stalking down the aisle on four legs.

"You and I are actually Lady Odette and Lady Trudchen, you see. We may also be descended from a baron on the German side of our family."

I gave a murmur and a blink, and the silhouette swung its large and beastly head our way. I smelled something foul—charred wood. The stink of a building burned to ashes. That baby cried again, and a chorus of snores erupted down the train. Somebody belched.

"Once upon a time," said Od, her voice drowsy, distant, "you and I . . . Lady Trudchen . . . Lady Odette . . . hellhounds . . ."

A low growl rumbled from the other side of the curtain and vibrated across every vertebra in my spine. I thought I saw my sister grab her hatpin and stick it through the curtain. Something whined in pain in response. No, I must have dreamed it, for the next thing I knew, I was opening my eyes in the dark on a rocking train that carried us thousands upon thousands of miles away from Oregon.

CHAPTER SIX

Odette
June 20, 1896—California

Uncle Magnus and I reached an endless sea of rolling hills. The air out in the wide-open world smelled pure and wild and licorice sweet, and I inhaled it down to the bottom of my lungs.

My uncle slowed Glancer to a trot and asked, "Are you all right, Od?"

I nodded but could not speak. Never in my life had I realized the vastness of the world—the magnificent possibility that life could exist miles and miles and miles beyond our ranch house and the olive groves, which had seemed such a giant realm unto itself before that day. My legs itched to jump off Glancer and hurtle over the chaparral like the jackrabbits bounding in the distance. The bushes around us rustled with winds and earthly magic. A falcon screeched high above a golden summit, and beyond him rose a black and purple mountain range, painted against the blue sky like one of Papa's oil paintings.

My uncle passed me a canteen for a sip of water that tasted hot, but the liquid moistened my throat. It cooled my steaming skin when it dribbled down my chin.

I passed the canteen back and asked, "Are we safe without Mama's special case of tools?"

"She needs it more than we do." He looped the canteen's strap back over his right shoulder. "And I never said it carried tools. Remember?"

"Will she be very mad at us?"

"Yes." Uncle Magnus cleared his throat. "Quite mad."

"Do you think she'd like it if we brought Papa home?"

"No."

"Is he truly rich? Does he live in a castle? Is he a king?"

"You'll see."

We rode even farther, and the hills and mountains rolled onward. Every few miles a ranch house or an adobe proved civilization still existed, but otherwise we voyaged through a land ruled by wildlife. I spied more jackrabbits, as well as road-runners, rattlesnakes, and flashes of larger creatures I didn't recognize, their pelts blending in with the golds and browns of the summer grasses and soil.

At times we seemed alone. At others, the gaze of a thousand unseen eyes made the hairs on my arms bristle. My uncle's protective arms barricaded me on both sides from the dangers below us. Still, I feared getting gobbled up by sharp teeth.

We rode for twenty days (although Uncle Magnus claimed it to have been just under six hours) and at long last stopped at an inn that looked like an old horse stable with weathered boards for walls. A redheaded woman—older than Mama, less wrinkled and gray than Papa—brought us tin plates that contained our "meal": stale bread and tough strips of meat she claimed was goat. She also served us cups of rusty water that tasted like metal. Uncle Magnus and I sat on three-legged stools instead of chairs and ate at a table that gleamed with grease.

"We know your uncle well from his travels to and from your house, little missy," the woman who served us told me with a smile that exposed yellow teeth. "He reads me the cards and makes this little part of the world a tad lovelier every time he passes through."

After we ate, Uncle Magnus, indeed, laid out a trio of cards for the woman. All three revealed pictures that entailed gold coins, which pleased the woman so immensely, she allowed the two of us to eat that god-awful goat leather for free.

After Glancer rested a bit and drank his own orange water from a trough, Uncle Magnus hoisted me back up to the saddle and climbed on behind me.

"How much longer?" I asked when he steered the horse back to the trail.

"We'll be riding until sunset."

"Are you sure we'll see Papa?"

"I know precisely where he lives when he's in the city. Your mother used to work there."

"When?"

"When she first brought me down to California. She was his maid. That's how they met."

"No." I shook my head. "You're wrong, Uncle Magnus. Mama said they met at a party."

"Mama lied."

Uncle Magnus clucked his tongue at the horse and sent us trotting to San Diego, down the long road rippling with waves of heat.

✷

We traversed a valley teeming with dairy cows that grazed on yellow grasses, and the sun dipped down behind more hills, these more verdant than all the others. The air now tasted of salt—"of the sea," said Uncle Magnus. "We're almost there," he promised.

We entered neighborhoods—actual city neighborhoods populated by rows of houses with fences dividing lawns of green grasses that stretched to cement sidewalks. In the final, fragile strains of daylight, we rode up to a tall white house with great arched windows. A mansion. A wooden overhang cut in the shape of a lady's lace hem sheltered the front door, and lush trees and bushes nestled the residence in a coat of waxy leaves and pale pink flowers.

Uncle Magnus brought Glancer to a halt and dismounted. Before helping me down, he tied the horse to a black post and glanced back at those arched windows.

"Is this where Papa stays when he's not with us?" I asked, unsettled, for the house seemed awfully giant for just one man, even a large man like Papa. I wondered if it might have been a hotel or a boardinghouse, and that's why Mama had once worked there as a maid. On the lawn lay a pair of child-size bicycles, both blue.

Uncle Magnus reached up and grabbed me beneath my arms to help me down. I was getting so big by that age that his hands hurt as they dug into my armpits. When he plopped me on the ground, I discovered that my legs had grown sore and chafed.

"May I see him now?" I asked.

My uncle kept his eyes upon the house. He took my right hand, his skin hot and slick.

"May I?" I asked again.

"Od"—he peeked down at me out of the corner of his eye—"this little visit might not be pleasant. Whatever happens, know that you're loved a great deal."

The air turned colder when he said those words. The sun dipped beneath the houses an inch farther. I shivered.

"Come along." He squeezed my hand. "Let's go."

We climbed up three short steps to the front door. A brass lamp hung next to the door, and it appeared to contain an electric lightbulb, although it wasn't yet glowing.

Uncle Magnus took a breath and straightened his posture. He rapped against the door with the brass knocker.

Footsteps approached. I tightened my grip on my uncle's hand and gaped up at the rich wood door, which swung open a second later. A pretty young woman with brown eyes and a white cap stood on the other side, holding the glass doorknob. She wore a plain black dress with a white collar and a white apron.

"May I help you?" she asked.

Uncle Magnus breathed a short laugh. "You look an awful lot like my sister. What are you, sixteen or seventeen, just like she was when he hired her?"

Her cheeks colored. "I beg your pardon, sir?"

"Tell Mr. Grey," said my uncle, "that Miss Odette Grey is here to see him."

The young woman dropped her gaze to me. Her dark eyelashes fluttered with confused blinks. "Is she a relative, sir?"

"Yes," said Uncle Magnus. "Please go straight to the master of the house and tell him she's here."

"Is he expecting her?"

"Please"—Uncle Magnus shifted his weight between his feet—"tell him she's here."

"Who's calling, Annie?" asked a golden-haired woman who approached from the hallway behind the servant. She carried a curly-haired baby, a cherub, like the drawings on Papa's cigar boxes. A blond little girl in braids clung to the woman's blue skirt. A moment later, a blond boy in knee pants also appeared from somewhere behind the woman, as well as an older boy with red cheeks and a rugged build who didn't look much younger than Uncle Magnus. They all had blue eyes and hair the color of Tru's, and the soles of their fine patent leather shoes made impressive claps against the floorboards.

"Are you looking for someone?" asked the woman, her heart-shaped face pleasant and motherly and equipped with a smile that made me feel welcome.

Uncle Magnus took another breath. "Please tell Mr. Grey that Miss Odette Grey is here to see him."

All those blue eyes turned my way, and yet another child—a girl of about ten—showed up at the far right edge of the gathering.

"Is she a cousin of some sort?" asked the woman, the smile faltering. "My husband didn't say—"

"No, she's not a cousin," said Uncle Magnus. "Is Mr. Grey at home? May we see him?"

"I don't understand." The woman shook her head. "Who is this child?"

"I hope to God she's not who I think she is," said the oldest boy in a growl that made me recoil.

"What's going on down here?" asked a voice I recognized as Papa's. The deep timbre of his question rang out from high near the molded ceiling of this strange house with its scents of waxes and polishes. Footsteps thumped down a staircase I couldn't see, and before I could even ask if that was my father approaching, Papa nudged his way through the throng of blond strangers and beheld me with eyes that expanded into the size of silver dollars.

"Oh, Christ." His attention switched to Magnus. "What are you doing, Magnus? What in God's name are you doing?"

My uncle lifted his chin. "I think you should tell Od the truth, Louis."

"Who is this?" asked the woman, whose forehead now crinkled and whitened. She clasped the baby to her chest, as though we might hurt it.

I simply stood there, rooted to the ground, shrinking down, down, down into the pristine white boards below my scuffed old shoes that squeezed my toes. All those piercing blue eyes—*oh, Lord, two more pairs just emerged!*—stared me down as though their owners expected me to sprout claws and jagged teeth.

Everything that happened next unfolded like a terrible dream. Papa grabbed Uncle Magnus by the lapels of his brown coat and slammed his back into a post. He cursed at my uncle and called him words that caused the woman to cover as many ears as she could, her free hand flying from child to child until she was hitting more than protecting. The oldest boy lunged at my uncle with a raised fist, but Papa held the boy back, warning, "Stay out of this, son."

Son, he said. He'd called that awful, red-cheeked man-boy "son."

"It's bad enough we all knew this was happening," said the boy to Uncle Magnus, "but you didn't need to come shove it in our faces. Get this little bastard away from our house. Take her back to her whore of a mother."

"Stop it, Lou." Papa shoved the boy toward the house. "You're not helping."

"How could you have done this to Mother?" asked the boy— *Lou*—and he swung an outstretched hand toward the woman in the doorway, who now trembled and cried, her eyes scorching red. "How could you," he asked Papa, "you selfish, selfish man?"

All the beauty and goodness of my childhood shattered across the ground, too broken to ever be mended. I ran to Papa and squeezed my arms around his thick waist.

"I want us to go home," I said into the thin wool of his summer coat.

"No, Odette." He pried my arms off him. "We can't do that. You must leave with your uncle right away."

"Why are you here with these people?" I asked through tears. "Why aren't you with us?"

"I'm sorry, monkey." He continued to push me away with a gentle nudge, his eyes damp, his voice shaking, his fingers cold against my wrists. "This is my real family."

I swore I'd never speak to my uncle ever again for showing me what he'd showed me. He scooped me back up to Glancer's saddle and took us to a bright yellow house in a part of the city that wasn't as nice as Papa's neighborhood. The houses were smaller and butted up to the street, with strips of weeds for yards. Bottles of booze littered the road. A rat scuttled down a gutter, away from us, its long pink tail so large, I thought it was dragging another animal behind it.

We entered the yellow house through a back door, where we were welcomed by two women with lips painted bloodred, in rooms wallpapered in gold and jade green. They wore jewel-colored dresses cut so low that their bosoms were falling out of the tops, and they reeked of the flowery perfumes that clung to my uncle's clothing whenever he visited us. We ate supper with four such women in a kitchen, and Uncle Magnus read them their cards in a voice that no longer possessed any enchantment to me, although it clearly mesmerized the ladies. They smiled down at his nimble fingers and sighed over his predictions. One of the women, a younger one, stroked his left leg beneath the table. I watched her ring-clad fingers knead his inner thigh over his black trousers until he caught me staring and pushed her hand away.

I spent the entire meal choking down a peppered stew that stung like firecrackers on my tongue, and afterward, Uncle Magnus insisted I stay with him at all times, even though one of the women wanted to brush my hair and paint rouge on my cheeks. Another kept saying how much I looked like him. "Are you sure she's not your daughter?" she asked. Uncle Magnus guided me out of the kitchen by my shoulders and told her, "She's definitely my niece, but she's my girl, and I love her dearly."

He laid out blankets in a corner of a dark room, not far from an upright piano.

"Lie down here," he said. "It's going to get crowded soon. Close your eyes and go to sleep. This isn't a place for children, but I've got nowhere else to stay."

With a huff, I rolled over and pulled a scratchy blanket over my shoulder.

"I love you, Od," he said, a hand on my head, but I ignored him.

The floorboards creaked and sagged beneath my left hip and shoulder. If I wiggled too much, the ground would split open, and I'd collapse into a cellar squirming with more rats with fat tails. Or so I assumed.

Behind me, Uncle Magnus played ragtime music on the piano and drank whiskey from a short glass, but I pushed him out of my head by telling myself stories of castles and fathers who never left home—stories that kept ending poorly, no matter how hard I gritted my teeth and pretended my visit with Papa had never happened. If those blond people were his "real family," as Papa had told me, I wondered if that made Mama, Tru, and me his phantom family. My body felt empty, made of nothing but gauze and air. I possessed no substance. No bones. No breath.

I didn't know it then, but that was the last night I'd ever see my uncle, let alone my father, during the long and difficult years of my childhood. When Uncle Magnus and I returned home the following day, Mama ran at him and hit him in his face and his chest and told him she was tearing him out of our lives.

"Don't follow me! Don't write to me!" she'd yelled as she pummeled him with her fists and knocked him back against his horse, as though she were still a bigger person than he. "I'll never forgive you for taking her away, Magnus. You've ruined our lives, and I'll never forgive you. Don't ever come near me and my children again."

Mr. Alvarado drove us and our belongings to the railroad station in the mouth of another canyon, a mile and a half below downtown Fallbrook. Mama left the MarViLUs case behind at the house.

When I asked her about the case, she sat up straight in the carriage seat beside me and said, "Forget that case. Forget everything your uncle ever told you about it. Forget him and your father. We're through with everything."

CHAPTER SEVEN

Trudchen
January 18, 1909—Illinois

Od and I arrived in Chicago's Union Depot at nine o'clock on a Monday night. A constellation of electric lights glimmered from skyscrapers across the Chicago River and looked nothing at all like pitch-black, nighttime Carnation, Oregon.

My sister helped me walk through a lobby lit by chandeliers shaped like clusters of enormous glowing grapes, but the dark wood of the benches, the ceiling, and the pillars made the space look rather dim and suffocating, as though we were trapped inside a wooden chest. Both of my legs felt stiff and sore, and neither of them worked quite right at the moment. The soles of my shoes squeaked and skidded on the black and white tiled floor.

Od lugged her canvas bag and the MarViLUs case and slowed her pace to match mine. I grew self-conscious about the way the upper half of my body rocked from side to side when I walked. Everyone else glided across the floor with the grace of ice-skaters.

"I'll ask if they have any sleeping accommodations," said Od. "These armrests on the benches won't do for slumbering."

"I miss my wheelchair," I said. "I'm not sure how I'll be able to manage in cities without it."

"We'll buy another one."

"But . . ." I winced at a burning sensation that flared in my right hip from flinging the leg forward with such force. "I just talked you into spending most of your money on train tickets."

"We'll earn money. Don't worry."

"'Scuse me, ladies," said a gentleman who seemed to materialize from the shadows among the other passengers. "If you need a guide, I can help you find where you're going."

He approached us with his hands tucked into his potato-brown coat, and Od and I both stopped and surveyed his appearance. He wore a green derby and a three-piece suit that bagged at the knees. His face was youngish and long, whiskery and scrawny, and his eyes seemed too big for the rest of his features.

"Areya partada Sailvation Airmy?" he asked in an accent so nasally and unfamiliar, it took my ears a few moments to realize he'd asked, "Are you part of the Salvation Army?"

"No, wait—" He snapped his right fingers. "Those ladies wear navy blue, not purple. What organization are you with?"

Od stood up tall. "We're . . ." She cast me a brief glance. "We're with a group of researchers."

"Researchers?" The fellow's eyebrows shot up. "What do you mean? Scientists?"

Od's gaze shifted to the other travelers around us. "Do passengers from Philadelphia often come through this station?"

"Sure." The fellow nodded. "Yeah, sure they do. Why do you ask?"

Od's eyes followed a young family with four small children. "Have any of them brought word of anything abnormal occurring in that city?"

The fellow shrugged. "I haven't paid close enough attention."

"Has anything abnormal occurred in Chicago of late?" she asked.

"Abnormal how?"

Od cleared her throat. "Otherworldly."

The fellow lifted his chin. "Oh, boy, you're Spiritualists!" He pointed straight at her. "I knew there was something spooky about the two of you the minute I saw you. Those purple coats caught my eye, and—"

"We're not Spiritualists," said my sister. "Our interests extend to all things metaphysical and mysterious. We find otherworldly entities, document them, and exterminate them. For a fee."

The man cracked a lopsided smile. "Are you pulling my leg?"

"No," said Od, "not at all."

"Od." I tugged on my sister's left elbow. "I need to sit down."

"Our police stations are all haunted," said the fellow. "It's been in the papers. Chicago's got a ghost epidemic."

Oh, bother! I thought. *There goes our chance for a good night's rest.*

"A copper in the Hyde Park station fired six bullets into a wall because of a lady ghost," continued the man. "She stared him down with one eerie, solitary blue eye, and *bang, bang, bang!*" He pantomimed shooting Od with his right index finger. "That happened 'bout two years ago, but the bullet holes are still there."

Od tightened her hold on the bags. "Are the policemen looking to rid the stations of these spirits?"

"'Course they are. It got so bad at one station, they had

cart one of the patrolmen off to an asylum. My brother's a copper, and he's witnessed the horrors." The man tucked his hands
into his coat pockets. "Why? You got something that can help?"

"We do." My sister nodded. "Are any of the stations nearby?"

"We could walk to them real easy . . . Oh, I mean . . ." He
glanced at my cane and scratched the back of his neck. "How
far can this little lady walk?"

"Od," I said, "I'm not awake enough for this right now."

Od turned so that she faced me alone, her back to the man.
"We could help the officers—see if they would pay us for capturing the ghosts in our mirror. That's the best way to rid a
place of spirits. You know that as well as I."

I gritted my teeth. "Police officers—law-abiding *police* officers—aren't going to pay us for ghost-hunting, Od."

"These people sound desperate. You heard the man! One of
them shot six bullets into a wall. One's in an asylum." Od glanced
over her shoulder at the fellow. "What is your name, sir?"

"Johnny Reeves, miss."

"Mr. Reeves"—Od swiveled toward him—"I'm Odette Grey,
and this is my sister, Trudchen. We'd be happy to offer our
assistance to your brother and his fellow officers."

"Well, then, Sisters Grey." He smiled and withdrew his
hands from his pockets. "I thank the Good Lord that I stumbled upon you."

Outside in the darkness, a train zoomed overhead on an ele-
vated track with shocking loudness and suddenness. I flinched
and dropped my cane, which Od helped me pick up, while
wheels continued to thunder across the sky in a fog of chimney

smoke and steam. Wind and snow gusted into my eyes. I spotted two hotels across the cobblestone street and longed to escape into one of them.

Od handed me the MarViLUs case so that she could take hold of my right arm with her gloved left fingers. "I think we should hire a hackney carriage to make my sister more comfortable," she said to Johnny Reeves.

"The first police station isn't far. Just over by Van Buren." He slowed his stride to avoid walking too far ahead of us. "You want me to carry your bags?"

"No, thank you," said Od—the first rational thing I had heard her say to this stranger.

A block or two later, Johnny Reeves seemed to tire of slogging along at the pace of a girl with a leg in a brace. He kept turning around to check on our progress, his jaw clenched in a grimace of frustration.

"What's wrong with your leg?" he asked.

"I had polio."

"Oh, Christ." He winced. "That's a hell of a disease. It killed a little kid in the neighborhood last year."

"Oh, I'm sorry," I said. My eyes dampened, and I gave thanks that death hadn't been my fate.

Od tightened her hold on my arm.

Johnny Reeves led us around a corner, onto a street marked Van Buren. All the streets in that region were named after deceased presidents, which reminded me of my old schoolhouse days, when we were made to stand in front of the classroom and recite the names of the presidents by heart up until Theodore Roosevelt.

Washington, Adams, Jefferson, Madison . . .

Mr. Reeves stopped at the head of an alley. "The back door's down here." He nodded toward the dark wedge between two brick buildings. "We'll find my brother inside. He'll tell you all about the ghosts."

Od crept forward with her tan Gladstone bag gripped in her right hand. I squeezed my fingers around the handle of our mother's old case of tools.

"Isn't there a front door?" asked Od.

"The back door's where we can find my brother. He keeps the night watch. He's sleeping in there."

Od shook her head. "I'm not taking my sister down an unlit alleyway."

Johnny Reeves snorted. "I thought ghosts didn't scare you."

"Tru"—Od pivoted toward me—"we're going to—"

Before she could finish speaking, Johnny Reeves grabbed her bag and tried to yank it away from her.

She wheeled back around. "What are you doing?"

"Give me your bag."

"No!"

"Give it to me!" Johnny pulled out a knife and pressed the blade to my sister's throat.

For a moment, I just stood there, frozen, gaping at Od stuck in that horrifying position, her head and upper back tilted away from her attacker, the knife shining against her throat. Both she and the thief clasped the bag that carried all our belongings, including Od's money. The man breathed in her face and rustled her hair.

"Let go, or I'll hurt you," he said, tugging harder. "Give me the bag!"

Suddenly, I remembered the MarViLUs case. I snapped it open, reached inside . . . and touched nothing but velvet.

Oh, no! Oh, no, no, no, no, no!

The case was empty. A rich green lining made of velvet met my eyes, but not one single tool—not even a simple butter knife!—rested against the fabric. I didn't see any hooks or pockets for securing tools, nor any indentations or scratches from blades and handles.

"Od, the case!" I cried out, my voice echoing across the buildings.

Johnny Reeves pulled back from my sister. "Hey! What do you have in there?" He inched toward me, the knife raised. "What's in there? A gun?"

Something—a large shadow—flew through the air behind him and slammed him to the ground. I held my breath and saw Od readjusting her grip on her iron-bottom bag, which she had swung into Johnny's right shoulder, I realized. He rolled onto his back and tried to stand up, but she swung again, this time at his face, whacking his chin so hard, I heard the crack of a bone. He curled onto his side, his teeth covered in blood, and whimpered into the shadows of the sidewalk.

"Come on." Od grabbed me by my right arm. "We need to go."

Somehow, I managed the strength to walk at a trot on my stiff right leg. We didn't dare peek over our shoulders; we didn't speak a word. Snow chilled my nose and cheeks and set my teeth chattering.

Two blocks later we slipped into one of the inns across from

Union Depot on Canal Street: the Oxford Hotel. Od urged the man behind the front counter to get us a room as swiftly as possible because I wasn't feeling well—which was, in fact, the truth.

Od and I recovered on opposite sides of the bed in the hotel room, both of us seated on the edge of the mattress, both panting. I pressed a steel lever through my skirts that unlocked the brace and allowed my right knee to bend. I clamped my hands around my upper legs and stared at the bedroom door, willing it to stay closed and free from the knockings of Johnny Reeves.

"Od," I said after five minutes had passed. "The MarViLUs case was empty."

She didn't answer. I shifted around so I could see her, my leg brace creaking.

"Od," I said again, struggling to keep my voice steady. "Where are the tools?"

She tilted her head so that I saw her face in profile, her eyes cast downward, toward the white eyelet of the bedspread.

"*Why* is the case empty?" I asked. "I really needed a weapon."

Od swallowed and said, "The case is extremely special."

I dug my nails into the eyelet and tried with all my might not to yell, not after she'd just experienced the horrors of a knife blade pressed to her throat.

"A Protector," she continued, "must decide what tool she needs to face her foe, and after she calls out, 'I require . . . ,' and then she inserts the name of the device she requires, the tool will appear."

I turned back around and again stared at the door. "We must absolutely reach our mother when we get to Philadelphia."

"Don't let that jackass out there spoil our travels, Tru. Remember, we're on a quest to fight evil."

"How much do you think you hurt him?"

"I don't know." She shrugged, or, at least, I sensed her shrugging behind me from the slight movement of the bed. "I may have broken his jaw. At the very least I knocked out some teeth."

"No one will arrest you, will they?"

"We were defending ourselves. He would have taken everything we had—our money, our journal, Mama's hand mirror, my story in the box . . ."

I looked over my shoulder at her. "What's in that story?"

She got to her feet and unbuttoned her coat. "It's the story of our lives. I was *not* about to allow him to have it."

"May I see it?"

She shook her head. "Not yet."

"Why not?"

She sighed. "I don't want anything else ruining our adventure."

"Why would it ruin it?"

She shook her arms out of the coat. "Are you hungry?"

Again, I eyed the latched door. "I'm scared to go out there right now."

"I'll fetch you some food."

"No! Don't go out there, Od."

"I'll leave the coat behind and unpin my hair to look less recognizable, but I doubt an unbathed thug who just suffered a beating by a girl is going to show his mangled face in a respectable hotel." She lay the coat upon the bed. "What would you like from the dining room downstairs?"

I rubbed my arms, which tingled with gooseflesh. "Soup and tea, please."

"That sounds good. I'll see if we can find any roses for the tea. Mama taught me that rose petals ease fears." Od tugged on the small pearl decorating her hat and pulled out the ten-inch hatpin.

I cleared my throat. "I once heard a story about a woman—a Pennsylvania woman, if I remember correctly—who accidentally punctured the heart of a gentleman caller with her hatpin. If the MarViLUs case is useless—"

"I didn't say it's useless, Tru."

I angled my face away from her so she wouldn't see me roll my eyes. "We should keep in mind that we have a ten-inch weapon tucked inside your hat, in addition to the damaging heft of your Gladstone bag, should anyone, or anything, try to attack us again. We're somewhat prepared, but let's not ever again follow a stranger through the streets of an unfamiliar city. I can't run."

"I know you can't run, Tru." She yanked the hat off her head. "That's why I've been teaching you how to fight. As I said, the darkness will be coming for you, but you can't let it win. You mustn't let it turn you into either a victim or a villain. You must always be the hero—always! Even when you're being attacked, or ridiculed, or thrown out on your own with no one else in the world to help you, you need to rise up from the pain and transform into a victor, no matter how much of a struggle it is, no matter how much it hurts. Always be the victor, Tru. Do you hear me?"

I nodded and shrank back a bit, for she seemed so impassioned at the moment, I didn't quite know what to make of her. My eyes moistened with tears over her belief in me—and yet, I still found myself not believing in her. I still worried about her sanity, dreadfully.

Od unpinned her hair until every strand of her brown locks tumbled to her waist.

"I'll be back with soup and tea," she said, and she slipped out the door, armed, I noticed, with that hatpin.

Od returned fifteen minutes later, accompanied by a man in a white coat and black trousers who steered a cart carrying two bowls of chicken and rice soup, two teacups, and a pot of tea into our room. He placed our meal on a small table in front of the shuttered window and then rolled the cart back out. Od locked the door and pulled out a chair for me. The broth and the tea seemed to warm the room or, at least, made it smell a bit like home. No rose-petal scent wafted from the teapot, but even if it had, I doubted the perfume could have warded off my fears, as Od had claimed it would.

"Tru"—Od sat down in the chair across from me—"I asked the hotel staff about the local police stations, and they confirmed that they're haunted. The man at the front desk showed me a newspaper clipping from two years ago that involved artists' renderings of various apparitions. It included a drawing of the policeman who shot at the ghostly woman."

I spread a napkin across my lap. "I want to enjoy my soup without thinking about that."

"I also discovered the name of one of the ghosts."

I picked up my spoon and dunked it into the soup. "Please don't tell me it's Phil."

"No, it's Johnny Reeves."

I flinched and splattered broth onto the table.

"Johnny," said Od again, "Reeves."

I dabbed at the table with my napkin.

She leaned forward. "Did you hear what I—"

"Of course a criminal isn't going to use his real name, Od. He must have decided to have a bit of fun with us and pulled a name straight from the ghost tales he was telling."

My sister frowned and snaked her spoon through her bowl. "I think we might have just fought off a spirit."

"I heard that 'spirit's' jawbone crack."

She winced, and I felt rotten for bringing up the gruesomeness of her counterattack. I wondered, quite macabrely, if the sickening vibration of his damaged bone had ricocheted off her hands.

I sipped a spoonful of soup and then added, after swallowing, "I'm frightened enough of a mortal man banging down our door. I don't want to think of him as a phantom who can slip through the walls."

Od's shoulders stiffened, and her gaze veered toward the door. A moment later, she jumped to her feet, fetched the hand mirror from the Gladstone, and hurried it onto the windowsill. She also wiped down an oval mirror that stood in a corner, flapped out our purple coats and lay them in front of the doorway, and parked her shoes so that the toes faced the door.

"When I was in Missouri"—she padded back to the table in her stockinged feet—"I met a girl from Savannah, Georgia, who said her family painted their doors, shutters, and the ceiling of their porch a color they called 'haint blue.'" Od sat back down across from me. "Evil spirits and vampires would get confused and think they were approaching the sky, not a house, and would travel elsewhere for their hauntings."

I cocked my head at her. "Why were you in Missouri?"

"I told you in my letters." She lifted the silver pot from the table and poured freshly brewed tea into my cup. "I joined a circus there."

"And"—I blew away a cloud of steam from another spoonful of soup—"what, precisely, did you do in the circus?"

"I learned how to tell fortunes." She poured herself a cup of tea. "I also fell madly in love."

"You did?"

She nodded and set the pot back down on the table.

Jealousy stung my heart. All that time she'd been gone, I'd pictured her as being as miserable and lonely as I was. I never imagined her kissing and cuddling some boy from Missouri.

"Why aren't you two together anymore?" I asked.

She lifted her spoon from the table. "We were forcibly separated."

"How long ago?"

"Almost a year." She slid the empty spoon into her mouth and stared down into her bowl.

"Well . . ." I scraped my teeth across my bottom lip, jealousy still burrowing inside me, making me feel cross and cruel. "If this *person* wasn't kind to you or—"

"Kindness had nothing to do with it." She lowered the spoon. "We just weren't meant to be together. At least . . . that's what I was told."

I took a sip of tea and watched my sister continue to stare down into the depths of her bowl, as though she searched for the future in the lumps of rice and chicken floating around in the broth.

"The world's so vast, Tru," she said with a tremble of a smile. "This country's impossibly large—I know that now after crisscrossing it so often. But I sometimes wonder if I'll see my beloved again . . . during one of my travels. I wonder, if you and I could one day manage to publish our book, *Odd & True Tales*, if somehow . . . we could meet again . . ." She blinked away tears. "I could perhaps dedicate the book . . ."

I dropped my spoon to the table with an obnoxious *clank*. "Is that why you're on this quest—to find some boy who didn't even think the two of you should be together?"

"No, that's not what I'm saying at all."

"Did he say you weren't good enough for him?"

"Tru, no . . . that's not what I meant."

"I thought this was *our* quest."

She squirmed in her chair. "Well, I'm glad you're now seeing it that way instead of calling it my quest."

"Is this journey for us or for someone else?"

"It's for us, of course. I told you, I've been planning this trip since the day Aunt Vik booted me out of the house, and nothing's going to get in the way."

I sat up straight. "Unless you find this 'beloved' of yours."

She slouched. "Tru, there's no need for jealousy. I would just . . ." She raised her shoulders to her ears. "Uncle Magnus always told me I possessed the ability to form special connections to people . . . connections that would allow me to find missing loved ones."

"Where is this 'connection' telling you to go right now, then?"

She shook her head. "It's not telling me anything at the moment. I don't think the northeast is the right place . . . but . . . I can't be certain. As I said, this country's so ridiculously huge. I hate how small and helpless I feel inside it."

I resumed drinking my tea, and I closed my eyes to ask the leaves to show me what would happen to us next.

Show me, show me, show me . . .

The tea scalded my throat, but I endured the burn to hurry the process. My search for answers amid clumps of soggy brown leaves did not seem quite so silly in the confines of that hotel room after our encounter with "Johnny Reeves" . . . after Od's talk of her mysterious beloved. My fingers shook, and my heart rate doubled. I spun the cup, turned it over, held my breath, and flipped it right-side up again.

Oh, Lord.

He was back. The bat-winged creature. And his cracked bell.

The beast hovered at the top of the teacup, still in the east, and the crown of his bread-loaf-shaped head now aligned with the rim. Watery tea bled from his hooves. Another word sur-rounded his body, this time not *Phil*. This time it was a word that chilled my soul, written in a jumble of capital and lower-case letters.

"Tru!" called Od, for what may have been the second or third time. "What's wrong? Your eyes are bulging."

I slid the cup across the tabletop and scratched the wood grain by accident. "L-l-look what it says."

"Where?"

"That word . . . the word surrounding the creature."

"I don't see any word."

"There!" I pointed to a lowercase *d* to the left of the thing's wings. "On this side it says, 'dE . . .'" I then shoved my right index finger toward the other side. "And over here it says, 'vIL.' 'Devil,' Od. It says, 'Devil'!"

"Don't worry."

"We were attacked by a man with a knife, and now I'm see-ing the devil."

"Tru." She grabbed my left hand. "Don't worry."

"How can I not worry? How can I even feel safe leaving this room?"

"We're prepared."

"No, we're not."

She took hold of both my hands. "We are. We've been pre-paring to face the devil our entire lives. In fact, we've already faced worse."

I recoiled. "Wh-wh-what do you mean?"

"We've been through hell."

"No, we haven't. My life has always been so sheltered, so simple and safe and comfortable."

"That's not true." She squeezed my fingers and looked me in the eye. "We can face whatever we need to face, because we've done it before. We've already proved we're strong, Tru. We're lionhearted. Both of us."

CHAPTER EIGHT

Odette
June 26, 1896—Oregon

Mama moved us to Portland, Oregon, at the end of June of 1896 and stuffed us into a crowded building that she called a "tenement house." Our apartment smelled like cheese—*stinky* cheese, not the good kind—but it afforded us a small parlor, a kitchenette, and a bedroom, all wallpapered in a green that looked black in the scant light of the rooms. Instead of olive groves and canyon hills for our playground, we now had cobblestone streets that whirred with electrical streetcars attached to webs of overhead wires. Horse-drawn delivery wagons clopped past the building from dawn until dusk.

Mama, Tru, and I slept together in one bed, but the springs in the mattress groaned whenever we moved the tiniest inch and dug into our spines and stomachs. Every morning, we woke up tired, sore, and snappish. We shared a water closet with two other families, and during our second night there, a naked man ran down the hallway, calling, "Sorry, ladies. Desperately need to use the toilet." Mama covered our eyes so we wouldn't see him, but I caught sight of his backside wobbling.

The tenement house made me sick to my stomach.

Mama strung up charms shaped like eagles and lions in front of our door and placed her hand mirror in the bedroom window, but her magic couldn't chase away the ugliness.

The week after we moved in, Mama fell ill in the middle of a Tuesday night. She brought Tru and me next door to stay with a Swedish family named the Karlssons. Mr. Karlsson helped Mama get to a hospital, and Tru and I were told to climb into bed with these strangers' children—all of them blue-eyed blondes, like my father's "real family." Once again, I felt as though I didn't belong. I felt hollow and strange. The children's feet were so cold, they woke me up every time one of them turned over, and the girl beside me sucked on her hair in her sleep. I squeezed my eyes shut and sent a message of distress to Uncle Magnus down in California: *Please, please, please come help us. I'm still mad at you a bit, but please,* please, *we need you!*

Mama didn't return home from the hospital until the following evening. When she entered our apartment, pale-faced, doubled-over, she staggered as much as Uncle Magnus did when he came home drunk. She went straight to the bed and collapsed.

I climbed up beside her in the sea of blankets. The coiled bedsprings bruised my knees and wheezed beneath me like an old man snoring.

Mama stared straight at me with moist brown eyes. "There isn't going to be a baby anymore, Odette."

"Why not?"

"It's gone."

I gulped, and my skin went cold. "Wh-wh-where did it go? Did it disappear?"

"This one simply wasn't meant to be." She closed her eyes, and her lips flinched with a surge of pain. "You're going to need to take care of Tru until I feel better. And then I must find a job. Mrs. Karlsson will watch over you during the days."

"You said we were going to live on a farm with your sister."

"I decided not to bother her. It's not worth seeing the disappointment in her eyes."

I scratched at my cheek and sulked, still not quite understanding where her new baby had gone off to, unsure why we always lived without the relatives who loved us.

"Can we write to Uncle Magnus and ask him to come take care of us?" I asked.

"No."

"Why not?"

Mama opened her eyes. "You know why not. Plus, he's not allowed to live in Oregon anymore."

"Why not?"

The skin between her eyebrows puckered. "Don't ask so many questions, Odette. Go feed your sister supper."

"Should I light the stove?"

"No! Go feed her some bread and some cheese, and let me sleep."

"May I kiss you?" I scooted closer. "Would that help?"

My question, to my surprise, unleashed a flood of tears. "Oh, Odette." She took my hand and pushed out words through bursts of sobs and gasps. "Life's been so hard for me . . . ever since I turned fifteen. I've been forced . . . to be so strong. I promise you . . . I'll do what I can . . . to make sure you don't get trapped in such darkness."

I leaned down and gave her wet cheek a kiss. She smiled for a moment, but then she closed her eyes and wept so much, I feared she might never stop, just like the sink that leaked in the water closet.

Three days after she lost the baby, my mother picked herself up and lumbered off to work in a shoe factory somewhere in the midst of the concrete forest of Portland. Tru and I stayed next door with Mrs. Karlsson, a woman much taller and tidier than Mama. She took in sewing for extra money, and I enjoyed watching the needle of her big black sewing machine attack innocent swaths of fabric. She pumped the machine into action with a foot pedal sticky with cobwebs.

At the end of summer I entered the first grade, and each morning I trooped off to school with the older Karlsson children: a ten-year-old girl named Agatha, and seven-year-old twins, a boy and a girl, Silvester and Ida. In the afternoons I went home with the children and read Swedish books I didn't understand with them in their apartment, which also smelled of cheese. Their mother's sewing machine hummed in the corner, and the voices of other neighbors rattled through the vents. Two-year-old Tru chatted in short sentences with the Karlssons' baby, Milo, whose greatest pleasure in life was gnawing his way through the family's furniture. I pulled Tru away from him every time his vicious little teeth got anywhere close to her.

My favorite thing to do in the Karlssons' apartment was to interrogate Mrs. Karlsson about the monsters she'd grown up with in Sweden. The woman would be changing one of Milo's wretched diapers or sweating over a stack of ironing, but she would tell me stories of elves and trolls and a beautiful woman with the tail of a cow who lured men into the woods.

"My mother slays monsters," I told her in her kitchen the evening before our first Halloween in Oregon.

"So you've said," said Mrs. Karlsson while she fried a white fish in a pan. "I wonder how she has time to work in the factory *and* take care of you if she's so busy scaring away monsters."

"I don't think she's found many monsters here in the city. So far, I haven't heard or seen anything peculiar, but you should sleep with the toes of your shoes pointed toward the door all the same."

Mrs. Karlsson arched her blond eyebrows. "And why is that?"

"Because"—I put my hands on my hips—"creatures called *Alps* like to mount people in the middle of the night."

Mrs. Karlsson froze and stared at me as though I'd just uttered a swear word without realizing it. "They *what*?"

"They press down on people's chests," I said, "until they can't breathe and give them terrible nightmares."

The fish sizzled in the frying pan and stank up the kitchen with a stench worse than the cheese, and Mrs. Karlsson held her spatula two inches above it without moving.

"That doesn't sound like something a little girl should be talking about, Odette."

"It's true, though," I said. "They enjoy climbing on top of sleepers in their beds or entering their mouths as mist."

"I don't want the other children hearing you say such things.

No filthy monster talk in this house, do you hear me?" She pointed toward the kitchen door with a plump finger.

I backed away, surprised by her use of the word "filthy" to describe a monster. I'd always considered such creatures terrifying yet clean.

Silvester, the boy twin, just a year older than I, must have overheard me speaking of *Alps*, for he asked if I wanted to play monsters in his bedroom.

"Yes, of course," I said, and I followed him into the room that he shared with his sisters and Milo while the other girls played with the little ones.

Silvester had a cap made of navy blue tweed that dangled off a chest of drawers in his corner of the room. I grabbed the cap from the knob and fitted it over my head, for I knew *Alps* drew their powers from a special hat called a *Tarnkappe*. Silvester lay down on his bed with his arms by his sides, and I crawled toward him across the floorboards, which squeaked and settled beneath my hands and knees. It was all rather perfect and sacred.

When Mrs. Karlsson walked into the bedroom to tell me my mother was at the door, she caught me straddling her son in his bed.

"What are you doing?" She yanked me off her boy by my braids. "You little heathen! What are your parents teaching you?"

She dragged me out to the front room and shoved me at my mother, who was lifting Tru into her arms.

"This one's not allowed to come back here."

"What happened?" asked Mama.

"She was on my seven-year-old son, pretending to be a monster. On him! In his bed."

Mama glared at me and marched me to our apartment, where she slammed the door so loudly, she made Tru cry. "You're not to play like that, Odette."

"But I was an *Alp*."

"Where am I supposed to put you and your sister if Mrs. Karlsson won't watch you? What am I to do now?"

"I'm sorry. He asked me to play with him."

"He's not the one who has to worry about his mother losing her job. This is a fine mess you've gotten me into."

"I'm sorry."

She pushed me toward the bedroom. "Go to your room and think about what you've done."

"It was only a game."

"Go to your room!"

I did as she asked and hoped Mrs. Karlsson would find an *Alp* in her bedroom that very night. I hoped she would go to bed without the toes of her shoes pointed toward her door, and she would lie next to her husband with her blankets clasped to her chin, shaking, her big blue eyes protruding from their sockets as she listened for the *clomp, clomp, clomp* of an odious creature plodding toward her in the dark.

Something entered our own bedroom that night.

No sounds warned of the intruder's approach. We didn't know it had crawled into our bed with us when we first snuggled beneath the sheets and blankets. It didn't disguise itself as mist, or animal, or human, or anything else we could see or touch.

Worst of all, it attacked my little sister.

My Tru.

"My head hurts," called Tru from the middle of the bed around midnight, and I woke up to her left arm burning my skin through my nightgown. "Mama!"

Mama fumbled with matches and lit the kerosene lamp. We found Tru flushed and shivering with a fever.

"My head hurts," she cried. Her teeth chattered. Her nose ran. Heat radiated from her as though invisible flames crackled across her body.

Mama looked to me. "Go get a washcloth. Soak it in water."

I did as she asked and didn't even spill one wasted drop when I poured cold water over a cloth in our washbasin.

Mama dampened Tru's face and chest, and she sang "Rock-a-bye, Baby" until my sister's eyelids fluttered closed. I crawled back beneath the sheets and sweltered from the fire burning across her.

The following day was a Saturday, so Mama could stay home and tend to Tru. Tru couldn't eat or sleep, and her blond hair looked sweaty and dark. Mama held her against her chest in her lap most of the day, and I read them both tales from our book by the Grimms—benevolent tales, not the murderous ones. "The Fisherman and His Wife." "The Frog-King." "The Star-Money."

On Sunday, Tru would not open her eyes. She couldn't wake up, no matter how hard we shook her. I burst into tears. Mama flew into a panic. She wrapped Tru up in blankets and ran with her out into the street to hail down a hackney carriage. We hurried to a hospital that frightened me with its hushed voices and harsh footsteps.

Tru was still alive, a doctor said, but unconscious. He called her sleeping state a "coma."

For days and days and days thereafter, Tru lay in a strange metal bed without waking. Doctors observed her, and they told us, in deep voices, of an extreme coldness in her right leg. They talked about a tube they stuck up my sister's nose to feed her and discussed pulse rates and temperatures and small voluntary movements of Tru's eyes.

I met Aunt Viktoria for the first time in that hospital. She marched in with a black umbrella dripping with rainwater and reminded me a bit of my mother, but with less color in her hair and eyes. She had a sharp nose and thick eyebrows that pursed together when she saw Mama and me huddled together in the waiting room.

"Oh, Maria." She walked over and clasped her arms around my mother. "Why does trouble always follow you?"

That evening, Aunt Viktoria took me back to our tenement apartment and packed my belongings into the gaping mouth of a black and gold bag made of carpet.

"You're going to stay with your uncle William and me for a while," she said, and she stuffed my rag doll from Uncle Magnus into the belly of the bag.

"Is Tru going to die?" I asked.

Aunt Viktoria cleared her throat. "I don't know. The doctors aren't certain what's wrong with her just yet."

"Can't Mama do anything to save her?"

"I'm afraid not, dear. This is a matter for the hospital."

We rode a train through the tree-smothered slopes of the

western hills that rose above Portland. A mustached man in the seat across from us recognized Aunt Viktoria from childhood.

"Do you remember that boy our age who was killed when we were seventeen or eighteen?" he asked with the same sort of smile that Papa used when telling ghost tales in front of the fireplace. "That boy Rufus Todd, a pushy fellow who was always stirring up trouble . . . remember they found him in the woods . . . a knife wound in his back? I always wondered who attacked him."

"Please, there's a child here." Aunt Viktoria clamped her hands over my ears, but I heard her snap at the fellow, "What's wrong with you? Don't speak of such things in front of a six-year-old girl."

"Did a monster kill him?" I asked. "Uncle Magnus told me all about the monsters in your woods, and he said that Mama—"

"You see?" asked Aunt Viktoria. "You've frightened the child."

I longed for the man to talk more about Rufus Todd and whatever it was that had murdered him in the woods so I would stop thinking of my sister with tubes up her nose.

Instead, he apologized and murmured, "Well, it was nice to see you again, Viktoria. Tell your brother and sister hello for me."

The doctors gave a name to the thing that had attacked my sister: *acute poliomyelitis.*

Polio.

Tru regained consciousness a week after she arrived in the

hospital, but she couldn't move her right leg any longer, and she suffered from agonizing muscle spasms. She lay there in that bed for two entire months before they allowed her to go home, just two weeks before her third birthday. Mama brought her on a train out to the farmlands to stay with me and our aunt and uncle. Uncle William, a man with a woolly strawberry-blond beard and arms and legs thicker than those of any person I'd ever seen, rigged a chair with a rope and a pulley so he could hoist Tru up to my attic bedroom. I'd fetch her at the top and help her get settled on the crunchy straw mattress so she could rest as much as she needed.

On the night Tru turned three, she and I lay side by side in bed, swallowed up by the darkness of January nights. Her good leg warmed my left thigh, but her other leg, the cold leg, rested on the mattress without the tiniest twitch of a muscle. It didn't act like a leg at all. And yet the doctors weren't sure how to help her.

I hugged my rag doll against my chest, the perfume no longer embedded in its hair, and Tru cuddled a white dog made of yarn that Mama had knitted while she worried away the hours in the hospital. Mama had stayed in Portland without us, for she had bills to pay, debts to face, demons to battle . . .

"Do you want to hear the story about the day you were born?" I asked Tru.

"Yes," she said in a whisper.

I inhaled a long breath and closed my eyes, and for a moment I tasted the licorice-sweet winds of California and heard the gallop of horse hooves speeding past jackrabbits.

"Once upon a time," I said, "three years ago today, a girl named Trudchen Maria Grey was born in a castle built to look like a stone Scottish fortress called Dunnottar."

I said the words, and I believed them. Tru believed them—I knew because she told me so. She would walk again . . . soon. Mama would return. Papa would leave his real family and join us in Oregon, and so would Uncle Magnus. We would all live happily ever after, just like every proper story ought to end.

"Papa hurried home," I said, my voice rising with excitement. "He'd been selling one of his grandest paintings to a rich ranchero who lived in an old adobe by the Pacific Ocean. He loosened the reins and urged his handsome black stallion forward, and he smiled when he spied the first stone tower of the palace he had built high on the side of a California hill . . . and this all happened the day you were born. Every single part of it is true, I promise you. It's all true."

"What happened next?" she asked, and I told her.

CHAPTER NINE

Trudchen
January 20, 1909—Pennsylvania

On the Wednesday following my fifteenth birthday, the final train of our journey arrived at our destination, Philadelphia—a city far taller and centuries older than Portland and all its frontier-flavored saloons and wildness. As dusk settled over the city, the locomotive chugged across a river, steamed through the heart of downtown, and stopped in an aboveground enclosure with a dramatic, arched roof made of glass and wood. We might as well have rolled onto another planet.

Without rushing me one bit, Od walked by my side through the station's lobby, which echoed with footsteps and voices that spoke in another strange accent—one different from the Chicagoans'. It struck me as brash and confident and a little twangy. Od carried the Gladstone bag and that empty leather case, while I limped through a sweltering swarm of passengers bundled in dark winter coats, some with hats and shoulders speckled with snow. I noticed several people sharing newspapers with one another, pointing to the front page, as though America had, perhaps, just declared war, or someone had shot President Roosevelt. Tension buzzed across the air. I tripped in nervousness, but Od caught me and steadied me.

"Are you all right?" she asked.

I nodded but couldn't manage to answer out loud.

A passing gentleman in a gray suit banged a steamer trunk into my good knee. I winced and panicked about losing the use of that leg, too, but a few steps farther, the throbbing eased, and my eyes stopped watering.

"How will we get to Mother's?" I asked Od, who'd just been shoved by a woman with elbows she couldn't seem to control.

"I think we should find a hack," she said, regaining her balance. "I don't know a thing about this city and would hate to put us on the wrong streetcar by mistake."

Another passerby bumped her with an elbow, this time a young man with light brown hair, almost blond. He'd been striding at a brisk pace with two other lads in pressed suits and silk neckties, all of them clutching newspapers and luggage. The offending young man turned his head toward Od and said, "Oh. Sorry."

She turned her head, as well, and both she and the fellow came to an abrupt stop. They pivoted toward each other in a strange, surreal, dancelike spin, their arms hanging at their sides, their torsos stiff. The young man's mouth fell open, revealing a set of perfect, pearl-colored teeth. Five feet away, his friends halted in their tracks. I lingered behind Od, viewing the back of her head and the blaze of recognition burning in the young man's hazel eyes. The other passengers swept around them in a roiling sea of black and gray wool, and yet Od and the fellow didn't seem to notice anyone else. My heart stopped. I worried she'd just found *the* boy—her "beloved." The missing paramour from Missouri.

"Odette?" asked the young man, his lips quivering at the corners, as though deciding whether to smile. "What are you doing here in the East?"

"What are *you* doing here?" she asked, her voice so strange—breathy, higher pitched than normal. She backed away from him, I noticed.

"My parents sent me to that prep school in New York near my grandfather—the one I told you about." The fellow inched closer. "And now I'm at Columbia University." He loomed closer still. "I don't understand . . . Did you somehow hear I'd be visiting Philadelphia today?"

"No, not at all. I wouldn't have come if I did. My mother recently moved here. We've . . . we've come to visit her. This is my sister, Tru."

The young man wrinkled his forehead and lowered his luggage to the floor. "Tru? I thought you weren't able to see her again."

"Until last week I *hadn't* seen her—not since . . ." She closed her mouth, her jaw tight.

The fellow gave a little cough into his right hand, and his cheeks and neck reddened.

"I spent a great deal of time in Kansas City," added Od.

"Kansas City, was it?" he asked, but he looked at his shoes when he spoke and scratched the back of his neck with the newspaper.

"Well . . ." Od drew a breath and shifted toward the exit. "We must get going. No time to chat."

The fellow raised his eyes. "Have you heard about the devil?"

Od and I exchanged a look of stunned horror.

She swiveled back toward him on her heels. "What did you just say?"

"Do you remember me telling you about the legend linked to my family's name?" he asked. "The Leeds Devil?"

I clutched my stomach.

Again, Od cast me a glance, her face so pale, it matched the collar of her blouse that poked out from the top of her coat. "Of c-c-course I remember. Why?"

"Well . . ." He shifted his weight between his legs. "The newspapers from here to New York are saying the Leeds Devil is running amok all over the Delaware Valley. That's why we traveled to Philadelphia. Everyone from here to eastern New Jersey has claimed to see the thing." He handed Od one of the newspaper pages. "He's killing livestock, mauling dogs, terrifying eyewitnesses . . ."

Again, Od and I checked in with each other, our eyes wide and unblinking. The floor seemed to roll beneath me. I lost my balance and pushed my full weight against the cane.

Od set down her Gladstone and took the newspaper. We both leaned our heads to read an article about a slew of recent sightings of some sort of beast called the "Leeds Devil," which the writer referred to as a "jabberwock" in the article's opening line.

"Are you coming, Cy?" asked one of the young man's friends, slapping him on his left shoulder. "We're going to miss all the excitement if you stand around flirting. Who's the girl?"

"I know her from home," said the fellow—Cy, apparently.

Cy Leeds.

Cy from Oregon.

Cy, whom I never saw but whom I'd heard all about when Od started working for the family named Leeds in Hillsboro. The boy who'd made her sigh with a lovesick sound. Not her "beloved" from Missouri but, still, a potential distraction.

In case it might compel him to leave us alone, I shifted the crucifix on my cane in his direction.

"Are you in a theater production?" asked Cy's other friend—a taller fellow with an oily face and rust-colored hair parted straight down the middle. He was looking at me when he asked the question.

"N-n-no." I shrank back. "Why?"

"Because you're both wearing those purple coats," said the first friend, the one who'd slapped Cy's shoulder—a short fellow with a brown wisp of a mustache not much thicker than the hairs above Aunt Viktoria's lip. "And you've got that cane. You look like you're in costumes."

Od shoved the newspaper back at Cy's chest. "Your university friends are rude, Cyrus."

"I'm sorry," said Cy. "They don't know about your sister's leg."

"Be cautious if you go chasing after your devil cousin." Od grabbed her bag. "I know for a fact that you lack courage."

Cy leaned close to my sister and dropped his voice to a whisper. "My parents shipped me back here right after you left. No one told me where you were."

She swallowed. I turned my face away from the two of them, not caring at all for the intimacy of his tone.

"Come along with us tomorrow," he said. "We're about to check the timetables to decide if we want to venture into the

Pine Barrens in the morning or stay for a while here in the city. Rumor has it, the Devil's been running around in the snow all over Philadelphia today."

Od peeked at him out of the corner of her eye. "Is this really true? Hordes of people actually believe they're seeing this creature?"

"Here"—he handed the newspaper back to her—"keep the article. Read for yourself what they're saying. We've heard there might even be organized posses and a reward for this thing's capture."

My sister and I exchanged yet another glance. Our supply of money in Od's bag was growing so terribly scarce.

"Meet me back here, right at this very spot, tomorrow morning," said Cy, and he tucked the rest of the newspaper beneath his left arm. "Say, around eight o'clock. We'll have made our plans by then. Have a bag ready in case we're journeying into New Jersey. We're going to shop for rifles and netting tonight."

"The last time I followed you on an adventure," said Od with a bite to her voice, "my life fell into shambles."

"I know, but—"

"Good-bye, Cy," she said, and for the first time in my fifteen years of life, my sister turned her back on a monster tale.

"Did anyone else come with you?" called Cy from behind her. "Is it just you and your sister?"

Od's eyes dampened, and her bottom lip shook, but she simply kept marching away from handsome, hazel-eyed Mr. Leeds of Hillsboro, Oregon.

Tucked inside an enclosed hackney carriage and yet chilled by a draft that allowed the snowy air to steal inside with us, we rode through Philadelphia just as the streetlights awakened. I gazed out the window at all the Colonial bricks and columns and lifeless statues that watched us from buildings I was certain I'd seen in schoolbooks. Four or five blocks away from the train station, I spotted a bookseller's shop with a wide display window. In it, dozens of copies of that same crimson-bound book with the gargoyle on the cover were stacked in a pyramid.

I twisted around in my seat and watched the building disappear from view around a corner. "I think I just saw that book again," I said to Od. "*Marvelous and Monstrous.*"

Od studied the newspaper Cy had given her, ignoring me. She had fallen ever so silent after her encounter with the fellow and read beside me without any reaction whatsoever.

Another block later, she handed the newspaper to me, and I pored over the article that reported the escapades of the so-called "jabberwock," who'd purportedly left tracks in the snow all over southern New Jersey. According to an eyewitness—a paperhanger named Nelson Evans of Gloucester City, New Jersey—the Leeds Devil stood about three and a half feet tall, and his head resembled that of "a collie dog," his face, that of "a horse." He had two-foot-long wings, a long neck, and he walked on his hind legs, which ended in horse hooves. His front legs were short, and Mr. Evans saw paws at the ends of them. The beast tried to break into the man's back shed, but Mr. Evans yelled "Shoo!" from an open window, and the thing barked at him before flying away.

"My teacup visitor has wings and hooves," I said, my throat dry, my voice small, just barely audible over the clamor of carriage wheels.

Od turned to me. "How long did you say you've been seeing this visitor?"

"A couple of weeks now."

She knitted her eyebrows and nodded, and then she said, quite cryptically, "I think Uncle Magnus may have been wrong."

"About what?"

"I'll tell you another time."

I reread the article and asked, "Do you think our mother is the reason the Leeds Devil has ventured into Philadelphia? Has she attracted him to her?"

My sister cast me a sidelong glance. "You sound like you finally believe me about our family."

"It does seem an awful lot like destiny, the two of us guided here by the 'PHIL' in my teacup . . . and then Mother's address . . . directly after my fifteenth birthday. Do you suppose we're meant to kill this 'jabberwock'?"

"Oh, Tru." Od wrapped an arm around me and squeezed me against her. "There's the Lowenherz blood talking!"

"I'm not saying I *want* to kill it." I folded the newspaper in my lap, my gloves marred by ink, my nose itching from news-print. "What if this creature is actually an exotic animal that's escaped from a zoo? Or just a person dressed in a costume?"

"We stand to earn reward money if it is the genuine Leeds Devil, so let's hope that's what it is."

"I don't remember anyone we interviewed ever talking about this Devil."

Od slid her arm off me. "Cy told me about it when I knew him in Oregon. He said it was the thirteenth child of a woman named Mother Leeds, who tired of having so many children.

When the baby was born, she cried out, 'Let it be a devil!' And the child changed into a monster and flew up the chimney— possibly after eating his family. Possibly not. It depends on whom you ask."

I read the article a third time, surprised that such a preposterous-sounding legend had led to the current sightings of an odd animal in the city. The newspaper stated quite emphatically that all eyewitnesses appeared to have been sober.

"I think we're here," said Od, leaning forward.

The driver steered the hack to a low curb to our right and brought us to a stop in front of a brick building with rows of doors reached by steps with iron handrails. Black shutters framed the tall windows. Lumps of snow topped the hedges lining the front wall. The building looked like a collection of connected homes. "Town houses," I believed they were called, although we most certainly didn't have any such thing in our rolling Oregon farmlands.

"Will you wait here for a moment, just in case our mother isn't home?" Od asked the driver as she paid him our fare.

The driver nodded. I plunged the heel of my left boot through the snow's crust on the ground and then dared to balance my right foot beside it. Using the tip of my cane, I tested the slickness of the surface before following Od to a set of steps that led to a lime-green door bearing our mother's address. Each time I thrust my right leg forward, my right hip socket erupted in pain, as though someone were grinding an ax against the socket. I imagined sparks flying, bone searing inside me.

Od lowered her bags to the ground and braced herself against the handrail.

"Are you all right?" I asked.

"This is a mistake."

"Od, please." I leaned my weight against the cane. "I think she could help us."

"Fate's just handed us a monster hunt, and we're going to get stuck here with a person who'll bring up all sorts of awful things that'll ruin the fun."

"No, she won't. She loves us. Isn't that right? She'll protect us, or else we'll protect her."

Od sighed and hesitated a tad longer, but those particular words of mine must have inspired her, for she climbed up to the stoop and knocked.

I held my breath, and she seemed to do the same, drawing air through her nostrils. The street smelled of horse droppings and burned trash, but no other signs of life stirred. I glanced over my shoulder, fearful of something creeping up from behind. My breath crystallized into fog, creating the illusion of movement in the dark.

"I feel a little sorry for the Leeds Devil," I found myself saying.

"Why is that?" asked Od.

I dropped my voice to a whisper. "His mother wasn't able to raise it."

My sister turned her face my way with a frown. "Don't empathize with monsters, Tru. That only gives them more power."

"But . . . still . . ."

"Shh! We're standing right in front of Mama's door. I don't want her to hear you talking that way."

Od knocked again, but no one answered. She then raised

herself on tiptoe and peeked through a glass panel at the top of the door. "I don't think she's here right now. I wonder if she moved in with a cousin or an aunt . . . I can't remember how old she was when she and her family migrated west to Oregon."

"Should we leave a note?" I asked.

"I don't have paper to spare."

"Use my cane, then." I lifted the cane up to her, holding the stair rail for support, fearful of slipping. "Write a message in the snow."

"All right." She backed herself down to the second-topmost step and dragged the tip of the cane through the layer of powder in front of the door.

Using the railing, I climbed up to the first step and craned my neck forward to read what she wrote.

OD AND TRU WERE HERE. WILL RETURN LATER.

"Add a little heart," I suggested.

"A heart?"

"It would be nice, in case she's devastated that she missed us . . . or if she's exhausted from this Leeds Devil business. Do you think that's where she might be? Looking for him?"

"I don't know." Od scratched a heart into the snow. "Let's go find some supper and get you a cup of tea. I'm curious if we're meant to join that hunting party in New Jersey . . . even though the last thing I ever wanted was to see Cy Leeds again."

"He's not your beloved from Missouri, then?"

"No." She handed the cane back to me.

"Does Mother know about Missouri? Is that why you're

worried about seeing her? You weren't married in that state, were you? Did you elope?"

"Oh, Tru." Od squeezed her eyes shut and gripped her head in her hands. "How you do bubble over with questions."

"Can we exchange another secret for a secret back in the hack?"

She picked up the bags and trudged back toward the awaiting vehicle and horse.

"Od?" I asked.

"Oh, if we must. But don't ask me about Missouri."

She helped to boost me back into the hack, and then she climbed in beside me with a grunt.

"Where to now?" asked the driver.

"A reasonably priced restaurant suitable for two young ladies," said Od.

"I know just the place." The driver swung the door shut, climbed up to his seat, and off we went, back through the nighttime world of Philadelphia.

"Here's my secret," I said, and I picked at the yarn of my left glove. "I received a valentine from Peter Hofwegen last year. Do you remember him? His parents were from Holland."

She nodded. "I do."

I shrugged. "That's my secret. A special valentine. He rode a bicycle out to the house to deliver it to me, even though I hadn't attended school in almost a year."

"Did he come by often?"

"Not really. All the other kids were so busy with school and their own farms." I chewed on my bottom lip. "He told me he missed me and wondered how I was doing."

"Well, my esteem for Peter Hofwegen just doubled."

I smiled, but a block later my mouth turned downward as I considered what I wanted to ask her.

"I want to know at least one truth about our mother," I said. "It can't be anything I already know about her, and it can't have anything to do with monsters."

Od leaned back against the padding of the seat, and her face deliquesced into darkness. "One truth you ought to know"— she took a deep breath—"is that she's made thousands of sacrifices for us. It might not seem like it, but she has. She loves us more than anything."

"Does she?"

"Yes." Od gulped. "She does."

"She wasn't hiding from us back there, was she?"

"No, of course not. She simply wasn't home."

I searched for the expression on my sister's face in the dark, unable to see her eyes or her mouth, only the outline of her cheeks and chin. I worried that she'd spied our mother when she peeked through the glass at the top of the door. I worried that Mother had hesitated in her entry hall, somehow knowing it was us, and she'd crouched behind her furniture so we wouldn't discover her at home, as though we were phantoms from her past, come back to remind her what she'd done.

CHAPTER TEN

Odette
January 14, 1905—Oregon

T ell me the story again," asked Tru in the nighttime blackness of the bedroom we shared in Aunt Vik and Uncle William's farmhouse.

I closed my eyes and breathed without a sound. The weight of shadows from our past pushed down on my lungs with a wheeze and a crackle.

"Od?" Tru lifted her head. "Will you tell it to me again?"

"Oh, Tru." I sighed. "You've heard the story for eleven years now. You must know it by heart."

"It wouldn't feel quite like my birthday without it." She rolled onto her side and bumped her good knee—her warm knee—against my right leg. Her other leg remained flaccid when she wasn't wearing the brace and ice-cold to the touch, even after all these years. "Please," she added, but she didn't whine. Tru was polite—far more so than I.

I pressed my front teeth into my bottom lip and vowed to never tell her the truth about our father's absence on the day of her birth, or of the fact that he had kept our mother hidden away in a remote part of the world for more than seven long years while married to another woman. Tru didn't need to know that our mother continued to work in the city to pay off debts and that Aunt Vik referred to Mama as "immoral" and "sinful" whenever she spoke about her to Uncle William, when she didn't know I was listening. I didn't know how Mama earned money. Aunt Vik kept us so sheltered, I wouldn't have understood it if she ever named our mother's profession. I preferred to still imagine her in her long purple coat with flared sleeves, stealing out into the nights with the MarViLUs case.

"Od?" asked Tru again. "Are you awake?"

I opened my eyes and saw the stillness of my sister in the dark as she waited with bated breath.

"Once upon a time," I said, my voice strained, "on a cold January morning, a girl named Trudchen Maria Grey was born in a castle built to resemble a stone Scottish fortress called Dunnottar . . ."

Later that evening, long after Tru had fallen asleep with a birthday smile lingering on her lips, someone banged on the front door. I gasped and shot upright in bed.

On the other side of our bedroom wall, Uncle William and Aunt Vik murmured to each other in worried tones. Their footsteps groaned across the floor of the front room. I heard the click of Uncle William's rifle leaving its mounted post, and my chest tightened.

"Who's there?" asked my uncle, his voice gruff. If I hadn't known him and his gentle ways, I most certainly wouldn't have wanted to encounter Uncle William and the long barrel of his rifle in the pitch of night.

Careful not to wake up Tru, I slid off my side of the bed, slipped my hand beneath the curtain shielding our window, and gripped the handle of our mother's copper and gold mirror, which felt as chilled as if it had been sitting in the icebox. I then tiptoed over to our bedroom door.

Uncle William and Aunt Vik were now talking to someone. A female voice—one that sounded familiar—spoke with urgency, but I couldn't make out the woman's words.

I squeaked open the bedroom door.

"I'm terrified," said the stranger. "Odette turns fifteen next month."

"What happened to you won't ever happen to her," said Aunt Viktoria. "I'll make sure of it."

"Magnus hasn't come back here, has he? If anyone ever hurts him . . . or the girls . . . I still think about what happened in the woods . . ."

"Don't!" said Aunt Viktoria. "Don't speak of it. Nothing's ever come of it, so stop dwelling on it."

"Please, promise me you'll watch over Odette now that she's older," asked the woman. "Teach her how to stay safe."

"Mama?" I asked, and I bolted to the door, my bare feet smacking against the floorboards.

Aunt Vik spun in my direction. "Go back to bed, Odette! Your mother's not fit to be seen."

Aunt Vik held a lantern that cast a dim light; Uncle William toted his rifle. Both of them wore robes and nightcaps and concerned faces. Both struggled to hold me back.

"No, Odette," they said, their hands pushing at me to keep me from the door. "Go back to bed."

"Mama?" I asked, but my smile soon fell.

Outside the door stood a woman who looked nothing at all like my mother. Her cheekbones were sharp, her brown eyes sunken, her coat a heap of mangy fur. She smelled of liquor, and she rocked back and forth, as though either nervous or drunk.

"Odette." Mother reached a bony hand toward me, but I drew back. "No, darling . . ." She shuffled forward. A feathered green hat teetered on her head. "Don't be afraid. It's me. It's Mama." Her eyes dropped to the mirror shaking in my right hand. "Oh, look, you smart girl. You still protect yourself from monsters."

"Leave her alone, Maria," said Aunt Viktoria, wrapping an arm around me—the only time I'd felt the woman hold me close. "Please, you'll break her heart."

"Don't say that, Vik." Mama wiped her nose with the back of a sleeve. "I came all this way . . ."

Aunt Vik nodded toward a stocky figure in the dark who lurked by a horse and buggy. "Who's that?"

"Just a friend."

My aunt pulled me closer. "I don't like the looks of him."

"He looks like a werewolf," I muttered under my breath, believing I spotted long tufts of hair on the backs of the man's hands.

Mama laughed. "Oh, Odette, you're still so much like your uncle Magnus. He would have said the exact same thing about him."

My aunt nudged me behind Uncle William. "You can't show up here in the middle of the night and expect a reunion with your daughters, Maria. Not when you're as drunk as a fiddler and running around with strange men. Until you've changed your ways and become a decent woman—"

"I don't want anything to hurt them," said Mama, now crying, her eyes red. "Odette, you're a special girl, filled with wonder . . ."

"She's an ordinary girl," said Aunt Vik, "and the sooner she learns how normal and vulnerable she is, the better off she'll be. Now go home, Maria, and stop drinking. You're killing yourself."

"Vik!"

"Go home! Stay away until you're well."

Aunt Vik slammed the door shut in her sister's face and fastened the latch.

"No!" Mama banged a fist against the wood. "Open the door. Please. Open the door. Odette. Odette!"

My aunt drew me backward, while Mama screamed my name with an agonized wail that felt like a hand squeezing down on my heart. I covered my ears with both hands and believed that our mother—our loving, dauntless protector from childhood—had transformed into the Weeping Woman herself, shrieking about the loss of her children. I cried and choked and wished her away.

"What's that noise?" asked Tru from behind us.

I turned and found my sister on her crutches. She favored her good leg, her face pale, her blond hair a tangled bird's nest from sleeping. Even at eleven years old, she seemed such a fragile sparrow who might crumble from the slightest tremor of sorrow.

"It's *La Llorona*," I said with a swallow that hurt my throat. "But don't worry, we're all making sure she leaves. You're safe and loved. Don't worry."

You're safe and loved; don't worry, I told myself, as well, while my aunt gripped my shoulders and dragged me away from the door my mother still rattled.

CHAPTER ELEVEN

Trudchen
January 20, 1909—Pennsylvania

The driver of our hack deposited Od and me at a restaurant on the banks of the Delaware River, in a region of the city with narrow streets made of bricks and cobblestones and buildings with ancient wooden doors. Next to the restaurant stood a hotel that looked as if it had been delivered from a village in Europe. I imagined the Brothers Grimm sleeping inside it.

Od and I sat in a dining room with dark wooden tables and chairs, and we supped upon Yankee pot roast, served to us by a rather handsome young waiter with black hair and blue eyes.

While we ate, my sister scanned the restaurant with great care, as though she again searched for that lost love of hers—a task that, at the moment, seemed a thousand times more impossible than finding an actual monster.

A white-haired couple beside us was discussing a sighting of the Leeds Devil on a local street called Sansom. They perused a copy of the *Philadelphia Evening Bulletin*, and when they flipped the page, I glimpsed an almost comical-looking illustration of an animal with a head that looked like a cross between a horse's and a camel's, a long neck, the sticklike legs of a stork, and the wings of a bat, the last of which were roughly one-third the length of its body. I crossed my eyes to see if a blurred version of the creature resembled the silhouette of my teacup visitor.

Good God, I believed it did.

"This newspaper is calling this thing the 'New Jersey What-Is-It,'" said the gentleman of the couple when he spotted me staring at the page.

"How are the people of Philadelphia reacting to news of this intruder?" asked Od.

The gentleman shook his head. "No one knows what to make of it. I've got neighbors pulling out shotguns and locking up their dogs, children, and wives."

My sister cleared her throat and offered, "If anyone is looking to hire a team of monster-hunt—"

"Od, *shh!*" I said, for just then that blue-eyed young waiter returned with a pewter pot of tea.

"Here's your tea, ladies," he said, and he filled Od's teacup first. He spoke in that peculiar-sounding Philadelphia accent—an accent somewhat less nasally than the ones in Chicago, I realized, but it involved highly unique pronunciations. "The wooder's hot," he said, which I believed meant *water*. "Be careful."

I moved my cane around to the other side of my chair so it wouldn't trip him when he came over to me. He leaned over and poured a sweet-smelling oolong into an ornate white cup with a red sailing ship painted upon it.

"I don't mean to pry," he said with a nod toward the cane. "But I see you use a cane."

"I do." I squeezed my hand around the hickory handle, wishing the thing gone.

He lifted the pot and stood up straight. "My five-year-old sister just got put into a wheelchair. She's real frustrated, not being able to play with the other children."

"Oh, I'm sorry," I said. "Was she recently injured?"

"No." He rested the pot in the center of our table. "She had something called polio."

Od and I both winced.

"Tru had polio, too," said my sister. "She was just two at the time. It paralyzed her right leg."

"It attacked both of Celia's legs." The waiter hiked up the long white apron he wore around his waist. "Her muscles won't budge."

"Mine didn't either for the longest time," I said.

"How long did it take for you to recover, if you don't mind me asking?"

"A while, but when I was ten years old, the doctor spied little muscle movements and put me in a leg brace. Eventually, I moved from crutches to a cane, and now"—I sat up tall—"here I am today, journeying across the country with my sister."

"Really?" The waiter lifted his eyebrows. "Where you from?"

"Oregon," I said with a smile.

"Oh, yeah?" He put his hands on his hips. "I was wondering why you had that accent. You're able to travel long distances, then?"

"Oh, she's planning to do more than just travel on this journey," said Od, raising her teacup to her lips.

"What else are you doing?" asked the waiter, his entire face expectant, those bright blue irises brimming with hope for his five-year-old sister.

I shrank back, unsure what to say, not wanting to disappoint him. Out of the corner of my eye, I saw Od sipping her tea and watching to see what I would do.

"I'm sorry—I shouldn't have pried." He backed away. "Enjoy your supper, ladies. I'll return in a—"

"Tell little Celia you met a polio survivor who now hunts monsters," I said before he could leave us.

He turned back around, his lips parted, a wordless question seeming to hang upon them. The couple next to us lowered their newspaper.

"Tell her you met a fifteen-year-old girl named Trudchen Grey," I said, "who uses a cane and a metal brace, but she's here to save the city from the Leeds Devil."

The waiter's eyes crinkled with a smile. "Oh, boy. She would be happy as a clam if I told her that." He stepped closer. "What did you say your name was?"

"Trudchen Grey. It's spelled *T-r-u-d-c-h-e-n*."

The smiled broadened. "My sister's Celia Blue. We've both got 'colorful' last names."

"There's nothing too 'colorful' about *Grey*," noted Od.

"I'm Ezra, and—"

"Mr. Blue!" called another waiter, who passed by as a blur of black fabric and snapping fingers. "Table seven is waiting for you to take their orders."

"Sorry, sir." Ezra Blue ducked his head, excused himself, and scuttled away.

I realized I was just sitting there, grinning like a ninny, and I noticed my sister still stared at me over her teacup, which she held with both hands.

"He looked at me with so much hope in his eyes," I said.

"I think it was more than hope. I think Peter Hofwegen might lose out to a rival this Valentine's Day."

"Oh, Od." I waved away her comment, my face and neck burning. "Don't be ridiculous."

I tasted my tea—the sweetest tea I'd ever sipped, and I hadn't added a single lump of sugar.

A few minutes later, Ezra returned with a piece of paper and a pencil. "Will you write Celia a note, telling her what you just told me? She's so miserable lately. I think you'd inspire her."

"Yes, of course." I took the paper and pencil, and that same silly grin insisted upon stretching across my face.

Ezra tapped the table with his fingertips. "I've got to rush off and fetch some meals, but I'll come back straightaway."

"That's fine," I said, and I watched him dash away again.

Od eyed the blank paper. "What are you going to write?"

"I'm trying to remember what I just said to him. I think I'll let little Celia know we're considering venturing into New Jersey to find the monster in his very own home."

Od recoiled. "I never said we were doing that for certain."

"I thought you wanted to. If Mother's still not home—"

"The more I consider it, the more I know I don't want to follow Cy and his posse of spoiled Columbia University boys."

"But . . . I thought we were on a quest for monsters, and I've *led* you to a monster."

"I'm not following Cy Leeds into the woods, Tru. Do you understand me?"

"Yes, of course," I said.

Nonetheless, I leaned over and penned my note to Ezra's sister.

Dear Celia,

I fell ill with polio when I was two years old. Even though I do not remember much about my long stay in the hospital, I have lived my entire life recovering from the paralysis in my right leg. Despite this obstacle, despite my need for a leg brace, a cane, and, for longer outings, a wheelchair, I have traveled all the way from Oregon to hunt down this "Leeds Devil" that has been seen around Philadelphia. I intend to save Pennsylvania and New Jersey from the monster. You will stay safe because of me, and I am a girl just like you. I hope you, too, will one day embark upon bold adventures.

Yours sincerely,
Trudchen Grey

I risked Ezra thinking me off my rocker, but I knew it would cheer his sister.

His eyes moistened a bit when he read it.

"Thank you." He blinked several times in a row and folded the paper into the breast pocket of his coat. "That message'll mean the world to her. I wish you all the best with your adventures, ladies."

"If we're successful," I said, "we'll be sure to return here for our celebratory dinner."

"I hope you do." He patted his pocket with a rustle of the

paper within the black fabric and returned to the other cus-
tomers and their meals.

"I'm going to arrange for a room at the hotel next door,"
said Od.

"What about Mother?"

"After you're situated and comfortable, I'll look for her, and
if she's at that address, we can always come back and fetch
you. But I don't want to keep dragging you around in the cold.
I think we both could use some sleep."

"Let me just finish my tea. After writing that note, I'm almost
hoping the leaves will show me . . ."

"Show you what?" she asked, her eyes narrowed, suspicious,
as though she believed I was about to utter the name Cy Leeds.

"Never mind." I shook my head, and I finished warming my
insides with the beverage. I then closed my eyes and willed the
leaves to guide me yet again.

*Show me answers about this bizarre and troubling crea-
ture that's frightening this region of the country*, I wished.
*Show me why I'm here and what I'm to do. Reassure me that
I'm not simply behaving like a fool.*

I rotated the teacup three times, turned it upside down, and
inhaled the lingering whiffs of oolong.

When I repositioned the cup in its upright position, the
damp leaves glistened in the yellow glow of the electric lamp
hanging over the table. A thicket of triangles lay pressed against
the eastern section of the cup, near the top. A series of lines
squiggled away from them, down to the tea-stained bottom.
Across the way, in the west, a lopsided *M* hung half an inch
beneath the rim.

I breathed over the cup, my mouth open, and the leaves shimmered against the china. The triangles reminded me of trees. Of a forest. The lines resembled trails leading in and out of the woods. As for the *M*, I wondered if it represented our mother, Maria. Or magic. Or maybe another monster.

What are you doing, Tru? I asked myself. *What on earth are you doing?*

Trapped in an enormous city, thousands of miles from home, with no mother, aunt, or wheelchair—I was allowing myself to drift closer and closer to the realm of superstitions. It was as though Od and I still huddled together in our attic bedroom, and the familiarity of her stories enveloped me, protected me, warmed away the chill.

"What do you see?" asked Od.

I jumped at the sound of her voice, having almost forgotten she was there. I removed my hands from the teacup, which I realized I'd been squeezing enough to leave grooves from the rim in the middles of my thumbs.

"What was the name of the part of New Jersey where Cy said he might go tomorrow morning?" I asked.

My sister's face sank at yet another mention of Cy and the hunt. "I don't quite remember. The Barren Pines, maybe. The Piney Barrens."

"I see trees in my cup."

She crossed her legs beneath the table, but one of her knees banged against it and rattled the dishes. "Do you, now?"

"Trees and trails, to the east of here. Is New Jersey to our east?"

"I don't know. Our forefathers crammed so many states together back here, it's hard to remember."

"I'm meant to kill him, aren't I?"

Od cracked a small grin. "Do you mean the Leeds Devil . . . or Cy?"

I flinched. "Why do you ask that?"

She shook her head. "I'm only teasing."

The half smile on her face told me she only half teased.

"Od?" I asked. "How, precisely, do you know Cy? I know you met him when you went to work in Hillsboro . . ."

"Let's stop talking about Cy, please. This is *our* journey, not mine and his."

"I think the leaves are urging us to follow him."

"Well, tell them to stop. I hadn't expected to ever see him again, and it seems terribly unkind of fate to hurl him at me at a Philadelphia railway station, of all places."

"You did say you have a knack for finding people close to you . . ."

"I'm not close to him, Tru. I'm not even sure I like the idea that the creature you're seeing in your teacup is *his* creature. For heaven's sake, stop talking about Cy Leeds."

My gaze strayed again to the tableau of leaves. I bent my head over the cup and inhaled a long breath.

Out of the bottoms of my eyes, on the portion of the cup that faced away from me, behind the handle, I saw him, standing in profile.

My creature.

He was back—yet again—but hiding from me. Taunting me. Tempting me into finding him.

In our Philadelphia hotel room, I did not tremble in terror and swallow down vomit, as I had when Od and I cowered in the hotel room in Chicago. The mattress didn't groan when I sat upon it to unbraid my hair, and the walls didn't smell of dampness and mildew from Oregon rains saturating the boards nine months out of the year. It was the most comfortable bedroom I had ever occupied.

Framed paintings of the Liberty Bell and Independence Hall decorated walls a deep shade of blue that struck me as being as Colonial and patriotic as the rest of the city. A miniature American flag stood on a marble-topped table next to the bed. I thought of Ezra bustling around with plates of food in the restaurant next door and wished I could go home with him and hand that note to his sister in person.

"I'll go try Mama's door one more time," said Od, buttoning up her plum-colored coat. "Stay here and rest. I'll be back soon."

I combed my fingers through the ridges left behind from my braid. "Will you be safe on your own?"

"I'll take another hack, and I'm wearing my *Hexenspiegel*. I've put the hand mirror on the windowsill so you'll stay safe."

"What about protection for you against robbers and murderers?"

She plunked her black hat upon her head. "I'll remain alert and prepared." She threaded the pin through her hat and her hair. "Get some sleep." She kissed my cheek and swept out of the room with her coat billowing behind her.

I changed into my nightgown, unstrapped the brace from my leg, and lay down on my back on the bed. I scrunched my eyes closed to bear that lingering pain in my right hip. A fireplace sizzled beside me, and an alabaster clock on top of the mantel ticked away the seconds of my sister's absence.

One. Two. Three. Four. Five. Six. Seven. Eight . . .

The next thing I knew, I was with Od in a cabin in the middle of a forest thick with trees and darkness. We sat on spindle-back chairs set in a circle, waiting for the Leeds Devil with Cy and his college friends. A fire burned in a stone hearth behind the boy with the wisp of a mustache. All three of the young men held lanterns that quivered with flames, and the air smelled of smoke and a swampy sort of dampness—the scent of flower stems moldering in a vase.

On the floorboards between Od and me sat the MarViLUs case. The silver letters engraved upon it twinkled in the lantern light.

"Go on," said Od with a nod.

I realized I'd been sipping another cup of an oolong tea that may or may not have been poured by Ezra Blue. I alone could determine where the Leeds Devil lurked—how close he prowled, when he would find me. Upon my sister's lap lay the hand mirror, and its oval glass reflected the dark rafters of the ceiling.

Again, she nodded.

The boys didn't seem aware of my ability to track down danger with a simple cup of tea. They kept turning their heads toward the windows and the door, for the wind rattled the hinges and toyed with their nerves. On the roof above our heads an owl hooted and flapped away with a sudden screech that made our shoulders jerk.

I drank the last sip of tea, flipped the cup over, counted ten seconds, and turned it upright again. My eyes then widened so much that they hurt.

Dozens of versions of my tea-leaf creature filled the entire cup. North, south, east, west, rim, bottom—my nemesis with bat wings and hooves appeared *everywhere*. The cup quaked against the saucer in my lap, and a pressure in the air squeezed my chest, warning that either I or the cabin would implode.

"We need to go." I lowered the cup to the floor and grabbed the case. "Now."

"Now?" asked Od, rising to her feet.

"Now!" I said, which drew the boys' attention. "He's in this cabin."

Without warning, something barked from the rafters. We all looked up, and the lanterns blew out. A boy screamed. A shadow pounced. I heard a struggle in the darkness, along with cries of pain, shouts, and scratches. Chairs toppled and smacked the ground.

I fumbled to unlatch the case.

"I require a lantern!" I cried, and the latch snapped open. My right thumb found a metal handle. I yanked a lantern out of the case, and a blaze of light erupted across the room.

The dark figure from the rafters lunged for the fireplace. Before I could see what it looked like, the thing shot up the chimney, killing off the flames in the hearth in its wake.

Cy and his friends lay on the floor, claw marks bleeding across their faces. The boy with the mustache clasped his head and said, "He was on me. The Devil! He was on me!"

Od shook my arms and begged me, "Do something, Tru! Tru! Tru!"

"Trudchen!" I then heard her say from someplace farther away, and my eyes fluttered open. I saw our hotel room in Philadelphia and smelled the fireplace in the corner. Od leaned over me with a hand on my right arm, her hat speckled in snow. She felt cold and damp.

"Are you all right?" she asked. "You were thrashing about in your sleep."

I fought to catch my breath, my heart racing, my back soaked in sweat.

"Tru?" she said. "Were you having a nightmare?"

"Was our mother home?"

"No." Od dropped down onto the bed, next to my right leg. "A neighbor lady stepped out of the house next door and told me she's gone."

"Gone?" I lifted my head. "Gone where?"

"She didn't know. Sometime last week Mama climbed into a carriage with a steamer trunk and hasn't been home since."

I furrowed my brow. This was *not* part of my plan.

"Did the woman verify it was actually our mother?" I asked.

"Yes, I mentioned her name, and I described her in detail."

"How long has the Leeds Devil been spotted around here?"

Od peeled her gloves off her fingers. "I believe the newspaper stated since Saturday. This would be the fifth day of sightings."

"You don't think . . ." I pushed the blankets off me. "Her disappearance isn't related to the Devil, is it? Did she go to New Jersey? Or maybe she went to Oregon." I wiggled myself up to a seated position. "Od, I saw an *M* in the western section of my teacup. Is our mother trying to find us?"

"If she hasn't come to fetch us in twelve and a half years, I doubt she'd finally do it now."

"I just had a dream about that devil." I picked at a string at the edge of the blanket. "Cy was in it, too."

At that, Od turned away from me, and the mattress shifted beneath her. She still wore her plum coat, and snow peppered the sleeves, darkening the wool with smudges in the spots where the flakes melted on the fabric.

"He's not the reason Aunt Viktoria sent you away, is he?" I asked, softening my voice. "I know he's not your beloved darling from Missouri . . . unless you two eloped to Missouri—"

"I'm not married to Cy Leeds, Tru!" Od rubbed her forehead and hunched her shoulders. "He's not my beloved darling, and I don't know why fate would be pushing and pushing for me to follow him. He's not the one I'm looking for. In fact, he's the last person in the world I ever wanted to see."

The sense of excitement I'd just started feeling about the mysteries of our journey thawed with the same swiftness as the snow on her coat.

"Those little pine trees in my cup," I said, "they might mean nothing."

Od lowered her hand to her lap, her head bowed. "He called it the Pine Barrens. I remembered when I was out there walking. The Pine Barrens of New Jersey. He once told me that's where the Leeds Devil was born." She kept her face away from mine, her head bent, her hands now braced against the mattress on each side of her legs. Long strands of her hair had slipped out of pins and dangled across her neck and upper back.

I adjusted one of the pins that poked out above her left ear. "We don't need to go to the Pine Barrens."

"We could probably manage the train fare to New Jersey."

"But . . ." I shook my head, confused. "I thought you just said you never want to see Cy again."

"I know you want to keep your promise to that little girl with the polio." She sighed with a frustrated sound. "I don't know what to do, Tru. It does seem like the opportunity of a lifetime—joining an actual, organized monster expedition. I just don't know . . . I'd have to face something I don't want to face if Cy's there. And the date . . ." She stiffened. "It's so near to an anniversary I'm trying to forget."

She said no more about the subject.

I asked no further questions.

She leaned her head against my right shoulder and drew deep breaths. I wrapped my arms around her and held her close, as if I were the older sister and she my little Odette.

CHAPTER TWELVE

Odette
February 1907—Oregon

Uncle William died of pneumonia on December 28, 1906, exactly two months before my seventeenth birthday. He had been a man of few words, but we dearly missed the deep timbre of his voice rumbling through the house and the jokes he'd share over supper—jokes that weren't always all that funny, but Tru would laugh at them until she hiccupped. We had to teach ourselves to stop expecting him to tromp into the house in his mud-caked boots that always caused Aunt Vik to shake her head with a sigh, and, gradually, time erased the scent of his pipe smoke from the furniture and the walls.

One Saturday night in February 1907, after Tru went to bed, Aunt Vik sat me down at the kitchen table. A rather-more-serious-than-usual expression hardened her face.

"I've found you a job," she said. "A good job. I'm hiring you out to a lawyer and his wife. They have three sons, and you're not to get close to any of them."

I flinched at that anvil-size load of information dropped into my lap. "Wh-wh-where am I going?" I asked. "Why am I to worry about someone's sons?"

"Millie Fischer from up the road used to work as their hired girl, but she eloped with her fiancé last week. Her father helped

me secure the position for you. You'll be cooking and clean-
ing for the Leedses and living in their house in Hillsboro. Mrs.
Leeds is asking that you work for a week on trial to ensure
you're capable of meeting the needs of the household. But they
do have those three young men residing under their roof, and
you're not to go near them."

I peeked over my shoulder at the closed door of the room I
shared with my sister. "What about Tru?" I asked. "What about
school?"

My aunt folded her callused hands upon the table. "I stopped
attending school when my mother died, when I wasn't much
older than you. The death of my parents forced me to grow up
and take care of my younger siblings, and I don't regret a single
second of my sacrifices."

I wondered if the sharpness of her voice—the harsh set
of her jaw—wouldn't have been so severe if she hadn't been
forced to make those sacrifices. I remembered Mama and
Uncle Magnus heaping a hundred times more affection on Tru
and me than Aunt Vik ever had, even when Mama suffered her
darkest moods.

"But . . ." I massaged my temples. A headache erupted; veins
pulsated. "Tru won't survive in school. How will she get there
without me pushing her in her wheelchair?"

"Her teacher has offered to ride out here in her buckboard
every morning to take Trudchen to school. Tru has enough
friends of her own to help her, so please don't worry that she'll
struggle without you. What she needs most is three square
meals a day, but now that Uncle William isn't here to help with
the orchards . . ." Aunt Vik swallowed and rubbed at the back

of her neck. "I'm not certain I can manage the farm the way he did. The Leedses will pay you four and a half dollars a week. That's good money. You can send it home for the care of your sister."

I squeezed my face between my palms. "And why am I to also worry about three sons?"

"Because you're a pretty young woman, that's why. Do not ever place yourself alone in a room with any of them. Do not get close to them. If you find yourself . . ." Her face and neck turned pink. She stammered a moment before continuing. "If you find yourself in the family way because of one of them, the humiliation would ruin us. I would be forced to send you away in disgrace, without your sister. Do you understand me?"

Now, I hadn't the slightest inkling how one could become "in the family way." Aunt Vik wouldn't even allow Tru and me to go to the pond during the spring, when she said the ducks grew "too flirtatious." Most of the other children at our schoolhouse grew up on farms, as well, but no one ever told us girls how babies, human or animal, suddenly appeared in their mothers' bellies.

My mouth went dry. "How does one become in the family way, exactly?" I asked.

Aunt Vik averted her eyes from mine. "That's something your husband will teach you on your wedding night."

"But . . ."

"I'm not going to speak of such things with you, Odette. Just stay away from those boys."

I sighed, loathing the new job, suffering pangs of homesickness, even though I hadn't yet stepped one foot out the door.

"Do you understand me?" she asked.

"Yes," I murmured.

"What was that? I didn't hear you."

"I said, yes, I understand."

"Good. Now go to bed." She stood up, the bottom of her chair legs growling against the floorboards. "You're to start your trial week on Monday morning. We'll pack a bag for you tomorrow, after church."

On Monday morning, when the sun first gilded the edges of the hills to the east and the cold chilled the marrow of my bones, I walked to the train depot in Carnation, my bag packed, my heart cracking in half. A railcar then toted me to Hillsboro, just seven miles northeast, but the journey felt like a voyage to another hemisphere. My job would not permit me to travel home much at all. Aunt Vik mentioned something about Mrs. Leeds offering to give me every other Sunday off. I would scarcely see Tru.

My aunt had written down the Leedses' address on one of her blank recipe cards, but I didn't know my way around Hillsboro, so it took strangers pointing me in the right direction before I found the Leedses' house, a wedding-cake-white behemoth of a building with towers and fish-scale shingles. It was parked in the heart of a tree-lined neighborhood with lawns so green, they looked painted. My stomach churned. The place reminded me of the home my father shared with his "real family" down in San Diego.

I rang the bell, and a rather surprised-looking woman with copper hair opened the door. She wore a tailored checked dress with cream-colored appliques adorning her shoulders and cuffs.

"Hello?" she said. A question, not a greeting.

"Good morning." I tightened my hold on my bag. "I'm Odette Grey. My aunt Viktoria instructed me to come here to work as the hired girl. She said you'd be expecting me."

The woman nodded to her left. "The servants' entrance is located in the back."

"Oh." My face warmed. "I'm . . . I'm sorry . . ."

"I'll meet you over there."

"Yes. Thank you."

She closed the door, and I hustled through a garden of hibernating roses to the other side of the house, certain I'd be fired before I even uttered another word.

I knocked on a brittle brown door in need of a coat of paint. Two seconds later, the woman answered, her face more relaxed.

"I'm sorry," I said again.

"No more apologizing. I like my girls to display confidence."

"I have more confidence when I'm not knocking upon inappropriate doors."

Her eyes smiled, even though her lips didn't quite agree with the response. "I'm so glad Mr. Fischer found me such a swift replacement," she said. "His daughter quit rather suddenly, and I've been managing on my own. He spoke highly of you and called you an innovative girl."

I didn't know Mr. Fischer well, but I appreciated his speaking kindly of me, and I quite liked his use of the term *innovative*. He had been friends with Uncle William. I remembered from my story-collection days with Tru that he had grown up hearing strange tales of famous pig-women who strove to fit in with European society.

"You'll work for a week on trial," said the woman, whose own facial features were far from porcine. "Won't you come in . . . Odette, was it?"

"Yes. Odette Grey."

"I'm Mrs. Leeds." She swung the door open two feet farther.

I stepped inside a kitchen almost twice as large as the bedroom I shared with my sister, and I do not exaggerate. The soles of my shoes clicked against white and blue tiles, and my eyes soaked up wondrous sights: a modern gas range! Built-in cabinetry! An electric toaster! Unlike our kitchen with the ancient wood-burning stove, the air wasn't clogged with smoke. I relished breathing without the need to cough up soot and spit out ashes.

Mrs. Leeds closed the door behind me. "I pay four fifty a week, with Thursday afternoons and every other Sunday off. I have three sons, ages fourteen, sixteen, and eighteen, all of them still in school, with the oldest bound for Stanford in the fall."

"Congratulations," I said.

She opened her mouth as if to continue with her introductory remarks, but a moment later she stopped and blinked at me. "Congratulations for what?" she asked.

"Stanford. That's impressive. You must be bursting with pride."

She closed her lips, another smile flickering in her green eyes. "Yes, I am. My boys are highly intelligent and well behaved, for the most part. But I must warn that they do ride horses year-round, and they play football in the summer and fall. Dirt and mud are constant nemeses for my hired girls."

I nodded. "I understand. I'm no stranger to battling stains."

"I'm glad to hear that." She fussed with her hair, which she'd pinned up in intricate twists and knots. "As long as you're not the one bringing the mud indoors . . ."

"Of course not, ma'am," I said—an outright lie. Just the week before, I'd been exploring a peculiar set of tracks in the mud behind the orchards and had spent an hour scrubbing my ensuing footprints out of Aunt Vik's rugs.

My employer proceeded to give me a tour of the entire house. Her lawyer husband and sons had already skedaddled off to work and school, so she alone guided me through the sunlit rooms, which included five bedrooms, a parlor, a dining room, a sitting room, a library, a study, a kitchen, a butler's pantry, two indoor toilets, and two bathtubs. Millie Fischer had kept the place immaculately clean, it seemed, every item tucked away on shelves or stored inside cabinets, every bedspread smoothed flat, each table and sideboard dusted. The air smelled of fresh hothouse flowers that bloomed in vases throughout the house.

In the middle son's bedroom, dozens of books lined a set of shelves mounted above a walnut-colored desk. The titles on a few particular spines caught my eye: *The Book of Werewolves*, by Baring-Gould; *Myths and Legends of Our Own Land*, Volumes 1 and 2, by Skinner; *Demonology and Devil-Lore*, by Conway; *Myths and Myth-Makers*, by Fiske.

Upon the desk, a text lay open. An illustration of a werewolf with bared fangs leered from the leftmost page. My heart pounded from both the elation and the terror of finding a potential kindred spirit in one of the very individuals Aunt Vik had commanded me to avoid.

"This one seems to be a reader," I said in the most professional, uninterested tone I could muster.

Mrs. Leeds rolled her eyes. "This one has strange interests. Pay no attention to Cy."

Mrs. Leeds opened a door in the kitchen, next to the larder, and led me down a dim flight of stairs so rickety, I worried they might disintegrate beneath my feet.

"This is where you'll stay," she said, and she led me into a small bedroom, also dim.

She switched on an electric lamp, revealing walls the yellowish beige of the condensed milk pumped out every week by the factory up the road from my house. The furnishings included a bed blanketed in a thin quilt, a wardrobe, and a washstand with a yellow pitcher and basin. Sunlight strained through two horizontal windows near the ceiling. A tan rug covered dark floorboards that soaked up all light.

I surveyed the room in silence as the gravity of my situation sank in. I was now this woman's servant. She expected me to sleep in this chilly, subterranean chamber, all alone, without the warmth and comfort of my sister beside me.

"I've hung your aprons in the wardrobe." Mrs. Leeds clicked open the cabinet door and revealed a starched white pinafore and a blue gingham apron. "The gingham is for everyday chores; the white, for lighter housework and guests."

"Thank you," I said. I kept my posture straight, knees locked, for Aunt Viktoria had warned against slouching on the job. A spell of dizziness hit me, but I forbade myself from fainting in front of this woman.

Mrs. Leeds turned for the door. "You may unpack your bag, tie on your apron, and then meet me upstairs, where I'll instruct you on your duties."

"Yes, ma'am," I said.

"I'm an extremely busy woman who isn't home much." She took hold of the door's brass handle. "I'm the president of the Hillsboro Coffee Club, as well as an active member of the Women's Christian Temperance Union and the Rathbone Sisters of the World. Most of the time, I will not be here to guide you, so please listen carefully to all I expect of you."

"Yes, ma'am," I said again, and I wondered if I should curtsy. Nothing I'd read or heard ever hinted how hired girls were to behave around their employers.

A head bob seemed a safe choice. Mrs. Leeds made no objection when I offered it.

She left, and I stood there on my own, breathing the basement's musty air, peering around at the bare walls and spiderwebs.

I'd started off in life with a fine upstairs bedroom, I realized. Then I'd moved to an attic loft, a ground-floor bedroom, and now down to an underground burrow dug deep into the earth. Still feeling I might faint, I sank down on the bed and held my head in my hands for at least five minutes before gaining the strength to tie on that gingham apron.

✺

By the time evening arrived, my hands stung and had turned bright red from washing endless mounds of trousers, underclothes, and masculine shirts with glass buttons. My left thumb smarted from burning it on a pan while checking the temperature of a roast. An explosion of flour and butter marred the gingham apron that drooped around my waist after a mishap with my biscuit batter.

Mrs. Leeds asked me to serve dinner at half past six, after the return of her sons from riding their horses at stables in the countryside and her husband from his law office. At six o'clock sharp I heard the squeal of rubber tires careering around a bend. A thunderous clicking noise approached, like a swarm of insects descending upon the house. Intrigued, I peeked out the kitchen window at the gravel drive in the side yard and witnessed the sudden approach—and jerking stop— of an extraordinary, cherry red, four-seater automobile with a hood that stretched at least six feet long. Gold trim gleamed in the beams of a lamp in the drive. Bug-eyed headlights illuminated the hedges before the driver switched them off, and four gentlemen—three younger fellows in tweed caps and an older man in a gray derby—climbed out of the car amid a ruckus of laughter. The oldest gentleman swore at the driver, who couldn't have been any older than I. The driver smiled so much, his eyes disappeared into crinkles, and I heard him say, "Admit it, Pop, you love it when I shoot us down the street like one of your racehorses. You're smiling while you're clinging to the door."

"It's a grimace of terror, Cy," said the fellow beside him, who looked a tad older, and all four of them chuckled.

The fourth one—a shorter boy with blond hair and freckles —caught me watching from the window. I wheeled around and returned to my biscuits, my back stooped, despite my instructions not to slouch.

Mrs. Leeds did not introduce me to her passel of males until I served the family dinner. Too concerned about placing dishes on the wrong sides of the diners or spilling gravy into laps, I couldn't pay much attention to what anyone said. The oldest boy asked in confusion who I was, Mrs. Leeds called me something such as "Odette, the new hired girl," and I believed I heard that the sons' names were Art, Cyrus, and Thomas, with Art being the oldest and Thomas the youngest. Or perhaps it was the other way around. After I finished serving everyone, I couldn't remember anyone's names, including my own. When I swept the downstairs hallway after scrubbing the dishes clean, the youngest boy asked if my name was Annette, and I answered, "Oh, probably," while my head sagged with exhaustion.

That night, down in the hollows of the basement, I slept like the dead. I had assumed I would lie awake, fretting about the ghosts of Leedses past roaming around in the dark, but I didn't even remember to park my shoes next to the bed with the toes facing the door. An *Alp* could very well have settled on top of my chest and breathed nightmares down my throat. A vampire could have broken through my window and gorged on my blood and my soul.

I didn't care. Domestic work sucked all the life from my body. I had nothing left to give.

✶

The first day following the end of my trial week, the middle boy, Cyrus, whom his family called "Cy," caught me reading that werewolf book that still lay open on his bedroom desk. I'd been dusting the cloth spines of the rest of his scrumptious texts, and my gaze strayed down to passages that described the long history of lupine creatures attacking villagers and livestock in Europe, including incidents in my family's native Germany. My hand that held the feather duster froze mid-swipe, and I drank in the words as though sipping ambrosia. For the first time since I'd knocked on the Leedses' wrong door, I felt like myself again.

"Hello," said a voice behind me.

I spun around and found Cy standing in his doorway, smiling—that boy was always smiling. He brushed a hand through his hair, which was a shiny golden brown, like caramel apples, and his brownish-grayish eyes shimmered with amusement. He wore a white shirt with thin navy stripes and a vest and trousers, both charcoal gray. I'd personally washed, dried, and ironed every stitch of his clothing.

"Are you interested in werewolves?" he asked, still smiling, although his tone didn't suggest he was laughing at or patronizing me. He sounded genuinely interested to know my opinion on people who transformed into murderous wolves.

"Yes," I said, and I darted out of the room with the feather duster tucked beneath my left arm. Aunt Vik's voice snapped inside my head: *Do not ever place yourself alone in a room with any of them. Do not get close to them.*

That night, when I returned to the basement, I found the werewolf book sitting outside my bedroom door, propped against the wall. My stomach fluttered. No boy had ever given me as much as a single hand-picked flower, but, to me, that book with red claw marks embossed across the front cover surpassed even a bouquet of roses.

During the next two months, book after book appeared outside my door. The mornings after I had finished reading one of them, I'd set the text in the same place where I had found it and trudge upstairs to start breakfast. That very evening, another book would appear in its stead, and I'd spend at least an hour diving into worlds of beasts and hobgoblins before drifting off to sleep. Cy and I never stood inside a room alone together, as my aunt had instructed. We never talked. We simply exchanged glances now and then, and, wordlessly, we shared monster legends.

One afternoon toward the end of April, as I was hanging laundry in the backyard, I heard footsteps squishing toward me across the damp grass. A human-shaped shadow bled across the bedsheet I'd just pinned to the line. I stiffened, every muscle alert and poised to either flee or fight. A hand reached out between the laundered cloths. A second later, the fingers pulled back the sheet.

"Boo!" said Cy with a suddenness that made me shriek.

"Don't do that!" I cried. "You scared me. I could have socked you in the nose."

"How do you like the books?"

I tugged the sheet out of his hands and draped it back in place to impede our view of each other.

"I love them," I said to his shadow, my voice low, so as not to attract the attention of neighbors.

"I thought you might." He ducked beneath the laundry and stood on the opposite side of my basket of clean linens.

I grabbed another sheet and sidled down to an empty section of the line. "I'm not supposed to talk to you. I'll lose my job."

He stepped forward, his hands in his pockets. "Did my mother tell you that?"

"No, my aunt. She threatened to permanently send me away from my sister if I spoke to you or your brothers."

He snickered. "I don't think I'd mind if anyone shipped me away from my brothers."

"It's not like that with my sister and me. We're close friends. And she has trouble walking because of an illness."

"Oh." He rubbed the back of his neck. "Sorry to hear that."

I pinned the edges of the fabric to the taut and quivering line. "Every cent I earn is going to her."

He drew another step toward me. "Well, Mother Leeds isn't home for at least two more hours. She's busy waging wars on saloons with other rabble-rousers in Portland."

"I thought you and your brothers visited your horses after school."

"I told my brothers I didn't feel well."

I glanced at the pinkness of his cheeks and the vividness of his eyes. "You don't look sick."

He smiled. "I'm not. I came here to finally speak with you alone. I want to show you something."

I inched backward, my pulse racing. "Show me what?"

"I want to introduce you to my family's monster."

✄

I stood in the hallway outside of Cy's bedroom while he rummaged around in his bottom desk drawer. Papers crinkled, metal clanked, and candy wrappers flew about in the air behind him.

"My parents don't know I keep this box in here," he said, "but no one cares about it as much as I do."

He excavated a black wooden box from the depths of the drawer.

"Come in," he said.

I tensed. "I can't."

"Odette"—he peeked up at me, still kneeling—"I told you, my mother is in Portland."

"What about your brothers?"

"The stables."

"Your father?"

"Prosecuting hoodlums in court, feeling highly important about himself." He carried the box to his bed and lowered it to the mattress with great care, as though it was made of glass. "No one is home right now, and no one will be for at least another hour. Come here." He waved me over. "I've got a nearly two-hundred-year-old document to show you."

I eyed the hallway for any signs of his family before daring to venture into his room with him. Ignoring a person who was willing to share his personal, two-hundred-year-old document, I reasoned, would be exceptionally rude.

Cy lifted the thick lid off the box. "A distant cousin of a cousin of mine—the great-great-great-great-grandfather of a fifth cousin once removed, or something like that—was an almanac-maker in New Jersey named Daniel Leeds, and so was his son, Titan."

I lifted my eyebrows. "Titan?"

"Yes—I think that's what my parents should have named me."

I laughed.

As did Cy.

"Anyway," he continued, his cheeks ruddier than before, "Daniel Leeds published astrological predictions and other occultist ideas, and the New Jersey Quakers had a big old conniption and called him 'Satan's Harbinger' in their pamphlets. When Titan inherited the almanac from his father, *he* caused an uproar by changing the masthead to the Leeds family coat of arms, which, as you can see right here, involves dragonlike creatures."

I leaned over the box and perused a brittle yellow paper titled TITAN'S NEW ALMANACK, dated 1729. The masthead, indeed, included a shield inhabited by three strange creatures with wings, two legs, and a tail.

"Are they wyverns?" I asked.

Cy's jaw dropped. "You've heard of wyverns?"

"My sister and I conducted research on the supernatural as children."

"I'm deeply impressed."

"Thank you."

Cy lifted those beguiling, fragile pages, which smelled of older people's houses. "Beneath the almanac I've got letters from my ancestors that describe the feuds between the Quakers and the Leedses. Even Benjamin Franklin joined the anti-Leeds crusade and spread rumors about Titan being a ghost—both before and after old Titan actually died."

"Oh, dear," I said. "Poor Titan."

"Poor Titan! And here's the best part of all"—Cy sat down on his bed—"the people of New Jersey started witnessing a diabolical beast in their midst. They claimed he was the son of a Leeds woman—maybe one of Daniel's many wives—who cursed her thirteenth child after she tired of having so many babies."

I straightened my neck. "You're related to a devil?"

"I might be." He grinned, and his fingertips crinkled the edges of the papers. "It would explain why I'm always getting into trouble—why my father's always threatening to send me off to a strict prep school near my grandfather's house, clear across the country."

"You're that much trouble?"

"Sometimes." He lowered his gaze to the box, still smiling, of course. "Mainly when I'm bored."

"You should find some more hobbies."

"I might enjoy getting in trouble is the thing. Art's the remarkable oldest child, and Thomas is the baby, which leaves me stranded in the middle."

"You don't seem so strange to me," I said, despite the fact that his hands were wrist-deep in papers about devils and occultists—and despite a rather terrifying burlap mask I spied on his bedside table out of the corner of my eye. "What is that thing?" I asked with a nod toward the mask, which seemed a cross between a jack-o'-lantern and the empty-eyed face of a scarecrow.

"Oh, that's my Herbert mask."

"What's a Herbert mask?"

Cy withdrew his hands from the box and picked up the lid. "Herbert was one of my friends from childhood—a neighbor from across the street. He fell off a horse and died from a broken neck when we were both ten years old."

"Oh." My shoulders tightened. "I'm so sorry."

"Sometimes, when I wake up at night, I catch him standing at the foot of my bed, watching me. Sometimes he even tugs my blankets off me. But the mask . . . it scares him away." He fitted the lid back over the box, the wood scraping into place. "I don't usually tell people that." He kept pushing down on the lid. "I'm not sure why I just told you."

"Try putting a mirror next to your bed when you sleep," I said, noting how chalky white his face had turned as he'd spoken of his late friend. "Mirrors capture the souls of the dead—among other unwanted visitors."

"That doesn't seem a nice thing to do to old Herbert. He's still just a kid."

"Leave a dish of vinegar on your bedside table, then. It'll smell terrible, but it'll repel him, and it's better than lying there with burlap on your face."

"All right. I'll give that a try."

I shot a look over my right shoulder, believing I'd just heard a floorboard whine from a footstep.

When I turned back around, Cy was standing again, raking a hand through his hair, gazing at me as though he saw me as more than just a "hired girl" with fingers so cracked, they kept bleeding and a back that wouldn't stop aching.

"I've never met anyone quite like you," he said, and he

stepped nearer—close enough to wrap his right index finger around my left pinkie.

My eyes dropped down to our linked-together hands, and I found it difficult to breathe. My pinkie looked so small with his finger snuggled around it. I was so used to the sight of my hands appearing like giant paws when they held Tru's petite fingers.

I swallowed. "I can't let anything come between my sister and me."

"No one will be home for at least fifty more minutes."

"What about Herbert?"

He reddened again and stifled a laugh. "Don't bring up poor Herbert when I'm trying to be romantic."

"Is that what this is about?" I grinned. "You're wooing me with these tales of devils and dragons?"

"Is it working?" he asked with another one of his famous Cy smiles that shrank Aunt Vik's warnings down to mere whispers.

"I'm afraid it might be. But don't you dare tell my aunt."

"I'm a little afraid of this aunt. I wouldn't dare."

I snickered, and he leaned closer still. He cupped a warm hand around the back of my head and kissed me with lips soft and smooth and yet as incendiary as matches. Fire burned up from the middle of my chest to the roots of my hair.

"I need to finish the laundry," I said when we stopped for a breath of air. "If I fall behind . . . your mother . . . she'll notice . . ."

He stroked a thumb along the length of my left collarbone, over the coarse muslin of my plain brown dress that reeked of

Borax and Lux laundry soap. "Let me visit you down in your room tonight," he said near my ear. "I want to kiss you for hours."

I lowered my eyes. "I can't."

"You're so far away from the rest of the bedrooms. No one else in the house will hear us . . . I can't tell you how many times I've snuck out the back door and wandered around town in the middle of the night without anyone hearing me."

I breathed a small laugh, rather impressed with his adventures.

He kissed me again, this time with more hunger.

I nudged him away. "The laundry, Cy . . ."

"If I can't visit you in your room, then I'll have to keep pretending I'm sick so I can come here and see you when everyone else is away."

"Your family will fret over your health."

"I don't care." He stroked the small of my back, and a flash of his own devilish nature shone in his eyes. "I just want to be with you. Alone."

When I served the family their apple-glazed pork chops that evening, all I could think about was Cy's desire to kiss me "for hours"—and of the heat he'd kindled inside me. I couldn't stop perspiring, even though Mrs. Leeds asked me to add another log to the fire to fight the chill in the house. When I leaned over Cy to set his plate down in front of him, he didn't look at me, and I didn't look at him, but I could have sworn I saw wisps of smoke rising from our faces, from our chests and our arms and thighs. As I maneuvered myself around him, I noticed the sweat on the back of his neck, and I dabbed my damp forehead with the cuff of my right sleeve.

That evening in my bedroom, down in the basement, Cy knocked on my door.

"I told you," I said after I opened it, "I'm not supposed to be alone in a room with you."

"I realized"—he wrapped a hand around my waist—"that if I pretend I'm sick and come home all the time, they're going to figure out I'm here with you, all alone. However, if I sneak down here at night . . ." He bent forward and warmed me again with a kiss on the lips.

I shouldn't have allowed him to shut and lock the door behind us—I knew that then, and I certainly know that now. I should have kept my thoughts on Tru at all times and found relief from my loneliness elsewhere. But he was there to comfort and hold me, and all my other nights down in that basement hollow had proven so cold and desolate.

We sat on my bed and kissed and caressed until I found myself wanting to get closer and closer to him. Our legs kept climbing over each other; we gripped each other's backs as though we were wrestling. I felt restless and strange, my stomach heavy with a feeling somewhere between sickness and excitement.

Cy laid me back against the cool sheets of my bed and lifted my skirts past my thighs. Not knowing what he was doing to me, never having been told about such behavior, I allowed him to climb on top of me, to spread my legs apart, to rub some part of himself inside me with an intense sensation of pleasure unlike anything I'd experienced before.

"How did you do that?" I asked him afterward, when we struggled to catch our breath, our hearts banging against each other.

"Magic," he said with a sigh of exhaustion, and, by God, how I actually believed him.

CHAPTER THIRTEEN

Trudchen
January 21, 1909—Pennsylvania

S hall we go to the Pine Barrens?" I asked my sister when
we awoke in our hotel room the next morning.

Od blinked her drowsy eyes open. "Tell me about your
Leeds Devil dream first." She stretched her arms over her head.
"How did we fight it?"

"You had the mirror, and I had the MarViLUs case, and I
used the case to fetch a lantern, which scared the Devil up a
chimney—after it attacked Cy and his friends."

"Oh, Lord . . . *Cy.*" Od propped herself up on her elbows
after hissing his name. "I still have a sinking feeling about all
of this."

I held my breath, so certain she would insist we abandon
the Northeast altogether. No more Leeds Devil. No more Ezra
and Celia Blue. No chance of catching our mother should she
return to her house.

"But . . ." Od ran her tongue along the inside of her left
cheek. "A visit to the Pine Barrens *would* make for an excellent
chapter of *Odd & True Tales*. Our experience while partaking
in a posse might even warrant its own book."

I nodded. "I'm certain it would."

She tipped her head back and pondered a moment longer.

"I wouldn't want to stay long. We mustn't get too comfortable in one place. And if they're talking about hunting with guns, I don't want any part of that. That's not how we were raised to fight devils."

My smile froze at those last words of hers, and again I heard how irrational this all sounded.

Still, my heart craved this test of my bravery, for Celia. For me.

"I wouldn't want to stay long in the woods with the Leeds Devil, anyway," I said. "But, my goodness, Od, the number of times I've seen his shape in my teacup. . . I can't imagine it being a mere case of coincidence. Something wants me to find this creature."

Od sat up in bed. "The moment either of us feels miserable or at risk of dying, we'll leave. We have our hand mirror, the *Hexenspiegels*, the MarViLUs case, my iron-bottom bag, my hatpin, your crucifix, and your talent with the leaves. Heavens, I wonder if we'd be better off trekking into the Pine Barrens on our own."

"No! We need company. And I wouldn't mind having the rifles there, just in case our own weapons aren't enough." I took hold of Od's left hand. "I think this might be fun, Od. Can you imagine, when we were little, hearing about two sisters who marched into the woods to search for a beast that was terrorizing several states?"

"We did hear such tales. Uncle Magnus told them to me about him and his sisters."

"But this is real, Od."

"*That* was real," she snapped. "We're Protectors. It's in our blood."

"All right, don't get angry." I withdrew my hand from hers.

"I'm not angry. I'm just nervous about seeing him again."

"Cy, you mean?"

She gritted her teeth and turned her head toward the sun-brightened curtains of the window.

"We might find our mother in the Pine Barrens," I said. "Who knows how many people are heading to the region to track down the Leeds Devil? We'd regret missing this opportunity."

Od gnawed on her lip and nodded. "I know. It would be frustrating if Cy caught the Devil and not I."

We returned to Philadelphia's Broad Street Station by eight o'clock that morning, in search of Cy Leeds and his friends. Od's face lacked color, and she winced from a headache, and to add to our decidedly un-posse-like appearance, walking proved almost impossible for me. The bones and muscles of my right hip screamed at me to stop slamming my foot against the floor.

The boys awaited, gathered around an opened newspaper, their dark caps bent together, their postures tense with anticipation. Supplies rested at their feet: suitcases, rifles packed in leather cases, and a thick coil of rope.

Od called Cy's name.

He lifted his head, smiled, and hustled toward us with powerful strides and impressive-sounding clicks of his soles against the tiles.

"An animal trainer here in Philadelphia is offering five hundred dollars for the Devil's capture," he called out before even reaching us. "He wants to display it in a museum."

"Good morning to you, too," said Od with a grimace.

Cy stopped in front of us, his hands on his hips. He eyed the bags Od carried. "Are you coming to New Jersey, then?"

Od lifted her chin and forced her eyes all the way open. "I had no desire to ever see you again, Cy. I hope you know that. I didn't follow you here."

Cy's elbows drooped. "I never said you did."

"We came here because our mother now lives here."

"I know. You told me yesterday."

"And Tru witnessed visions of the Leeds Devil in tea-leaf readings. She saw the Devil, and the word *Phil* appeared beside him."

Cy blinked several times in a row. "She did?"

"Just last night she foresaw a forest of pines, to the east," said Od. "And she spied the shape of the Devil hiding in the south. I think she and I could fare just fine on our own in the Pine Barrens, but Tru would prefer company. Will you and your friends be kind to us if we join you?"

"Yes, of course." Cy adjusted his cap on his head. "They call you the Purple Posse, but if you don't mind that"—he flashed a grin—"you can certainly join us. I'd hate to think of the two of you wandering out there in the woods on your own."

"Are you planning to shoot the Leeds Devil?" I asked with a gesture toward the rifles down the way.

Cy glanced at the pile of weapons and tugged on his right earlobe. "Uh, well, right now our plan is to injure this thing with a bullet, tie it up with rope, and drag it back to Philadelphia for the reward money. But if your tea leaves suggest anything better . . ."

"Isn't this your great-great-great-great cousin of a cousin we're talking about?" asked Od.

Cy bent down and picked up our bags. "It is."

"And you're comfortable shooting it?" she asked.

"I think a Leeds man ought to receive this money as a sort of inheritance. Don't you? I'll share. Come on." He walked backward.

Od looped a hand through the crook of my right elbow and helped me press onward.

My right leg lurched forward, and my shoe with the thick heel whacked the tile with such a jolt to my hip that I gasped.

"Tru?" Od stopped. "Are you in pain?"

My mouth stretched wide open from the impact. I caught a little brown-haired boy in knee pants watching me while he held his mother's hand.

Cy slowed his pace. "Is she in pain?"

Od nodded. "I think she might be. Normally she uses a wheelchair for longer distances, but it's still in Oregon. We couldn't bring it."

"Here . . ." Cy strode toward me and plopped our bags on the floor. "I'll carry you to the platform."

"No!" My face simmered. "N-n-no . . . you don't need to . . . it would be quite embarrass—"

Before I could finish sputtering my objections, Cy, to my horror, scooped me up, cane and all. My sister grabbed the bags, and he led her through the throng of passengers, many of whose shoulders crashed against the segments of my back that weren't shielded by Cy's right arm. My escort smelled of shaving soap or cologne—something spicy, strong, overpowering, even—and I craned my neck at an odd angle to avoid looking him in the eye.

"You're like carrying a baby bird," he told me, his breath near my ear.

I didn't know how to respond, but my eyes watered with humiliation. People stared. The lever I needed to push to bend my right leg was trapped against his stomach, so my ugly raised shoe—now fully on display—bumped against dozens of people.

"What's with the heroics?" asked the taller of his friends, the one with red hair.

"She's in pain," said Cy, "but they're coming with us."

"If she's in pain, then why is she coming?" asked the brunet boy with the slip of a mustache. "Shouldn't she be visiting a doctor instead?"

"She's fine if she doesn't need to walk far," said Od. "She's determined to do this, so please don't stop her."

"I don't need to be carried," I said. "Please—everyone's looking!"

The redhead shot Cy a glare loaded with disapproval. "We don't have time for this."

"Odette here knows a great deal about folklore, and her sister apparently has a talent for divination." Cy readjusted his hold on my legs. "They know how to find the Devil. We'll be far better off with them than without them."

The mustached one muttered something inaudible under his breath. The redhead must have understood him, for he snorted and said, "I completely agree. He's not thinking with his full brain."

"Quick introductions," said Cy, ignoring them both. "This

lovely young woman beside me is Odette Grey, and the little bird in my arms is her sister, Trudchen. Ladies, the tall bean-pole here is Ned, whom we all call Red, for obvious reasons growing out of his head. The shorter fellow—the one desperately trying to grow a mustache—is Andrew."

I did manage to smirk at the mustache comment.

"Tru," continued Cy, "since you and I haven't been formally introduced, I'm Cyrus Leeds, or Cy."

My face tightened. "Yes, I know who you are."

"We *all* know who you are," added Od. "Now let's please catch this train before you and your friends lose your nerve."

Red and Andrew's jaws dropped at the very idea of Od implying they might be cowards, but Cy chortled and steered me past them.

"Help me with my bags, will you, fellows?" he said. "I'm carrying delicate cargo."

"Truly, I'm not delicate," I said with a squirm.

"Your delicate cargo is going to slow us down," called Red after him.

Cy simply smiled and continued carrying me toward the platform, obviously trying with all his might to impress us girls.

I was not impressed in the slightest.

"I bought you something, just in case you decided to join us," said Cy to Od from the passenger seat across the aisle from us in an electric train bound for New Jersey. He reached into a worn leather satchel on his lap and pulled out a book with a crimson cover.

"Oh, dear Lord," said Od with a shiver. "Don't tell me that's *Marvelous and Monstrous*."

"You've heard of it?" he asked, and he handed it to her.

Od set the book on top of her thighs, and we both stared at the cover. The author's name, set in the style of lettering befitting a story of castles and knights errant, stretched across the front cover, beneath the golden gargoyle:

L. N. HARDT

"We saw it displayed in a window featuring brand-new books after we left the station yesterday evening," said Cy. "The book-seller said it's a captivating horror story about devils and beasts, so people are grabbing it up by the dozens this week. He just ordered a new shipment. I thought of you when I saw it."

Od pulled back the front cover with a delicious crack of the spine and rifled through the first pages until she landed upon a prologue:

The tale you are about to encounter is a true one, but I must warn you, dear reader, that the facts have been sugared with whimsy, marinated in daydreams, and seasoned with a generous salting of exaggeration. I will leave you and your clever brain to decipher the myths from the realities, but do bear in mind that the truth, as Lord Byron once wrote, is "stranger than fiction," and fantasy is a gilded mirror that reflects the dangers, the oddities, and the marvelous wonders of our own true world.

I peeked up at my sister. "This sounds like something you might write."

She shook her head. "I swear, I didn't."

"The word *marvelous* is certainly emphasized."

"The only book I've ever written, besides our catalog-in-progress, is locked in that box in my bag."

"A book you'll allow me to read sometime soon?"

"Tru." Od turned to me. "Thus far you've talked me into traveling to Philadelphia, searching for our mother, and climbing aboard this very train—all tasks that have made me highly uncomfortable."

"Don't forget, I wasn't comfortable embarking upon this trip to begin with."

"I know, but my point is, I'm not yet ready to share that story. We're supposed to be fulfilling our destiny, not—" Od's face darkened. She glared down at *Marvelous and Monstrous* as though the book suddenly reminded her of an appalling memory. "What am I doing? Cy!" She turned and tossed the book at him. "I don't want this. I've vowed never again to receive any monster books from you."

Cy managed to catch the book after it grazed his chin—an action that made my stomach clench, for it reminded me of Od slamming her bag against our attacker in Chicago and that hideous *crunch* of his jaw.

"I actually wanted to read it," I said to Od.

"We'll find another copy." She stood up and climbed around my legs amid the rocking of the train. "Scoot over so I can have the window seat, please. I don't know why I agreed to sit across the aisle from him. I can't even breathe on this train."

I did as she asked, my skirt snagging and swooshing against

the seat's fabric, and Od sank down beside me next to the window.

"I'll sneak the book to you later," said Cy in a whisper, but I shifted away from him and joined Od in peering out the window for signs of the Leeds Devil. In fact, I soon found myself unable to tear my eyes away from the snow-covered world streaking past our window, certain the flash of a face would appear amid the pine needles and branches caked in white.

A half hour after we boarded the train, we arrived in a southern region of New Jersey that had the word *Township* in the name. A map in Broad Street Station had shown numerous New Jersey regions called "Something-or-Something Township," which fascinated me to no end, since it wasn't at all what one called towns or counties in Oregon. In this particular township, witnesses had spotted the Leeds Devil on more than one occasion that week, according to Cy and his stack of newspapers.

We departed the railcar and stepped into a quaint world of church steeples, striped awnings, and winter trees stripped of their greenery. Snow coated the streets and frosted the rooftops.

The town did not strike me as the playground of a monster.

Before Cy could carry me again, I had stood and walked off the train on my own. Od had followed with our luggage, and behind her Cy, Red, and Andrew tromped down the railcar's steps with their rifles and bags.

We hadn't gone more than ten feet before a dark-whiskered man helming a farm wagon called out, "You young men with the rifles, there. Are you here to hunt the Devil?"

"We are," said Cy with a nod.

"Climb aboard," said the man, and he brought his horse, as gray as ashes, to a rocking halt in front of us. "We're forming a posse at an inn just west of here. We need more men."

"How do we know *he's* not the Leeds Devil," asked Andrew under his breath with a snicker. "He's awfully eager to lure us out into the woods."

I bristled at such a question. The man looked human enough, with his pockmarked cheeks and bulging Adam's apple, and his wagon appeared sturdy. The steel wheels had rolled through the snow without getting stuck.

Od put a hand on my back. "What do you think?"

My fingers tightened around the handle of my cane. "He seems harmless, as far as I can tell. And we're not alone this time like in Chicago."

"Are you ladies comfortable coming along with us?" asked Cy.

"Yes, of course," said Od.

"Do you want me to carry you again?" he asked me.

"No!" I pushed forward with the help of my cane.

The driver shook his head at my sister and me. "You young women shouldn't be traveling in the woods right now. We don't call this thing the 'flying death' for naught."

Od boosted me into the back of the wagon by gripping my arm and my waist. "If you want the flying death to make an appearance, sir, you'll want to take this one with you."

Red asked what Od meant by that remark, but Cy just jumped into the wagon bed beside me and hoisted me the rest of the way up, which caused my leg brace to jangle louder than ever. I must have resembled a fish flopping about on dry land, so limp, so awkward, for when I lifted my head, I caught the driver frowning at me.

My hands and left knee sank into a mattress of a spongy, pale-green moss piled into the wagon, as though the driver had harvested it, as one would wheat or barley. I sat up and remained in the spot where I'd arrived to avoid the task of crawling.

My sister clambered up behind me with my cane and the bags and situated herself on a hump of moss on my left side. The boys settled in across the wagon from us and unfastened their rifles from their leather coverings.

I leaned toward Od and asked near her ear, "Do you think they know how to use those things?"

"I don't know." She drew air through her nose. "Let's hope they don't shoot one of us by mistake."

The driver carted us to the far reaches of the town and then farther onward, to a forest of pines that looked different from the thick clusters of evergreens in Oregon. The trees stood far apart. We would be able to view anything that darted between them. The air thickened and smelled piney sweet yet also dank, dangerous, like an unfamiliar cellar. My eyes flitted left and right, catching movements and shadows that made my heart flinch. My sister's right arm stiffened against me, and when the sun melted behind the winter-white clouds, she looked me in the eye and seemed to say with a glance, *It's out there. I can feel it.*

I felt it, too.

Across the way, the boys craned their necks and kept a watch on the trees behind their backs. Our driver's head swiveled back and forth, as though he were scanning the wilderness for signs of attack.

"Am I endangering everyone's lives by being here?" I asked in a low voice. "If I'm attracting the Leeds Devil—"

"We're armed with rifles, mirrors, charms, and our case," she said. "If he comes, we'll be ready, *especially* if you're here."

Her confidence bolstered mine, and I reminded myself that Lowenherz blood burned through my veins. *Lionhearted*, she'd said the surname meant. Again, I thought of my note to Celia Blue.

I intend to save Pennsylvania and New Jersey from the monster. You will stay safe because of me, and I am a girl just like you.

Up ahead rose a two-story wooden structure that looked old enough—and remote enough—to have served as a meetinghouse for perpetrators of espionage during the Revolutionary War. Three brick chimneys puffed plumes of dark smoke into the sky, and another wagon, an empty one, waited out front, its horse still harnessed, parked in ankle-deep snow. A moment later, a group of five men embroiled in discussion trooped out the front door, each one of them older than Cy and his friends. They held rifles and vicious steel traps. Bear traps, if I had to guess.

The man at the front of the gathering, a clean-shaven fellow in a brown woolen hat, plodded toward us. "You only found three volunteers?"

"Three eager ones, Mr. Munro," said the driver, and he slowed the horse and wagon to a stop. "They climbed off the train with those rifles slung across their chests and jumped straight into the wagon."

"Why did you bring those two?" asked this Mr. Munro, gesturing a long, crooked thumb toward Od and me.

"The older girl insisted I bring them." The driver fussed with his hat. "The younger one . . . she, um . . . she might be a witch."

Od cast me a wry grin, her eyes narrowing with amusement.

"I'm trying to protect my inn from trouble, Gus," said Mr. Munro. "Take these girls straight back to where you found them."

Od stood up in the wagon. "Why, precisely, would we mean trouble, sir?"

"Any fool of a woman who dares to come out here this week should be locked up indoors for her own good."

"You're wrong, sir." Od tucked the leather case beneath her right arm. "My name is Odette Grey, and this is my sister, Trudchen. We're descended from a grandmother who guarded her village in the darkest depths of Germany's Black Forest, ridding the streets of werewolves and vampires and other foul spirits that attacked the innocent while they slept."

The gentlemen with the traps broke into chuckles, even though they themselves were hunting down a monster.

"Go ahead and laugh," called Od. "We'll see who's still alive and in one piece in the morning after the Devil's ravenous appetite has been sated."

At that remark, the men fell silent. I noticed some of them shrinking back, their traps swinging from thickly gloved hands.

"The Leeds Devil will be going after you first, sweetheart," said a younger member of the group, a squeak of terror in his voice. "And if he doesn't"—he grinned—"I will."

Cy jumped to his feet. "Are you threatening her?"

"He's just scared," said Od, "as he should be. He's unprepared for the supernatural, like the rest of them. You can't catch this creature with steel traps and bullets, gentlemen. If you're wise, you'll listen to the guidance of my younger sister here. She sees the Leeds Devil in tea leaves and can tell us exactly where to find him. Hold your traps and your guns and allow us to set up mirrors that will send the beast back to its true realm."

"What in hell is going on, Cy?" asked Andrew, rising to a standing position, struggling to keep his balance in the wagon. "Is your Oregon girl a crackpot?"

I shrank down in the wagon, horrified that the entire world might now question Od's sanity.

Cy stepped closer to my sister. "Odette? What, exactly, are you going on about?"

"What am I going on about?" She spun around with a jostle of the wagon. "Didn't you listen to anything I said in Oregon, Cy? Aren't you taking what I said about Tru and the tea leaves seriously, or did you just bring me along for sport?"

Cy forced a thin smile. "I'm happy to have you here so you can see if this thing is real, but you're speaking to men with weapons and fear in their eyes. Don't go telling them wild stories about yourself."

Od's fingers tightened around the handle of the leather case. I watched her face redden, her knuckles whiten. Her entire body quaked with a fury that rattled the wagon, and just as I reached up to offer a calming touch, she exploded at Cy, shouting, "You ruin everything, Cyrus! Do you realize that? This was supposed to be a quest for Tru and me alone, and once again you've shown up and spoiled our happiness."

"You young men, jump out of the wagon," called Mr. Munro with a beckoning wave toward the boys. "Gus, drive these girls back to town immediately. We don't need any more hysterical women in our midst right now. My missus is already spooked after hearing bloodcurdling screams last night."

"No!" Od climbed over the wagon's edge and landed on her feet in the snow with a *thump*. "I swear upon all that's holy, you need my sister's guidance. Serve her a cup of tea. She'll show you where the Leeds Devil is hiding. We're here because she predicted the arrival of a creature with bat wings and hoofed legs. She witnessed the word *Phil* for *Philadelphia* and the Liberty Bell, too, and two nights ago the word *Devil* manifested in her cup. She can find him."

"Od!" I slunk down farther into the bed of moss. "I don't want to read the leaves for these men."

"You have more of a right to be here than anyone." She reached over the side of the wagon and fetched our belongings.

"P-p-perhaps we should talk in private, Odette," said Cy, although the rigidness of his stance in the wagon betrayed his reluctance to do any such thing.

"We will later, Cy. Not now. I'm not in the mood." Od hustled around to the back opening of the wagon and reached out a hand toward me. "Come along, Tru. We're wasting time. This thing's not going to wait for us to stand around arguing."

"We're laying traps before nightfall," said Mr. Munro, marching past the wagon with his small army of men, who eyeballed Od as though they didn't know quite what to make of her. "If you boys want to sit around playing tea party with these young ladies, you're free to do so. But if you're joining us—"

"Oh, we are," said Red, leaping over the side with a dramatic bound that, by some miracle, didn't cause his rifle to fire, thank God.

I scooted myself through the moss on my backside, while the wagon wobbled and whined from Cy's and Andrew's exiting footsteps. Od grabbed my hand just as Cy slid off the back, beside me.

"Are you all right, Odette?" he asked.

"Don't lose a foot in one of those traps," said Od. "I have a feeling you don't know what you're doing." She wrapped her arms around my waist and lowered me down to the snow.

Cy wandered after the other men but with far less gusto than the rest of them displayed. Od hooked her right hand around my back and guided me to the inn without another word about him or his family's Devil. The men's voices trailed off into the trees, and for a slip of a moment before we reached the front door, it was just she and I again.

She and I and the New Jersey pines and whatever waited for us within them.

CHAPTER FOURTEEN

Odette
June 4, 1907—Missouri

P*lease don't grow up and make the same mistakes as your mother,* Uncle Magnus had asked of me all those years ago, when he'd protected me from *La Llorona* in Papa's studio after Tru first entered the world. Yet there I sat, thousands of miles from both our California canyon and the fertile farms of Oregon, in the front office of a Kansas City maternity sanitarium. I swallowed down the taste of bile and squirmed in a leather chair that squeaked beneath my backside.

A youngish brunette in a tailored blue jacket laid a sheet of paper on the mahogany desk between us.

"Well, Miss Grey," she said, unscrewing the cap of a fountain pen, "have you seen a doctor about your condition?"

I cleared my throat. "The mother of the baby's father—my employer—sent me to a doctor as soon as I showed signs of illness."

"And did the doctor say how far along you are at this point?"

Dazed and overwhelmed by her questions, even though she had just started asking them, I stared at the woman without answering. She wore her hair in a low pompadour that gave her head the shape of an acorn, her hair being the cap, her oval face the nut. A loud, buzzing commotion sawed through my brain.

The woman lifted her eyes to mine. "Miss Grey?"

"The baby is expected to arrive the week of January 19."

"Oh, that's excellent." She scribbled down my response, her eyebrows lifted. "We send out postcards to prospective adoptive parents every Christmas. Most of our babies find homes in December and January."

"I'll get to meet the baby, though, won't I?" I laid a hand over my still-flat stomach. "You're not going to take her away immediately?"

She smiled. "You don't yet know whether this child is a 'her,' dear."

"How much time will I get to spend with her?"

"Let's wait and see if you can afford to stay with us at all during your convalescence." She removed a pair of reading glasses from the bridge of her turned-up nose. "I know this former employer of yours insisted you come to this particular facility, but, quite frankly, Miss Grey, the Willows is reserved for only the finest young ladies—well-bred girls and women who have made a misstep and seek to avoid social ruin. You will be working in the kitchen to earn your keep. You will not receive the full benefits of a regular Willows girl, and that includes forgoing our essential massages that lessen the signs of pregnancy on a woman's body."

I swallowed, not at all caring for the notion that I would be treated as an inferior, especially in the midst of other girls who had mucked up their lives and were avoiding "social ruin."

"Is there another home I could go to instead?" I asked.

"Mrs. Leeds said in her letter that she wants this baby to find exceptional adoptive parents. Upstanding couples travel miles and miles across the country after reading our advertisements. They're the crème de la crème of prospective parents."

My eyes brimmed with tears over the thought of Mrs. Leeds's compassion for this baby, despite what I'd done with her son. It was she who first made me aware of my "unfortunate condition." One week earlier, she'd come home from one of her Coffee Club meetings to find me throwing up in the downstairs bathroom.

"Are you sick, Odette?" she had asked.

I sank back on my calves and said, "I'm not sure. I'm so hungry, but I can't stop vomiting."

Mrs. Leeds's forehead creased when I said those words. I remembered the fright in her eyes and how she cupped a hand over her mouth.

"Do—do you have any other peculiar symptoms?" she had asked, rubbing at her throat.

I averted my gaze from hers and didn't dare mention the painful swelling of my breasts, which neither Cy nor I had understood when we'd pondered them together in the weak light of my basement bedroom the past couple of weeks.

"Where were you born?" asked the sanitarium woman.

I straightened my posture, remembering where I was. "California."

"Where was your mother born?"

"Germany."

"And your father?"

"England."

"Oh, wonderful. An English heritage is highly desirable in the eyes of adoptive parents. Blue-eyed, blond-haired babies tend to find homes first, but a brunet of Western European stock will quickly follow."

The woman made a note of the baby's pedigree. The sound of her pen's nib scratching across the paper made my skin crawl, and, again, I almost got sick to my stomach.

"Do you know the nationality of the baby's father?" she then asked.

I muttered under my breath, "New Jersey Devil."

She started and lifted her face. "I beg your pardon?"

I squeezed my lips together to keep from grinning. "I believe his family came from England, too. At least on his father's side. They were Colonists."

"Oh, how lovely. Prospective parents adore Colonial heritages."

I placed my other hand on my stomach and could have sworn I felt the baby twitch inside me, as minuscule as the poor thing was.

After I answered a hundred other questions about Cy and me and our religions, our health, and the color of everyone's hair, eyes, moles, warts, and big toes, the woman showed me to a room with five metal beds crammed together inside.

"You'll share the space with nine other young women," she said. "The beds are quite comfortable."

One of the young women, in fact, was sleeping in the room. She lay stretched out on her left side on a bed beneath the window, her belly huge and quite fascinating. I feared the idea of my own middle stretching and hardening and squirming, the way Mama's did when Tru kicked and shoved her elbows about inside of her, but it had been more than thirteen years since I'd witnessed such a sight. This girl snored louder than even Aunt Vik, and that impressive stomach of hers rose and fell beneath the sheet with each grizzly-bear roar of an exhale.

"That's Helen," said the woman, not bothering to whisper to avoid waking the girl, who looked a year or two older than I. "You'll be sharing the bed with her until she's in confinement."

Helen occupied roughly ninety-five percent of the mattress. How I'd manage to squeeze in beside her was beyond me.

I deposited my bag in a tiny space between two of the beds and followed the woman to another room, one with dark paneled walls and no windows, where a physician examined me with cold, intrusive fingers and asked a great many questions that made my head ache. By then I was shaking and sweating, and I worried I suffered from a fever. The physician told me, "It's just nerves," and recommended a nap before I started work in the kitchen.

I curled up on a bed across from Helen the Snorer and awoke to the sight of three more girls with astounding pregnant bellies. They stared down at me with curiosity in their eyes and asked who I was, inquiring if I still loved the boy who'd led to my "misstep," wondering if he had offered to marry me (no, he hadn't). The youngest girl was fourteen, just a year older than Tru. She wore a loose gown that draped a stomach so rotund, it drooped down to her thighs—and that's what set me crying for the first time during my stay at the Willows. Not my own fear and loneliness. Not the pang of Cy's denial of having had anything to do with the baby, even when his mother caught him skipping school to be with me the same day I went to her doctor. But the sight of that poor girl, Becky Walsh, with blond curls and big gray eyes, caused something inside me to break. Every trace of magic lingering inside my body spilled out of my fingers and toes and bled into the walls, staining the wallpaper in shadows.

In my letters to Tru, I called the Willows "The Circus." Among other renowned performers, our prestigious Kansas City big top boasted such headliners as Gloria the Tea Leaf Reader, who claimed she could predict the gender of all our babies by studying piles of leaves soaked in a combination of tea and her own spit; Ruby the Robin Hood of Unfortunate Girls, who stole extra food for us in the kitchen; Psychic Sal, who could hear the approaching taxis that carried the adoptive parents from the train station; and Flying Gertie, a sixteen-year-old girl who leapt from bed to bed in an attempt to give birth to her baby early so she could return home to her mother.

No one knew what to make of me. I didn't tell any stories. I didn't speak much at all. When I lay in bed, wedged against Helen and her stomach, I wondered in silence if the Weeping Woman might be stalking the nursery downstairs, her breath icing the window as she waited, waited, waited, her clawlike hands eager for one of us unfortunates to provide a new child to steal.

Some of the babies born in the home died. The doctors and nurses never told us of these tragedies, but we knew from the arrival of a certain black carriage whenever a girl had lost an infant during childbirth. The nurses' faces looked puffier on such days. The cook in the kitchen scolded me less. Fear breathed down my neck with a heat that soaked my skin with sticky perspiration. My Lord, I had lost so much. So, so much. Pain had hollowed me out into a husk of a girl, but I swore, with every ounce of breath in my body, that the little one I carried—Trudie Marie if it was a girl, Duncan Magnus if it was a boy—would be the healthiest baby the world had ever witnessed.

We would all live happily ever after.

Ever after.

After . . .

After the New Year, false labor pains attacked me in the nights. The nurses put me in confinement, but I couldn't sleep without the other girls squirming and snoring around me. I felt sick. Wrong. Sometimes the baby kicked my organs with so much strength, I cried. At other times, the baby fell still for hours on end, and I cried again, believing it dead.

Finally, at two o'clock in the morning on January 18, 1908, fourteen years and four days after Mrs. Alvarado pulled Trudchen Maria Grey into the world in our California ranch house, Trudie Marie Leeds came squalling into existence in the bright electric lights of the delivery room in the Willows of Kansas City, Missouri. She weighed seven pounds, three ounces, and unlike her father's distant cousin of a cousin, she didn't transform into a beast with bat wings and fly straight up the chimney. On the contrary, Trudie personified all that's marvelous and good. I pressed my lips against her silken left cheek, ran my fingers through the soft blond fuzz sprouting out of the top of her sweet head, and magic rushed back out of the shadows on the walls and flooded my heart.

CHAPTER FIFTEEN

Trudchen
January 21, 1909—New Jersey

Tomorrow is January 22," said Od when we sipped tea by a fireplace in the Pine Barrens inn. "It's a day we must face with great courage."

I lowered my cup to the pearl-colored saucer. "Why do you say that?"

Od gulped a sizable swallow of her drink, her hands wrapped around the bone china.

"Do . . . do you feel that's when he'll cross our paths?" I asked. "The Devil?"

"Yes." She placed her right elbow against the table and held her forehead, her eyes squeezed shut.

Something moved outside the window. I saw the lowest branches of the nearest tree swinging as though disturbed. Snow tumbled off the needles. My breath caught in my throat.

"Tru," said Od, an ache in her voice.

"What?" I forced my attention away from the trees.

She opened her eyes, now bloodshot. "I am far more than just a troubled young woman. You are far more than a timid girl with a limp and a cane."

My throat tightened, and my own eyes stung. "I know that."

"Do you absolutely believe it?"

"Yes, of course. We wouldn't be here otherwise, would we?"

She reached across the table and threaded her fingers through mine.

The woman who had served us the tea—the innkeeper's wife, Mrs. Munro—returned with steaming bowls of a rabbit stew that reminded me of a long-ago time in a house buried in the muddle of my earliest memories. Mrs. Munro's arms, four times wider than mine, looked mighty enough to snap the Leeds Devil's neck in two, but she set the bowls before us with trembling hands, her gaze transfixed on the world outside the window.

"You haven't heard anything out there, have you?" she asked.

Od and I turned our heads and listened. Not a sound met my ears, aside from the woman's shallow breathing.

"I heard the thing last night," she said. "It gave the most bloodcurdling scream you ever heard, out by the woodshed. This morning we found its tracks in the snow."

Od scooted her chair backward with a loud squeak of the wood. "The Leeds Devil's tracks are out there?"

"I'd show them to you"—Mrs. Munro wiped her hands on her apron—"but I'd have to open the door, which doesn't seem wise with the menfolk gone."

"Tru . . ." Od tossed her napkin onto the table. "I'm going to fetch our hand mirror and coats. You concentrate on walking toward the door, and do make sure you keep the crucifix pointed outward."

My mouth fell open. "But . . . sh-sh-she just said we shouldn't open the door."

Od leapt to her feet. "In which room did you place our belongings, ma'am?"

"The first one at the top of the staircase, but—"

Od shot off for the staircase before Mrs. Munro could speak a word of objection.

The woman looked to me. "You should have heard it," she said. "This thing's not natural."

I gripped my cane and got to my feet, unsure which I feared more—those footprints in the snow or the long climb up to a second-story bedroom. "We'll keep you safe. I promise." A sharp nod punctuated my proclamation of feigned bravery.

"Child"—her eyes dropped down to my cane—"forgive my bluntness, but you can scarcely walk. That creature out there will devour you. Things like that always go after the weak ones first."

The cane wobbled beneath my left hand, and my left leg quaked against my skirt from bearing the bulk of my weight. At that graceless moment, I saw myself—*truly* saw myself—in this stranger's eyes. The pity, the doubt swimming in her dark pupils, painted me as a helpless, misshapen wretch.

"My appearance of weakness is what makes me such a threat." I swung my right leg forward and stepped away from the chair. "The creature will never suspect I'm prepared to destroy it."

The woman's eyebrows shot up into two identical arches, and she inched backward, which inspired me to stand even straighter.

I heard Od galloping back down the staircase, and before Mrs. Munro could remember to blink, my sister jogged into the room with the hand mirror, the MarViLUs case, and my purple coat, the last of which she handed to me.

"Lead the way, Mrs. Munro," she said after helping me wriggle my shoulders into the toasty purple wool. "We're ready."

"Y-y-yes . . ." The woman gaped at both of us. "So I'm told."

Mrs. Munro led us to the kitchen at an uneven pace, striding as if she needed to rush, yet dragging her heels whenever she saw how far behind her I lagged. I walked faster than was comfortable so her bravery wouldn't falter.

"The tracks are out here." She opened the door, her knuckles white, and stepped outside.

Od clutched the handles of the mirror and the case and followed the woman. I steeled myself against a gust of cold air that blew into my right hip, but it still drew a whimper from my lips. Nausea writhed within my bones.

Out in the shade of the woods, our boots and my tall right shoe disappeared halfway into snow, and it took me a moment to remember how to walk in such conditions—how to lift my leg with the brace just right so it would not get stuck. By the time I caught up to my sister and our hostess by the woodshed, I was out of breath, and sweat covered my neck beneath the collar of my blouse, despite the freezing temperature.

"See here," said Mrs. Munro, and she pointed at the snow. "They're like the hoofprints of a small horse, but instead of in fours, they're made in pairs, and they jump around, as though the thing leapt and flew."

I edged close enough to observe the markings to which

she referred. The prints, indeed, appeared to have been made by a miniature, two-legged horse that walked upright like a human. They led to the woodshed, disappeared, and then manifested again in the distance, rambling toward a chicken coop clucking with orange hens. We could view the hens through a wire screen at the front of the coop, and none of them looked harmed.

"My husband found tracks on the shed's roof, too. Those rectangular marks are from his ladder." Mrs. Munro pointed toward the indentations from the ladder on the ground. "It must have sprung to the roof, then spotted the chickens and bounded toward them. Mr. Munro opened the window and fired a bullet into the night before it could attack them."

"Did he see the creature?" asked Od.

"No, but as I said, we heard it. It screamed like a fiend from hell."

A moment later, a horrific cry ricocheted across the woods. My stomach dropped to my toes, and all three of us jumped and turned toward the part of the forest into which the men had marched. Another cry rang out, this one filled with agony.

"It's coming back!" Mrs. Munro tripped through the snow toward the kitchen door. "Run!"

I remained frozen to the ground, my gaze trained on those woods.

"Someone *is* coming—a person," said Od, and I, too, saw a male figure sprinting toward us, arms flailing. More screams of pain howled from the trees behind him, and a flock of birds scattered out of the pines.

The figure rushed closer. I recognized his tweed cap and short stature.

Andrew. Tiny-mustache Andrew. Splattered in blood.

"Fetch gauze bandages!" he called to us. "We need bandages. Miles of bandages."

"What happened?" asked Od.

"Just fetch them. Now!"

Od shoved the case and the mirror into my arms and stumbled through the snow to the inn.

Andrew bent over with his hands on his knees and fought to catch his breath.

"Was it the Leeds Devil?" I asked.

"No." He wheezed. "A steel trap. Oh, God, it was awful. He stepped in it."

"Who?"

Od threw the door back open and dashed out with rolls of gauze cradled in her arms.

"Whose blood is it?" she asked, thrusting the bandages at Andrew. "What did this?"

"Can't talk." Andrew turned and bolted away.

"Andrew!" she called after him. "Answer me—please!"

"Have the wagon ready," he shouted over his left shoulder. "He'll lose his foot. Steel trap. So much blood!"

Od waded through the snow. "Is it Cy? Andrew, is it Cy?"

Andrew tore across the snow without falling even once and flew back into the woods. More shrieks of pain shot across the earth . . . and undoubtedly chased the Devil away.

Od paced the whining boards of the front porch and wrung her hands, muttering, "I haven't yet told him. I should have told him."

When I asked, "Told him what?" she shook her head and said, under her breath, "Oh, what does it matter, anyway? Nothing can come of it."

Voices spilled out of the woods. I rose to my feet and followed Od to the wagon, which Mrs. Munro had readied before sequestering herself back inside the inn.

Four of the men hauled a limp individual whose backside slumped toward the snow. His head flopped behind him; from my angle he looked headless. He no longer made even the tiniest groan, and I supposed he was unconscious. His left boot and the hem of his pants were soaked in fresh blood that glistened in the weak haze of daylight. I had imagined that the trap would still be dangling off his ankle like a mouth clamped around his bone, but someone must have freed him from the steel in the woods.

"I see Cy!" said Od, and she launched herself off the porch. "He's carrying the body. It's not him!"

I assumed she was merely relieved that she hadn't cursed healthy, pink-cheeked Cy with her snide remark to him about the traps, but the way she ran up to him and placed a hand on his back made me wonder if something deeper simmered between them.

Cy, Red, and Mr. Munro hoisted the injured man into the back of the wagon. Mr. Munro then climbed up into the driver's seat. Just as he flicked the reins and set his horse into motion, Gus, our driver from the depot, pulled up again with his wagon, carrying four more men with rifles.

"Send them all out into the woods, Gus," called Mr. Munro

as he sailed past him. "We're down one steel trap and need more of them laid. That Devil's probably laughing at us from the trees."

After the men again left, Od talked poor, stunned Mrs. Munro into letting us borrow the farm's sleigh and a horse, as well as a blanket for warmth, and she even persuaded the woman to teach her the horse's vocal commands.

"You really shouldn't go out there," called Mrs. Munro from the kitchen door, seeming to just then come to her senses as we trekked to the stable beyond the chicken coop. "You'll get yourselves killed."

"We traveled all the way from Oregon because of this monster, ma'am," called Od over her shoulder, Mama's copper mirror secured in her right hand. "We're not going to simply sit inside and wait for the men."

I glanced back at the lack of faith in Mrs. Munro's expression and prayed that Od and I weren't tromping out in the snow to our deaths. I kept rehearing the shrieks of the man who had stepped into the trap and seeing the blood on his trousers. I wondered if he would now walk worse than I . . . if he could still walk at all.

I stopped for a moment to catch my breath, the bunched-up blanket tucked beneath my right arm. "Are you certain you remember how to manage a sleigh?" I asked my sister from several feet behind. "It's been a while since you drove Uncle William's."

"You don't forget that sort of thing, Tru." My sister hoisted open a red stable door, her skirts catching in a breeze that also threatened the hat on her head. "I'll keep the horse at a walk so we don't miss hearing or seeing anything out there."

"We will stay away from the part of the woods where the men are creeping around with their traps and guns, won't we?"

"Yes, most definitely." She disappeared into the stable, but I heard her voice from within. "Those tracks in the snow suggest the Devil is hiding near here in the woods. Anyone with any sense can see that."

Od hitched a horse to an open black sleigh with room for two riders. I managed to maneuver myself into the vehicle and sat back with my cane wedged between my legs. My sister scooted in beside me, but not before resting an ax with a short handle on the floor.

I yanked my left foot away from the tool. "Why is *that* here?"

She dropped down on the seat. "I'm bringing it along just in case."

"I thought you insisted the Leeds Devil couldn't be fought with regular weapons."

"It's just in case, Tru. Now pull your *Hexenspiegel* out from beneath your coat. If only we had bells to tie to the horse . . ."

I scooped the little mirror at the end of the silver chain out from its hiding place between my coat and my blouse. We draped the woolen blanket across our legs and tucked it around our laps. It was a green and red plaid that reminded me of the curtains in Aunt Viktoria's kitchen.

Od grabbed the leather reins and made a clicking sound out of the left side of her mouth to set the horse walking. Off we glided into the thicket of trees behind the stable, and, as promised, Od kept the horse at a gentle pace. The sleigh's steel runners sliced through the snow with a whisper, but nothing else stirred out there in the frozen, moss-clad world of the barrens. Our purple coats stood out as stains of color amid the whiteness of the ground and the powdered branches. Even the horse pulling us along was as pale as fresh cream.

I scanned the empty spaces among the pines and the oaks. The whooshing of the sleigh started to sound like breathing.

"Do you sense that we'll find her here in New Jersey?" I asked.

"Who?" asked Od, so apparently startled by my question, she jabbed my left side with an elbow.

"Our mother. Do you think she's here?"

My sister settled back against the seat. "I suppose there's a strong possibility that she is."

"Od . . ." I tightened my fingers around my cane. "How long ago did you last visit her? And where was she?"

"Oh, Tru." My sister sighed. "Our full attention should be focused on movements in the woods right now."

"Was she still in Oregon? What was she doing?"

"As I've always told you, she was and still is a Protector. Now stop with the questions."

"I don't think Cy would share the reward money if he caught whatever this thing is," I decided to add. "Despite what he promised."

Od readjusted her position in the seat. "Would *you* share it with *him*?"

"Would you?"

She met my eye. "He has plenty of money and doesn't require special care for his legs."

"Do you love him?"

"Don't ask that, Tru."

"Do you?"

"No." She peered ahead. "Once we're done in the Pine Barrens, I'd like to travel to Tennessee and seek the Bell Witch. Have you ever heard of her?"

Her sidestep into yet another legend to avoid speaking about reality made me question why I was allowing her to lead me into an unfamiliar, uninhabited portion of the world, where no one would even hear us scream. The farther she steered us into the shadowy coldness of those woods, the more I started to doubt even my visions in the teacup. Perhaps I'd heard Aunt Viktoria mention that our mother now lived in Philadelphia. Perhaps I only saw what I wanted to see in the leaves: an adventure with my long-missing sister, a reunion with our mother, a chance to be more than delicate Trudchen.

I peeked over my shoulder. "How will we find our way back?"

"The stable is where the horse gets his food. He'll know the way back."

I turned back around and gazed into a black tunnel of trees up ahead. "Should we try stopping and seeing if I attract the Devil to me? I don't think there's really any need to go farther."

"Hmm, we could try that," she said. And she called out to the horse, "Whoa!"

We stopped in a portion of the barrens blanketed in snow several inches deep. I felt trapped but tried not to panic, reminding myself to breathe. The frigidness of the air stung my lips, and I shivered deep in my bones.

We sat with postures straight and stiff. Od reached down and grabbed the ax from the ground.

"Why did you say 'Who?' when I asked if you felt we'd find her in New Jersey?" I said.

"Keep a watch on your side, Tru. I'll monitor the left side."

"Tell me more about your beloved in Missouri."

"Tru, enough! You're not taking this seriously. You were the one who dragged me into the Pine Barrens. Now be respectful and listen for any signs of the Devil."

We sat in silence for at least five minutes, which unfolded as an excruciating eternity. I kept spying the ax in Od's lap in the outer edges of my vision, and I imagined one of the men sneaking up on us with a gun, to which Od might respond with a swing of the blade.

I also feared the devil—not the bat-winged, horse-faced caricature in the paper—but *the* devil from hell, screaming over our heads with a contorted face as we waited in our vulnerable position in the sleigh, two purple targets sticking out against the bleak backdrop. The words *Be gone!* hovered on the edges of my lips. I squirmed and fidgeted and wasn't quite sure if this was adventure or torture.

"How much longer should we stay out here?" I asked.

"Are you getting cold?"

"Yes."

"I was hoping to view more than just tracks during the daylight. It would be a disappointment to go back to the inn with nothing to report."

"Well," I said, "if you want to stay a mite longer . . ."

"Would you mind?"

"I suppose not." I pulled the collar of my coat farther around myself and breathed into the wool to warm my lips.

We stayed out in the middle of the woods for at least a half hour.

No Devil devoured us, nor did a wolf or a bear.

We slunk home with nothing to report, and the men did the same. Od and I spent the afternoon in the warmth of our upstairs bedroom—which took me about twenty minutes to reach and involved gripping the rail with both hands. We read through our old notebook of creature legends. We plotted what to do next.

At one point, Od ran downstairs with some of her hair bows and tied Mrs. Munro's silver spoons to the eaves outside the doors in hopes they might tinkle together like bells. We posted the mirror in our window. Od fetched me supper so I wouldn't have to struggle back down the stairs, and she promised to switch rooms with one of the men on the first floor if we decided to stay another night. We spoke of monsters, and only monsters, while the story of our lives hid in the box inside her canvas bag next to the bed, secured by a lock—so close yet so forbidden. The key to the lock dangled from Od's neck, the golden metal near enough for me to grab as we read side by side.

If I were a person capable of leaping and sprinting and stealing secret boxes, I would have yanked the key straight off her at that moment.

That night, I fell asleep without much trouble.

Around midnight, however, some sort of sound—a loud

clunk—yanked me into a lesser stage of slumber, the type of half sleep where everything turns jumbled and your skull feels too heavy to lift from the pillow.

Through my cracked-open eyelids, I saw the creature made of tea leaves, and he was plastered against the beams of the ceiling above me. The longer I stared at the image, the more he shifted from the shape I had viewed in my cups into a dragonesque figure with glowing red eyes and a grin so devious, it stole the breath from my lungs. I heard its heart thumping, thump, thump, thumping. *Thump-thump. Thump-thump. Thump-thump.*

Od jumped up beside me. "There's something on the roof!"

I blinked, and the shape on the ceiling dissolved.

"Tru!" Od shook my right arm. "Do you hear it? Are you awake?"

I struggled to sit up, and I heard it—footsteps, creaking across the rooftop. I dared to raise my face toward the ceiling.

"Oh, God—it's right above us," said Od.

Darkness obscured my view of the boards overhead. Not even moonlight risked entering our room.

"Is—is the hand mirror still in the window?" I asked.

"Yes."

"Where's the case?"

"I don't remember."

"The Devil's on the roof!" shouted someone from somewhere inside the inn.

A rifle fired.

I shrieked and covered my ears.

Moments later, a herd of people—or at least I prayed those

footsteps belonged to people—ran through the hallways, both upstairs and down, and voices traveled out of doors.

Another gunshot cracked across the darkness.

"The chickens are all gone!" called one of the men from a distance.

Od leapt out of bed and lit a candle. She threw her coat over herself, which blew a cold gust of air over the bed.

"Where are you going?" I asked.

"I want to see if it's still out there."

"No! Don't go outside!"

"I'm just going downstairs."

She spun around with a ripple of deep purple and dashed through our doorway.

I fastened my leg into the brace, climbed out of bed, and fumbled my way out to the landing.

Down below, Od stood in the open doorway, her hand on the door's iron handle. A kerosene lamp on the wall beside her cast restless rays of light across the back of her hair.

"What do you see?" I called down, the T of my cane pointed outward.

"Everyone's running around with their rifles." Od stuck her head farther out. "I'm not sure if anyone actually saw it."

A breeze snapped through the inn and tasted of bitter-cold darkness.

"Come inside." I inched forward. "Don't get shot! Please! I don't want them to shoot you by mistake. And I don't want the Devil—"

The sudden gonging of a grandfather clock down in the lobby drowned out my words. Od spun around and stared at the contraption with dark and haunted eyes. Her lips drained of all color. I feared the Devil stood in front of her.

"Od!" I eased myself down the first two steps. "What do you see?"

The clock chimed eleven more times, but my sister did not blink through any of the bongs. It was now midnight.

"What's wrong?" I asked, now, somehow, halfway down the stairs. My cane slipped from my hands and clattered down to the main floor.

Od lifted her face to mine. "Today's the day," she said, her voice strained, her legs unsteady. She closed her eyes and covered her face with shaking fingers.

"Od?" I clutched the handrail with both hands. "What day? What do you mean?"

Her fingers wouldn't stop quaking. "It's January 22," she said. "Oh, God. It's here again."

CHAPTER SIXTEEN

Odette
January 22, 1908—Missouri

T rudie wouldn't sleep that fourth night after she entered the world. The nurses gave her drops of a syrup to settle her down, and they administered a spoonful to me, as well. The cries of my baby, along with the chaos of the wind slamming against the window, made me watchful and wary. I struggled against the effects of the tonic. I squirmed and strained to lift my head, and yet the numbing fingers of the medicine crept across my skull and pulled down on my eyelids. They lured me away from the rest of the world, including my Trudie's cries.

I awoke at dusk with a thick feeling fogging up my head.

A sense of panic seized me. Something wasn't right in that room.

Against the too-bright window stood the silhouette of a nurse I did not recognize. She wore the starched white uniform of the other nurses at the Willows, with the cinched waist, the high collar, and the skirt that ended two inches off the floor, revealing a pair of polished black shoes. As she stepped nearer, however, I noticed that she didn't wear her hair pinned back in a tidy chignon beneath her white cap, like all the others. Her midnight-black locks hung over her face and trailed down to her waist in wet tendrils. She smelled of stagnant pond water. Of rivers. Of drowning.

I scooted myself upright in the bed and clutched my pillow and blankets. "Who—who are you?"

"It's time for her to go," she said in a whisper, and her fingers reached for Trudie's cradle. "They want her."

"Stay away from her!"

"You agreed to give her away."

"Stay away from her!" I yanked my *Hexenspiegel* out from beneath my nightgown and flashed the round mirror at the wraith. "Be gone! Be gone!"

"Hush, Odette."

"Be gone!"

"Hush!" The woman lunged at me and pushed me down by my shoulders with claws as cold as the frost outdoors. Behind all that damp hair, black eyes protruded from a face with pale flesh that rotted off skeletal bones.

I froze, paralyzed by the horror of the woman's gaze, crippled by the fumes of sulfur she breathed into my mouth.

"You signed the papers," she said, those eyes looming over me, her tongue flicking like a rattlesnake's. "This is for your own good and, more importantly, for hers."

She released me, and yet, still, I couldn't move. I lay there, motionless, helpless, while she scooped my Trudie out of the cradle and carried her away.

When I summoned the ability to scream—to holler that the Weeping Woman had stolen my baby—no one believed me. No one showed me the smallest sliver of sympathy. The staff told me it was an employee named Nurse Hitchcock who had fetched Trudie and delivered her to an awaiting married couple in the lobby. The adoptive parents had received a postcard from the Willows at Christmastime and couldn't wait to take the child to the nursery they'd been preparing since December. They thought Trudie was a perfect angel.

"Where is she?" I shouted in the superintendent's office, but the nurses dragged me away by both arms and told me that that information wasn't for me to know. They packed me up, shoved me into my scratchy winter coat, and shipped me off in a hack to the Kansas City Provident Association, where a woman who spoke in too soft a voice told me she'd help me get home. I got sick to my stomach from the medicine the nurses had poured down my throat the night before, and the panic of missing Trudie made it impossible for me to sit still in a chair, let alone to think where my home ought to be.

"Portland, Oregon," I sputtered when no other answer came to me. I leaned forward in the chair, my hands clasped behind my neck, and rocked back and forth. "My mother's there. I want to see my mother."

"Of course, dear," said the too-quiet woman. "A mother's love is the perfect salve to soothe a broken heart."

"She should have been there for me." I brushed tears from my eyes. "She would have killed *La Llorona*."

The woman offered a tight smile and simply replied, "I'm sorry, I don't speak Italian."

When Aunt Vik had put me on the train to Missouri the previous spring, she'd crammed an envelope into my hand. "It's your mother's address," she said. "Now that you've done what you've done, you ought to know what she is. After you've given birth, go to her, not me."

It rained in Portland on the day I arrived. My body still hadn't quite recovered from giving birth, and I saw the stooped reflection of myself in the windows of the storefronts I passed, my bag by my side, my left hand pressed against my chest. Kansas City had cast out a wan and hollow-eyed thing, a wretch in deep pain, weeping for the loss of her child.

I wandered to Davis Street and stood on the northeast corner of the intersection with Third. Rain streamed off the brim of my black hat with red rosettes—a hat I'd found on the train and now wore as if I'd bought it. The silver hatpin that accompanied it secured the felt to my hair, which I hadn't bothered to brush until that morning.

For the hundredth time since I departed Kansas City, a panicky sensation that I had forgotten something shot through my heart, and I clutched at my coat and peered around me. I had to remind myself, *It's Trudie. You're missing Trudie. And Tru. Oh, my Lord. They're both gone.*

To my left, an automobile puttered around the bend from Second. I turned my head and watched the slick black vehicle approach, reminded of Cy steering his father's cherry-red car to a squealing stop in the Leedses' side yard the first time I laid eyes upon him. I wondered if Trudie would possess her father's daredevil nature and our shared fascination with monsters. I imagined her growing into a child as quiet and curious as Tru, with a penchant for magic and storytelling. Someone needed to inform her that her great-grandmother had protected a village in Germany and that her grandmother hunted *La Llorona* in the canyons of California. Someone needed to teach her about *Hexenspiegels*, hand mirrors, tarot cards, charms, and a secret society called MarViLUs. Otherwise, she wouldn't know what to do when the bogeyman crawled out of her nightmares and into the shadows of her bedroom—wherever that bedroom might be.

The car passed me by, and my eyes, still directed to my left, caught sight of a name I recognized, painted in white on the bricks of the building across the street.

DUNNOTTAR HOUSE

Dunnottar, the inspiration for the castle on the hill in the canyons.

Dunnottar, one of my favorite words—the reason Trudie would have been named Duncan, had she been a boy.

Dunnottar, a word familiar to my mother.

I fetched Mama's address from a pocket of my coat and compared the numbers to those painted on the building.

A match.

I lifted the hem of my skirt, dashed into the street, hurdled over a pile of ripe horse dung, and veered around two puddles before swinging open the door to the establishment that bore the name of the castle in Scotland. My footsteps thumped to a stop, and every occupant of the saloon I found inside the door lifted his head with a start.

"I'm looking for a woman named Maria Grey," I said to a man who poured glasses of beer from bottles behind the bar.

Without the slightest hint of a smile, without even looking up from his pouring, the bartender said, "There's a Maria Pearl who runs the hotel upstairs. But I don't know any Maria Grey."

I knitted my eyebrows. "Pearl? Oh . . . um . . ." My heart sank, as did my shoulders. "Well . . . is . . . is she the one who named Dunnottar House?"

The man shrugged. "It's been called Dunnottar House since I started working here six months ago."

I chewed my lip and peeked over my shoulder at the dozens of men throwing back drinks at the unvarnished tables. Most of them watched me with eyes bleary with liquor. Their heads bobbed. Lewd grins crept up the sides of their flushed faces. A pack of stained, unshaven wolves was what they were. I choked on the fumes of all that alcohol and sweat.

"How do I get up to the hotel?" I asked the bartender.

He gestured to his left with an empty bottle. "Stairs around that wall."

"Thank you."

I walked at a brisk pace around a corner and climbed up a staircase with my only belongings in the world—the canvas Gladstone crammed full of clothing that had fit me before the pregnancy and the handwritten catalog of monsters I had created with my sister. Again, my heart stopped. I'd forgotten something. Again, I ached for Trudie and Tru. In the bend in the staircase, my legs buckled, and I fell against the steps, my left palm landing in something damp. I pushed myself back up, rubbed my sore knee, and continued upward.

A narrow hallway bathed in afternoon sunlight stretched before me at the top of the stairs. The air up there smelled less of booze, more of perfume and mold, of loneliness. Of sin. I pressed forward, my footsteps now hesitant.

Behind the first door I passed, a mattress squeaked. Someone emitted a low, throaty moan. I hastened my gait, not daring to imagine what was happening in there. Two rooms down, a door opened, and a blonde who couldn't have been any older than twenty sauntered into the hall, wearing a cotton chemise, a pair of black stockings, and absolutely nothing else. Her hips were quite round and pronounced, her waist trim, despite a paunch in her stomach—a prime example of a figure that had bent to the will of corsetry.

She flashed a welcoming smile, albeit one with three crooked teeth, and meandered my way with the strut of a cat, those wide hips swinging.

"Are you here for the open position, honey?" she asked.

I shrank back. "No, I'm looking for someone named Maria."

"Well, Maria's the one hiring. We don't have enough girls to accommodate our patronage, so you'd be busy and paid well for it. We're three- to five-dollar girls, not those one-dollar tarts."

I shook my head. "No, you don't understand. I'm looking for a woman named Maria who's my mother."

The blonde's green eyes widened, and her ruby-red lips spread into a cockeyed grin. "My goodness. Is Mama Maria an actual mama?"

"Has your Maria ever stated that her last name was once Grey? Or Lowenherz?"

"Most of us don't use our real last names, sweetie. But *Pearl* would be a prettier version of *Grey*, don't you think? Isn't 'pearl gray' a color?" The woman wandered close enough for me to cough on her perfume.

I backed two steps away. "Has Maria Pearl ever mentioned having any daughters?"

She stopped and peeked over her shoulder, dropping her voice to a near whisper. "She never mentions much of anything about herself. Everything's a secret. All I know is that she was born in Germany."

My pulse raced.

The blonde cocked her head like a wren. "Did I say something important? You look like you just swallowed a straight pin."

"M-m-may I meet her?"

"She's probably in her office, if she's not entertaining a gentleman." The woman pivoted on her stockinged heels and beckoned for me to follow with a wiggle of her right index finger. "Right this way."

"If she's entertaining a gentleman, I don't want to see her."

The blonde laughed. "Oh, I'll knock first, sweetie. One always knocks in a place as respectable as Dunnottar House."

She led me down to the very last door on the left, a closed door with a brass knob that was slipping out of place, bowing down toward the bare floor below. She gave a short rap with the back of her right knuckles and tilted her head toward the wood.

"Miss Pearl?" she asked. "You have a visitor."

"Who is it?" called a woman from the other side, and my ears strained as I tried to remember if I recognized the voice.

"What's your name?" asked the blonde.

"Odette." I hugged my bag to my chest. "Od to some, including my mother's brother and my sister."

"She says her name's Odette, ma'am," said the woman. "Called 'Od' by her uncle and sister."

A chair moved within. I held my breath and waited for more movements. Blood rushed to my toes.

The blonde locked eyes with mine. "I'm sorry. Maybe it's the wrong Maria . . ."

Footsteps charged toward us from inside the room, and the door swung open.

A woman with hair the same reddish brown as mine stared at me without moving. She looked fleshier than the scarecrow who'd arrived on Aunt Vik's doorstep three years earlier, and older, lustier, bolder. Her cheeks and lips were rouged; her burgundy gown just barely covered her body.

"Mama?" I asked.

Her chin quivered. "Odette?" she said in a gasp. "What are you doing here?"

I lowered my head, my skin burning.

"Odette?" Mama stepped forward and cupped a hand around my left shoulder.

"I had a baby," I said, and before I could quite yet burst into tears, she drew me into her room and allowed me to release my story.

Mama's rooms contained a kitchen with a set of table and chairs, a blue cookstove, a sink, and four or five cupboards. She heated a kettle on the stove and dumped a can of chicken noodle soup and some water into a pot, while I sat at the table, my hands folded on the chipped wood, lulled by the sight of her stirring a spoon through broth for me. All around us hung paintings of pastoral green settings that might have been rural Oregon. Or Germany. Or the homes of one of her lovers. I didn't ask. A silver charm shaped like a bird dangled from the eave outside the kitchen window, and a gilded hand mirror lay propped on the sill.

Mama set a steaming bowl and a cup of tea with a splash of cream in front of me. "I brewed rose petals and lemon balm into the tea," she said, her voice tender, her movements gentle. "They'll ease your fears and heartbreak."

"Thank you." I picked up my spoon but couldn't yet eat. My arms again tingled with the panic of forgetting something.

Mama sat down beside me with her own cup of tea, although hers smelled as if it contained a dash of something stronger than cream and herbs. "I know you said you haven't seen Tru in almost a year," she said, "but how was she when you left? How is her leg?"

I swallowed down a sharp spot in my throat. "Well . . . her poor right leg never grew properly. It's about two and a half inches shorter than the left one. She wears an iron brace and a special shoe to even out her legs. She can't walk without the brace and a cane."

Mama cradled her forehead in her right hand. "Oh, Odette. I wanted more than anything to raise you two girls on my own."

"I know."

"I'm sorry."

"I understand." My throat clamped up and prohibited any more words from passing. I blew on a spoonful of soup and accidentally whistled.

I longed to ask my mother about MarViLUs and Uncle Magnus, about Aunt Vik's denial of monsters, despite all the bells and the amulets shaped like boars and lions chiming from her eaves. Such questions sounded foolish in my head, though. Mama's pinched lips and distant eyes didn't look in the mood for magic.

I swallowed a spoonful of broth. "Should I return to my sister, do you think?" I asked. "Never mind Aunt Vik's rules, do you think it would be best if I went to her, took her away . . . ?" I closed my mouth, for I noted Mama's silence and the downward turn of her mouth.

"Odette," she said, and she took one of my hands in hers. "You have no money, no job. And you're not yourself—I can tell, even though I haven't seen you for years. You wouldn't be of any help to your sister if you took her away."

"Perhaps . . ." I glanced around me, ignoring a dead mouse stuck in a trap next to the cookstove, the cigarette stains dirtying the sink. "Perhaps I could work here for a spell."

"No! Absolutely not." Her fingers tightened around mine. "You'll stay no longer than this afternoon, and you'll never think of working anywhere like it again."

"Then why do *you* work here?"

"Because it's allowed me to pay off my debts and live in comfort. A woman can make more money in a place like this than from most other available means of employment, but she has to sell her soul to do it."

"Then what should I do?"

"Return home. Find yourself again. Heal from the pain of letting go of that baby."

I frowned. "How can I return home if I'm unable to see Tru?"

"I mean your California home."

"I . . . I don't understand." I shook my head. "We left it years ago."

"Magnus moved into the house a few years after I brought you girls to Oregon, after he spent some time wandering the country. Your father abandoned the ranch and left it to the bank, and Magnus decided that's where he wanted to settle."

I sat up straight. "Is Uncle Magnus alive, then?"

"As far as I know, yes." She squeaked a finger around the rim of her cup. "He wrote Aunt Viktoria a letter two years ago, and she forwarded it to me. He wanted us to know he's healthy and safe and that he's been married to Mrs. Alvarado's oldest daughter, Josefina, for several years now."

I sat back, remembering pretty, dark-eyed Josefina squeezing one of her sisters' boots over my foot when I ran to the Alvarados on the day of Tru's birth.

Mama slid her hand out of mine. "Go to them. Breathe the fresh air. Work in the outdoors. Remember who you are."

"Why didn't he ever come back here to find us?"

"Because I told him to stay away from us." Mama rubbed her cheeks, her elbows now on the table. "And because it's not safe for him to return."

"Because of his asthma, you mean?"

"Yes." She rose to her feet, her voice terse. "His asthma. He shouldn't ever come back. It's too dangerous. Too risky."

I watched her walk over to a low cupboard and heard her knees crack as she bent before it. I remembered the night Uncle Magnus had gotten drunk at our house down in California, and how Mama had held him back, as though she feared he'd kill our father.

"He didn't cause some sort of trouble up here, did he?" I asked, my skin now cold, for her silence emitted a chill. "I know you left when you were almost sixteen, and he thirteen . . . I remember some of his stories about monsters in your house."

She breathed a short laugh. "Monsters, yes. There was a monster, all right."

I stirred my spoon through the soup, my eyes cast down at the bright yellow droplets of oil floating across the surface. Steam rose from my teacup. The soothing scent of the rose petals emboldened me to keep questioning her.

"What type of monster?"

"I'll give you enough money to help you get by for several weeks." Mama had opened the low cupboard. "Lord knows how much cash I sent for you and Tru over the years, but your aunt always mailed it straight back, calling it 'tainted with sin.'"

I remembered the day Aunt Vik first took me to her house on the train when I was six, and how we'd sat near a man who had known her and her siblings when they were all younger.

Do you remember that boy our age who was killed when we were seventeen or so? he had asked her. *That boy Rufus Todd, a pushy fellow who was always stirring up trouble . . . remember they found him in the woods . . . a knife wound in his back? I always wondered who attacked him . . .*

"Did . . ." I swallowed. "Did you kill the monster?" I asked my mother, not quite brave enough to come out and say the name Rufus Todd.

Mama froze, still bent over the cupboard, her back toward me.

"Mama?" I asked. "Is that why Uncle Magnus can't come back? Is that why you hurried down to San Diego and stayed there all those years? Did someone die?"

She stood up straight and turned toward me, her face older than before, more creased and thin and gray. "There was a boy," she said. "A jealous boy. He didn't like that I'd found a new sweetheart. He hurt me badly in front of my brother, and my brother stopped him." She drew a long breath and exhaled through her mouth. "That's all you need to know."

The air had thinned when she said the words *my brother stopped him.*

A knife wound to the back, that man had stated on the train.

"Was . . . was Aunt Viktoria there, too?" I asked.

"I said, that's all you need to know, Odette. We took care of each other, protected each other, and that's that."

I laid my spoon beside my bowl, my appetite gone.

Mama bent down in front of the open cupboard and spun a dial on a metal box in a series of whirrs and clicks.

"Write to me when you arrive at your uncle's house," she said. "Let me know how he's doing."

"You should come with me."

"I can't." She opened the safe. "I've been in this business far too long to do anything else."

"You're a Lowenherz. Lionhearted. A warrior who'd do anything to protect us." I rubbed my hands across my legs and searched for the right words to coax her into joining me. "It's time you protected yourself. Reclaimed your soul."

A small smile twitched across Mama's lips. "It's too late."

"If you're still alive, it's not too late."

She made a small murmur that might have meant agreement. Without another word about her past or her future, she bent back down and fetched the money that would allow me to return to the California canyon where I had begun my life. The canyon in which my family's secrets once hid.

"Tell me the story about the day I was born," I asked her, for I'd never heard my own story, and I wanted to trample down the ugliness that crowded my brain. "Who was there?"

"Well . . ." She sighed and stood upright. "You were born at eleven fifty-five at night on February 28, 1890, a Friday, almost midnight of March 1. Uncle Magnus was there, and he wasn't even yet sixteen, but he had to ride a horse through the canyon in the dark to fetch Mrs. Alvarado. The most glorious sound I'd ever heard in my life was the pounding of hooves when the two of them rode up to help me." She smiled and fussed with a loose lock of her hair. "I gave you the middle name Magnolia because it sounded like a flowery version of my brother's name, which upset your father, but I didn't care." Her expression turned pensive; she gazed out the small window at the faded bricks of the building next door. The bird charm danced in a breeze. "Always remember the people who were there for you, Odette. That's who you need to keep close to your heart."

I nodded and toyed with my spoon beside the bowl. "I'm going to find my daughter, Mama. I'm going to fetch her and Tru and take care of them both."

Mama pressed the stack of money to her stomach. "Oh, Odette, you've already taken care of that baby by giving her to people able to raise her."

"That's not enough."

"It has to be. I'm sorry, my darling . . . but it has to be."

CHAPTER SEVENTEEN

Trudchen
January 22, 1909—New Jersey

The morning after the Leeds Devil crept across the roof above our heads, after Od panicked about the clock striking midnight, my sister did not speak for the longest time. She yawned and fastened up the hooks on the front of her corset, and I yawned in response as I pulled my slip down over my head. Neither of us had slept much after the incident. I assumed no one in the inn had rested for long. From what I learned through the chaos and the commotion of the night before, *everyone* in the establishment had heard the footsteps on the rooftop. The first man who ran out—no one would specify which man it was—claimed to have seen a tall figure with an eight-foot-wide wingspan fly away into the night. In the coop, Cy and the other boys discovered the chickens missing, with "feathers strewn everywhere."

"You look tired," I said to Od while I braided my hair.

Od pinned up her own hair in front of a wood-framed mirror that hung a little cockeyed on the wall by the window. The reflection of her brown eyes glanced my way. "I slept terribly," she said. One of the pins stuck out of her mouth, so she had spoken through her teeth.

"Do you want to leave?" I asked. "You seemed so troubled last night when you mentioned the date . . ."

Od withdrew the pin from her lips and shoved it into the bottom half of a knot she had twisted onto the back of her head. She did not reply to my statement. The bags below her eyes, the curve of her back, stopped me from saying anything further.

Once our hair and clothing looked presentable, she helped me downstairs for breakfast by standing in front of me with a hand on my ribs to catch me if I fell.

"I'll insist we switch rooms with one of the men on the first floor," she said again. "I'm sorry I didn't do that yesterday. I wasn't thinking clearly. It was selfish. I'll bring our bags down soon."

"Thank you." I clung to the handrail and inched downward as best I could. Sitting and scooting down on my backside proved a less terrifying option, and, thankfully, no one witnessed me doing it besides my sister.

Down below, we found the inn emptied of most of the rifle-toting men from the day before.

"They've left," said Cy from one of the dining room tables. He, Red, and Andrew sat together with pencils in hand. In front of them lay a paper with drawings of some sort.

"Where did they go?" asked Od.

Cy leaned back in his chair with a creak of its joints. "Back to their homes. They got frightened and told Mr. Munro he can defend his inn on his own. Mr. Munro is currently driving his spooked wife to her sister's."

I lowered myself into the nearest chair.

Od walked up to the boys' table. "What are you drawing?"

"We're trying to design a trap"—Cy drummed his pencil against the paper—"using bait. One that would catch the Devil without us needing to tie ropes around it. At this point, none of us feels inclined to get too close to the thing."

Od pulled up a chair to their table and sat. "Tru and I used to build boxes with trapdoors to catch rabbits with our uncle William."

"Trapdoors?" asked Red with a lift of his eyebrows. "Isn't that a little . . . *complex* for the materials we have?"

"A trapdoor is quite simple, really," said Od. "The challenging part will be finding wooden boards—or a giant crate—large enough to house this Devil. Otherwise, we would simply need some wire and screws, along with a saw, a hammer, and nails."

"I'm sure if we dig around behind the kitchen," said Cy, "or in the basement, we'd find some large delivery crates."

"What would you use as bait?" I asked from my table behind them.

The boys all turned my way with contemplative gazes, and for a moment I feared they considered using me.

Od scooted her chair sideways to better view me. "Another chicken would likely work."

"Look at the carnage in that coop," said Red, leaning forward on his pointy elbows. "You'll see this greedy bastard is hungry. He doesn't want just one measly chicken."

"The newspapers all say there's another meal the Leeds Devil craves," said Andrew in a tone that made me shiver.

"What is it?" I asked, again worrying it would involve something to do with me.

Andrew's lips inched into a hesitant grin beneath that scraggly slip of hair. "Puppy dogs."

"Oh, no." Od sat up tall. "I wouldn't let you risk a dog's life."

"Not a purebred," said Andrew with a chuckle. "A cast-aside mutt we'd fetch from the pound. Something infested with fleas and maybe missing a leg. A cripple no one wants."

I flinched.

"Careful what you're saying, Andrew . . ." said Red through his teeth, and he cast a glance my way. "Not a cripple, per se," he then added, as though that made everything better. "Any old dog would do."

My eyes welled with tears over the idea of some poor, unwanted dog—a dog with a limp and no family to care for it—stuck in a trap in the middle of the night. I could never return to Ezra Blue and tell him and his sister what we'd done. I could never again raise my head with pride.

"Maybe we should stick Andrew in the trap," said Cy with a twirl of his pencil.

Od nodded. "I quite agree."

"I would like to see the chicken coop," I said, and all eyes again turned my way.

"There's not much left to see," said Red. "He ate everything."

I pushed my weight against my cane and stood up. "I want to see how real the Devil is—what we're up against."

"All right," said Cy. "If you insist."

"I do."

The boys led Od and me out through the kitchen, but they strolled with no particular hurry, as though they dreaded that coop. I could just about keep up with their pace.

Cy opened the door, and my sister took hold of my left hand and helped me step off the stoop.

We walked through the snow to the empty coop—now a mess of white and orange feathers, with not one single bird left for us to see. The wooden door hung off its hinges, the wood splintered beyond repair, the screen gnawed. The silence of the yard, the lack of all that clucking from the day before, turned my stomach.

"If we do manage to catch this monstrosity," said Cy, "we'll have to transport it with caution. I'd say that animal dealer would owe us at least a thousand dollars."

"Apiece," suggested Andrew.

"If you boys help me build the trap"—Od trod closer to the wreckage—"I'll split the reward money evenly between us. It was five hundred, you said?"

Cy nodded.

"That's one hundred apiece for all five of us here," said Od, "and that includes Tru, even if she can't do any lifting."

I stepped forward. "I'll help any way I can, but please promise we won't use a dog as bait."

"We won't." She took my hand again. "Will you help carve the peg from one of the logs in the woodshed? That peg's ever so important, remember?"

"Yes." I nodded. "Of course."

Cy sidled over to my sister and nudged her with an elbow. "I thought you said yesterday you didn't believe this thing could be caught with traps and rifles."

Od squeezed my hand with more strength. "It feels more substantial now. More like an animal. More reckless. I think we can do this."

Od and the boys carried in beverage and soap crates from behind the inn, and we debated how best to take them apart and fit them together to create one giant box from which the creature, theoretically, would not escape.

Mr. Munro returned from delivering his wife to her sister's and told us, "I've just the crate you need in the basement. Four mattresses arrived in it, and I've kept it around in case I ever required extra lumber. If you can carry it up the stairs, you can use it. I only ask that you set the trap out in the woods, not next to my inn."

The boys hauled the crate up to the dining room, and we all deemed it an exceptional find. Mr. Munro explained that the mattresses had each measured four feet by six feet, with thicknesses of six inches.

"Do you think it's big enough for the thing that wreaked havoc here last night?" asked Red.

Mr. Munro folded his arms over his chest. "I don't think you'll find any crate bigger. I will tell you this, though: if you do catch this killer who's ruined my chickens and my business—I don't care if that thing is fox, devil, or man—I'll give you free lodging for a week. And beer."

At that the boys grinned and laughed.

Od used the back of a hammer to pry off the nails on one of the ends of the crate and then sawed a slot for the trapdoor two inches behind the new opening. She instructed Cy and

Andrew to nail down the lid, and I helped Red measure spare pieces of wood for the fulcrum, the balance board, the trap-door, and a peg the Leeds Devil would hit when lunging after the bait.

In the thick of all that activity, my sister appeared less shaken than she had the night before. I was glad to see her so intent on building that box, but her refusal to confide in me about what January 22 meant to her upset me. I was getting so tired of her always pushing me away.

Late in the afternoon, Cy, Andrew, Red, and Od lugged the finished trap out into the woods. Mr. Munro guarded the front porch with his shotgun, and I watched my sister and the boys wander into the trees through a window in the new downstairs room Od had secured for us before she left. Cy had given me the copy of *Marvelous and Monstrous*, so I opened to the first chapter and read:

It all started with a set of footprints that ended five feet away from the front of the house. Margaret discovered the prints first. She opened the door to survey the depth of the snow that a storm had swept into their woods the night before. She spied the tracks, and her breath caught in her throat. The markings looked like human footprints, but they stopped so abruptly, as if someone had crept toward the door and then suddenly taken flight. She saw no retreating footsteps leading in the other direction. She remembered her sister, Viola, worrying about a sound on the roof around midnight, but all three of the children had reasoned it must have been a loose board, pestered by the wind that hollered through the hills.

The characters then debated the best means of preparing to defend themselves from that same ghastly visitor, should he approach again that night. Margaret pushed for the use of a sword that had been in the family since the Middle Ages. Viola insisted the intruder must be a vampire and claimed their crucifix would be the best weapon against him. The sisters also had a brother named Augustus, and everyone treated each other with honesty and respect, even under duress. No one buried or otherwise hid family secrets. No one lied.

I closed the book, seized by a dangerous bout of curiosity.

All those months of not knowing where Od was—the years of wondering why she behaved the way she did—the frustration of watching her keep close to this Cy fellow, despite the obvious fact that he bothered her—chewed me up and spat me out a person who no longer respected her sister's privacy. I could not stand my ignorance a moment longer.

I forced open the Gladstone bag and dug around for the locked box that held the story of our lives. Od's secrets. Beneath her underclothes, I found an oak box—the perfect size for storing letters—tucked beneath a playing card illustrated with a woman and a lion. The key to unlock the box still dangled from the chain around Od's neck, so I jostled and picked at the lock with my fingernails and fought to yank the lid open. I squeezed the oak between my knees, and I pried and pried and pried . . .

"Oh, come on, you stubborn thing. Open up!"

I thought of Cy knowing more of my sister's secrets than I did. I remembered he had understood when, two days earlier in the Philadelphia station, Od told him, *I spent a great deal of time in Kansas City.*

Kansas City, was it? he had asked, while I just stood there behind her, oblivious, expected to believe she had worked for circuses and fortune-tellers.

I lifted the box over my head and slammed it down to the floor.

With a crack that made my heart jump, the bottom split open. Sheets of white paper poked out from the oak base lined in brass beads, and the truth—sweet, sweet, tempting truth—lay within reach.

Cy's laugh rang out in the distance. A brief peek out the window revealed Od and the men returning without the trap. A desperate need to read something—*anything*—about my sister and our past blurred my mind of all sense and reason. I lowered myself to the ground, smashed the box against the floor with one more blow, and tugged out Od's full confession.

Footsteps reached the porch. I rifled through the papers, picked a random page from the middle . . .

All the beauty and goodness of my childhood scattered across the ground, too broken to ever be mended. I ran to Papa and squeezed my arms around his thick waist.

"I want us to go home," I said into the thin wool of his summer coat.

"No, Odette." He pried my arms off him. "We can't do that. You must leave with your uncle right away."

"Why are you here with these people?" I asked through tears. "Why aren't you with us?"

"I'm sorry, monkey." He continued to push me away with a gentle nudge, his eyes damp, his voice shaking, his fingers cold against my wrists. "This is my real family."

The front door opened down the hall. I flipped through the pages to another section, my fingers moistening the paper.

Outside the door stood a woman who looked nothing at all like my mother. Her cheekbones were sharp, her brown eyes sunken, her coat a heap of mangy fur. She smelled of liquor, and she rocked back and forth, as though either nervous or drunk.

"Odette." Mother reached a bony hand toward me, but I drew back. "No, darling . . ." She shuffled forward. A feathered green hat teetered on her head. "Don't be afraid. It's me. It's Mama." Her eyes dropped to the mirror shaking in my right hand. "Oh, look, you smart girl. You still protect yourself from monsters."

"Tru?" called Od from down in the entryway. "Are you still here? Are you all right?"

"Yes," I said, my voice screechy, nervous. "I'm fine. Mr. Munro is still sitting down there with his rifle, isn't he? No need to worry."

One more, one more, I told myself, and I skipped ahead, closer to the end.

When I summoned the ability to scream—to holler that the Weeping Woman had stolen my baby—no one believed me. No one showed me the smallest sliver of sympathy. The staff told me it was an employee named Nurse Hitchcock who had fetched Trudie and delivered her to an awaiting married couple in the lobby. The adoptive parents had received a postcard from the

Willows at Christmastime and couldn't wait to take the child to the nursery they'd been preparing since December. They thought Trudie was a perfect angel.

"Where is she?" I shouted in the superintendent's office, but the nurses dragged me away by both arms and told me that that information wasn't for me to know. They packed me up, shoved me into my scratchy winter coat, and shipped me off in a hack to the Kansas City Provident Association, where a woman who spoke in too soft a voice told me she'd help me get home. I got sick to my stomach from the medicine the nurses had poured down my throat the night before, and the panic of missing Trudie made it impossible for me to sit still in a chair, let alone to think where my home ought to be.

"What are you doing?" asked Od from the doorway.

I jumped and swiveled my knees to the right. My sister glared at me with an expression of horror and utter betrayal. The broken box—as demolished as the mutilated door of the chicken coop—lay next to my feet.

"What are you doing?" she asked again, this time much louder. She slammed the door shut behind her and marched over to me, her hands balled into fists. "I told you I'd show you that when I was ready."

"*I'm* ready now," I said. "I want to know. I want to help you."

"You're ruining our adventure, Tru. There's no place for *this*"—she yanked the pages out of my hands—"in the middle of our hunting party. Why did you break my box?"

"I'm sorry."

"I told you I'd show it to you eventually."

"Did our father truly have another family?"

She drew back, her lips parting.

"Is that why he disappeared," I asked, "and not because of our uncle? Did our mother turn to drink because of him?"

Od swallowed, and her cheeks turned red and blotchy. She bent over and collected the rest of the papers from the floor, her breathing erratic, her movements clumsy.

"Od, please . . ." I took hold of her wrist.

She shook me off her. "I can't believe you did this, Tru!"

I watched her cram the papers into her Gladstone, the tidiness and order of the stack now ruined. She slammed the divided compartments of the bag shut, but two corners of the papers stuck out like a pair of pointed ears.

She lugged the bag to the door.

"Od." I slid my left leg into a better position for standing up. "Where are you going?"

"I don't want to talk about any of this right now." She threw open the door and stormed out of sight.

I sat there on the floor without moving, and those words I'd just read—*her* words—pelted my head like brickbats. In the matter of one tiny minute, I'd suddenly become the daughter of a man who had another family and a mother ravaged by drink and life. Moreover, I was the aunt of a niece sent away to live with strangers. A niece named after me.

Trudie, she'd called her.

Her beloved from Missouri.

Before sunset, Mr. Munro drove away in his wagon to procure the bait for the trap. Red and Andrew sat in the back with a rope and a large burlap sack, which I did not care for in the slightest.

Cy stayed behind to "protect" Od and me, which consisted of him bringing out a carton of playing cards and teaching us how to play poker. We used pennies as our wagers and drank soda pop instead of whiskey, but despite Cy's enthusiasm, Od refused to smile or look me in the eye, even when I won three times in a row.

"Beginner's luck," said Cy. He collected the cards. "Congratulations, Tru."

I treated him with the same silence that Od bestowed upon me.

He reshuffled the deck.

I glanced out the window and noted how little daylight remained. The white of the sky had dimmed to a cold bluish gray and warned of a moonless night. The hairs on the back of my neck bristled.

I cleared my throat and dared to ask, "Are they fetching chickens?"

Cy and Od exchanged a look that turned my stomach.

"Od?" I turned toward my sister. "It's not a dog, is it? You promised you wouldn't let that happen."

She laid her palms against the tabletop and stared at her twitching fingers.

I leaned forward. "Od?"

"Two hundred dollars would allow for our comfort and safety, Tru," she said. "We wouldn't have to scrounge around for employment right away and take jobs we found demeaning. We would accomplish our goal of getting paid to hunt down a legendary creature."

I ground my teeth and shifted my eyes back and forth between her and Cy, the latter of whom dealt the cards and whistled. He moved with the ease of a person who hadn't broken a family apart—who hadn't put my sister in the position of giving up her home and a baby who clearly meant the world to her. My poor sister, roaming the country in search of her daughter. That's what she was doing, I realized. This wasn't a monster hunt. It was a quest to find a child hidden somewhere in this enormous country of ours.

"I should think Cy owes you a bit of money himself," I said. "And I don't mean pennies from poker."

Cy froze and peered at me with the look of a startled deer.

"I should think, in fact," I said, "he owes you a great deal of money. And apologies. And nine months of your life."

"Trudchen!" Od gripped the table with both hands. "What did you read in that box?"

The cards slipped from Cy's fingers. "I suppose, Odette, we should sometime talk about it."

The front door opened, and Andrew, Red, and Mr. Munro stomped inside from the cold. They joined us in the dining room upon the thick soles of their winter boots, bringing with them the scent of the pines.

Red peeled off his coat. "It's done. All set."

Cy breathed a sigh of relief, whether due to the idea of the trap being set or the fact that he'd avoided a conversation about the baby, I was not sure.

I got to my feet and braced myself against the back of my chair. "What did you find?" I asked. "What's in the trap?"

"Just a chicken," said Red, not meeting my eyes.

Andrew hooked his coat over the back of the chair next to Cy's. "I'm starving. Didn't you say there's a ham in the icebox, Mr. Munro?"

"There is."

Mr. Munro wouldn't meet my eyes, either. No one would. I strained my ears for the sound of barking in the distance, but the men's boots clomped around with such a to-do, I heard nothing but their galumphing.

"Sit down, Tru." Od pulled on the back of my skirt and looked at me without bitterness for the first time since she had caught me with her papers. "Don't worry. It's an adventure, remember? We're finally catching a bona fide monster that won't be a simple flash in a mirror."

"If it's a dog out there . . ."

"They said it's a chicken."

"I've been fed more than my share of lies, Od. I don't believe it's a chicken. I'm going to walk into those woods and—"

"Don't you dare!" Od jumped up and grabbed my left elbow. "Sit back down."

"It's going to tear apart that poor, unwanted animal. Don't you see? We're just like it, Od. It may as well be us out there."

"Haven't you listened to any of the fairy tales I've told you, Tru? You don't go wandering out in the dark by yourself—no matter who you are." She let go of my arm. "Please sit down and eat some supper. I'm . . . I'm going to . . ." She leaned close and whispered into my ear, "I'm going to speak to Cy, alone, after dinner. And then I'll sit down and talk to you."

I swallowed. "You will?"

"Yes, but don't go running off on your own. Stay inside. It's not a dog. Do you understand?"

I nodded, and I desperately wanted to believe her.

But I didn't.

The barking began at around ten o'clock that night. Outside my window, I saw the black silhouettes of thousands of trees, but nothing moved in the sky or on land. From somewhere in the depths of those pines, a dog yelped, pleading for someone to fetch it.

Od had left me alone in our new room to speak with Cy in private—in his bedroom, of all places, which further vexed me.

I knocked on Cy's door.

"Who is it?" he called.

"I'm looking for my sister," I called back.

Od opened the door, the rims of her nostrils red, as though she'd been blowing her nose a great deal. "I can't talk now, Tru."

"I hear a dog barking in the woods."

"Oh, Tru . . ." She slouched. "Not now. I can't worry about a dog . . . We're in the middle of an extremely difficult conversation."

"The newspapers all say the Leeds Devil tends to bark like a dog," said Cy from a chair in his room, his elbows hanging over the armrests. "Don't let him fool you. Stay inside with your window shut tight."

Od nodded and touched my left shoulder. "Keep the mirror in the window and the *Hexenspiegel* around your neck. I'll be back in a little while."

"But it's a desperate bark—a cry for help."

"Don't trust it," said Cy. "It's the Devil."

I stiffened. "I should offer those same words of advice to my sister, Cy."

"Stop it, Tru." Od nudged me backward. "Go back to the room. You're not helping."

Startled by the nudge, I took a second to regain my balance. "Please," she said. "Go."

I leaned toward her. "If Cy is willing to allow his friends to tie a helpless dog in the middle of the woods, leaving it to be destroyed, then what would he do to you?"

"He's already done that exact same thing to me, which is what we're now talking about, so leave us alone." She slammed the door in my face.

My sister—*Od*—slammed a door in my face.

I trudged back to my bedroom with my cane and my raised black shoe banging against the floor. Once again, I peered out the window, in search of movements and sounds. The dog no longer barked. Charcoal clouds smudged away the small sliver of the moon I'd seen earlier. Nothing lit the trees. My skin chilled in anticipation of the sound of feet thudding on the roof above us.

The dog barked again. No, it howled—a pitiful wail of distress in the darkness. I grabbed my coat from the bed and threaded my arms through the thick sleeves. I took a gold cord used to hold back the curtains and fastened it around my waist, and then I used the ends to tie the handle of the hand mirror against my right hip, like a gun secured in a holster. The dog yipped and barked, still alive and in one piece, as far as I could tell. After buttoning up my coat, I fished my *Hexenspiegel* out from beneath the purple wool and allowed the mirror the size of a half-dollar to dangle in the open. I also donned Od's hat, checking for the feel of the little pearl at the end of the hatpin. I even tucked the ax from our sleigh ride into the green velvet depths of the MarViLUs case.

Before leaving, I wrote a note and left it on the bed for Od.

I'm going to save that dog. Don't worry, I've brought all the tools.

All my love,
Tru

With the MarViLUs case in my right hand and my left fingers hooked around the handle of my cane, I strode down the hallway as fast as my legs would allow. My pain subsided, as though my body realized it was mighty. It was needed.

I opened the front door and journeyed out into the chill of that cold January night, and for the first time in my life I felt strong. Powerful. Invincible.

Lionhearted.

CHAPTER EIGHTEEN

Odette
January 2, 1909—California

I t took me eleven months to reach my uncle's home in Fallbrook, California—not through any fault of the United States railway system, but due to my own lack of courage. During my journey south to California at the end of the previous January, all I could think about was the faith Uncle Magnus had placed in me when I was a child, how he'd insisted I would grow up to be "something rather special." I also thought about what he had had to do to stop that "jealous boy" from badly hurting my mother when they were young—an act of violence that both horrified me and reminded me of my own failure to protect my sister and my daughter.

Instead of facing Uncle Magnus, I traveled to San Francisco, Sacramento, Los Angeles, Orange, Laguna Beach, San Juan Capistrano, and Carlsbad, among other towns and cities scattered throughout the ridiculously large state of California. I worked in shops and restaurants, lodged in the cheapest boardinghouses I could find, and saved up every penny that wasn't contributing to my meals and occasional train fare. I looked for Trudie in the faces of the babies in the parks and in the places of my employment, even though I didn't know what she looked like beyond my memory of her tiny features at four days old.

When my mood grew too dark and restless—when sitting and thinking kept me from sleeping and eating—I picked up and moved somewhere else.

By December 1908, I'd managed to save close to two hundred dollars.

Now, at long last, at the dawn of 1909, there I stood at my original destination, Fallbrook's Howe Station, which sat on three acres of land at the mouth of the Temecula Canyon. My sinuses hurt from the arid inland air, and my nose bled a bit from the dryness. I dabbed at my nostrils with a handkerchief and wondered if I should jump onto the next train west, back from where I'd just come from.

A mile-and-a-half trek up a hillside road to Fallbrook awaited, but, thankfully, so did an open-air coach, into which I climbed with four of my fellow railway passengers. The steep slope of granite and chaparral looked as alien as a moonscape. The afternoon sun stung my eyes, causing them to water.

"Are you visiting this region for the first time?" asked a woman in a glossy black hat in the seat in front of me. Her hatpin involved ornate jewels of red and blue, set in a cone of silver.

"I lived here years ago," I said, but I almost didn't believe my own words.

A pair of auburn horses hoisted the coach out of the canyon and delivered us to a grand hotel with sweeping porches and porticos. The driver called the place "the Naples," but I didn't remember much about it. Although quite magnificent, the resort had not impressed me as much as the castle inspired by a Scottish fortress that reigned over the golden canyons.

"Excuse me," I said to the driver after the other passengers climbed off with their bags. "Do you happen to know of a local olive farm owned by Magnus Lowenherz?"

"I do." The driver swiveled toward me on his leather seat. "This region now teems with olive ranches, but I know Magnus well."

"I'm his niece, Odette."

The man smiled. "Well, then, I'm pleased to meet you. My name is Watkins."

"How far of a walk is it to the ranch house?"

"I'd be happy to drive you over there."

"Oh, would you?" I sank back in relief. "Thank you ever so much."

The driver dropped me off in front of a two-story ranch house about half the size of the towering structure I remembered from the past, but the walls were still pale brown, like a chicken's egg. Olive trees thick with leaves shook in a breeze, and a handful of Mama's old amulets and bells rang from the eaves. The symphony of my childhood.

I climbed up to the front porch and knocked on the door.

The ensuing wait reminded me of standing on Papa's front step in San Diego, and I thought again of all those unfamiliar blue eyes gazing out the door at me while I squeezed Uncle Magnus's hand. I held my breath and wiggled my right fingers on the handle of my bag.

The door opened, and a woman with black hair, pretty brown eyes, and a warm, golden complexion appeared with a child of about two, a boy, balanced on her right hip. She tipped her head to her right, and the skin between her eyebrows puckered.

"Hello," she said with an air of confusion, but her voice carried warmth, nonetheless.

"Are you Josefina?" I asked.

"I am."

I swallowed. "I don't know if you remember me, but I used to live in this house when I was little. Your mother helped my mother give birth to my sister, and you pushed one of your sisters' shoes onto my bleeding foot after I ran through the canyon barefoot."

The pucker deepened. "Oh, my goodness. Are you . . ." She cracked a smile. "Are you little Odette?"

I nodded.

Josefina—now *Aunt* Josefina—covered her mouth and blinked several times in a row. "My heavens! Magnus will be so surprised to see you. We didn't know you were coming."

"I'm sorry I didn't write." My fingers slipped on the handle of my bag, and the Gladstone thumped against the porch.

"Are you all right?" She lowered the toddler to the floor. "You look so tired."

"It's been a long journey."

"Magnus just went into town for the mail, but he should be home for lunch any minute now. Oh, wait . . ." She shielded her eyes with her right hand. "Speak of the devil . . . here he is."

I turned and spotted a bottle-green automobile rattling our way through the groves with little pops and hiccups of its engine. The driver wore a cap and goggles, so I couldn't tell if he looked anything at all like what I remembered of handsome young Uncle Magnus. I inched backward, frightened again of disappointing him, wondering if any glimmers of enchantment still flickered inside me.

He cruised the car to a stop in the patch of dirt at the end of the front path, set the brake, and, with one last shudder of the engine, the vehicle quieted.

"Look who we have here, Magnus," called Josefina to him. "See if you can guess."

"I didn't know we were expecting a visitor," he said with a polite smile, and he yanked off his goggles and climbed out of the driver's side of the car. He didn't look as young as he used to, but not nearly as ancient as I imagined for a thirty-four-year-old uncle, either. His resemblance to my mother and me couldn't be mistaken. We all shared the same hair color, the same chocolate brown eyes.

The closer he strode, the more his face sobered, and the slower his pace grew. He stopped six feet away and simply stared with his goggles hanging from his right hand.

"Well?" asked Josefina. "Do you recognize her?"

He stretched his neck forward. "Od?"

I bit my lip and nodded.

He gasped. "Really?"

Again, I nodded.

"Holy smoke!" He stepped back on one foot. "My God . . . I can't believe this." He broke into laughter and grabbed me up in a hug.

I smiled and let him squeeze me as hard as he wanted, reminded again of how he'd taken such good care of me after Tru's birth, how Mama said he'd ridden through the canyon in the pitch-dark to fetch Mrs. Alvarado on the night I was born, and how he'd filled up my heart with tales of the marvelous.

"What are you doing here?" he asked. "How are your mother and sister?"

I slipped out of his arms, my face turned downward.

"What is it?" he asked. "Is something wrong?"

I shook my head. "Nothing's gone quite as planned."

"What happened? Is someone unwell?" He grabbed both of my arms. "Od? No one's died, have they?"

"No, it's not that." I gritted my teeth and tried not to cry in front of him.

Behind me, Josefina cleared her throat. "I'll go finish preparing the food, Magnus. Come in when you're ready."

"Thank you, Josie." Uncle Magnus loosened his hold on me.

I stepped back and hugged my arms around my middle. "Mama sent me down here to see you."

"She did?" He removed his cap from his hair. "When?"

I closed one eye. "Last January."

"Last January? You mean a whole year ago?"

I nodded.

He put his hands on his hips, still holding the cap and his goggles. "I don't understand . . . What's happened, Od?"

I switched my gaze to the house, imagining Renoir the cat flicking his tale on the porch. For a moment, I even thought I saw a flash of white fur.

"Od?"

"It's not a pleasant story, Uncle Magnus. I'm sorry . . . but it's not."

"Write it down for me at least. I need to know."

I rubbed my lips together. "I'm not sure writing it down would make it any better."

"It might be easier than saying it out loud."

"Maybe." I pulled on a thread that stuck out from the right sleeve of my coat. "I heard you bought the house after my father sold it."

"I did." He nodded and glanced up at the windows above us. "I took a while recovering from the loss of all of you, worked on some cattle ranches, grew up a bit, but . . . eventually . . . I wandered back here. The Alvarados took good care of me. They helped me get this place running again."

"Is my father still in San Diego?"

He shrugged. "I don't know."

"I have no desire to go see him in his other house."

"You don't have to."

I eyed Uncle Magnus's green automobile. "I don't know how long I'll stay in the area, but I wonder if you would do something for me while I'm here."

"Sure, I'd do anything for you, darling. Just say the word."

My heart filled up a bit more at that offer. "Will you drive me out to that castle in the hills? I want to see the stone towers again."

Uncle Magnus squinted at me through the sunlight. "Do you mean Woreland Castle?"

"Is that its name? The one built by an artist?"

"That's the one. I'll take you there this week if you'd like, but you've got to swear to tell me what's happened."

I ripped that stray thread from my sleeve.

"However awful it may be, Od, I want to know. I still care

deeply about you and the rest of the family. I've never forgotten you. I hope you know that."

"I've never forgotten you, either." I flicked the thread away and watched it drift to the ground. "I'll write it down."

"Good. Thank you. As I'm sure you already know, you're more than welcome to stay at the house."

"How many children do you have?"

"Five."

I choked. "Five? I have five cousins?"

He beamed and swung his goggles around his right index finger. "Pablo, Ana Maria, Jacob, Ansel, and Lola."

"Are any of them babies?"

"Ansel and Lola are twins who just turned two on Christmas."

I dug my nails into my palms and tried hard not to think of Trudie, who would be turning one year old in sixteen days. Twenty more days would mark the anniversary of our separation.

Uncle Magnus closed his mouth and lifted his chin. "Are you all right, Od?"

"Yes. I will be. Thank you."

"Well, let's get you inside so you can enjoy Josefina's extraordinary cooking. And, Od . . ." He stepped forward. "You have a little something by your ear."

I swatted at my left earlobe, expecting to find a fly.

He snickered and said, "No, it's here."

He reached behind my right ear, and I heard the flutter of a piece of paper in his left fingers. He took my right hand and lay a card against my palm, showing me the illustration of a woman in a red robe with her hair wrapped in a white head-dress. A regal lion lay at her feet.

La Force, he'd told me years ago when he showed me that same tarot card, *which foretells that you'll become a woman of great strength and courage.*

I smiled, and for a moment I believed again—genuinely believed—that I possessed the ability to become that woman.

I met my cousins, all younger than ten, in the dining room where I used to eat with their father when I was their ages. Aunt Josefina served us tamales wrapped and steamed in corn husks, spiced with exquisite, tongue-awakening flavors I'd never experienced in either Oregon or Missouri. That old house of ours that she now shared with Uncle Magnus bloomed with color and laughter and a palpable sense of love, but homesickness overwhelmed me as I sat there with all of them. For the first time since I'd left Oregon, people who cared about me enveloped me, and yet I was also a stranger, hovering on the edge of a world I'd lost. This Uncle Magnus wasn't *my* Uncle Magnus, the one who called me his girl and made sure we all stayed safe when Papa wasn't home.

"My mother still lives down the canyon," Aunt Josefina told me after we ate, while my uncle played piano for us in the front room, the smaller children hanging off him. "You'll have to see her. I know she remembers helping your mother give birth to you and your sister. She always said, 'I've never heard a baby squawk so loudly when she came into the world as Odette Magnolia Grey. That girl is going to have plenty to say in her life.'"

"And what did she say about Tru?" I asked with a smile.

Josefina's cheeks dimpled. "Mainly, she remembers you

vomiting all over my sister's shoes when you watched your mother push Tru out."

I covered my face with my hands and laughed for the first time in a long while.

That night, in the downstairs room that used to serve as Papa's studio, I sat on Uncle Magnus's old bedroll that he'd always brought along when he slept in that very same room. A pile of blank papers lay in front of me on the bedding. Uncle Magnus had given the pages to me, as well as a pen, and I imagined filling them with a tidied-up version of the last twelve and a half years. I drew a breath and cast a glance across the room at a box of old toys—dolls and wooden tops and a carved grasshopper Tru and I had pulled with a string. I imagined my sister tucked up beside me in our bed upstairs, her little snores breaking the silence of the room.

I pressed a hand against the papers and suddenly understood what I needed to write and for whom I should write it.

I leaned over, and I wrote the truth for the person I wanted by my side most of all.

My sister.

On the morning Trudchen Maria Grey entered the world, I wrote, *the eastern sky blazed with a magnificent orange light that made me believe someone had struck a match to the heavens . . .*

One week after I arrived in Fallbrook, Uncle Magnus drove me to a region twenty miles away that he called Moosa Canyon. By then, he'd read what I'd written for Tru. He now knew about my sister's polio, the tenement house, Aunt Vik's farm, Cy, Trudie, the Willows, my memories of him and my mother, the stories I told Tru, and my banishment from Oregon. He also knew that his beloved sister Maria ran a brothel called Dunnottar House and had prostituted herself for years. He knew she'd told me about the monster who'd attacked her, and how he'd saved her. He'd read the pages out on the front porch that Saturday afternoon, and afterward he'd taken a long walk by himself in the groves.

When he got home, he told me to lock up the story in a box and to only show it to Tru when she was old enough to endure it. "Please don't ever show anyone else the part about the monster in the hills," he said without looking me in the eye.

The following afternoon, he drove me to the place I'd longed to visit ever since I'd left California: the famous setting of Tru's birthday story.

He parked the car beneath an oak tree and pointed up at a winter-green hilltop, which I remembered as golden in the summer.

"There it is," he said.

Off in the distance, a single tower made of gray stones stood amid live oaks. I climbed out of the car and trod forward with my eyes locked upon that tower.

"Where's the rest of it?" I asked.

"The rest of what?"

"The castle, of course."

"That's all Mr. Frazee built. He probably ran out of money. Or stones."

"No, I remember it being an entire castle. That's why I always told Tru she was born in it. I loved gazing up at the place."

"It's always been just one tower, Od. Your imagination must have filled in the rest of it."

My arms dropped to my sides. "Next I expect you to tell me there's no MarViLUs case."

At that he laughed.

I whipped my head toward him. "What's so funny? Where's the case?"

"Still at the house, along with a purple coat Vik sewed for your mother's fifteenth birthday. Vik always said purple was one of the most mystical and protective of colors. And we believed her. Lord, how we relied on all those charms and superstitions to keep us safe from harm."

"What's inside the case? Why did you laugh?"

"Nothing's inside it."

I recoiled. "Nothing?"

"It used to contain a book we wrote to make ourselves feel better after our parents died. I should say, Viktoria wrote it, but we all contributed stories of how the most horrifying of creatures tried to devour us in our home, but we remained valiant to the end." He leaned his back against the trunk of an oak stripped of bark, a wistful smile on his face. "Vik sent it down with us when your mother and I escaped to California. She encouraged us to sell the manuscript to earn money, but . . . we worried . . ."

"Worried about what?"

He shifted his focus to the pale blue sky. "We worried people would think we were killers."

I wrapped my arms around myself and suffered a bout of chills.

"Besides"—he cleared his throat—"I don't think anyone would want to read our bunkum."

"Bunkum?"

"Yes, we were overflowing with nonsense, humbuggery, and bunkum. Just like you, Od, we were all storytellers. In fact, I've always wondered if we're descended from the famed Baron Munchausen of Germany, who claimed to fight lions and crocodiles and ride through the air on a cannonball." That last word turned into a chuckle.

I squeezed my hands into fists until my thumbs hurt. "You told me we're all descended from a woman who chased werewolves and *Alps* out of her village. You swore my mother could do the same. I even remember Mama leaving the house in the night to battle impossible creatures."

"Od . . ." His smile faded, and his forehead creased with an expression of concern. "Of course I told you such things. You were a child stuck in a remote house with an unhappy mother, and I was still recovering from the horrors of my youth. Imagining myself and your mother as heroes capable of fighting off evil always made me feel stronger. I wanted you to feel just as safe and powerful."

"You showed me magic. Your tarot cards . . . your promise that I could reach you with my mind if I needed you. You told me I'd grow up to be something quite special."

"You have, Od. You're a clever young woman with a deep compassion for others. I think you should return to your sister, despite Vik's command. Vik's turned hard because life's been hard and she's borne the brunt of responsibility. But she knows deep down what it means to be close to a sibling. She knows family should stand by family."

I sank down on a sun-bleached log and dug my elbows into the tops of my thighs. "Where's the book you said Aunt Vik wrote if it's not still in the case?"

"I stuffed it into your mother's trunk of clothing when she first started packing to return to Oregon."

"Mama has it?"

"She did when she left California with you." He scratched at the back of his neck and looked away. "Your mother's never once written to me since she moved all of you away. I haven't known a thing about her until I read what you wrote. I didn't even know she lost that third child."

"She was so, so angry at you for taking me to my father."

"I know, but you needed to see the truth."

I cocked my head. "Did I truly need to see that?"

He nodded, his face serious. "Yes, Odette. You did."

I flinched. It was the first time he'd ever called me "Odette" in my life, and more than anything else I'd experienced—including Trudie's birth—his use of my full given name made me feel as though I'd crossed over a threshold into the realm of adulthood.

I turned my gaze to that lone tower on the hill. How small and pathetic it looked up there. A grown man's unfinished dream, left for all to see.

"Do people live in that tower?" I asked.

"I think the original owner lives up there with his wife and children."

I wiped a splintery chip from the log off the palm of my left hand. "I hope he knows what a disappointment he is to all the former children who believed he was building a castle."

My uncle's eyes met mine. "Oh, I'm sure he realizes how difficult it is to bid childhood magic good-bye."

I clenched my jaw and peered down at my shoes.

"There's such a thing as grown-up magic, too, you know," said Uncle Magnus. "I think you've already glimpsed it, even if it's slipped out of your hands. You can find it again. You've just got to pick yourself up and go after it."

I scratched a nail across the log's gray bark. "That's exactly what I intend to do."

"Good."

"I'm going to fetch Tru, and then we're going to search the country for my Trudie. We'll need to teach my daughter all these stories about our family. She'll need to know she's a Lowenherz."

"Oh . . . no . . ." Uncle Magnus sauntered over to me. "No, Od. I'm sorry, but the world's much too large for that." He sat down on the log beside me. "I'm sure you love that baby with all your heart, but you've got to let her go. You'll drive yourself mad roaming the country trying to find her. That's an impossible task."

"You once told me we both formed connections to the people we love—connections stronger than regular bonds. Was that a lie, too?"

"I told you, those were just stories, Od. Things I wanted to believe myself."

I pushed the palms of my hands against the log, hearing

the wood crunch beneath my bones. "If I do ever find myself face-to-face with a monster, Uncle Magnus, do tell me, should I bother raising a silly hand mirror, or an amulet, or anything else our superstitious family ingrained in my head? Or are all those tools bunkum, too?"

He brushed bark dust from the hems of his trousers. "If you encounter a supernatural creature, there's only one thing I suggest you do, darling—besides taking a photograph and sending it my way."

I squinted at him through the sharp rays of the late-afternoon sun. "What is it?"

He cracked a grin. "Run. Run as fast as you can."

I frowned. "And if Tru encounters evil, what should she do?"

Uncle Magnus's face fell. "Well, if that ever happens, God forbid, let's just hope you're standing there beside her."

CHAPTER NINETEEN

Trudchen
January 22, 1909—New Jersey

The dog's barks led me deep into the forest. I held the leather case and my cane, which meant I had no room left for a lantern, so I navigated my way through the snow and the trees in absolute darkness. All those stiff and silent trunks surrounding me felt like an army of silent sentinels, watching me, barricading my path. Trees sprang up in front of me without my spotting them in advance, and I gasped, fearing a hand would grab me.

My right shoe dragged through the undergrowth, snagging on roots, slowing me further. The hand mirror smacked against my coat, below my right hip. I grew short of breath and developed a stitch in my left side, but I clambered onward, determined to reach the dog before anything silenced its yelps.

At last I came upon it. The poor thing's whimpers echoed inside the crate, which I saw as a shadow the shape of a bed on the ground.

"I'm here, puppy." I bent down in front of the opening. "Good dog."

The whimpers loudened and rose to a pitch that made my ears ring. I moved to the left side of the crate, set the case down in the snow, propped my cane against the wood, and ran my fingertips across the rough surface of the trap, in search of the fulcrum and balance board.

"I'm just going to adjust the boards . . . so the door won't slam shut and trap either of us inside."

Something splatted against the snow to my right. I winced and drew back, bracing for the pain of teeth against my neck.

Once fear stopped tingling inside my chest, however, I realized the sound had come from where my cane had stood. I lowered myself down to my left knee and rummaged around on the ground for the sturdy feel of hickory.

The dog's voice deepened into a growl, right there beside me in the dark. My skin broke out in gooseflesh, for I feared Cy was right when he warned that the Leeds Devil barked like a dog. *Don't trust it*, he'd said, but there I kneeled in the blackness, crouched like a rabbit on the freezing-cold ground, in search of a cane—unable to run, even if I found it.

I smacked the earth with both palms but felt nothing but snow.

My left hip knocked the dark shadow of the MarViLUs case, and I remembered the ax tucked inside. I scrambled to open the latch, but the metal jammed and wouldn't budge. A surge of terror rushed up my chest and fled my mouth as a shriek of panic. My fingers slipped all over the latch and seemed to swell into sausages that couldn't grasp a thing.

"Open up! Oh, Lord, open up! I require a lantern. I require a blade."

The dog yipped. My fingers thickened. The case remained stuck.

Without warning, a scream echoed through the woods. I

stiffened, and the dog scuttled backward in the crate, nails scratching against wood.

A second scream tore through the air, directly above me, and it sounded nothing at all like a noise a human would make. The scream wasn't of this world. I stopped breathing. My back ached from the terror washing through me, but somehow I managed to crane my face toward the sky and peer around for signs of movement.

Be gone! I said, but only in my head. No words formed on my lips. The muscles of my mouth refused to move. My legs prickled with the urge to run, but I lacked the ability to even stand.

"Tru!" I heard my sister yell from a distance—probably back at the inn. "Tru! Where are you?"

She didn't have the mirror or the ax, only her tiny *Hexenspiegel* necklace. My poor sister—as helpless as the dog cowering in the crate beside me.

"Tru!" she called again, her voice traveling toward the woods.

I finally found my cane and pushed myself to my feet. "Od! Go back to the inn."

"Where are you?"

"Go back to the inn. Please! Something's out here!"

"Tell me where you are!"

"I'm saving the dog." I untied our mother's hand mirror from the cord around my waist.

Something pushed through the trees with a rush of blinding light. I jumped back and raised the mirror the wrong way, catching the reflection of my own eyes.

"It's just me." Od ran toward me with a lantern in her right hand; in the other, she clutched a carving knife. "Come back inside. Quickly!"

"Not without this dog."

"You can't stay here, Tru."

"I've got the hand mirror. If there's any shred of truth to what you've said—"

"No, Tru, listen to me." She plunked the lantern and knife on the ground and clasped me by the shoulders. "That mirror will do nothing."

"But—"

"Listen! We're not daughters of a monster-hunter. We're not invincible. We're children who resulted from an illicit affair between a married man and his former servant, and our uncle Magnus is no more a magician than the mind-readers and fortune-tellers at carnivals. There's nothing marvelous coursing through our blood or shining from our charms and mirrors—nothing that can stop us from getting hurt or killed out here."

My hands remained frozen on the mirror, my fingers curled around the cold brass handle. I knew the truth, but at the moment I so desperately needed some of her tales to be real.

"And I wasn't ever at a circus," she continued. "Aunt Vik and Cy's mother hid me away at a home for unwed mothers in Kansas City. I gave birth to my Trudie four days after your birthday last year. A married couple—strangers—adopted her a year ago today. I don't know where she is. All I know"—she leaned her forehead against mine—"is that I needed this adventure with you. I want to find my Trudie so badly. I want to write our book so she can one day know my name and find me."

The words she confessed seeped into my ears and burned

down my throat with the sting of acid. Shallow breaths trembled through my lips.

"Why didn't you tell me about Trudie when you first climbed through my window?" I asked. "Why didn't you write about her in your letters? I could have helped you."

"Oh, Tru." Od broke into tears. "I miss her. I know I'm supposed to let her go, but I miss her so much."

My throat tightened. I wrapped my hand that held the mirror around her back and held her close to my chest, and she clutched me as though she were drowning. She cried with her shoulders shaking against me, and my own tears for her and Trudie rushed down my cheeks.

From the back of the crate emerged another whine. The dog's nails again scuttled across wood.

Somewhere behind me, a twig snapped.

I flinched and let Od go. "We've got to untie this dog."

Another snap.

"Now!"

Od grabbed the lantern and the knife. "I'll . . . cut the rope," she said, her voice still choppy, breathy. She bent down in front of the crate and shone the lantern inside.

The dog again whimpered.

"It's about forty-odd pounds," she said. "I wonder if it'll bite me if I reach inside."

"Something's nearby, Od. We can't take time to free it. Let's drag the case out of the woods."

She swung the light my way. "Can you? It's heavy."

"I'll push the crate. You pull it from the front and guide the way with the lantern."

We maneuvered ourselves into position. Od lay the knife on the crate and pulled; I rested my cane and the mirror on the lid and pushed with both hands while hopping on my left leg to avoid relying on my right one in the slightest. We left the MarViLUs case behind us in the snow. I peeked over my shoulder when I remembered it still lying there, but by then it had fallen out of reach of our light.

I turned my head back around and stopped in my tracks.

Od halted, too. "Oh, Christ."

Twenty-five feet in front of my sister stood the silhouette of a figure that did not resemble either animal or man. I could not tell what it was or what it looked like, precisely, but I knew it was enormous and that something hung off its back like a pair of unfurled wings. It breathed. It lived. It wasn't a tree or a figment of my imagination.

Two wide-set eyes stared out from its unseen face, and they shone with a strange luminescence, like the eyes of an opossum or a cat staring through the dark. Instead of yellow or green, however, this creature's irises glowed red. Bloodred. Two burning, bleeding embers.

The dog inside the crate growled from deep in his throat.

The creature growled back.

I sucked air through my teeth, and the lantern quaked in my sister's left hand, the flame wobbling and snapping, metal squeaking. Her other hand reached back and snatched the knife from the crate, and she turned the blade upward.

"Be gone!" I called out with a strength and a volume that made me wonder if someone bolder had just possessed me. I did not understand how I'd summoned the ability to unlock my jaw, let alone to speak, but I loathed seeing my sister stuck at the front of that crate, six feet closer to the figure than I.

"Be gone!" I said again, and I lumbered over to Od with the tip of my cane slicing through snow, the mirror at my side. "It's time you move onward. Be gone!"

After one more step, Od and I stood side by side—two ordinary young women in coats the colors of irises and plums, with no power in the world whatsoever. However, for some unknown reason, I continued to yell at those two chilling eyes.

"Be gone!" I directed the mirror at those eyes. "Be gone!"

The creature's growls deepened in the crook of its throat. It lowered its head in a position of attack—a wolf preparing to lunge.

"M-m-maybe it's j-j-just the boys playing a trick," said Od. "M-m-maybe . . ."

A sudden blast of wind pushed at my chest and tipped me off balance. The creature broke into a run—it barreled toward us with the thunder of a stampede of horses, and it screamed like the Weeping Woman who haunted Od in the nights. It unfurled its wings, and I saw it—the Leeds Devil. It resembled everything I'd ever feared in my entire life, all that hideousness and horror shrieking our way.

I grabbed hold of my sister, and she took hold of me, and with the mirror and the knife raised we stood up against it, for there was nothing else we could do.

"Be gone!" I screamed at the top of my lungs, and Od shouted something, too, her voice as sturdy as mine, but I couldn't understand her, for the impact was near.

She thrust the blade at its chest, I swung the mirror, and a heavy force slammed against us, knocking us to the ground. No longer holding the mirror, I yanked the pin from the hat on my head and forced myself again to my feet with the help of the cane. I ensured that the crucifix pointed toward the shadow that now writhed on the ground six feet away. The thing breathed as though hurt, but I still didn't trust it.

I steadied my balance and prayed my right leg wouldn't give way. The iron brace shook and jangled beneath my skirt, and the handle of my cane felt slippery and cold. My eardrums ached. My head went dizzy.

Od lifted the lantern and jumped to her feet, the knife now missing from her hand.

"Hide!" I yelled to her. "Hide behind the crate."

She ducked behind the wooden trap, and the shadow lunged again. "Be gone!" I cried, but I lost the nerve to swipe at the thing with a thin piece of steel a mere ten inches long. Instead, I threw the pin at its right eye, kneeled, and cowered behind my cane and the crucifix. The beast screamed straight over my head with a horrific cry that turned my skin to ice. Snow rained down on the crate from the tree overhead, and when I dared to open my eyes, I saw those burning red embers peering down over Od from a branch five feet above her.

"The ax is in the MarViLUs case!" I shouted. "Run to the spot we just left! Run!"

With a bleat of panic, Od tore through the woods, the orange flame of the lantern streaking through the darkness at her side. I backed away from the crate and stepped on the handle of the mirror with the heel of my lighter shoe. A rancid smell blew down at me from the tree—an ungodly stink, fetid breath. The thing snarled and barked and spread its black wings.

From within the trap, the dog growled, and the crate shook from its fight to break free. Pine needles and more piles of snow loosened from the branches and splatted against the wood. I gripped my cane until I thought the handle might break.

Without warning, the creature dropped from the tree and landed on the crate with a crack of the boards.

Od sprinted toward me. "I've got the case!"

The shadow clawed at the wood, snuffling, growling, ripping up planks.

Od forced the case open.

Wood splintered and snapped beneath the beast's paws, and below it, that poor dog came into view, tied down with rope, vulnerable, trapped . . .

Od struck the first blow with the ax.

The Leeds Devil hollered and turned on her. Before it could jump, I hit its face with my cane, and it shrieked and stood to its full height on the crate.

"Where's the mirror?" asked Od.

"You said it won't help us."

"Where is it?"

"Under my left foot."

Od handed me the ax and knelt down for our mother's hand mirror, but the Devil pounced and landed upon her. In shock, I dropped the cane. All I now held was the ax. The thought of swinging it sickened me—blood and violence was not what I desired—but this monstrosity was on my sister.

"Be gone!" I raised the blade over my head and brought

it down on its back with a *thwack*. The beast screeched, the handle burned, and a violent gust of black smoke blinded my eyes and singed my nostrils. Soot and screams engulfed me. I dropped the ax, stumbled backward, and covered my ears until the creature's piercing cries swelled to a shuddering crescendo and then disappeared with an agonized whimper.

Silence followed.

The earth settled.

When I opened my eyes, when they finally stopped watering, I found my sister lying on the forest floor, alone, awake but stunned. The lantern flickered near her head, and ribbons of smoke rose from the glass of the hand mirror she clutched and drifted from the bloodied blade of my ax.

The Devil was gone.

Od pried off the remaining boards on the top of the crate with the knife, which she found lying in moss near the lantern, then she cut the rope that tethered the dog to a metal hook inside. My hair smelled like a chimney, and the palms of my hands stung as though singed. Od's hair fell over her face, ripped out of its pins, and I noticed scratches bleeding near her left eye.

Still catching our breath, not saying a word, we trudged out of the woods with the dog, my cane, the lantern, and the MarViLUs case, the last of which I'd just filled with the knife, the hand mirror, and the wiped-clean ax. Our tools. I still wore Od's black hat, minus the pin, which I hadn't seen since I'd thrown it at the eye of the Leeds Devil.

Lanterns bobbed about on the edge of the pines. A tree

branch cracked beneath my left foot, and four figures spun our way with rifles cocked.

"Don't shoot!" Od lifted her hands. "Please—don't shoot! It's us."

"Odette?" asked Cy, and he lowered the barrel of his weapon and crept toward us, his boots crunching through snow. "We heard screaming. What were you doing out there by yourselves?"

Od lowered her arms. "We weren't by ourselves."

Mr. Munro backed toward his inn. "Is . . . is it out there?"

"D-d-did you catch it?" asked Red. "Is it in the trap?"

Cy stepped closer. "What happened? Are those scratches on your face?"

Od switched everything she held into her left hand and wrapped her right arm around me, warming me. "We fought it off. Tru delivered the final blow. The Devil's gone."

The men all glanced at one another in the light of their lanterns, as though checking to see the proper reaction to Od's claim. One by one, their faces broke into grins.

Cy adjusted his grip on his rifle. "Aw, you had us fooled there for a moment."

"But . . . no . . ." Od shook her head. "We fought it off—I swear we did. I'd swear under oath in a court of law. Look at the marks on my face. Look at the soot in Tru's hair. There might still be some blood on the ax . . ."

"Why'd you free the dog?" asked Andrew, nodding toward the pup hanging its gray head against my right leg. "Why are you bungling the plan?"

"To the devil with your plan, Andrew!" said Od, and she turned us around and urged me onward, back toward the inn.

"I thought you wanted that reward money," said Cy from behind us.

"To hell with you, too, Cy."

"Odette?"

She wheeled toward him. "You're never there when I need you, including tonight when I ran out that door to find my sister."

"You disappeared so quickly after screaming about her note."

"I didn't see you running after me to make sure I was all right."

"I was getting my rifle . . . and my shoes . . . and a lantern . . . and the rest of what's left of our meager posse. You can't just run into the woods and fight off a dangerous threat willy-nilly."

Od squeezed me tighter.

"Odette . . ." Cy inched toward her with one hand held out in front of him, as though he feared her a little. "Don't be mad. This is all supposed to be fun."

"Oh, yes . . ." Her hand dropped from my back. "Let's not dash Cyrus Leeds's fun, shall we? Let's make sure he can always keep having a good time."

He pursed his lips. "I know what you're driving at, but I wasn't ready for that type of responsibility back then. I was just barely seventeen when I faced all that."

"I know." Od resumed walking the dog and me toward the inn. "So was I."

"My mother knew, anyway," he called after her. "It clearly

didn't matter that I denied it. I'm here in the east as a punishment, if that makes you feel any better."

"Good-bye, Cy."

"Odette . . ."

"I'm done with this chapter. Go have your fun, Cyrus. Good-bye."

Together, along with our four-legged rescuee, Od and I marched through the snow, away from the woods, away from those who did not believe in us.

CHAPTER TWENTY

Odette
January 11, 1909—California

I remained at my uncle's house in Fallbrook, not yet confident enough to whisk my sister away from my aunt. I worried that the money I'd earned wouldn't be enough to keep Tru safe. I doubted my abilities. I questioned my plans.

A mere three days before Tru's fifteenth birthday, instead of climbing aboard a train and returning to her, I engaged in a morning broomstick swordfight with my six-year-old cousin, Ana Maria—an auburn-haired spitfire who reminded me quite a bit of my younger self. With our broomsticks knocking together and our bare feet mussing up the rug, we dueled in Papa's old art studio and pretended to be swashbucklers from the novel I'd been reading to her: *The Three Musketeers*, by Alexandre Dumas.

Uncle Magnus strolled into the room with a long purple coat draped over his right arm. In his left hand, he held a leather case.

"For you, Od," he said.

My broomstick fell from my hand at the sight of those two heirlooms. Even though Uncle Magnus had sworn that the MarViLUs case lacked enchantment, I found myself drawn to it. My feet moved on their own accord toward it, as though the voices of my grandmother and mother called to me from within the leather casing.

Uncle Magnus handed me the coat first. "It's a little old-fashioned, but I have a feeling it'll fit you."

I threaded my arms through the flared woolen sleeves and fastened the topmost buttons around my chest. A perfect fit. I'd never felt so warm in all my life.

"And here's the famous, old MarViLUs case." He passed the case my way. "Guard it well, Od. It really did come from Germany and belonged to your grandmother Trudchen."

My fingers slid into the smooth grooves of the handle. I still envisioned tools packed inside the case—crucifixes, daggers, pistols with silver bullets, mirrors, and even a bag of salt to repel vampires and witches.

"Thank you," I said, and I turned and spotted myself in a full-length mirror by the window.

My Lord. I looked exactly like my mother when she lived in that house and battled the canyon's darkness. I walked toward my reflection, the case at my side, the hem of the plum-colored coat swaying, my eyes shining with a hint of their former fire, for I felt Mama's strength inside me.

"Inside the case, you'll find a ticket for a train that departs this afternoon," said Uncle Magnus, a hitch in his voice. "It's time you return to your sister. Fulfill your destiny. I believe in you, darling. Always will." He cleared his throat and left the room.

Ana Maria crept up beside me and peered at the two of us together in the mirror, a finger hooked around her plump bottom lip. She wore an indigo dress, one shade off from purple, as well as a ruffled white pinafore that had slipped off her right shoulder from our swordfight. We had the same eyebrows and noses, I noticed. Her smile reminded me of my old mischievous grins.

"What do you think, Ana Maria?" I asked her. "Do I look like someone who could slay a wicked beast?"

She nodded and placed her hands on her hips. "Yes!"

All it took was that one magic word, spoken with gusto from a child, as well as a twenty-two-year-old coat and an old leather case from halfway around the world. I rolled back my shoulders, stood to my full height, and saw myself as a Protector.

CHAPTER TWENTY-ONE

Trudchen
January 23, 1909—Pennsylvania

T he day after the night of the Leeds Devil, Od and I
returned to Pennsylvania by train. Accompanying us
was the dog—a female, we discovered, a mottled gray
mutt with heartbreaking brown eyes. We absolutely could not
leave her at the New Jersey inn with the boys, even with that
trap ripped to pieces.

Late that afternoon, Od, the dog, and I took a hackney carriage to the Philadelphia restaurant where Ezra Blue worked.
Out in front of one of the establishment's windows, we tied the
pup to a hitching post at the edge of the brick sidewalk.

I draped my coat over the dog's bony back and said, "I think
we ought to name her Dulcinea."

"Where did you get that from?" asked Od.

"The novel *Don Quixote*. Dulcinea del Toboso was Quixote's
fantastical lady love."

"Hmm . . ." Od stepped back and studied the dog. "I like it.
It reminds me of California."

She tied the sleeves of the coat around Dulcinea's belly, and
we urged her to lie down on the bricks of the sidewalk, which
someone had cleared of snow.

"Will you pull my train ticket out of the right pocket of the coat?" I asked Od, and she complied. I then tucked the proof of our travels into the sash of my skirt.

Od picked up our bags, and we entered the restaurant. I kept my gloves on, for my skin hadn't yet warmed from the night before. Every now and then my teeth spontaneously chattered.

"Is Ezra Blue working here today?" Od asked the man who seated us at a table by a window near Dulcinea. I'd felt too nervous to ask the question myself.

"He is," said the fellow. "Do you know him?"

Od glanced my way and said, "Tell him Trudchen Grey has returned from the Pine Barrens and is here for her celebratory supper. And may we have a pot of tea, please?"

"Of course." The man turned and walked toward a door in the back of the dining room that seemed to lead to the kitchen.

At the table next to us sat a young couple. The gentleman of the pair fluttered open a newspaper.

"Here it is," he said in a thick Philadelphia accent, complete with that touch of a twang. "Just as I heard from Billy—that devil thing disappeared."

"No more sightings today?" asked the woman, a brunette around Od's age.

"Nope. None reported."

Od and I locked eyes.

The man folded the newspaper in half. "I'm a little disappointed."

"Well, you shouldn't be," said the woman. "That beast was a killer. Now we don't have to worry about it attacking the cat. Or us."

"Life is going to seem duller without it, though. It sure made the newspapers more exciting."

"You wouldn't be saying such a thing if that monster ate Princess," said the woman, and she took a sip of a drink from a mug.

A trace of a smile graced Od's lips, and I realized how much she looked like her old self again. Instead of pinning up her hair, she wore it down to hide the scratches near her left eye, and her brown locks fell to her waist. The muscles around her mouth had softened. Her eyes shone with more life.

"Tru," she said in a whisper. "You saw it and felt it as much as I did, didn't you?"

"Of course I did."

She leaned forward on her elbows. "We haven't spoken much about it . . ."

"I know the boys didn't believe us . . . but it was on you, Od! I thought it was going to kill you. How on earth did you survive?"

"I hardly remember. It felt surreal, like a dream. But I'm certain it happened."

"Oh, it most definitely happened." I reached out and took hold of her hand. "I don't care what anyone else says, we did something extraordinary out there. *I* believe in us."

She nodded, her eyes damp, and she wiped the moisture from her lashes. "I do, too. One hundred percent." Her gaze drifted to her left. "Oh . . . look who's coming . . ."

I turned my head and forgot to breathe for a moment, for out from the kitchen came Ezra Blue in his black vest and bow tie, both of which matched the inky color of his hair. He still wore the long white apron over his trousers, and he fussed with the waist a bit as he walked toward us.

"You're back," he said with a smile, his blue eyes focused on me. "Did you find the Leeds Devil?"

I sat up straight. "Yes, we did, as a matter of fact. Please tell Celia we traveled to the Pine Barrens and accomplished our mission." I plucked the train ticket from my sash and handed it to him.

The smile lingered on his lips, and yet his eyes darted between the two of us in confusion. "Are you serious? You . . . you saw it?"

"We have proof," I said. "It scratched my sister's face."

Od pulled her hair back and showed him the four red lines clawed across her skin.

"What . . . ?" He pointed at her with my ticket. "What did . . . *That's* from the Leeds Devil?"

"We know it sounds preposterous," I said, "but please tell Celia she's safe. We made sure that he's gone."

"Let's show him the hand mirror," said Od, and she leaned down to the floor beside her chair and picked up the MarViLUs case, which shed a cluster of pine needles. The receptacle smelled of leather and sap and appeared to be a tad sticky from the way she yanked her fingertips off one of the corners. She popped open the silver latch and pulled out the hand mirror from its resting spot above our copy of *Marvelous and Monstrous*.

A black spot—a burn mark—marred the center of the mirror. Other signs of the heat from the night before darkened the copper handle.

"It's from the heat of the Devil when Tru whacked it with an ax," said Od. "We could show the burn spots to Celia if you'd like."

I expected Ezra to either laugh at us or skedaddle in the other direction, but instead he asked to hold the mirror, and he ran his fingertips across the damaged glass.

He smiled. "Celia would love this. Here"—he handed the mirror back to Od—"I want to ask you so much more about it, but I need to fetch your tea. I'll be back with a pot before my boss gets mad, and I'll take your orders. Don't go anywhere."

"We won't," said Od, and she fitted the mirror back inside the case.

After he left, I peeked out the window at Dulcinea. The dog slept on the sidewalk, curled into a ball, nestled beneath the folds of my coat.

"Tru," said Od. "I made an interesting discovery last night."

I pulled my attention away from the pup. "What do you mean? In the woods?"

"No, later. But first I should explain something. You see, when I was in California, I learned that our mother and her siblings kept a handwritten book inside this case when they all were young. Aunt Vik wrote it, and Mama and Uncle Magnus contributed, all when they were living on their own after their parents died." Od pulled *Marvelous and Monstrous* from the case, thumped it upon the table, and slid it toward me on its crimson cloth binding. "I read this last night when I couldn't fall asleep. It was published in Philadelphia. The author's name is L. N. Hardt, which sounds suspiciously close to *Lionheart* . . ."

I pulled back the front cover and wrinkled my forehead at the word *Philadelphia*, listed beneath the publisher's name. "What are you saying, Od? You think *this* is their book?"

"Have you read it?"

"Just the beginning."

"The characters are three orphans in the woods named Viola, Margaret, and Augustus. They're all the same ages that Viktoria, Maria, and Magnus were after their parents died and left them alone on their Oregon farm."

"But . . . this book . . . this popular book . . . ?"

"Look inside." Od tapped a fingernail against the first page. "See for yourself."

I flipped to the prologue, which I remembered reading on the train to the Pine Barrens.

The tale you are about to encounter is a true one, but I must warn you, dear reader, that the facts have been sugared with whimsy, marinated in daydreams, and seasoned with a generous salting of exaggeration. I will leave you and your clever brain to decipher the myths from the realities, but do bear in mind that the truth, as Lord Byron once wrote, is "stranger than fiction," and fantasy is a gilded mirror that reflects the dangers, the oddities, and the marvelous wonders of our own true world.

I met my sister's eyes. "Are you honestly saying Aunt Viktoria wrote this?"

"According to Uncle Magnus, she was the primary author."

I shook my head, unsure I believed such a claim. "You mean to tell me that Aunt Viktoria was once a teller of tall tales?"

"That appears to be the situation." Od smirked and removed her elbows from the table.

"If this is true," I said, "then what on earth happened to her?"

My sister snapped the MarViLUs case shut and set it down on the floor beside her. "Life has a way of knocking the whimsy out of people, Tru. Make sure that doesn't happen to you."

Ezra strolled up to our table with two teacups and a pot balanced on a pewter platter.

"Here you are, ladies. A nice, hot pot of tea to shake off the chill of New Jersey." He placed the items on the table with nimble hands. "What would you like to eat?"

Od grabbed the teapot and poured herself a cup. "I'll have a bowl of your best soup, please."

"Me, too," I said, and I noticed that my train ticket poked out from the top of Ezra's apron, as though he'd tucked it there for safekeeping. "Thank you."

"Do you want me to pour your teas?" he asked.

"No, thank you; I'll manage," said Od, which sent him bustling away with the platter.

"Why was this book published just now, do you think?" I asked. "After all these years?"

"I saw Mama last year, after Trudie was born. Maybe our conversation had something to do with it. Maybe she sought out a publisher here in Philadelphia and decided to take a gamble on this old story." Od slid my teacup and saucer toward herself and poured. "It's actually a good story. You'll have to read it."

I flipped through the pages. "But . . . I can't believe . . . *Aunt Viktoria*?"

"Consult the leaves, Tru." Od rested the pot on the table. "I'm curious if they'll tell us more about the book and our mother, and what we should do next. I also wonder"—she held my cup and saucer out toward me, but her hands shook—"if this talent of yours could ever help me find . . ." She spilled a drop on the table and fought to lower the cup in front of me without dumping the rest of the contents.

I closed *Marvelous and Monstrous* and set it aside. "I don't know if I could find Trudie for you. I wouldn't want to see something wrong and send you on a wild chase to the wrong part of the world."

She nodded and placed her hands in her lap, her lips pressed together.

"I'm sorry, Od, but I'm not sure that would work."

"No." She nodded again. "I understand."

I shifted my focus to the steam curling into the air from the tea in front of me. If the leaves again showed me a bat-winged creature . . .

No, it's gone, I told myself. *What we experienced in the Pine Barrens I will never forget, but it was the type of anomaly a person only encounters once in a lifetime.*

I took a breath and brought the cup to my lips for the first sip of tea that day, and my teeth again chattered from the chill of the pines.

Ezra Blue made several more rounds to our table while we drank our tea and ate our soup, not only to serve us the food, but to slip us his address so we could make a personal visit to Celia.

"Tomorrow's Sunday, so we're home all afternoon. I'm sure she'd love it if you could come by. Your note made her smile so hard, my ma started crying."

"I would love to meet Celia," I said, and I placed a hand on the paper with his address.

Once he'd wandered off again, Od nodded toward my cup. "Is it time yet?"

"I suppose it is."

I performed my usual ritual that ended with my flipping the cup over and closing my eyes. I heard my sister breathing across the table. My teeth again hammered against each other.

I turned the cup upright and blinked.

What I viewed below me caused my lips to part with an audible *pop*.

Od leaned forward. "What is it? What do you see?"

I saw absolutely nothing. With both of our minds so pre-occupied, we'd strained the tea without allowing any leaves to slide into the cup.

"Do you see anything regarding our mother?" asked Od. "Should we go back to her house?"

"Yes," I said with a lift of my eyes.

"This evening?"

"Yes."

My sister scooted forward in her chair. "Is that what the leaves say?"

"No, it's what I say."

I tipped the cup toward her.

Od's face paled.

"We didn't allow any of the leaves to slip out of the pot," I said with a smile. "It's not a bad omen; it's a *tabula rasa*. Isn't that the right phrase? A blank slate." I clicked the cup back into the well of the saucer. "*I* want to go look for our mother, Od. I want that to happen, no matter what any tea leaves or tarot cards might predict. I want to start taking my fate into my own hands."

Od wrapped her long fingers around her own cup. "All right."

"We may find Trudie one day."

"I know," she said with a swallow.

"No matter what happens, I'll stay by your side. I promise you, Od. I'll be here."

That evening, when the streetlights shimmered and a calming hush fell over the snow-lined sidewalks of Philadelphia, we knocked upon the door of the town house we'd visited earlier that week. During that second visit, I noticed three silver bells hanging from the eave above the doorway and a little circular mirror made of copper positioned beneath the porch lamp. Od held on to Dulcinea by the rope we now used as a leash, and I gripped the leather case and my cane.

Footsteps padded our way from within the house. A woman with hair the color of Od's threw open the door.

"There you are!" she said, and she clasped us both to her chest with the fiercest, most protective embrace I'd ever experienced. "My girls! I was at Aunt Viktoria's when your telegram arrived. I'd gone to Oregon to find you—to give you money from a book that's been a bit of a surprise success. I didn't know you'd come to find me, but I'm so glad you're here."

I closed my eyes and allowed this woman—my mother—to

envelop me in her marvelous maternal warmth and strength, with Od tucked up against my left side.

We would ask all our questions later. We would speak of *Marvelous and Monstrous,* and Od's baby, and our futures, and our pasts, of love and forgiveness, of aunts and uncles and fathers and a ranch house nestled in a California canyon.

At that moment, however, we spoke no words, for no words were needed. Mama's silver bells jangled in a breeze above our heads, and the air tasted of hearth fires and magic.

CHAPTER TWENTY-TWO

Odette
January 14, 1909—Oregon

Now that I've pulled back the curtain on our family's mysticism, revealed our secrets, confessed our sins, I'm ready to lock these pages in a box, and, eventually, I'll present my memoir to you, the intended audience, my dear, sweet Tru.

Forgive me if I do not show you our story immediately after my return. Forgive me if I appear at your window like a spirit tonight, carry you off on adventures, and encourage you to savor the old Lowenherz legends for a longer taste than I probably should. My reasons are several.

Despite the bitter spoonful of reality forced down my throat ever since I was a young child, despite Uncle Magnus's insistence that our family is composed of storytellers and dreamers, not heroes and magicians, I still feel it, Tru—magic crackling through the air. I know Uncle Magnus, Mama, and Aunt Vik feel it, too, but now that they've grown into weary adults, they turn their backs on enchantment and pretend they don't sense it. In the world of grown-ups, you see, practical thinking is king; dreamers are fools and madmen. How ridiculous that is.

I've decided I'd rather be foolish than ordinary. I'd rather risk chasing monsters that might not exist, searching for a child I'm not meant to find, than to believe we're nothing more than mundane creatures, steeped in ordinary lives. I know I'm not supposed to see you anymore, for my foolishness has "ruined" me and turned me into an "unfortunate" girl, but today is your fifteenth birthday. You are on the brink of adulthood. Please trust me when I insist that it is too soon for you to turn your back on spellbinding wonders.

Think of all the tales we've heard people tell of their beliefs in bogeymen and beasts over the years. Remember the ghost tales, the fairy tales, the peculiar firsthand accounts, the people who've sworn up and down that they've faced the unknown. There must be something to these tales, Tru, and I want to explore their possibilities with you. I don't care how far we must travel, how much our knees knock together in fear, let's break free of the chains binding us to our fates and journey deep into the world of the unexplainable.

One hour remains before my train reaches Portland. I will now set down my pen and seal up these pages, but please bear in mind that the end of all stories aren't truly endings. Do not ever trust the words *And they lived happily ever after.* Do not believe that epilogues mark a final destination. Do not ever listen to an author who proudly proclaims, "I've finished the book!"

These are all lies.

Endings are beginnings in disguise, dear Tru. They signify one door closing and another one opening. They mark the point where the heroine transforms from a person who's been beaten and badgered and bolstered by life into someone who's about to shed her past and metamorphose into an entirely new creature. Even if we never read a second volume of a book, the characters continue to live on and on and on, and their stories merge into other stories, told by new generations of heroes and heroines.

Our own tale is quite unfinished, Trudchen Maria. Our adventures have not yet even begun. If I scribble down the words *The End* at the bottom of this page, do not believe me in the slightest, for this is not an ending at all.

Far from it.

For, you see, this is the beginning—the true beginning—of the marvelous tale of Odette and Trudchen Grey, two girls born in a ranch house, twenty miles northwest of one-sixteenth of a castle built to resemble a stone Scottish fortress called Dunnottar.

EPILOGUE

Trudie
January 18, 1923—Texas

For my fifteenth birthday, Ma handed me a book-shaped present, wrapped in paper the brilliant golden orange of our High Plains sunsets. Ma loved bright colors, but I preferred moodier ones, like the ebony of night after the sky purpled and darkened, when the wild dogs howled.

"Open it," said Ma of the present.

"Go on," said Pa with a nod, bracing his callused hands on the back of his chair. Both parents stood over me at the dining room table, their faces amber from the bright spell of winter sunshine breaking through the rain clouds.

I unfastened the bow made of twine and unclasped the gold seals holding the paper down. Inside the wrappings awaited a book with a midnight-blue dust jacket and a title that made my heart quicken:

Odd & True Tales:
A Guide to Monstrous Creatures & Spirits
of the United States of America
by Odette M. Grey and Trudchen Grey Blue

"Where did you find this?" I asked Ma.

"Mrs. Herzstein telephoned two weeks ago to say the book arrived in her store. I suppose you've talked off everyone's ears enough about the . . ." Ma rubbed the back of her neck. "Well, we all know about your fascination with legends."

I opened the book to the table of contents, which listed dozens upon dozens of fantastical creatures, demons, hobgoblins, and wraiths.

"Oh, how splendid this is!" I said. "I love it. Thank you."

Ma smiled. "You're welcome."

Pa walked over and kissed the top of my head, his lips cold from the near-freezing winds he withstood while plowing our prosperous fields of wheat in his combine. "Happy birthday, Trudie," he said in his husky Texas drawl. "We're grateful we were blessed with your presence fifteen years ago."

His words, though meant to be loving, cast a shadow over my excitement. I closed the book and refrained from asking the weighty questions that always lingered on the tip of my tongue, especially on my birthdays.

Who am I, really?

Where do I belong?

Why was I abandoned in Missouri back in January 1908, when I was only four days old?

That night, I curled up with *Odd & True Tales* beneath the scarlet bedspread in my upstairs bedroom, while the walls creaked and whined from a windstorm. Within the pages of the book I learned where to find and how to fight the Bell Witch of Tennessee, the mine-shaft monster of Van Meter, Iowa, the Leeds Devil of New Jersey, *La Llorona* of the states bordering

Mexico, the Hodag of Wisconsin, Rawhead and Bloody Bones of the Ozarks, and even a strange wolf in Texas. *Central* Texas, not our panhandle. The authors, these sisters Grey, had traveled down to the town of Converse and discovered the existence of an enormous lupine creature—part wolf, part gorilla—who ate a rancher's fifteen-year-old son in the 1800s. Poor fellow!

The book described purple as a mystical, magical color, and it instructed the use of red and a hue called "haint blue" for painting doors and shutters. Mirrors worked well for capturing ghosts and bogeymen, it claimed. If I hung bells and amulets on the eaves outside the house, I could ward off evil spirits and spells . . . although I couldn't imagine Ma allowing me to hang anything from our roof that our wild Texas winds might hurl through a window.

At the back of the book I found an old photograph of the authors—two pretty young women, not much older than I. They wore high-collared blouses and ankle-length skirts, like the ones Ma wore in pictures from when I was a baby. The caption below the photograph read, *Odette and Trudchen, photographed in January 1909, following their triumph over the Leeds Devil.*

One of the young women, the brunette, wore her hair up, and long scratches marked the left side of her face, near her eye. She held a hand mirror, the glass blackened as though struck by lightning, and her sister, a blonde like me with braided hair, gripped both a cane and an ax. The blade of the ax was a tad stained, but it gleamed in the light of the studio, in which they posed against a gray backdrop.

The young women looked delicate yet dangerous. I wanted to be them. I believed I *could* be them. Everyone in Dalhart, Texas, saw me as a lanky, freckle-faced misfit, but fierceness and fearlessness blazed through my blood—even though I had yet to prove it.

I sighed. "Miss Grey and Mrs. Blue, what I wouldn't give to join you on your adventures."

Wind slammed against the wall behind me, and the bulb in my lamp blinked off for a second before brightening once again.

I flipped back to the beginning of the book, and I froze when I saw a page I must have skipped before. Two lines I hadn't yet seen leapt out at me.

This book is dedicated to Trudie,
beloved daughter, born in Missouri,
sent to live with new protectors in January 1908,
dearly missed.
May she be courageous.

My heart pounded. My skin warmed. My fingers trembled against the page. All the jumbled pieces that had always hurled out of control inside me fell neatly into place, and a sense of hope, of recognition, of *belonging*, washed through me. I stared at those words, tears burning in my eyes, and I knew—I could feel it.

I was that Trudie.

FURTHER READING

Odd & True is a work of fiction, but many of the locations and historical events described in the book are based on real places and incidents, including the Willows Maternity Sanitarium, Woreland Castle, and the January 1909 sightings of the Leeds Devil. The following is a list of some of the resources I used while writing this novel.

BOOKS

American Monsters: A History of Monster Lore, Legends, and Sightings in America, by Linda S. Godfrey (Penguin, 2014).

By-Paths and Cross-Roads: Accidents of Fair Travelers on the Highway of Life, by E. P. Haworth (The Willows Maternity Sanitarium, 1918).

The Encyclopedia of Vampires, Werewolves, and Other Monsters, by Rosemary Ellen Guiley (Checkmark Books, 2005).

The Folklore and Folklife of New Jersey, by David Steven Cohen (Rutgers University Press, 1991).

The Girls Who Went Away: The Hidden History of Women Who Surrendered Children for Adoption in the Decades Before Roe v. Wade, by Ann Fessler (Penguin, 2007).

Images of America: Fallbrook, by Rebecca Farnbach and Loretta Barnett (Arcadia Publishing, 2007).

Images of America: Hillsboro, by Kimberli Fitzgerald and Deborah Raber with the Hillsboro Historic Landmarks Advisory Committee (Arcadia Publishing, 2009).

The Jersey Devil, by James F. McCloy and Ray Miller Jr. (Middle Atlantic Press, 1999).

The Official Guide of the Railways and Steam Navigation Lines of the United States, Puerto Rico, Canada, Mexico, and Cuba (National Railway Publication Co., 1906).

Polio Voices: An Oral History from the American Polio Epidemics and Worldwide Eradication Efforts, by Julie Silver, M.D., and Daniel Wilson, Ph.D. (Praeger Publishers, 2007).

Seven Days a Week: Women and Domestic Service in Industrializing America, by David M. Katzman (University of Illinois Press, 1978).

Small Steps: The Year I Got Polio, by Peg Kehret (Albert Whitman & Company, 1996).

NEWSPAPER ARTICLES

"A Condensed History," by Elias Gilman, *Portland Tribune* (Portland, OR), April 28, 2009.

"Death Drew Artist to Area, but Beauty Made Him Stay," by Vincent Nicholas Rossi, *San Diego Union-Tribune* (San Diego, CA), September 18, 2005.

"Fly Rival of 'Leeds Devil' Has Jersey People Frightened," *Trenton Evening Times* (Trenton, NJ), January 20, 1909.

"For Protection to the Erring Girls a Ban upon Deceptive Advertising by Maternity Homes Is Asked," *Chillicothe Constitution* (Chillicothe, MO), April 10, 1913.

"The Haunted Police Stations of Chicago," *Chicago Tribune* (Chicago, IL), May 5, 1907.

"Jab from Hatpin Causes Death," *San Francisco Call* (San Francisco, CA), November 12, 1906.

"'Leeds Devil' in N.J.," *New-York Daily Tribune* (New York, NY), January 22, 1909.

"New Jersey's Bogey," *Sunday Star* (Washington, D.C.), January 24, 1909.

"Strange Beast Seen," *Washington Herald* (Washington, D.C.), January 21, 1909.

"Traveling through the History of Portland's Streetcars," by Kristi Turnquist, *Oregonian* (Portland, OR), February 23, 2011.

"What Ails South Jersey?" *Sun* (New York, NY), January 21, 1909.

"Willows Maternity Sanitarium," *Kansas City Times* (Kansas City, MO), May 7, 1982.

JOURNAL ARTICLES

"Case of Acute Polio-Encephalitis," by Herbert P. Hawkins, M. D. Oxon., *St. Thomas's Hospital Reports*, Vol. 32 (1904), pp. 399–405.

"Oregonian Folk-Lore," by Albert S. Gatschet, *Journal of American Folklore*, Vol. 4, No. 13 (Apr.–June 1891), pp. 139–143.

"Treatment of Anterior Polio-myelitis," by Wm. Harvey King, M.D., *Medical Century: An International Journal of Homeopathic Medicine and Surgery*, Vol. 3, No. 13 (July 1, 1895), pp. 297–299.

LITERATURE REFERENCED

Don Quixote, by Miguel de Cervantes Saavedra (originally published in Spanish as *El Ingenioso Hidalgo Don Quixote de La Mancha,* 1605 and 1615).

Grimm's Fairy Tales, by Jacob and Wilhelm Grimm (originally published in German as *Kinder- und Hausmärchen,* 1812).

ACKNOWLEDGMENTS

I'm extremely grateful to the following:

Barbara Poelle, for believing in this book as soon as I sent you the original draft of the first chapter.

Maggie Lehrman, for using your marvelous editorial skills to once again turn one of my manuscripts into a coherent, finished work that's so much stronger than anything I originally imagined.

Nathália Suellen, for your gorgeous, haunting artistry.

Alyssa Nassner, for the book's utterly magical design.

Kim Murphy, for your superb critiquing skills and vast historical knowledge.

The Wednesday Morning Coffee and Writing Crew, for always listening to me and encouraging me, even when I'm pulling out my hair in full stressed-out mode.

The Library of Congress, for making a historical novelist's work so much easier by scanning thousands of newspapers, photographs, and rare documents, including a 1729 issue of *Titan's New Almanack* with "the Arms of the Family Leeds."

Manchester Township High School, New Jersey, for showing me that the legend of the Leeds Devil (a.k.a. the Jersey Devil) is alive and well to this day. Special thanks to Marjon Weber for inviting me to speak in Manchester Township and introducing me to the region.

Samantha Dempster, a descendent of the Colonial Leedses of New Jersey, for sharing your perspective of being a part of the family tied to the Leeds Devil legend.

My parents, for providing my sister and me with a stable, loving home that overflowed with books and imagination—and for protecting us from California snakes, black widows, brush-fires, and the monsters in my closet.

Adam, for moving with me to the canyons of San Diego when we were young and newly married, and for always standing by me, even when my schedule steals me away from the family.

Meggie, for cheering on my writing endeavors during your entire childhood and for your eloquent input on descriptions of pain. Don't ever lose your passion, strength, humor, and compassion, even as you now enter adulthood. I'm so incredibly proud of the young woman you've become.

Ethan, for listening to me read the first draft of *Odd & True* aloud (although I skipped some words and scenes to make the book more appropriate for your then eleven-year-old ears). Your honest criticism, enthusiasm, and extraordinary knowledge of literature for one so young made this novel a hundred times better.

Carrie, my little sister, for listening to all of my make-believe stories as we grew up in Southern California, for playing along with me, and for always being there for me, both then and now. This book is for you and our entire wondrous childhood. I love you to pieces and would slay monsters for you.